Awakening The Forgotten Goddess

Rebekah Sinclair

Warning

This book contains content that may be triggering. Mentions and depicts detailed accounts of death, physical abuse and torture detailed on page, refers to the threat of sexual assault, details non-consensual physical touch, child endangerment and death detailed on page. Contains explicit language, graphic sexual content, physical violence, and death.

To: Me

This one, is for me.

Enjoy listening to the Awakening The Forgotten Goddess playlist on Spotify!

A song has been added for each chapter to represent the tones or themes of the chapter.

I've gone by many names over the ages: Eve, Cleopatra, and Joan. But no matter what name I answer to during my missions for Ares, the goal is always the same: locate the missing Scepter of the Herald.

And last night, we got close, closer than we've ever gotten before.

Nestled in the soft bed with cool, crisp sheets wrapped around me, the breeze wafts in from the open patio door and caresses me as I watch the puffy clouds roll across the blue sky.

Ares has taken over Lupo's Tuscan villa for the funeral, and then we are to return to the Underworld.

It's a shame Lupo was one of the many deaths in last night's battle against the do-gooder elementals that follow the Mortal Council and their flimsy definition of rules. When Ares finally restores his stolen power, Lupo was to sit by his side, along with Lucas, and reinstate the Shifters to the top of the power chain.

I can't help but wonder if Ares will give his true son, Flint, the seat that will be unoccupied with Lupo's death.

My aching body of tight muscles is the only sign that remains from the fight and the wound that pulled me from the battle. The vision of Hermes' Sword of Truth hurling at me end over end until the gleaming tip ran me through flashes through my mind.

Rubbing the place on my chest where I was stabbed, I cement my promise for retribution: Hermes will pay for attempting to take my life. I'm thankful Flint and Terra got me to Ares' healers quickly.

As if my thoughts summoned him, Flint enters the room from the open balcony door with a wave of fresh Tuscan air.

"Oh, good. You're up. You were tossing and turning a lot last night. How is your chest?"

The white curtains on each side of the patio dance in the air currents as the sunlight shines through his red hair, making him look like a true fire lord.

My muscles scream at me as I bow my back and reach my arms over my head.

"I feel a boulder ran me over," I grunt as I relax back into the sheets.

Flint lays next to me, his lean body on display, wearing only sweatpants and no shirt. He pulls me into him reassuringly, promising everything will be okay. I nuzzle into his neck and take in his scent as I wrap my arms around his shoulders, stroking the hard muscles of his back.

"You smell like a wet dog." I wrinkle my nose at him. His chuckle rumbles against my chest, and he pulls me closer.

"I'm just glad you're okay. Do you need to see a healer again?"

"I don't think so. Do we have any healing oils for a bath? I'd kill to soak in the tub for a while."

"I'll see what I can dig up." He places a kiss on my temple with such tenderness, and it brings a soft smile to my face. A knot twists in my belly as I push away the thoughts of Hermes that try to ram their way into my mind and tilt my head to Flint. Mussy red hair runs through my fingers, and I cup his jaw. The short stubble of growth is rough on my palm as he leans into my touch, kissing my hand.

His chestnut eyes take in my body framed by the thin white sheets. Desire and longing burn in his gaze like he can possess me with a single look. Lowering his mouth to mine, his eyelashes drop, and his lips skim mine with the tease of a kiss, making my smile widen.

He positions his body along mine, and the pressure of his weight on me is soothing. I wrap a leg around his hip and pull him closer, holding his eyes with mine.

Flint tilts his head and grazes my lips with his tongue, demanding entry.

Turning my head with a groan, I try to hide my morning breath by speaking away from him. "I haven't brushed my teeth yet."

"I don't care about that," he answers, pulling my chin back to him and slipping his tongue into my mouth.

I wish he would just hold me, but I'm sure last night scared him, seeing me injured on the long sword of his enemy, so I return his affections and kiss him as well.

I slip my tongue inside his mouth, and he gives me an approving growl; his hips rock into me again. Despite my soreness, I arch my back, and he meets me with his hips.

Flint's need for me pulls at the knot in my stomach, and a spike jolts through me as he clenches my hip. Sliding his hand behind me, he grasps my bottom, pushing me harder into him. I release a moan in surprise at his cold touch on my bare skin, which he interprets as enthusiasm, and deepens his kiss against my lips.

My sore muscles and bones complain about the movements and expended energy, and I break the kiss, turning to the side.

"Flint," I begin to stop him when he runs his tongue along my neck, and before he can reach my collarbone, there is a loud knock at the door.

"Persephone?" Aunt Demi calls from the hallway. Flint releases a groan in protest, but I silently appreciate the interruption.

"Pers, I will feed your aunt to the wolves the next time she interrupts such a perfect moment." His mouth takes the crook of my neck, teasing me with a gentle nibble on my skin. I chuckle but push him off in the direction of the bathroom.

"Go shower, dog-boy."

He winks at me from the bathroom door before he calls over his shoulder. "It's open, Demeter!"

My aunt and her warm smile peek around the wooden door. She has replaced her favorite coveralls with a set of hunter-green linen pants and a matching tunic that makes her look much more relaxed.

My heart settles at the sight of my aunt. My Fae mother, her sister, died in childbirth, having mated with a mortal and passing her Immortality to me so that I may live a long life. When my father died of a broken heart, I was orphaned, and Demeter raised me.

"How do you feel, dear?" she asks as she sits next to me on the edge of the bed. I grunt as I turn over to hug my pillow again and close my eyes.

"Like crap."

"Did you sleep well?" she asks, placing her hand on the temple of my head as she has always done. Ever since I can remember, terrible dreams have plagued my sleep, and Demeter has often used the medicinal sap from her Life element to help treat me.

The gentle secretions from her vines soothe my headache and aching bones. The tightness in my hips lessens, and the tension locked in my body melts away with a deep sigh of relief.

"I'm just thankful Flint and the packs got to you in time." She leans over and takes me in her arms. Aunt Demeter's curly raven hair tickles my nose just as it has done my entire life. "Do you need anything?"

"Mm." I pause, thinking. "Just Hermes' head on a spike." A phantom sensation warms my chest at the mention of his name, and I place my hand over my heart.

"In time, honey." Her brown eyes are like melted chocolate as she looks at me with adoration. "We've got to focus on the Mabon ritual in four days and helping unlock the Lycan Shifters' ability to transform into their wolves."

I take the fluffy white pillow and cover my face with it, releasing a low growl at the mention of the upcoming ceremony.

In a rare lunar alignment between Gaea and Avalon, the cleansing Lumos has the power to forcibly unbind some Lycan Shifters, curing them of the mysterious affliction that prevents them from transforming into the wolf form of their own as pups.

As Demeter is full-blooded Avalonia Fae and I share her blood-line through my mother, we will harness the power of the moon's light and cast it over the Shifters, hoping to help as many of them as possible and further strengthen Ares's army.

The fear of failure and suffering punishment at the hands of Ares is something I would avoid at nearly any cost and tightens the anxiety, cramping my stomach.

"Here, I brought these for you." She hands me some vials of bath salts and oils.

"Oh, I could kiss you."

"Hey! That will be my job," Flint teases, returning from his shower with a towel wrapped low around his hips. I don't think I have ever truly taken in his form, and with most of his body unclothed, save the towel, I notice how long his torso and arms are compared to the proportions of his legs.

He catches me looking at him, and a boyish smile breaks out as he ruffles his wet hair, mistaking my observations for admiration. Embarrassed, he may realize the truth of my gaze; I quickly divert the room's attention back to the conversation. "Any word from Ares?"

"Yeah, any news from my dad if we'll be retaliating?" Flint returns to the double doors of the balcony and looks out over the Tuscan countryside.

"Yes, we'll be traveling to the temple after the funeral, and as soon as Rhe–" Demeter pauses and coughs before continuing. "Pardon me. As soon as Persephone is well."

The comment strikes me oddly, and I furrow my brows, replaying her response in my mind. My aching joints, feeling better with Demeter's sap remedy, beg me to stop talking and head to the bathroom for a soak. Blinking away the confusion from her answer, I bounce out of bed too eagerly, and my sore knees protest.

"I'm going nowhere without a long bath and a chat with Ares." I take more caution standing and twist my spine back and forth in a long stretch.

The glass vials of bath oils rattle in my hand as I escape for the bathroom and run a hot bath.

Demeter

That imbecile, Flint, snaps his shit-colored eyes at me when Nyx closes the bathroom door. Putting my finger to my mouth to keep him quiet, I flick my head towards the balcony.

"I know. I slipped up and almost used Rhea's real name." I bark at him before he can scold me. "It won't happen again."

"It better not." Flint stalks after me, and we head to the outdoor balcony on the villa's second floor. The sandstone bricks that form the outside reflect the bright sun as it rises in the morning sky.

"I don't understand why she has to go by *Persephone* anyhow. Why couldn't she keep going by Rhea?"

Flint has too small of a brain to understand the complexities of the mind and how to manipulate it properly.

"Persephone was an older reincarnation of Nyx. She walked these dark tunnels, never leaving the Underworld for the surface, and died within these corridors." I try to explain, but it's clear from his knitted eyebrows he doesn't understand. "It's an easier lie for her mind to accept because it's familiar to her soul. We'll have less resistance from her and a higher chance of finding the missing scepter."

I've become so sick of fabricating Nyx's memories. Life after life is wasted because she can't figure out her puzzle. And without knowing it, she has locked the twelve realms into a catatonic state of existence and marooned me within this realm in the process.

That small kernel of disdain has grown into a raging abhorrence with each of her reincarnations.

Last night, with my fingers spread in a web on each side of her head, buzzing with the sensation of my Life element, my vines weaved into the fibers of her mind like delicate lace. The poison from the carnivorous sap flooded her with new memories of my formation.

If Moros had survived last night, together, we would have invented an entirely new persona for Rhea, convinced all the inhabitants of the Underworld of her existence, and had her walk us straight to the scepter. Moros was the true mastermind of last night's successful mission, despite Flint walking around the tunnels of the Underworld with his chest puffed out in celebration of *his* accomplishment.

What a genius Moros was to cast his illusion at the same time Hermes cast his own. Believing he hid Rhea from us, Moros used the distraction as they bid each other goodbye to lower the curtain of his Mirage. Moros taunted the goddess in her young mortal shell, while Flint drove Hermes to anger. Goading him until he released his enchanted sword to strike through the reincarnation of Nyx and unleash the first of her powers.

Nyx should have drained the life from this sack of shit in front of me instead of Moros.

"All I want is the power that was promised to me." His shoulders begin to smoke like he can intimidate me with his little blazes. My fire lilies have more flames than he could ever muster.

"Don't forget my illusions have her thinking she is in love with you to distract her from the man she really wants. I can easily pierce her with a barb and change whatever I wish." I step toward him with my hands on my hips. My vines silently seep out from the bottoms of my pants. My power pulls at the hanging pothos decorating the verandah.

The green vines of the plant snap around his neck in a blink, and my largest vine flashes its three-inch barb a millimeter away from his eye. Poison threatens to leak from its tip, and if he dares to blink, he'll rake his eyelid against it.

"And what is your excuse for your selfish little moment of passion this morning, huh? I told you not to rush it. She has to want it, or it will break the illusion."

"Oh, she wanted it. Don't fret about your sentimental heart. I was about to have her coming all over my dick until you killed the mood. So, keep that perverted little nose in someone else's business, okay?" His tone rises, mocking me.

"Bold of someone who can only get laid when they poison a woman. Such a pity, *Little Flame*." The pothos pulls harder on his neck, and he strains against the vines. A smile creeps along my face as I allow some of my glamour to fall. The mortal facade I don in this realm dissolves, allowing my Fae features to show. My grey skin and razor teeth gleam while the pointed tips of my Fae ears protrude from my short hair.

Flint recoils away from me, swallowing hard as he watches my transformation. I soak in the discomfort that rises off his aura, letting it fuel me as I spread my smile uncomfortably wide.

He's too focused on my pointed teeth; he doesn't sense me pulling some of his life force and feeding it to the plant. The essence of his Fire Element seeps into me, warming the thin tendrils of the pothos.

He pales when he realizes I'm leeching him, and he relaxes. Raising his hands in surrender, he steps away from me. I loosen the vines around his neck, and one caresses his cheek as it retreats to its pot.

With it, my skin returns to the fresh peach color of the mortal complexion I have chosen, and my teeth flatten out as my ears return to a short, rounded shape tucked within my curls.

"Just keep to our bargain, and I'll keep to mine. And stay out of my way, old hag." He makes a point to bump my shoulder with his as he leaves the balcony. "I'm going to get my fuck buddy some breakfast. So why don't you piss off before I return?" Flint grabs his crotch like he actually has a pair of balls hiding in there.

I may just kill this little asshole before I return to Avalon.

Rhea

The steam rising off the water promises to cocoon me in a pool of relaxation. The oils work quickly to soothe my aching body, and I refresh the water several times, delaying the moment when I'll have to leave as long as possible. It's not until after my bath that I realize some of my soreness is from my period.

Right on time, I suppose. Having a period is one of the human traits the Fates could have spared me; even if it only comes once a year, it's still a nuisance and a constant reminder of the mortal blood that runs through my body, weakening me and making me an outcast.

There are big expectations of me during the Mabon ritual, and I'd rather not have to perform while I'm bloated and cramping. When adequately dried off, wrapped with towels, and sporting a tampon, I return to the room and thankfully find it empty.

My mind is a battleground, constantly thinking of last night's fight and the justice I will have when I find Hermes and make him pay for attacking me. I want nothing more than to plan out my vindication, but as much as I try to recall how the fight began or why we were ambushed, I can't remember.

Like trying to grab a whisp of smoke, the more I reach for it, the further the recollection floats away from me.

Clothes are set out on the bed, which has been made with the pillows stacked nicely. A tray of breakfast food is still steaming with a mug of black coffee, begging me to fill it with embarrassing amounts of cream and sugar. It would be my run of bad luck that there is no sugar. Flint knows how I like to prepare my coffee and should have requested some from the kitchen, but reluctantly, I add extra creamer, making it cooler than I would prefer. But it's hearty and filling.

I finish the fruit salad, popping small pomegranates into my mouth on the balcony, admiring the Tuscan view.

"Thought I'd find you out here. My shoulders jump as Flint returns to our small room and joins me on the balcony.

I feel the slight changes in the air around me as he approaches. One arm wraps around my waist, and the other rubs my hip as he gently pulls my body into his. I rest against his toned chest, and he moves my hair aside, peppering kisses down my neck.

His touch on my skin wears on my patience, and I blame it on my period cramps. I need to get some pain medicine, but for now, I lean out of his path. He ignores my movement, and his lips chase after me, trying to keep me in front of him, suffocating me in his arms.

"What's the matter? Do you feel like–you know, doing it?"

Doing it? What kind of question is that to ask? Even if I were feeling aroused, his question would have turned me off quickly. Before I can answer, Hermes' blue eyes flash in my mind, and my breath catches, startled by the unexpected intrusion.

"You okay?" Flint leans away to look at my face, and I work to clear my expression.

"Yes, just tired." I offer him a smile for a mask, and he resumes his work on my neck.

I shiver at his cold touch on my skin. A lover's embrace should be as hot as the flames he conjures with his element, but instead, it's a cold cauldron that hasn't been lit by a fire in centuries. It feels *wrong.* I clear my throat and set the fruit bowl on the table as a diversion, putting some distance between us.

"It's a shame we have to leave so soon. It's beautiful here." I look back at the landscape.

"Maybe we can come back after Mabon? Just you and I." Flint smiles, and his brown eyes gleam in the bright sun. The offer should make me glad. Any lover would want to spend time alone in this paradise, wrapped in nothing but sheets and each other. But that flash of bright blue eyes burns in my memory again and steals the happiness from the moment.

Perhaps last night's attack still has me on edge, clenching my jaw and trying to avoid being touched; maybe Hermes planted more inside my chest than his sword. Perhaps his enchanted blade severed something within me.

The missing pieces of last night's memories gnaw away at me. Still unable to recall why or how the battle began, I keep falling on the fact that Lupo died during my rescue. The second most powerful Shifter in the realm fell on Hermes' sword last night because of a half-mortal.

I already know what Ares is going to say. Lupo's life was far more valuable than mine.

"Hey, what's so intense over there?" Flint's question snaps me out of my thoughts, and I realize a gust of my Wind is circling the balcony with the beginnings of a small funnel. I tamper my element as my cheeks burn with shame.

"Sorry. I was thinking about things."

"Anything you want to talk about?"

I shake my head no and fiddle with my fingernails. "I'm okay."

After breakfast, Flint let me know Ares wanted to talk to me. With my heart thumping loudly in my skull and terrified to confront Ares, I open the door from our room and find two sentries from one of the wolfpacks on each side of the door. With a great roll of my eyes and a dramatic show of exhaling as loudly as possible, I cross my arms over my chest and lean a shoulder against the doorframe.

Ares placing guards outside my door is a clear sign that he is not happy with me, or perhaps the danger from last night is not yet behind us. I hope it's the latter to save myself from Ares' fire.

"Where is Ares?" I ask my two guards.

"We're told to guard you. Not him."

"Great." I huff under my breath. "Well, let's go, little puppies." I shouldn't tease the werewolves, but I can't help it. Having them assigned to follow me like I'm an incapable infant is annoying.

I may be part human, but I'm still a Fae with Wind elemental power and more adept at handling myself than they could ever be. All this fuss is over nothing, and as soon as I can talk with Ares, I'll be relieved of my babysitters.

Ares practically raised me alongside Demeter and trained me to be the assassin I am today. I'm hopeful his conversation will give me a chance to understand how last night's conflict began and if I can convince him to dismiss my guards.

The wolves follow me into the lift, and I find Ares at the top of the three-story villa. My security detail waits by the doors, and I walk onto the balcony to stand beside him.

His salt and pepper hair is always neatly trimmed and connects to his tidy beard. Patches of grey mingle with the dark hair and the occasional blotch of red glints in the sunlight. He wears a black ribbed tank top showing the tattoos of black flames running up both forearms.

Soul Fire; his specialty.

A sea of burning corpses reaching for salvation swims in the top of the flames as if begging for his mercy that he will refuse to give.

He's tense. His jaw tics as he eyes a hawk soaring across the blue sky, its caw bouncing off the Tuscan hills. Joining him, I lean on the iron railing and track the bird until it fades out of view; he spits over the rail.

"What's got your flames in a knot?" I regret the sarcasm as soon as it leaves my mouth.

"Quite chipper for all the trouble you cost me. Too many Immortals died last night coming to your aid, one of them, my most powerful general and his twin Betas."

I keep my eyes on the scenery, but it's a blur as my mind empties of the reasoning I thought of as I made my way here. Now that I'm standing before him, the heat of his temper radiating off him burns away the bravado I had mustered.

"How are you feeling?" He prods further when I remain silent too long.

I raise my shoulders dismissively as I look over the Tuscan countryside, unsure how to begin my request.

The golden sun shines on the green rolling hills, speckled with cypress trees. Narrow, winding roads connect villas that dot the panoramic view. Orchards of olive trees stand like steady soldiers lined up to sharply peaked mountains in the distance.

"You didn't answer my question." He turns to face me.

The weighted stare of the God of War is one I would gladly avoid, except I need to free myself of these guards, and I need his permission to go after Hermes.

"Annoyed."

He smiles as if he knew what my answer would be. "Ah. Getting restless already?"

"It's a little crowded, you know?" I look back at the guards, standing faithfully at their post by the lift's doors as an airplane flies overhead, spoiling the picturesque cobalt sky.

"It's for your protection."

I open my mouth to protest, but he holds his hand to silence me. I cringe, knowing he could very well slap me if I jostle his short temper even the slightest.

"You are a competent fighter, but our enemies are hunting us. The Mortal Counsel remains out of the conflict for the time being, but Atlas and his loyal mass of followers are desperate to stop the ritual, eager to keep the Shifters in their low status within the Immortal community. Do you think it was a coincidence that they attacked you last night? You were targeted. With Lupo dead, we need the family to stay close."

I fold my arms over my chest to cover the sting of the word *competent* and return to the Tuscan scenery again. This would be enjoyable if everyone weren't in such a foul mood because of me. But I know better than anyone that Ares can flip a switch quickly, and I don't want to be on the receiving end of one of his flames, so I consider my words carefully.

"I am an assassin, am I not?"

"You know I think very highly of your skills." He answers, taking away some of the sting from his earlier comment.

"So, you can understand I prefer a bit less company. Others get in the way, and unless someone goes after Hermes and takes him out of the fight, he will return and bring his squad of fighters with him."

"And you can understand, I'm not willing to lose more valuable fighters to our enemies just because your ego is hurt." He knows how to cut with his words and does it so casually. "Lupo already gave his life for a halfling, and you expect others to as well? This is not up for negotiation."

I release a frustrated huff and rest my weight on the railing. Ares reaches across and pats my head like I'm still a little girl, and he didn't just insult me with his constant reminders of my station within the full-blooded Immortals.

"You'll get your chance to kill Hermes soon enough, but I have another job for you first, and you need to focus on the ritual."

"Yes, sir."

The pit in my stomach drops further and not from the cramps of my period. I know what jobs he expects me to perform, and I steeled myself for his orders.

"Who would you like me to kill?"

I despise the sun and its envy of the moon. Why does it have to rise so fast and steal the night away from me? The time of day when I sense the power of my goddess, night embodied in a perfect human form, the essence of Nyx crosses the horizon, and my soul stretches out to reach her.

The dream of my mate fades with the darkness, chased away by the jealous daylight, and I hate it. Lying on my side in the dark cottage, I stare at the little bottle of black liquid that has been my companion through the long hours of this endless agony. The gold chain holds its small parcel with the simple request penned in dark ink.

"Find me."

Hours ago, I watched my sword fly through the air and strike the woman I love. I memorized the pain that etched along her beautiful face as my blade sliced her open. I held on to the earth as the power of Wind poured into her, and I wasn't fast enough to save her from being swallowed into the belly of the Underworld by a band of Ares' followers.

Sitting empty within this shell of a cottage all night, I fought with my element to find her. I projected my aura around the realm in bursts of angry Light, searching for Rhea, or Nyx, unsure which name she would prefer as the truth of her reincarnation circled the globe.

Like the Northern Lights under the auroral oval, my element shined in the velvet sky for hours, fighting to find the goddess of night against the break of dawn over the horizon.

As they dragged her into the earth of Terra's quicksand, I felt Rhea's presence slip away from me as she passed through the wards that would keep Ares's lair a secret, hidden somewhere within the realm.

The dull ache that throbs with each beat of my heart is a sign that Rhea has been healed, and with the climax of last night's battle, it's not just her that is different. It's as if the realm is holding its breath and waiting for the first break of daylight to see what will unfold next.

The faint pulse of a heart beating outside my chest is reassuring and agonizing. I know she is alive but in the hands of my greatest enemy and out of my reach. The man who has kept her in a perpetual state of torture for thousands of years. Dying and living, only to die again.

The agony over finding her again, only to lose her so quickly, squeezes me in a vice as my heart pumps blood through my body. Each second without her ticks by like a millennium, and I feel like

I'm punished to the banks of the River Styx, destined to roam the earth as a specter.

I place my hand over my chest, and warmth from my aura passes into my heart. I can sense the bond there, our fated connection, hanging heavy as the end of the line that should tether me to her is severed. I hope she can feel it and know I'm looking for her. In every life, it will be me and her, no matter the realm, and no matter the battle. In the end, it's going to be us.

Sitting up and stretching my sore body, the dull headache tapping the back of my eyes tells me I need to sleep. Cold breakfast sits on a cart in the portlet with a note, resting next to cooled coffee.

"Get out of the cottage. And shower."

-M-

I snort a laugh at Medusa's directness as the potion vial sits on the table, staring at me. Thoughts of what could happen if I drank it swim through my mind as I watch the dark liquid swirl inside the tiny glass bottle. It calls to me, and the room's interior seems to shrink on itself as if being sucked into the power held within the vial. The little pulse behind my eyes syncs up with my heartbeat, and the potion seems to take on the same rhythm as it thrums at me.

Gods, Callie is going to be so pissed.

I succumb to the beacon and break the wax seal, begging this small flask to give me the secret that will bring Rhea back to me. Pausing, I wait to see if I have released some ancient plague. When I'm satisfied that no swarms of locus or armies of frogs are descending upon me, I tip the bottle up and swallow the contents. The potion is cold as it travels the length of my throat and cools the aching in my mind. Like two satin-gloved hands caress my mind,

I feel the tendrils of Rhea's magic wash over me. Flashes of images strobe behind my eyelids.

The mountainous top of Angel Falls.

The misting pool at the base.

A wormhole glowing with iridescent starlight within the churning waters under the falls.

A chalice, golden with a jeweled handle.

It's the next piece of the spell, a memory, and my hand was holding the golden chalice in the vision. I bolt up from the couch, my eyes darting hastily across the objects strewn about the space.

Where are those fucking tarot cards?

Hecate left the four cards of her deck in the flaps of the book penned by my mother. The impacts of these cycles slam into me. I wonder what other clues have been left over the ages of the perpetual sequence of life and death of Nyx—the goddess, forgotten by the world who left little trails of breadcrumbs to follow. The hope of each of these clues breaks my heart, knowing they were left behind because there was an inevitability of another death looming over her.

The cards tip out of the book, and Hecate's words run across my memory...

"The first of her immortality was returned to her tonight, locked within the runes of your sword."

These four cards are the key to unlocking the rest of Rhea's powers and restoring her immortality. Suddenly, I realize all my hope of saving her lies within the images painted onto these small rectangles of ancient papyrus.

The ace of swords gleams at me as my Lord of Light is depicted in the brush strokes of the card. The blue topaz stone at the hilt and the gleaming runes that channel the power of starlight reflect on the blade. I wonder why my second sword is not depicted, but my eye travels to the ace of cups. As I suspect, it matches the golden jeweled goblet I just saw in the revelation.

The ace of pentacles rests upside down, and as I turn it correctly, the image of a large gold coin evokes no recollection as I look over the details of the painting. Last, the ace of wands pulls a gasp from my throat. My Caduceus floats in the card suspended by its power. The wood staff, entwined with two snakes, meet a pair of wings at the top. The eternal flame of peace burns above the staff.

The scepter of the Messenger.

I lost it when we fled Tartarus for Gaea during the battle of the Titans. If it's connected to Rhea's powers, this is something I'll have to worry about tomorrow.

My skin crawls each second I stay inside this cottage with the memory that plays through my mind from the potion. Sitting all night restlessly and knowing what I can do to move forward, it's taking all my restraint to delay a few moments while I grab some provisions.

I take the note from Medusa and flip it over to scrawl a message of my own on the back, letting Callie know what I'm doing. Leaving it on the table next to the empty potion bottle and tarot cards, I retrieve my scabbard of swords and my teleportation wand. With my course decided, I press a button at the top of the device. The quiet cottage is ripped away, replaced by the thunderous waterfalls and the Venezuelan forest.

I've been here hundreds of times, and now I realize the reason for the fondness. It's tied to my goddess, Rhea, my only reason for living. I stand at the edge as I look across the realm from this high vantage point. The images from the potion play again in my mind—the falls, the pools below, a wormhole, and a cup. The answer seems obvious, but I'm delaying the action to avoid being too hasty.

I should have eaten something before I left.

Shrugging my shoulders, I stand at the mountain's edge and look at the misting pools below. Securing my swords onto my back tightly, I watch the vapor rising from the crashing water that masks the pools and rocks beneath it. Projecting my aura downward, I close my eyes, feeling for any signs of where I should try to aim my entry. Everything feels the same. There is nothing in the rocky waters below that gives me any indication.

But then I find it.

A small opening where gravity is pulling more than it should. The sign of an unseen barrier resting at the bottom, behind the falls, and close to the mountain's edge.

I'll have to swim down and go behind the waterfall to reach it when I jump. I've leapt off this mountain before, but always with a chute and only for sport. Today, it's something else entirely. I have no idea what will be at the end of this or how to get back, but I can feel the pull of my partner here.

She constructed this. The silvery aura resonates from within the pool, and I trust I will have a way back to her. Grasping the portal wand firmly, I spread my arms outward and fall. I fall into a destiny that will bring her back to me, a destiny that will keep her from the depths of Ares' torment and safely out of the greedy hands of death.

The rushing wind beats against me, and I angle myself into a dive, then flip with my feet, ready to break the water's surface.

The falls are so tall that I count the seconds of freefall until I crash into the pools below. The violence under the surface is a stark contrast to the world above. Torrents of water pull me around, and large boulders, fallen from the mountain over thousands of years, are here like battering rams.

I open my eyes, but it's pointless with the murky brown water in constant battle with the waterfall. Keeping my eyes closed, I feel for that tendril of silver starlight. Finding it, my aura grasps it, and the bond's force thrusts me through the water. The currents rip away the portal wand in my hand, and I fumble for it aimlessly as the intensity of the bond pulls me away. I locate the hole in the rockface, just large enough for my shoulders and the hilt of my swords to squeeze through.

A glow on the other side of the rock invites me forward, and the sight before me is dazzling. Silver shimmering light glows brightly in the dark pool under the falls. The portal is warm as I approach it, and my body heats in the cool water. As I reach it, my outstretched arm contacts the barrier. It's thick and sluggish, like liquid metal, compared to the loose viscosity of the water around me. Pushing my hand into the glowing barrier, I pass into it easily.

When my head and torso have cleared the barrier, I push against the rock with my hands, propelling the rest of my body inside. Finally, fully submerged, the force of the wormhole pulls me blindingly fast. My lungs burn, still holding my breath, I shoot upward as the glowing tunnel turns. What should be the dark, rocky interior of the mountain has opened up into the vast expanse of outer space. As I propel through the wormhole, the universe's black velvet continues endlessly, housing the burning stars that glimmer against the dark.

It's beautiful, but my lungs beg for air. The thick liquid of the portal surrounds me as I shoot through the galaxy, sensing the approaching end above me. I reach behind my head for the hilt of my sword, but before I can wrap my fingers around it, the force of the wormhole shoots me outward into the open air.

I crash onto a rocky surface, spitting and sputtering the water from my lungs. A cold pressure, like slime mixed with fear, slams down on me, crushing me into the rock. My face grinds into the hard surface as the unseen darkness holds me. The cave's shadows crawl and sway, emanating from a dark corner. The chilling sense of dread wraps around my wrists like bindings, and the shadows pull tight. A pair of golden eyes with three pupils stare back at me from the deep shadows.

"Well, well. If it isn't the Herald."

My heart is booming in my mind at the sound of this monstrous voice that traps me, immobile and powerless within its shadowed growl.

The funeral priory stands solemn and prepared, the lifeless form of Lupo resting upon the polished wooden slats. His attire is a study in contrast, dressed in a pristine suit woven from the finest Italian silks, its immaculate pallor contrasted against his jet-black hair.

Surrounding him is a wealth of white lilies, roses, and peonies, adorning every surface of the villa's priory, chairs, and railings. A stone wolf, sculpted in the likeness of Lupo's shifted form, faces east, anticipating the first light of dawn, honoring the Onyx Alphas memory. A rock basin lies in wait at the base of the stone accolade, to be kindled into an everlasting tribute to Ares's second son.

How does Flint feel about these titles given to Lucas and Lupo? The werewolves, fashioned from Ares's power, hold a revered place by his side as his first two sons, eclipsing even the child born of his own blood. I imagine Flint must contend with the notion of living in the shadows of his father's creations, perpetually overshadowed by them.

The attendees, adhering to traditions of Ancient Greece, are garbed in pristine white. Ares's imposing presence commands the center of attention as he regards his assembled family. Lucas, the Zeta wolf, leads the somber procession, taking his dutiful place at Ares's right hand while the left side remains noticeably vacant, a poignant homage to Lupo.

Flint escorts me down the aisle with reverence, and we receive a solemn nod of acknowledgment from Ares as we find our seats. Following suit, the Betas of the great wolves march in solitary procession down the aisle, their respective packs trailing behind them in rank order.

As the congregation gathers, Lucas positions himself across the aisle from me, a silent sentinel of grief. Ares, the embodiment of stoic strength, commences his eulogy, his words punctuated by the gravity of the occasion. Much of the speech wafts over me as I replay the moments of yesterday's battle, taking myself minute by minute to unravel the haze of my memories. A sudden eruption of flames behind Ares snaps me back to the present.

In the blink of an eye, a vivid memory unfolds within my mind—a cave and the visage of Lupo, his lupine form drawing close to mine. In an uncanny metamorphosis, Lupo's features momentarily transform into those of Hermes before reverting to his own. The vivid recollection seizes my breath, swift and poignant as the roaring flames that heralded its arrival. Sensing my unease, Flint places a comforting hand on my knee, his clammy touch unsettling despite his attempt to comfort me.

"You okay?" he whispers, irritation etched in his eyes as I catch the attention of others around me. I respond with a faint smile and a nod, accepting his gesture as I encase his hand in mine, resting it in my lap. The residue of his sweaty palm on my knee sets my skin on edge, every nerve tingling and brittle.

Perhaps I should have taken a nap and some more pain medication for my period before this afternoon's funeral.

The fiery tribute consumes Lupo's remains with swiftness, his Immortal essence reduced to ash that gracefully descends into a channel below, collecting into a funerary urn. These remnants are humbly entombed in the earth at the base of the statue, a final resting place for the once-mighty wolf.

Ares steps forward, his face etched with sorrow, his eyes closing in a silent prayer for his fallen son. As a mark of respect, the gathered mourners also rise to their feet, and Lupo's pack of loyal wolves, ever faithful, encircle Ares and the statue. Shedding themselves of their clothing in solemn unity, they shift into their primal wolf forms, a sea of ebony and obsidian fur, echoing their Alpha's striking appearance.

A warm, orange glow emanates from Ares' chest, culminating in extracting his vibrant, orange aura with a black center. With a reverent toss into the awaiting basin, the air ignites in a brilliant burst of flames, settling into a steady, somber blaze of black fire. Ares' voice resonates through the gathering as he solemnly speaks, "This Soul Fire shall burn eternally, as will the memory of this valiant warrior and beloved son." His words evoke an aching howl from the wolf pack, a mournful chorus echoing their grief into the skies of Gaea.

Lucas joins Ares, offering a silent presence and a respectful hand upon his shoulder. Together, they turn and walk up the center aisle, leaving behind the smoldering pyre of Lupo's memory. Lucas extends his wrists to his Beta, a tall and statuesque woman whose ancestry traces back to the indigenous peoples of America, predating the arrival of European settlers that forever altered the continent's course.

I wonder whether appointing a female as Beta raised eyebrows within the wolf community, but surely none would dare to question the decree of the Wolf King himself. Lucas, his hazel eyes meeting mine briefly, repeats the same gesture, and an intense vision, perhaps a dream, rocks me, nearly pulling the breath from my body. My skin tingles where our skin touches.

Another cave, another pair of hazel eyes belonging to an enormous wolf, and then, abruptly, Lucas rips his hand away, glaring at me with a hint of repulsion. With an air of disdain, he stalks away down the aisle, his pack trailing in his wake.

In that flash of memory, I saw a woman reflected in the large orbs of the wolf. Bright pink hair, purple eyes, and pointed ears looked back at me as if I was looking at myself, but the stranger mirrored in the eyes of the wolf was not me, and yet somehow familiar all the same.

The somber aftermath of Lupo's funeral carries on as the pack selects a new Alpha. Normally determined through challenges, the loss of both Lupo and his twin Betas in the previous night's rescue mission leaves a gaping void within the ranks of the wolves. Another heavy burden to add to the ever-increasing weight of my own unending debt to Ares.

Tonight, they offer the role to the Cappa wolf, Gabriel.

In the ensuing reception of food and music, the female Shifters begin vying for Gabriel's attention while the rest of us quietly attempt to partake in the post-funeral dinner. Lucas left with his packs to prepare for Ares's arrival in Mexico for the Mabon ceremony, leaving Lupo's packs to celebrate.

They will revel in drunken orgies throughout the night until they reconvene with us in Mexico, nursing the inevitable hangovers that follow such celebrations.

Ares sits alone at a table for one. An array of food surrounds him with a goblet of deep, red wine that remains filled by the Lycan servant who stands several feet behind him. His sharp, brown eyes, kissed with a ring of orange near the iris, take in everything.

Flint walks up to his father with a wine glass of his own, shifting nervously on his feet. Flint inspects his wine as if expecting it to change colors. He's avoiding the prospect of meeting his father's gaze, though I don't expect Ares will bother to look at his son.

"What brings you to disturb my meal?" Ares asks as he spears a roasted tomato and crushes it between his teeth. The juices run into his grey, peppered beard, dripping back onto his plate before he wipes his chin with a napkin from his lap.

"Father, I've been thinking a lot lately, and I believe I'm ready for more responsibility. I want to take Lupo's position by your side and lead his former territories."

Ares raises an eyebrow, his expression stern as he remains observant of the wolves and their merriment. "Take Lupo's position, you say? And what would you know about the sacrifices Lupo made to serve in his position? This is no mere game for a boy to play, Flint.

The sting of Ares' words is as palpable as a slap across the face. Flint jerks his head and squints his eyes; the corners crinkle with the pain of Ares's cold tone. As Flint's partner, I sympathize with his father's dismissal, but as a solider of Ares, I question Flint's ability.

Surely, his father would reward him with increased rank and opportunity if Flint proved himself worthy. As I ponder the thought, I begin to wonder about the aspects of Flint's qualities that drew me to him, considering if these merits are only obvious to me. Just as I'm trying to recall the start of last night's battle, I'm trying to get back to the beginning of our relationship and find nothing but darkness.

It's as if my life began last night, birthed when the sword of Hermes pierced me. Shuffling through my mind, searching for memories is like filtering through a filing cabinet that has long been abandoned. Disorganized recollections and fractions of images float to the top with no real familiarity.

"I understand, Father. But I'm ready to prove myself. I know I can do this."

Ares pitches his fork onto his plate and turns to regard his son. Irritation hangs heavy on his brow as he picks at the food between his teeth with his tongue. His tone is harsh as he answers his son's plea. "You did well in your last mission, but do you think leading packs is only about fighting, Flint? It's about strategy, discipline, and the ability to make tough decisions. It's about understanding the balance between strength and restraint. Have you truly learned these things?"

Flint inflates his chest and lifts his chin, defeated but resolute. "I've been studying you, Father. I'm an experienced warrior, and

I've tried to understand the bigger picture, if you would only trust me with your full vision–"

Ares snorts, cutting Flint off with a wave of his hand as he turns back to his food and the crowd of wolves, celebrating the life of their fallen Alpha.

"Understanding the bigger picture, huh? Flint, you are incapable of understanding anything, much less the greater plan I'm working hard to achieve. In any case, it doesn't revolve around you and your desire for power. We will soon be on the brink of a war that will shape the fate of this realm. I will not entertain distractions."

"Father, I can prove myself to you," Flint takes a step closer, "I want to make you proud."

Ares rises from his seat, his towering presence casting a shadow over Flint, who holds his position, meeting his father's judgmental eye. "Unfortunately, you are incapable of that too."

Flint lowers his head, his voice barely a whisper, "I just thought..."

Ares doesn't wait for the sad retort from Flint and turns his back. With a final wipe of his mouth, he tosses a white cloth napkin to the plates of half-eaten food and walks toward the villa, leaving the reception to the wolves for the rest of the evening. He pauses at the double doors and puts his arm out expectantly.

Demeter stops her conversation with two Elementals and walks ahead of Ares into the villa. He follows behind her, and two Lycans close the doors after them.

Flint stares at the vacant spot where his father was sitting. His face burning red with Ares's abrasive rejection of his appeal. Releasing a deep breath, Flint turns toward the stone memorial, walking to the edge of the gardens to look out over the Tuscan hills.

I thin my lips in empathy for his pain. It's not an easy feat to approach the God of War with a request, especially one that holds so much weight at the former position of general and Alpha over the packs of the Eastern regions.

At times, Demeter can be harsh or dismissive to me, not nearly as cold and rejecting as Ares. But I also know Flint has never experienced the *conditioning* Ares puts his soldiers through. I have suffered Ares' punishment for failures many times and understand perfectly the expectations of the God of War.

As a halfling, indebted to Ares for allowing Demeter to raise me within the Underworld, taking me into his ranks, and training me as an assassin, Ares demands perfection, and he ensures he receives it, or he consumes your soul with his fire, delivering you to the Shadows that lurk in the depths of the Underworld.

Flint, at least, should acknowledge his father has spared him from that level of brutality, and I believe that in itself is a mark of fatherly affection.

The roar of the party slams into me, stealing my attention as three Shifters walk in front of me back in human forms and partially dressed; they slosh beer and wine into the grey gravel at my feet. Stepping back, I narrowly miss being sprayed by their clumsiness, and they are too drunk even to register I'm here.

"More like a pack of hyenas than wolves, don't you think?" Lexi's voice cuts through the stillness, her tone laden with sarcasm.

Lexi is the cousin of Lupo; her father was his uncle and another general of Ares' army. She has no mother that I'm aware of, but we don't have a relationship that warrants knowing much about each other.

With long raven locks and even longer legs, I feel the inadequacy of my appearance with my simple white stola, brown sandals, and informal hairdo, letting my golden-brown trusses relax into the warm winds of the evening. I instinctively pull in my bloated stomach, knowing I could never compete with someone as naturally beautiful as Lexi.

I reply, my tone cool and measured to control my irritation at her undermining tones when speaking to me, "Lupo certainly had a tight leash on his packs, so I'll be interested to see how Gabriel fills those shoes as the new Alpha."

Red is her signature color, complementing her dark hair and tan skin. She always looks like she's dipped her lips and fingers in blood, as the color always adorns her, either with her clothes, lipstick, or nail polish. It's all three tonight, and she looks like a walking blood clot against the sea of funerary white.

"I had to change out of those horrid white clothes." She rubs her hands down the sides of her full breasts and tight stomach, laying perfectly flat in her sleeveless tube dress as she stands impeccably in red stiletto heels, even in the rough gravel. Her unapproving eyes roam down my body. "I hate looking pasty."

"Yeah, that's a tragedy." I fold my arms over my chest partly to cover my lumpy body and to keep my irritation from leaking into my Winds.

Lexi, always a source of friction, meets my words with a dismissive smile, her glossy red lips curving with self-assuredness. Her antagonism toward me remains baffling, a simmering rivalry that seems to exist solely within her mind, though I have never been a direct threat to her. The only wound against her is inflicted by herself for failing assassin training, where I excelled.

My only redeeming talent is my ability to be invisible in a room full of people. Being part-mortal, I'm easily dismissed or forgotten as a weaker member of the Immortal society, and it gave me a lot of practice in honing my observation skills. My mortal blood-line shining in my dull appearance makes me equally forgettable among humans.

Lexi thrives on being consumed by the eyes of everyone in the room she steps into. Blending into the background and actively working to remain out of the throngs of attention, a critical skill for an assassin, could never be something she hones to perfection.

Lexi believes her appearance or family stature should be enough to give her the position of her choice when others, like me, have to fight tooth and nail even to be considered.

Thank the goddess I have an elemental ability of Wind, and a powerful one at that, to add to my stealth and make me a deadly weapon despite my low station.

Gabriel locks eyes with Lexi from across the party. Sitting in an armless white garden chair, his legs spread wide; he looks at her with an animalistic gleam in his eye. The expression on his face is all but inviting her to ride him right now as he tips a wine glass up, draining the red liquid.

"I'll bring some semblance of order to this evening," she declares with an overly broad grin, clearly aiming to assert her dominance over the she-wolves, but as she looks down her nose at me, it's clear she intends to include me in the control she expects to exude over the Shifters.

"Undoubtedly," I respond, my irritation palpable as I return a glare of defiance, begging her to try and control me. My Winds flare, hugging close to my body, prepared to lash out at my beaconing.

Two men force Gabriel to break his stare when they approach him, bowing to declare their allegiance and congratulate the new Alpha.

Lexi turns back to me, her mask of seduction slipping to show the viper underneath.

"I know you're Ares's favored little *pet*," she says in a low tone, a veiled threat laced within her words. "But be vigilant. Once you've fulfilled your purpose for Mabon, you'll be expendable. Try not to get in anyone's way, and, for your sake, don't get anyone else killed."

At that moment, my patience snaps. I turn toward her, allowing my Winds to encircle her, my anger manifesting physically. Though she towers over me, I refuse to be intimidated, and my currents spiral up her body, constricting around her throat. Realization dawns in her eyes, panic stirring as my Winds smother her mouth and nose.

"I'm sorry," I taunt her with a cold smile, "I didn't quite catch that. Would you care to repeat yourself?" I click my tongue at her when she doesn't answer, and her eyes swell with alarm as I steal her ability to breathe. "What's the matter? Cat got your tongue?"

Flint intervenes, his arrival defusing the escalating situation. I didn't plan on killing her, but watching her panic just a moment more would have given me sweet dreams tonight.

Flint seizes my elbow, urging restraint while offering a knowing wink to Lexi. The movement pulls the final thread of my annoyance, and I wrench my elbow from his grasp. Releasing Lexi from my hold, I leave her gasping and clutching her throat in the wake of my power.

"Bitch," she spits out in anger as I depart and head back to my room within the Villa.

My fury is a burning ember in my stomach, and I am left with a restless, unsettling need to release it. The thirst for bloodshed festers within me; a dangerous hunger demands to be fed.

I need to find someone to kill, and thankfully, Ares has prepared a target for me.

The ethereal being before me radiates a dark, mysterious power that surpasses any I have ever encountered. Strands of raven-black hair frame her face like tendrils of obsidian. Her presence is cloaked in an aura of pure darkness, as if she is woven from the shadows lurking in the depths of caves.

Pallid skin bears an unnatural, sickly yellow hue devoid of the warmth that courses beneath the surface of mortal flesh. Piercing golden eyes, each adorned with three pupils, fixate on me with an unsettling intensity. Her voice, a jarring cacophony of whispers and distorted screams converging into one, emerges from her throat.

A suffocating void of darkness ensnares me with icy tendrils coiling around my body, and I'm powerless within their frigid grip. As I lie on the rocky platform, I attempt to burn the shadowed tendrils that bind my hands behind my back. The gentle lapping water against the rocky surface provides a haunting backdrop to the echo of droplets that fall from stalactites. Moonlight filters in from above, casting eerie shadows within the cavern.

The enigmatic woman crouched with feline grace in the darkest corner perches upon a massive boulder. Her unwavering golden gaze remains fixed on me as she raises her palm, conjuring a wisp of shadow that takes the form of a black bird. With a mesmerizing transformation, the shadow solidifies into a crow with obsidian feathers and orbs mirroring the golden eyes of its creator. With an inquisitive tilt of its head, the crow regards me before taking flight into the open night sky, its echoing caws resonating in the stillness.

We remain locked in a state of silence as I keep working to free myself from the darkness that ensnares me. The woman is unnervingly still and could be mistaken for a statue were it not for the gentle rise of her shoulders and the shifting of her pupils as she guards me.

My Light is locked firmly within me under her power, and never have I been so inadequately matched against another Immortal. I was rash and unprepared for what I would find on the other side of the portal that was left waiting for me within the tumbling pools of the falls. I can hear Callie's voice now, scolding me for my impatience.

As I work to pull my Element to me, absorbing the pearly light of the moon, I detect the aura of three beings residing within her body. The Light of each, one gold, one maroon, and one grey, like fog on top of a still lake, begin to stand out within the three pupils of the woman's eyes.

Never have I beheld a being capable of combining the souls of others into a single form, and my mind races with the dark magic that would be conjured to perform that feat.

"We don't appreciate wet clothing," the shadowy being finally breaks her long silence from within her shroud of obscurities, her voice a disconcerting blend of whispers and conflict. I open my mouth to speak, but the sound of approaching footsteps on the cave floor behind me halts my words.

"Thank you, Mor. You may release our guest," a male voice intercedes.

Instantly, the glacial shadows recede, releasing their icy grip on me. I rise to my feet swiftly, drawing both swords as I pivot to confront the source of the voice. The tip of my glowing blue blade hovers mere inches from the man's eye as the shine of my starlight returns to me. He regards me with a stoic expression, unmoving in his stance.

His alabaster complexion and stark-white hair shimmer in the moonlight's embrace. Shaved sides reveal the unmistakable pointed ears characteristic of the Fae. His almond, ebony eyes with oversized pupils match the dark swirling tattoos on the left side of his face, an intricate design that extends to three scarred slashes that run from his scalp, down his forehead, and over his left eye. A brown leather vest conceals the tattoos that continue down his neck, running the length of his left arm. A quiver of arrows rests casually over one shoulder while a longbow dangles idly from his hand.

"Tsk, tsk," he clicks his tongue in mock reproach, his black eyes dancing with amusement. "To threaten me with the very sword I gifted you? How rude, Hermes."

A third person has entered the caves, joining the creature of darkness behind me and the white-haired man before me.

"You were quite right in your assumption, Hypnos." My target speaks to the newcomer. "It appears the goddess is still in slumber. Most intriguing."

With my blades poised for battle, I tense at the mention of a slumbering goddess.

Nyx.

I inch forward, putting my blades closer to the man before me. Extending my aura throughout the cave, my Light remains aware of the man's other two companions.

"Indeed, my prince." The newcomer answers.

The figure stationed at the cave's entrance, possesses a complexion as dark as midnight under a new moon. Like the man I've been holding in my sword's path, his alabaster hair cascades in long, twisting locks. His eyes resemble the interior of an oyster shell, creamy white with swirls of silver and gold.

They are formidable warriors by their attire and the array of blades adorning their biceps, thighs, and waist. Each weapon tells a tale of patience and precision, a mastery that commands respect.

"Perhaps we can have a more reasonable conversation when the Lord of Light is not pointed at my eye."

"How do you know my sword's name?" The reference to Nyx and the mention of my sword by name pushes the blood within my body to race faster as an uneasy familiarity begins to creep along my spine.

My Light maps out the cracks and divots of the cave walls and pushes out to the surrounding island. When I jumped off the top of Angel Falls into the void Nyx created long ago, I hoped to find the salvation to her curse on the other side.

As I continue to search this realm with my powers, recognition stirs within me, and I'm becoming more certain I've visited this land before, perhaps many times, in search of aid for Nyx and her eternal battle with the God of War.

"As I said, I gifted it to you. During your *last* visit here." Crossing his arms over his chest, he exposes two leather cuffs encircling his wrists, revealing a striking symbol—a union of two overlapping circles pierced by an arrow, encompassed by a larger circle embellished with delicate vines and white roses.

"My mother wore a necklace with this symbol." I drop my swords as understanding slams into me like the waves crashing against the rocks within the caves. "This is Avalon. I have returned to the Realm of Avalon, home to the Titan Artemis. We thought it was destroyed."

The scarred man smiles, patting my shoulder jovially at my statement. "Come, cousin. We have much to discuss."

"Cousin?" I cock an eyebrow at the familial mention.

"Sir, we'll excuse ourselves if you have no further need of us." The dark woman with the souls of three resonates from the dark corner behind us.

"Of course, Mor. Thank you." The prince answers.

Like a cube of sugar dissolving in hot tea, she melts into the shadows and is gone.

The pair of men exit through the mouth of the cave with a chuckle as if they are enjoying a private joke between the two of them. My mind is reeling understanding that Avalon remains. It was the first realm destroyed in the battles of the Titans as the goddess of the hunt was killed, her Titan essence drained from her Immortal body.

Stepping off the stone riser, I turn behind me to take in the cave and contemplate a way to return to Gaea but the questions that darken my mind give me pause.

Nyx knew of this realm and gave me a connection to return. There is something here important to her; otherwise, she would not have left the vial or created the portal that delivered me.

Trusting in my mate and her plan, I follow them.

Their delight is unabated; the pair of Fae lead the way up a well-trodden path that runs parallel to the edge of a forest, guiding me toward a medieval castle that materializes through the mist.

The fog hangs low, an ethereal veil above the earth. Above, the colossal moon is golden and full as it shines brilliantly, its light amplifying the brilliance of billions of stars that blanket the night sky. So much closer and larger than the moon of Gaea, I can nearly see the details within the rings of craters as if I could reach out and run my hand along the rim of one.

The castle, perched on a cliff high above the shore of a vast lake with a central boulder outcrop crowned by a solitary tree, draws closer into view.

"I shall send word for dinner, my prince," Hypnos offers.

"Your thoughtfulness is appreciated, Hypnos," the white-haired prince replies.

Both men stand impressively tall, surpassing even my considerable stature. Their lean, muscular forms resonate with an otherworldly strength as we march up the trodden path.

The air smells of honeysuckle, and a salty breeze ushers in from the west, jostling my dark locks. Waves soak beaches made of black sand that glimmers with a deep hunter green as if a billion emeralds have been crushed into a fine powder. Wood flutes and crickets put on an orchestral arrangement of nighttime; the melancholy tune is almost playful at times, like children telling secrets and snickering.

"The wood sprites are–*excited* to see you return, cousin." The prince calls over his shoulder with a cocked grin of amusement. "They enjoy watching your gait in your fighting leathers, though they wish you had brought the goddess with you." His smile extends further, and I crane my neck toward the tight collection of trees, seeing nothing in the woods but the occasional whisp of shadow that darts from branch to branch.

"Are you telling me the wood sprites are looking at my ass?" I gruff as I follow behind them, casting a look of warning into the dark woods. My host bursts into a roaring laugh, tipping his head back; it echoes into the night.

"I am Orion, Prince Consort of Avalon, since you do not recall me." He introduces himself. "Our companion in the cave is The Morrigan or Mor. She is my most formidable warrior, I'm sure you would agree. And this is Hypnos, my most trusted Regent and friend."

Orion chuckles heartily, casting his dark gaze towards the castle. "We are very much alive and thriving, as you can see. Though we find ourselves in a delicate situation with our queen amiss."

"How does one misplace a queen?" I inquire, my curiosity piqued.

Now thoroughly amused, Orion grabs at his sides. "We will answer all your questions, Hermes. But first, let us retire to the dining hall. It has been a long while since we last had the pleasure of your company, and there is much we would like to know."

He nods toward the castle that seems to emerge straight from my memories of medieval England, its stone walls adorned with climbing ivy and white jasmine. Torches line the ramparts, casting an eerie orange glow, and soaring towers pierce the fog and mist above.

Before us, two monumental stone carvings flank the castle entrance—a pair of colossal scorpions, twenty feet in height, poised to strike with raised tails, hold the thick metal chains of the drawbridge.

An imposing barrier indeed.

On either side of the path leading to the bridge, looming stone figures are sculpted overlooking the castle. As we approach, the path widens, revealing a magnificent phoenix, wings outstretched in mid-flight, while a hare stands at its feet as if poised for escape. Two stone basins flank the phoenix, with flames curling brightly to guide our way.

Orion pauses and faces me, gesturing toward the castle. "Welcome back to Starfall."

A previous rendezvous surges into my memory as if the moon's light clears my trepidation. We have all been here before. A vision of my mother, Nyx, Calypso, and Achilles waves like a flag in the breeze, ushering me onward.

The vision of the chalice in my hand flashes like someone passing a burning torch in front of my eyes. As if the realm provided me with the answer, I speak the words that bounce in my mind with a fond smile on my face.

"Well, I'll be dammed. The Castle of the Grail."

Washington, DC, is beautiful in September, but I wish we were here in another month when the leaves change colors. I also wish we were here under different circumstances, but the alternative for defying Ares is death, and I came close enough to that two nights ago.

Seeing the splashes of yellow, orange, and red along the tree lines and the crispness that fills the air with hints of fall, ushering in a change to the season would lift some of the crushing weight bearing down on the shadows within my mind.

Instead, the leaves are mostly green as they hang within the trees, jostled by the delicate currents of air that dance between the limbs.

I lay back on the roof of the building Flint and I are using as we wait for the signal to start our attack. With my hands behind my head and one ankle crossed over the other, I bask in the warm sunlight as the Wind plays through my hair.

Since the Elementals attack, my mind has been covered in a thick blanket of fog that refuses to leave. Flashes of fragmented memories tease me with recognition of events that I can't recall or visions of people I have never met play in my mind.

It's creepy.

Flint occupies himself with a simple mortal game on his cell phone, sending small digital troops to attack a warring clan's castle. Meanwhile, my senses are alive with tension as my Winds monitor the lively city rushing along its day, oblivious to the shift the world will take in a matter of minutes.

Every sound, every flicker of movement, is a potential threat. The distant rumble of a subway train, the hushed whispers of passersby, and the occasional siren in the distance all contribute to the symphony of urban life but also overwhelm me as I work to quiet my mind.

I allow myself to daydream, following the path of the breeze; it paints a picture of couples lounging on picnic blankets in short green grass, wrapped up in the day and each other as they share stories, laughter, and affections.

A sense of loneliness blankets me as I long to feel the heat of passion that these couples share.

As I think about the sticky sensation left by Flint's touch on my skin, I imagine what it would feel like if the burn of his flames ignited the hunger that lies dormant within me when I look into his brown eyes.

I envision a strong hand holding mine, full of warmth and security, as we walk the National Mall and find a shaded place to sit under the groves of trees. Spreading out a picnic blanket, we would lay together, wrapped in each other as we talked and laughed, snacking on our basket of food.

The vision in my mind is so real I close my eyes and let the day's sunlight play the Mirage through my eyelids. The hazy image slowly comes to focus as my fingers thread through my companion's hands.

Running my palm up his arm, corded with muscles, I cup a man's cheek. Lifting my eyes to meet the face of my fantasy, I rip myself out of the daydream when it's Hermes' deep cerulean eyes that gleam back at me.

I sit up quickly from my resting position as Flint idly keeps focused on his phone, unaware that I startled myself.

Calming my racing heart, walking to the edge of the building, I rest my elbows on the brick and let the Winds caress me in the embrace I wish I could feel from Flint. I feel like I'm tumbling into the Void, desperate to reach out and grasp anything for salvation.

With my head in my hands, I think back to the past occasions throughout mortal history when Ares used Wind Sirens as a catalyst to start a war of the mortals, and I pity the coming days of the world nations.

In the mortal year of the 1770s, a Siren sat in trees while Red Coats from Britain faced off against farmers who would eventually unite. The Winds at Lexington, Massachusetts, echoed off the trees like a bullet and launched a series of gunshots and bayonet charges that would take years to quiet.

A hundred and fifty mortal years later, another Siren sat on the corner of a busy street in Sarajevo's beautiful city center to do it again, and the world felt the echo of Winds as the Archduke and Duchess's deaths became the cataclysm for the first World War.

The mortals have become so bloodthirsty that Ares rarely has to ignite the wars now. He can sit back in the luxury of chaos he's manufactured and move across lines, enflaming one side and then moving to the other. Billowing the flames of war hotter and hotter to keep the fighting going.

At the end of the Second World War, humans were given a false sense of security when the Mortal Treaty was amended to state no Immortal may hold a position of power for the countries of the realm, directly or by marriage. They may only be held by mortals, which doesn't really matter because most of the world's leaders work for Ares anyhow.

Except for the brave few who try to resist the God of War.

Occasionally, the high spirits of the mortals elect someone who thinks they will be the agent of change in how this realm works. They reject Ares' orders and the lavish spoils of Immortal riches he offers. In return, he revels in the madness he causes to their countries before he sends me in to deliver the final message. Disease, famine, and poverty plague them. Then his assassin arrives on the gentle currents of Winds that circle the globe, and I rip their minds from their skulls.

The bearded president in the theater and the young president in the convertible both had high hopes for change before they met their end on the Winds of Ares' Sirens.

Another one will join them today.

The American President Sims took control of the Oval Office and has been working to create a coalition of other world leaders who would oppose Ares. The ones that fight over the crumbs he cast down at his feet think they can rise against him and become the powers at the top of the food chain. Little do they know how far down the chain they truly are.

They'll find out today.

Ares's methods are volatile and harsh, but he sees a future where mortals and Immortals live in harmony together. Tired of hiding within the shadows and watching the Shifters get trampled on by the stronger Elementals, Ares will fight until we are all seen as equals.

Being a half-mortal, I would like to see a day where I'm accepted by the Elementals as a fellow Siren. Not just a human with half the soul of a Fae who can control the Wind.

Flint curses and clicks the side button on his phone, darkening the screen and sliding it into his pocket. Stretching his back, he yawns and looks over the streets. I roll my eyes at his lack of willingness to help me keep watch and wish I was alone up here.

He tried to petition Ares yesterday for control over half the Shifters, and now that we are on a mission, he just plays on his phone. Releasing a heavy sigh, I return to the capital and the long shadows stretching over the monuments.

"Can't you just tell me why you're upset, Pers?"

"It doesn't matter," I answer dully as I watch two birds dance on the airstreams together.

The Greek restaurant on the corner tortures me with the aroma of fresh lamb searing on a grill as kebabs are prepared for the dinner rush. Seared cheeses cooking in pans reach my nose, and the crunch of crispy phyllo echoes out of the establishment as the patrons savor the delicious food.

My stomach grumbles, and I measure the sun on the horizon, feeling the light of the day making its way across the sky. I wish

I were enjoying the city below instead of waiting to thrust it into chaos.

Another five minutes, and we should be ready to begin.

"It matters if you're upset," Flint pleads with me, but I sense the irritation in his tone. He doesn't actually care to know why he pissed me off because he would have sided with me last night instead of rescuing Lexi.

"Do you realize what it feels like when you defend everyone else except me?" I turn my eyes from the large mansion that houses the sitting President.

I don't need to watch the White House. My Winds tell me exactly where everyone is within the buildings. Running through the air conditioning vents, my currents keep tabs on the President as he goes through his day.

Flint takes in a large breath of air and pauses for a second before releasing it.

"You don't get what it's like for me." His chestnut eyes watch the traffic light change from yellow to red, and the cars stop to hear how he'll turn this into something about himself.

"I've never been good enough for him. He's always shoved me aside to focus on his other pets. All the while, I only want my father to–" Flint purses his lips together, watching a new line of cars take off toward their destinations before continuing. "– to be a father to me."

The light turns green, and the realm carries on, not knowing in two minutes, it will all flip upside down; today's events will only be an appetizer of the coming havoc and will hopefully distract the mortals from the Mabon ceremony.

Flint's words should strike sympathy in my heart, but resentment rises to the surface.

You have no idea what his wrath feels like. My chest burns where Ares has carved his anger into me with his Soul Fire for disappointing him in the past. Even though the last time was more than fifty years ago, I still feel the phantom burn of his Flames—marks left on my soul that never my body.

Only one Immortal ever challenged Ares's directive publicly. Triton, a Water Elemental, and the Architect of the Underworld. He was ushered away screaming at Ares, and while it's common knowledge he was allowed to live, no one has seen the Water Elemental in ages.

Triton is the cousin to the Goddess of War, Athena. His ability of Aquatic Adaptation keeps the Underworld safe under the crushing pressure of water, but no one would dare ask what happened to him.

I imagine he lives within a quiet corner of the Underworld, keeping himself busy maintaining the wards and shields that protect Ares' secret base at the bottom of the ocean, and I can't help but wonder if he still disagrees with Ares. If given the chance, would he rise against him or choose a different path?

"You know I don't even know who my mother is?" This is the typical speech Flint goes into. First, it's his inattentive father and then the absent mother figure. "I once overheard two of the Betas talking about secret breeding chambers hidden in the Underworld. They said Father keeps powerful Elementals down there to mate with, trying to produce an heir that could succeed him one day." Flint forces a laugh through his nose, shaking his head back and forth in denial.

I've never heard a rumor like that.

"He'd never let anyone be stronger than he is but what hurts is they act like I don't already exist."

Flint finally looks at me as I've been watching him, waiting to see how he'll twist my hurt feelings around to something minuscule to keep the pity about himself.

"We're on the eve of a big shift in this realm, Pers, and we've all got our part to play. You only see your short-sighted assassins' missions and think you know the bigger picture. You don't know anything. Too much has been put into motion, and no one will be able to stop what is coming."

It's ironic Flint wants to lecture me about the *bigger picture* his father refused to share with him yesterday.

The President finishes his meeting in his Oval Office.

My Winds rise around the area, so the hired Elementals that provide security for the rebel leader of the United States can't pick up on our position.

The streams of my breezes twist through the trees and buildings. The crowd assembling at the rear of the White House gathers to see their leader and hear his speech about astronauts who will depart for a new mission to the moon. My gentle torrents dance and sway around all living beings in the city *except one.*

I lock eyes with a woman as Flint wails about his childhood and unapproving father. She is standing on the opposite street corner, looking directly at me, watching me with squinted eyes against the setting sun.

Tan skin and a streak of grey hair frames her face. Rings and bangles rest on her fingers and wrists, and a long, wine-colored stola dances in my breeze. As I fix my eyes on her, I see the whisps of smoke and shadow that undulate within my breezes.

This is a Dark Mirage, and this woman is not really here, merely projecting her aura to observe from afar.

"Who are you?" I ask her, whispering in her ear with my Wind, carefully ensuring Flint is not alerted. Though, I don't know why I worry. I could hurl myself off this building, and he wouldn't realize it for several minutes.

While her presence is unexpected, something within the black hue of her eyes holds me in reassurance, as if promising she'll keep my secrets.

"Hecate." She answers. *"Who do you believe you are?"* She replies within my mind.

Her question makes me recoil in shock, my brows pinching together, almost offended. Of course, I know who I am. I am Persephone, Wind Siren and assassin of Ares. I don't answer her and only return her indifferent stare.

"I've never seen a sleeping goddess walk the realm before. You should–WAKE UP." Hecate's final two words blast into my mind as a series of flashes bombard my eyes.

Visions of screaming, burning, drowning mortals of ancient days crowd me in an instant.

A placid soldier lays on a two-thousand-year-old battlefield, eyes open staring at me. A war I helped start for Ares, where thousands died. A skeleton, wrapped with tight skin and standing at a fence, wearing a uniform of stripped clothes that swallow the emaciated figure. Sunken eyes look at me with the years of haunted memories in their hallowed gaze.

A passenger ship is drug to the seafloor by an unnatural whirlpool that consumes the ship like a hungry giant. The swirl of the great vortex drowns out the banging and prayers of the mortals who only have a few more seconds of life left.

The water that floods their lungs chokes me, and I gasp for air.

"What the fuck is wrong with you? Are you even listening to me?" Flint crinkles his eyes and shows no concern for my sudden panic. Only his irritation, knowing I didn't hear his whining at our position on the rooftop.

I look back and search with my Winds, and only a plastic bag rustles by the street corner where the woman had been standing. The caw of a crow bounces off the buildings, and my eyes try to find it.

The President exits the balcony doors, raises his hands, and smiles at his fans. Members of the press click their cameras, and news anchors perform their practiced introductions.

My skin warms as my mind pushes against the direction I need to carry out.

I don't truly want to do this.

The Wind dies on my thought, and the world stills as if pausing, allowing me to decide. Every leaf in every tree waits, holding its breath. Flags high on poles hang limp as if they are sleeping. The gentlest ruffle of birds' feathers thunder as loud as a car engine in the stillness.

You must do this. Ares will kill you if you let this president live. I give myself the reminder I need to unfreeze the brief moment of free will that wants to take over my actions. I long to run as freely as the airstreams that dance in the clouds, but no corner of this realm would be dark enough to hide me from Ares' Fire.

President Sims is the one trying to lead the others against Ares's efforts for equality. The example *has* to be made. That is why Ares sent me, his executioner.

Closing my eyes, I allow the currents of the realm to rise again, and a single surge of Piercing Winds races through the realm.

The combined actions of the Wind Elementals stationed across the globe, just as I am, form a single zip that runs through the atmosphere as they act at once, and I join them.

With only a pinprick at the front of President Sims' skull, my Winds easily cut through his flesh and bore through the hard bone. He's dead in an instant, but Ares needs dramatics.

Inflating like a balloon, I expand my Winds, and he loses the back half of his skull as his brains and blood paint the wall behind him. Unfortunately, his Vice President and NASA Administrator are also behind him.

Their red-streaked faces of shock will make excellent news clips that will circle the realm before we return to the Underworld.

"I'm finished. Let's go," Coating my words with false boredom as I swallow the magnitude of what I just did. A hand of remorse grips my neck, and I want to add my own to it and tighten the hold.

Flint grabs my arm, firm but gentle, and rubs his thumb across the taut fabric of my tactical shirt. "You need to drop this childish game of resentment for attention. The last thing we need is to be at each other's throats when the world starts to go to shit.

An earnest fire burns behind his brown eyes and wants me to understand. He hopes I'll push down my feelings for the greater good of what he and his father are working toward.

"It's already gone to shit."

"Where are my blades?"** A deep voice booms from within the castle. "I can feel my babies have returned to Avalon."

"Hephaestus is not going to be happy when he sees what Hermes has done to the Daggers of Darkness, sire," Hypnos says quietly as Orion removes a wide leather belt containing several blades from his waist. His eyes track my sheath, and I glance back to the dark hilt of my mother's blade.

We take seats around a long wooden table in a dining hall, and I repeat the name of the approaching man in my mind, searching for a shroud of recognition but finding none.

The ghosts of past celebrations have long quieted among the old tapestries and ornate paintings that line the tall stone dwelling. As I take them in, the whispered memory of a lute floats in the stale air above us as a musician plucked a tune. The smiles of patrons packed into the halls warmed the space much more than the fire that burns today.

Instead, a grey shroud hangs heavy over the castle, and cobwebs have ebbed their way into the rafters of the high ceilings. A cold draft creeps by, hanging low to the ground despite the large logs crackling in the vast fireplace, working hard to warm the cold fortress.

It's as if the realm is starving and one day will soon wither into a layer of dust to be blown away into nothing. Perhaps it is the absence of their queen; perhaps it is an effect of the spell Nyx has cast.

Echoes of the kitchen staff making final preparations for the dinner Hypnos ordered and the booming voice of the man stomping down the halls are the only other signs of inhabitants aside from us.

The double doors at one end of the room burst open. A portly man, soaring over eight feet in stature, bounds in. He limps on a metal peg as he stalks up to the table. It thumps against the flat stone floor of the castle as he takes long strides toward me.

A long red beard is peppered with streaks of white. Thin braids house small metal cuffs hanging at their ends in his long hair and beard. He smells of fire, and soot stains his white tunic and brown pants.

"Hermes! My boy! It's good to see you." The man embraces me, overshadowing me in his large arms and picking me up like a child. I can't help the grin that forms with the stranger's affections as Orion stands and addresses the giant with a half bow.

"Heff, Hermes has no memory of this place."

"Oh, what a pity. How is my best girl?"

This man is the definition of *jolly* if the word was ever used to describe someone. Round and large, he makes no attempts to hide his big stature or personality. I tilt my head and pause, assuming he means Rhea–or Nyx. Perhaps she went by another name when these people knew her.

"My mate is not well, and a clue she left behind hundreds of years ago has led me here."

Orion and Hypnos exchange glances, but Hephaestus flicks his eyes to the scabbards at my back. His expression shifts from jovial to murderous in a blink.

"I wouldn't be well either if you turned my blades into a decrepit sword! What have you done to my babies?" The pitch of his booming voice turns up at his question. Without waiting for a response, he rounds my chair and extracts the Mistress of Darkness from my scabbard.

I pitch the chair behind me with my foot, sending it screaming to the wall. Pulling the Lord of Light and holding the hilt firm within my hands, I point it at the man's chest. The enchanted blade glows blue at my touch.

"Give me back my sword," I demand. He stops inspecting the sword and raises a bushy red eyebrow as he shifts his downcast eyes to mine.

"Not–your–sword." The large man says each word slowly, like a challenge.

"I came here for clues about Nyx and the cup I saw in my vision. I did not come here to have my faithful swords taken by a red-bearded giant."

As I reel my arm back, ready to lunge, the large man presses a hidden clasp in the hilt of the dark blade in his hand. The sword erupts, and a casing of dark metal splits into two halves, falling to the floor with a clamor.

The sword's hilt now has two handles, and he holds a pair of daggers in each of his hands, shining with a silver glow. The momentum of my sword carries it forward, but an unseen force stops me. Cold encases my arm, holding me in place.

"Glad we got here in time for the excitement. Hermes still comes in ego first." The woman from the cave, The Morrigan, saunters into the room. Her cold tendrils of shadow twist around my wrist, holding my arm back. Her appearance in the dining hall starkly contrasts the creature crouched in the cave.

With a flare of blue starlight, my Element eats away at the thin shadows encasing my wrists, dissipating the moment's tension.

Still discolored with grey skin, gone is the pale-yellow complexion that looked like a disease had overridden her body. The harrowing voice of darkness now sounds like that of a typical woman. She no longer has yellow eyes with three pupils as she pierces me with a crimson stare.

She is clearly not my biggest fan.

"Mor, can you believe what they did to my precious babies?" The round man holds the two daggers in oversized hands, making them look like nothing but cutlery from the dining table.

"How did you do that?" I ask, returning my sword to my scabbard. The weight against my back is thrown off by losing its companion sword, which is now in pieces. I approach him and take the daggers.

"Oh, there is not a weapon in all the realms that does not speak to me when I am near it."

Mor sits in an unoccupied chair opposite Hypnos and next to Orion, who sits at the head of the table.

"Hephaestus, I'd love to hear what brought my cousin back to Avalon. Why don't you join us for some supper?" Orion offers the giant man just as platters of roasted meats, potatoes, and vegetables stream out of another set of doors. The smell of fresh bread and the red glow of wine bring water to my mouth as servants place the food on the grand table.

"I'd rather take my babies back to the shop for a sharpening and a good cleaning." Hephaestus turns to me, placing his hands out expectingly. I flick my eyes to Orion, and he gives me a pleading look.

The symbol on his leather cuffs peeks at me and reminds me of my mother. Putting my trust in her, as if her spirit is present here, I hand over the daggers, but he waits with a patient, wide smile.

"The sword, too, my friend. I forged these blades and imbued them with their magic. No one takes better care of their babies than I do." His jolly demeanor has returned and lightened my resolve.

These swords have long been important to me, weapons that protected me in battle, and I owe them the same as they guard my back.

We're on the edge of war with Ares, and the coming days will be fraught with conflicts. I could use freshly sharpened blades; if Hephaestus forged them, he would have the right tools and deft skills to care for them.

I remove my scabbard and release my weapons to him.

He exits the dining hall, one booted heel thudding the stones as the metal peg clinks in his retreat.

Servants fill wine goblets, and Mor has already helped herself to an extensive food offering, devouring mouthfuls nearly whole, hardly taking the time to chew. Hypnos delicately cuts his food and eats at a dignified pace as his alabaster eyes roam the hall. Slumped in his chair, resting his elbow on the armrest, Orion holds a wine goblet, swishing the drink.

"So, dear cousin. Tell us how you got back here after all this time. It's been nearly five ages since we saw you and Nyx last."

"So, you knew her as Nyx?"

Orion smiles. "As you well know, the soul of the goddess takes any form, but to see her is to know her. She has come here with many faces over the ages. The last was a queen of the mortal realm called Guinevere. You went by Lancelot and were at battle with your foe. A rival king known as Arthur."

Guinevere, with her strawberry golden hair and flowing gown of green and gilded thread, is a hazy wave within my memory. Holes are burned through the image like it's incomplete, and I fight to pull together enough to recollect that lifetime.

"Perhaps The Lady should attend to his memories, sire?" Hypnos pauses with food on his fork.

"Perhaps." Orion agrees. "Tell us, Hermes. What is the news from Gaea?"

I spend the next half hour telling my newly reacquainted cousin and his companions of our time on earth—everything I can recall from the age when my partner went by the name Guinevere until now.

I don't miss the tossed glances of Orion to his companions when I mention the work Hecate and Demeter have done over the lifetimes of Nyx to fight against Ares, my sword restoring some of her power and immortality, and the portal that landed me here.

"So, you have come again for the Grail?" Orion says with a pleased smile. "Wonderful, indeed. It seems the spell of the goddess has evolved, Hermes. If you have no recollections of Avalon and your ties here, that is a new facet of the spell that didn't exist before."

"What exactly is our relation, Orion?"

Admittedly, the genetic resemblance is not striking enough between Orion and me to make any familial connection on my own. The magic of the Fae comes from nature, and the moonlight of Avalon creates an opaline shimmer to Orion's cream-toned skin that glints against his long, pointed ears. He is more a creature of the forest than the mortal appearance of my form.

"Our mothers were sisters." Orion drinks his wine, and I cut into roasted boar and spear a steaming potato. "Half-sisters, actually. Our grandmother, Pandora, was Fae, apprentice to the great Artemis and first queen of Avalon."

Orion recounts my mother's family lineage. These facts I perhaps once knew, but I suppose my mate had a reason to weave the memories of Avalon into a vault of protection. One we need to unravel to understand.

"Pandora first married for duty to a Fae named Percival, and he was killed in battle before he saw the birth of his daughter, my mother, Elaine. The second time, Pandora married for love. Her second husband was an Elemental named Galahad, who gave her three more daughters, Hecate, Demeter, and your mother, Daphne.

"My mother was heir to the throne, and her sisters were to serve as her maidens. After Artemis was slain, Pandora lost the legions of the Valkyrie defending Avalon, but the realm survived. Hecate and Daphne found their callings on other realms, and Demeter remained behind, taking care of Pandora as she fell ill with an incurable affliction of her mind."

Orion drops his gaze, and a shadow falls over his brow as he recalls the memories.

"The same suffering would take over my mother's mind until it consumed her, and Demeter inherited the throne." He clears his throat, taking a large gulp of wine. Hypnos has finished eating, but Mor is still ingesting food at a ravaged pace, as if she has starved for days.

"Then, one day, you arrived with your new bride, Nyx." An expectant gleam shines in Orion's eye as if hoping this too would be a revelation.

My eyebrows shoot into my hairline, and I choke on the gravy-soaked bread I had just popped into my mouth. "Bride?" My gaze travels off, losing focus within the cracks between the tightly lain stones that make up the floor of the dining hall. A vision of Nyx with a thick braided crown of raven hair and eyes that shine with silver starlight is looking at me. She looks down with both of my hands in hers and gives them a nervous squeeze.

"We can't wear rings; we're going into battle."

Instinctively, my hand covers my sword necklace that has dangled from my neck with faithful allegiance all these ages.

Orion breaks out into a coughing spell as Hypnos reaches for a handkerchief. Dots of red and black blood soil the garment, and Orion waves Hypnos off with false reassurance as he continues.

"Grandfather had nearly lost his mind, broken-hearted with grief after grandmother passed so painfully slow, going insane. He became known by the Sprites as the Fisher King as all he did was sit by the lake, casting his line in repeatedly and mumbling to himself.

"Nyx couldn't stand to see him so grief-stricken, and as if she plucked Pandora's soul out from all the stars in the sky, she created a Mirage over the lake, and grandfather was reunited with a projection of his greatest love. His eyes lit up with happiness as he spoke to the image Nyx conjured, and he died peacefully in his sleep that night."

"How did the cup come into play?" The story is fascinating to me, and I want to hear more about Nyx, about my mother and her life here, but time is something I don't have at my disposal.

Finished with my dinner, I sit back in the wide, wooden chair, resting my elbow on the arm and bouncing my boot on the rung to alleviate some of my tense nerves. The sound of a metal tray scraping the wood sings within the empty hall as Mor slides one of the platters of roasted meat and root vegetables to her and uses it for a plate.

"The goddess returned to Avalon, blazing through the sky like a celestial comet with a staff and a dying Herald, crashing into the lake."

My unblinking eyes remain on Orion; all I can do is stare.

"I was dying?" My voice is barely above a whisper.

"The goddess pulled you from the lake, which shimmered silver with her aura as Nyx's powers seeped into the waters. She demanded a cup, and in her haste, your mother retrieved the wedding chalice of Pandora.

"Nyx lifted your head so you could drink the waters laced with her power from the goblet and healed you."

A bright expanse of pearly moonlight fills the dining hall and sears my eyes as a memory plunges into my mind, stealing my breath as if my heart were being ripped from my chest.

♫ *"Please Don't Go" by: Stephanie Rainey* ♫

Coughing and sputtering, I sit up. *"You can't do this, Nyx."*

My chest burns from the gape that is stitching itself closed with my mate's healing powers. The Dark Spear that tore through me feels like it's still impaled within me.

But it's not the spear making me feel this way. It's Nyx; she is injured.

The fibers of my flesh knit together, and the strength of her power warms my cold body. My chin quivers, and tears replace the droplets of water that race down my face. "You can't leave me," I whisper.

My throat closes with despair as I watch the color drain from her skin and ease her onto the ground—Hecate sprints here from the castle and drops to her knees, watching with wide eyes. Demeter remains standing with her arm around my weeping mother. Three beings with the power of moonlight join me as we witness the goddess of the realms give up her battle with life.

My eyes rake over her body, hurrying as I search for her wounds, but I find none.

Every moment of happiness I've ever experienced has been moments with her, and it's as if I'm watching them weep out of her as pools of silver ooze from her body onto the soil. The grey shimmer of her immortal ichor remains on the surface as Avalon refuses to soak in her power, rejecting her death as well.

"It's the only way." Her hoarse voice cracks as she looks at me with dreary eyes. Some of the light has already dimmed within them, and I feel my heart fracture.

The scabbard on my back starts to suffocate me, and I remove it, dropping it to the ground next to her.

Leaning over her, I summon the moonlight that coats the night, lifting the particles of Lumos and bending them to my will. I beg my power to save Nyx as I blanket her in a Shield of Light, but her aura continues to escape her as if her very soul is cracked in a dozen places and unable to contain her lifeforce any longer.

"Tell me," she whispers, blinking her eyes so slowly I fear they won't open again. "Tell me."

"I–" My voice won't work. I know what she wants to hear, but if I say it, she'll leave.

Her hand goes slack, and my Caduceus rolls out of her grasp.

Desperation is a boa constrictor, wrapping around my body and wringing me of all thought.

This can't happen. Not to her.

I jumped in front of the spear to save her so she could save everyone else.

It can't be Nyx; it's supposed to be me lying here.

My pain and fear for the next moments builds to an apex and I erupt. "Help her!" I scream into the dark Avalonia night, and my hopelessness bounces back, mocking me.

My hands shake, and I'm afraid to touch her for fear of hurting her. My trembling touch hovers just above her skin before I can't bear the distance anymore and lay next to her, wrapping her tenderly in my arms.

My mother drops to her knees beside us, the chalice falling from her hand. She knows Nyx is dying, and even if there is nothing to be done, I have to beg. "Help me." I whisper a plea to my mother.

She lowers her head, touching her forehead to the ground, sobbing. An amber pendant from her necklace drops onto the grass as Hecate tries to pull her up, to bear witness, to give us space.

Why, I'm not sure. I can't think of anything beyond this moment with Nyx.

The Immortal goddess plucked from the fabrics between the realms to be my mate, the being who was sent to save the twelve realms, is dying.

"Tell me." This time, when Nyx's eyes close, it takes effort to raise them again, her dark eyebrows straining to help open her eyelids. I look into the silver pools of her gaze, knowing I'll never look upon them again, and a part of me begins to die with her.

My soul tears itself within me, knowing I should be the one laying on the ground while my ichor seeps from me. She saved me, tearing herself into pieces to let me live; to let all of Gaea live.

But my life is not worth hers. A life without Nyx is one I don't want to live.

I failed her. I failed to fight hard enough, fast enough. I failed her as a mate, and she is dying for it.

Touching my her forehead to hers, I invoke the power of Light. I stretch her final seconds to burn slowly like hours, so I can memorize her, relive every moment we shared, and etch every molecule of her within the fibers of my soul. I beg the Fates to delay her last breath as long as possible, but they are too eager to rob me of her.

We had such little time.

In the lives of immortals, our few years of together are like the last flash of light at sunset, blazing in intensity but gone in a blink. Hundreds of Immortal lifetimes with her would only begin to be enough.

I feel her drifting away; I sense the light of her soul floating into the Void.

The silver starlight of her power is being siphoned out of her, and four channels of Immortal Ichor flow through the cyan-colored grass of Avalon, darkening as the blood and power of the goddess travel to the four relics lying around her body.

The sword, the chalice, the pendant, and the staff.

"Tell me."

Her body twitches as she fights to remain alive just long enough to hear the words.

"I'll find you." Tears burn hot in my eyes, and I demand they remain in place. I force them to be strong for her and pause in silent salute as she makes her procession out of this life. "I'll always find you."

I hold her as the last breath leaves her body, kissing and loving her as her life fades away. All the light of my existence dims with her death, and darkness settles over my soul.

⊱ ────── ⊰

A tear rolls down my neck into the dampened collar of my shirt where others have fallen before it.

Orion studies the fire while Hypnos inspects the table's wood-grain. Mor's eyes are fixed on me as she slows her chewing, studying me as the memory returns to me as if it were a torturous gift from Avalon's moon.

When Rhea was pierced by my sword, the memories of her lifetimes raced out of her. The power expelled announced to the realm, the identity of the returned goddess, demanding it remember her. But I suppose the fabric of my mind is not fully whole, and it would seem this journey still has many secrets to reveal.

The Fates have designed a cruel and twisting path that we must traverse, and I promise myself now, should I ever encounter the Fates, I'll run them through with my sword for putting my mate through the torment of a thousand deaths.

Wiping my damp cheek, I straighten myself in the chair and reach for the wine goblet, indicating for Orion to continue.

"It's quite alright, cousin." Orion's dark orbs are heavy with solemn understanding. "The Lady of the Lake took possession over the chalice, heavy with the divided powers of the goddess, and entrusted it to the caves of Pandora.

"Your mother safeguarded the pendant, and you kept sentry over your sword and staff. Promising to return with the goddess to restore her powers."

"What happened to Nyx's body?" My jaw tightens with anger over the thought of a priory of flames that would consume her body. The god that hunts her is a Flame, and my heart can't bear the thought of fire being the last thing to touch her.

"The Void opened up, and all the souls within came for her. Covering her body like firebugs, they led her funeral procession until the day she would return."

I close my eyes as I lift my chin toward the ceiling. Relief flooding me, knowing the gentle light of souls carried her into the next realm provides a trivial measure of reassurance.

My time on Avalon is wearing on my patience to return to Gaea with the object that holds the power of my goddess, and a resolute promise settles within me as I regain my composure.

If I have to send every soul in the twelve realms to the Shadow Realm, mine included, Nyx will not suffer another death. I send my prayer into the fibers of Light that connect the realms.

This time, you will not die, my love.

7

The oversized moon casts a pearlescent light over the **lands of Avalon.** It's a beautiful realm. The castle is perched on one end of an island. A low fog covers everything outside the castle walls, concealing the dark ocean and its white caps as they smash against the cliffs. Across the drawbridge, a short walk delivers us to a lake, its calm waters contrasting with the rough sea around the island. A dense forest hugs the lake and covers the rest of the land.

We walk the black and emerald sandy beach, hugging the shoreline of waves that lap eagerly at our feet.

Mor is perched on a rock, breaking a twig into small pieces and throwing them at the ground. Hypnos and Orion stand tall, watching the lake.

I follow their gaze to a cropping of rocks with its single tree in the lake's center. Massive in circumference, roots grip the rocks like large, spindly fingers. Nestled inside a cove of roots, a woman sits within the water, peering up at the moon. Her deep hair flows behind her with a sheen of dark blue color, even though the wind is still.

I look between my companions, curious about what we are waiting for. As a cloud covers the large moon, the light dims, and the woman turns to us. She nods her head once, and Orion returns the gesture. I look around the shore for a boat inquisitively, but my wonder is quickly resolved when the woman dives into the water.

In a beat, her head rises from the dark lake before us, her eyes the only thing not immersed in water. The surprise causes me to jump back, startled. *Gods.*

Orion stifles a grin as he turns toward me. "Please meet The Lady of the Lake. She wants to take you into the waters and see if she can help restore your scattered memories." He says this like following a strange woman into a dark, murky lake is typical.

"How about, fuck no."

Hypnos coughs to conceal his laugh and returns to his stoic demeanor quickly.

"You have been in the lake's healing waters before, my friend. You'll survive it again." He gestures with his hand for me to walk into the lagoon.

"That is exactly why I don't want to return to them now."

The Lady rises from the waters; her hair and dress appear dry immediately and billow in the windless night as if moved by their own accord.

As if the shimmer of our silver and blue auras still shines within the lake, the residue of Nyx's death coats my mind, and I can envision her dragging my body from the water at the very spot where we are standing now.

Just a few feet away is where I said goodbye to the woman who completed my soul for the first time, and as if touching the waters will bring the memory back to life, I hesitate.

But knowing how Nyx planned my return to this realm to seek the artifact that holds her power propels me forward.

With trepidation, I take a step into the lake, followed by another. The Lady stretches her hand out. Her skin is a pale aqua-blue color, and the shimmer of iridescent scales glistens in the moonlight. More humanoid than amphibious, she is a strange being living life under the break of the water's surface.

The moment my hand touches hers, a flash of pearlescent moonlight bursts, and I'm alone in the deep waters, the bright moon high above me. Bubbles swell from my mouth at the disbelief as I kick and push myself to the surface. Burning tears through my lungs as they scream for air, I struggle to reach the top.

As the corners of my vision darken, I break the surface, sputtering for air as I continue kicking to stay above the murky depths. Turning directionless in the lake, I spot Orion kneeling in the water. The Lady of the Lake is with him, still submerged. Hypnos and Mor stand at the shoreline looking at me, and Hypnos begins waving his arms, signaling me to them.

Confused, angry, and humiliated, I swim back to the shore with no improvement to my memories from when I first entered the lake.

As I reach the shore, a smug smile spreads across Mor's face as she relishes the spectacle.

"Enjoying this?" I ask as I emerge from the water and trudge through the shallow waters.

"Immensely."

"Apologies for asking you to enter the lake, but I appreciate your willingness to try and clear your memories, Hermes. The Lady could not remove the barrier the goddess had placed on your mind. But thank you for letting us try."

"I'm never getting in that lake again," I tell him. I nearly died, crashing into that lake goddess knows how long ago, and after practically drowning in it tonight, I'm declaring this lake a bad omen. With a flash of blue light, I dry my clothes and run my hands through my hair.

He smiles at my irritation and gestures toward the caves.

"Come, let us get your cup so you can return."

We walk a short distance to the cave; water dances and sways inside a cove in the rocky interior. Familiarity strikes me as I have more time to view the cave walls, and a memory with Rhea warms my mind. Sitting on a park bench before entering Damien's apartment, Rhea showed me a vision of locking her powers inside a box and stuffing them inside the walls of a cave.

This cave.

"I know this place," I say to no one specific. Walking around the walls, I feel the dark stone with my hands for the break that should hide the interior chamber. Invisible, the cave wall hides an opening into another section.

"By all means, lead the way to the chalice." Orion smiles and waits for me to continue. Following the path to an interior chamber, my hands pat the rocky wall, searching for the hollow section that houses a wooden box, just as it did in Rhea's mind.

Metal fixtures hold the lid in place with a lock. Mor moves ahead of me and retrieves the box, placing it in my hands. It's heavier than expected, as if it carries solid gold bars.

"This is Pandora's cave, our grandmother," Orion says as he nods to Mor. She approaches the box and holds out her palm. A key of shadow solidifies in her hand, delivering it to Orion. "There is a powerful celestial event on the horizon—the alignment of the Triple Moons. Avalon and Gaea will align first. I feel it is no coincidence you arrived here just before. Soon after, the moon of Tartarus will fall into alignment and the three realms will be in syn chronization."Orion opens the lid and reveals a chalice. It's golden in tone with a wide foot for a base and a thin stem of a handle. The bowl of the cup holds various precious gems, emanating a glowing radiance, unlike the pearlescent glow reflecting off everything here. This aura is the silver starlight of my mate. I can feel the goddess Nyx imbued within this chalice. Orion holds the cup to his eye level and spins it slowly.

"The final night of the alignment was the night Nyx surrendered her soul back to the Void. Upon her death, Hecate, Demeter, and your mother, Daphne, swore an oath under the triple moons of the realms to protect this chalice. They became the Maidens of the Grail, the Goddesses of the Triple Moon.

Orion hands me the cup, holding his breath, and I take it in my hand.

"Gods, it's heavy."

"It carries the powers of an immense being. Of course, it's heavy," Mor interjects with a dull tone as she leans against the cave walls. I spare her a irritated glance before returning to my inspection of the cup.

"On Gaea, there is a mortal fable that Pandora's box contains the downfall of mankind: famine, disease, death," I tell my companions as I turn the chalice in my hand, taking in the beauty of the craftsmanship and the intricate vines that encircle the precious jewels.

Orion snickers. "On the contrary, it holds our salvation."

My mother used to laugh so much at that story, and I understand it because she knew the truth about the cup and her mother, Pandora.

Hecate, Demeter, and my mother, born of this realm, were present at the time of Nyx's death and connected to the artifacts that contain her immortal spirit. I understand how Hecate knew what she said about Rhea's death and unlocking the spell.

My aunts and my mother are tied to the spell of Nyx, and as she emerges in a new lifetime and my soul is beaconed to her, so are they called to bear witness, just as they did the night of her death.

The glow of the cup sings to me as I hold it. I sense the aura of my mate locked within, and a salty spray of water carried on the cool breeze of the velvet night caresses my face in recognition of me.

"Pandora's box safeguards the chalice and a vial of water from the lake. The goddess must drink the waters from the grail. It will restore the powers locked within back to her."

A gentle hum comes from the cup, the very tune I heard on the Winds when Lupo captured Rhea. The song that brought me to her, and I can't look away from it.

"Are you going to spin this goblet in your hand all day, or can we get on with this?" Mor snaps me out of my trance, fixated on the silver glow of the chalice. I give her an unamused look as I drop my shoulders in irritation.

"She'll grow on you," Orion says with a smile before I can retort.

"Doubtful."

"In fact, Mor and Hypnos will accompany you back and assist you in your endeavors. I only ask a small favor in return when you have accomplished your missions."

"What? How in the realms are we supposed to get back?" Recalling I lost my portal device when I jumped into the waters, I realize now there is no way the small wand could have ported me back to another realm.

"The Lady has a gift for you that will help in that matter." Orion gestures to the waters that lap in the center of the cave. Beneath the dark waters, the face of the Lady startles me for a second time, and I jump back.

Gods help me; that is unsettling.

"Kneel down, please."

I return the chalice to Orion, who affixes it back in the wooden box. Locking it, he returns the key to Mor. Instantly, the box and key both vanish into the shadows within her hand.

Kneeling at the water's edge, I grip the dark rocks, hoping she doesn't pull me under again. The Lady rises, placing webbed hands on the rocks and lifting her body. She touches her forehead to mine, and an explosion of bright blue light knocks me back.

The flash of carnelian dragon eyes singes my vision.

Searing through my very bones, burning light, so bright it's blinding, races through the canals of my veins. My body heats as a force enters me, so hot my clothes begin to smoke.

"Great Hermes, Herald of the realms," Orion says, evoking the noble tone of a Prince as he squares his shoulders to me and places a hand on my shoulder. "The goddess also left some of your powers to be safeguarded in Avalon. Once given to you as a gift, we return your power to you again. Teleportation has always been your special ability, and you shared it with us as you built a portal in the cave of our grandmother to forever connect you back to your mother's heritage. The goddess entrusted The Lady to hold your power until you returned." He smiles, and the revelation floods my mind with memories of my ability.

The blue power of starlight courses through me as if it were buried, waiting to be unlocked. My skin imitates the radiating blue glow of my aura like a Shield of Light around my body. It settles as the power absorbs back into me. A piece of a puzzle I never knew was missing clicks back in place.

Closing my eyes and leaning my head back to let the light of the great moon fall upon me, I feel the fibers of the realms woven throughout the night. I would only need to pluck a single thread, and I know my power would instantly deliver me anywhere I desire.

"Thank you, Orion." We clasp wrists, and he covers my other hand with his. The genuine smile of a friend is warm on his face, and I wish I could return the sentiments with the memories he has. He pulls me in and whispers a request in my ear—a favor he needs doing. A queens escort back to Avalon.

Exiting the interior chamber, Hephaestus is waiting with a new sheath that holds my sword. Slung over his shoulder is a pair of thigh holsters containing the daggers.

"Good as new." The giant smiles at me as he hands me my weapons. "Your Adamantine sword has been sharpened; the runes refreshed. I think you'll find the enhancing and protecting properties will be more potent now." Hephaestus says, wagging his bushy red eyebrows up and down.

"And give my best girl her daggers back." His tone turns serious. "They are Stygian Iron. The goddess will need their protection."

"I promise."

With a goodbye from their prince, Mor and Hypnos join me on the platform.

The sweet scent of vanilla and berries, a vision of golden hair, and eyes made of warm honey summon the command that brings the portal to life, glowing with the blue starlight of my element as I evoke the word that will bring me back to my mate. To Rhea, to Nyx.

Home.

The dark water envelopes me, its warmth a comforting embrace as I float on the surface, entranced by the night sky above. Billowing clouds as soft as pillows form a slow parade across the velvet sky, made bright by the oversized moon.

Usually, an acquainted friend, the unfamiliar cratered face of the moon above me, holds a mysterious allure. As I gaze upward, a shooting star blazes white across the obsidian sky, leaving a trail of florescent glory in its wake. A smile unfurls on my lips, drawn out by the sheer beauty of the cosmic spectacle.

Green streaks of light burst forth, racing after the falling star like emeralds painting the heavens with their brilliance. Another star follows suit, its tail resembling rubies, adding a fiery flourish to the procession above. Twelve stars dash across the night sky, their radiant journey spanning from one end of the cosmos to the other.

The voice of an old woman, her timbre laced with wisdom and a touch of whimsy, cuts through the stillness. "Beautiful, aren't they?" Her words resonate in the open space, reverberating back to me.

I nod, though she can't see it as we lay on our backs, looking up at the sky. "They are," I reply, my voice a mere whisper in the vastness of the night. "If I could, I would steal them from the sky and place them around a goblet so I could admire their beauty every day." My answer elicits her gentle, musical giggle, like the tinkling of wind c himes.

I enjoy the waters and relax as I float on top of their serenity. My tired limbs and aching mind settle as I drift alongside the calming presence of my companion, and I find I don't mind that I'm unaware of who she is. Just as much a stranger as the new face of the moon high above me, yet there is a familiar knowing I can't place.

The woman stands, disturbing the still water as it drips and splashes around her. She gracefully emerges, a white nightdress clinging to her old body, heavy with the weight of the water. She envelops herself in a thick purple robe hanging from a tree's branch on the shoreline. Adorned with the emblem of two conjoined circles, pierced by an arrow, embroidered in silver thread, the symbol gleams in the soft moonlight.

Wearing a wistful smile, she gazes at me with eyes holding the wisdom of ages past and something deeper—an unspoken love transcending the boundaries of time and space. She knows me and is fond of me.

"I miss your visits, dear," she confesses, her words laden with a longing that tugs at my heartstrings.

Tilting my head, I try to recall her name, to recapture the elusive threads of memory. "I don't know who you are," I admit softly.

"P–a–a–andora–a–a," the name enters my mind with an echo as if the realm itself whispered it to satisfy my curiosity.

Her smile is tinged with a melancholy sweetness as she approaches me. Gently, she cradles my face in her wrinkled, loving hands, her touch as soft as a murmur. Our foreheads meet in a tender, intimate gesture that fills me with a whirlwind of emotions—adoration and sadness, hope and despair—all swirling together in a tempest of sensations.

In an instant, a spark arcs between us, a connection forged long ago is rekindled with the touch. I recoil instinctively, but her grip remains firm, and her sapphire eyes bore into mine, their luminous glow searing my soul. The intensity of the moment is undeniable and seeps into my bones.

"The Herald has his powers," she declares, her voice a solemn whisper, tinged with an urgency that sends a shiver down my spine. "He's coming for you."

Her face and head splatter open, like the skull of the President I assassinated, and the spray of brain and bone assault me.

✦✦✦

I awaken abruptly, my body drenched in sweat, my heart pounding a furious rhythm in my chest. Flint stirs beside me, his voice heavy with sleep as he mumbles, "What is it?"

"It's nothing. I'm fine," I murmur, my voice trembling with remnants of the dream that still cling to my consciousness. I swing my legs over the edge of the bed, the cool tiles beneath my feet grounding me in reality. I long for another day in Tuscany, where the fresh breeze could sweep away the lingering tendrils of the nightmare.

The air conditioner clicks to life, filling the room with a gust of stale, grey air, ruffling the strands of the unruly mop on my head. The image of the woman's blue-glowing eyes, etched into the canvas of my mind, reminds me of another pair of eyes, their radiant azure orbs harboring an identical Elemental Light.

I make my way to the bathroom, the gold hue of the night-light casting a soft glow across Flint's face as he slumbers. "Shut the door," he mumbles into his pillow, seeking respite from the intruding light and sound.

With a roll of my eyes, I oblige, closing the door behind me. The water from the faucet splashes onto my face, cool and refreshing but unable to wash away the lingering unease that clings to me like a second skin. I bring a gentle breeze to fan the water on my face, cooling and calming me. The reflection staring back at me in the mirror, wears an unfamiliar visage, haunted by the past few nights.

Deep purple sits like an unwelcome friend under my puffy eyes, and my skin is ashen, enhancing the brown freckles that splatter my cheeks and nose with annoying persistence.

The memory of my Winds cutting through the President's skull sends a chill coursing through my spine, and I force the thought into the recesses of my mind, locking it away. Over the years, I've mastered the skill of sealing away the darkest corners of my past inside a complex vault within my mind, each box containing a fragment of my pain safely concealed behind mental barriers.

But sometimes, the past breaks free, one of those boxes detonating in my mind, spilling its contents like corrosive acid. Panic surges through me like a torrential flood, and I am powerless to halt its advance.

I leave our room, my steps echoing in the dimly lit corridor. Cappa and Delta are nowhere to be seen, replaced by a new guard perched on a metal folding chair. The guard leans against the wall, a dark blue ball cap pulled low to shield their eyes from the artificial light. With gentle snores escaping their parted lips, they are oblivious to my presence as I tiptoe past them.

The sprawling tunnels of the Underworld, with their intricate twists and turns, have long been my home. I recall decades when we rarely ventured to the surface as Ares awaited the simmering down of mortal conflicts, concocting new schemes for sowing chaos.

I need to busy myself with something to erase the haunting dream and the vision of the old woman. Flint's cryptic comment about hidden chambers harboring Elementals has consumed my thoughts since he uttered those words. I want to explore some of the vacant corridors of the Underworld and see if there is any merit in the gossip.

I release gentle torrents of my Winds, dispatching them through the corridors and chambers, each carved out of the very earth to conceal Ares and his formidable armies. The levels above and below me house the inhabitants of the Underworld, a diverse mix of permanent residents and wandering visitors, leaving fleeting imprints of their presence before returning to the surface.

On this level, my Winds sense the large commercial kitchen, its stainless-steel surfaces resting quietly for the night. Above, a colossal laundry facility roars to life, ceaselessly washing and drying the garments and linens of the Underworld's occupants. Each floor serves as a substructure, cultivating fields of crops in condensed spaces or providing pasture for livestock. The Life Bearers of Ares' legions utilize their Elemental power to enhance the growth of the Underworld's sustenance, ensuring bountiful harvests that feed its people.

As my bare feet trace the rugged path, I run my fingers along the hewn walls, sending my powers downward. It stands to reason that any secret captives would be concealed beneath these common areas, a labyrinthine web designed to ensure both secrecy and hinder escape.

Around ten floors down, I encounter an insurmountable barrier—a wall of shadow, thick and unyielding. It halts my progress, and I pause, a furrow creasing my brow. My heart beats in my ears like a drum, my curiosity piqued. This inky darkness is undoubtedly where Ares would sequester secret captives.

Anyone who comes close to the level would detect a growing sense of dread that would ultimately convince them to turn away before nearing the area. I lack that sense of self-preservation, and I press my powers forward.

Closing my eyes, I extend my aura down the path of my Winds. Like silken ribbons, I intertwine the silvery power of my Immortal aura with the currents of Winds, striving to penetrate the enigmatic Dark Shield.

A formidable creation of mystical energies, it's unlike any barrier I have ever encountered in the depths of the Underworld. It pulsates with a dark, sentient energy, a malevolent presence hiding the mysteries behind its inky facade.

As I focus my attention on this obstacle, the very presence of the barrier draws me deeper into its paradox. The Dark Shield is an intricate tapestry woven from the threads of shadow and magic placed here with intention.

What is Ares hiding behind here?

I send my Winds closer and feel the frigid cold that seeps off the Shield. Curls of frost drop from the surface and disappear into nothing. A haunting cacophony of whispers and faint echoes fill the air, like the murmurs of restless souls confined in the darkest recesses of the River Styx.

Voices wailing a long-forgotten message travel on the current of my Wind, bringing me a tragic tale of imprisonment and despair that has been hidden away for centuries behind this darkened corridor. It brings me to my knees, pressing me down with sorrow and pain as it cries out for release.

The shadows come alive as I push my aura against the Dark Shield. They swirl and dance, taking on shapes and forms that resemble the wraiths and specters of Elysium, the realm of Darkness.

In my mind, I see the flickers of ghostly faces and phantom figures trapped within the confines of the barrier reaching out for me. Souls that have ended within the obscurity, trapped within the shield of energy and begging for release.

And there are children. So many children.

A mix of earthy decay and stale air barrels into me where I stand, levels above the Shield, as though I were standing in front of it. Bile threatens to spew out of me, and I fall to my knees by the pain and anguish that feeds this barrier.

I can taste the bitterness of thwarted ambition and the lingering stench of failure that has permeated the Shield when it was created. It is as if the very essence of Ares has been distilled into this malevolent obstruction, an embodiment of his ruthless determination to protect his secrets at any cost.

It's almost as if I can see the track he travels in and out of this secret chamber. Angry and frustrated as he fails at something. Over and over again, his disappointment has tainted the entire floor containing the Dark Shield.

As I open my eyes and focus my will, I see the wall before me as if I had teleported directly in front of it. All of my senses and elemental powers are fixated on this shield as if something beyond it is beaconing and calling for help.

The compulsion to get beyond this blockade and see what lies within overwhelms me, and I send my aura like a knife slashing through it.

In an instant, I'm caught in a vortex, a whirlpool of sensations that engulf my senses. The tunnels vanish, and I'm squeezed, like plunging through the neck of an hourglass, trapped by a palpable darkness that constricts me, threatening to crush the very life from my body.

Panic surges, my eyes feel like they might burst from their sockets, and my stomach plummets faster than my body through this unseen void.

And then, as abruptly as it began, the darkness releases me. I find myself clutching the tunnel's railing, my knuckles white with tension, my body drenched in sweat. My breaths come in ragged gasps with a heaving chest from the effort to regain my composure as I stand. I'm back where I began, my eyes darting warily across the rocky crevasses, searching for any signs of life.

"What are you doing out so late?" The voice, suspicion tinged with a hint of curiosity, shatters the quiet, startling me.

W**e arrive in a strange location, as nighttime blankets the day.** A warm wind, sticky with humidity, blows through the columns of a stone building, wrapping around my legs and swirling up my body as if welcoming me back to the realm. Silver starlight glimmers faintly within the breeze, and my heart jumps into my throat.

She's here.

Delivering us from Avalon, Hypnos and Mor stand by my side within an interior chamber of an ancient structure. The peeling glyphs on stone walls show ages of decay within a square room, open on all sides and showcasing the night sky. An altar is in the center, with a large stone table. Around the edges, a channel runs along the side with a divot at one corner.

It's a sacrificial table that drains the Immortal Ichor from Elementals, siphoning the aura from their blood to be consumed by another.

I'm about to project a faint ribbon of Light in all directions to map the area and find Rhea. Not knowing where we are, I have to be careful. The essence of my power is easier to see in the darkness. Before my thin wave of blue Light escapes me, Mor sends a pulse of obscurities across the stone floor that climb up the walls.

Like a heartbeat, the wave of darkness spreads out in all directions, deepening the shadows that cling to the walls and dimming the night a shade darker.

"Step into the shadows," Mor says, taking a few steps back into a corner of the man-made structure. Hypnos and I follow her command, and the darkness swallows us. Like a thick gel, the shadows encase us. It's like being underwater; the cool touch of the dark wisps takes my breath away.

My stomach pulls tight, and my chest warms before I hear the angelic voice of my mate wrap around me like satin garlands.

Rhea and Demeter climb the steps that deliver them mere feet away from where we are hiding. I move toward her, but the tendrils of darkness hold me in place. Snapping my head back at Mor, she shakes her head back and forth. Hypnos holds his finger to his mouth, telling me to remain silent.

"A powerful Elemental, surrounded by Shifters, is approaching."

My heart is a mighty drum echoing across the realm as I get a sense of who she is referring to.

"I couldn't sleep, is all. Promise." She's lying.

I hear the deception in Rhea's tone as she hides the truth from her confession. She may not have been able to sleep, but the tremor in her voice tells me something upset her.

My arms ache to wrap around her and pull her into my body to keep her safe. My Light pushes against Mors shadows and begs to be released to encase Rhea in a shield of protection that will guard her from the terrors that pull at her mind and the monster that is approaching.

I tremble with anger. *They are both right there.* All we need to do is step out of this darkness and bring them back to Kenya. The moment I open my mouth, a wisp of darkness clamps over me. Odd fingers of nothingness feel like the wet tentacles of an octopus sliding across my skin. Disgusted, I attempt to wipe them away, but nothing is there. Mor jerks her head to the left of our position as an elevator door opens. The God of War steps out with two Shifters in human form flanking him. The man I have hunted for thousands of years. The man who has hunted my mate since she stepped foot onto this realm.

Ares.

My instincts move before my mind can catch up, and I start for him with my hand reaching for the hilt of my sword. Slimy darkness engulfs me, wrapping around me like a snake coiling around my body and squeezing me tighter.

If the sensation before was like being emersed underwater, this is like being dropped to the bottom of the Mariana Trench. The pressure has multiplied and pushed against me, both holding me in place and warning me to remain still.

"Everything okay?" I haven't heard Ares' smoky voice in four hundred years, and my body nearly vibrates with fury, held back by these revolting shadows.

"She's okay." Demeter reassures him.

The two Shifter guards hold the elevator doors open as my mate and the Queen of Avalon step inside, with Ares following them. The doors close, and I feel Rhea's aura retreat away from me. Diving into the earth, under Ares' protective wards, she is gone.

Mor holds me in place a moment longer before finally releasing me. Cold like reptile skin, the dark coils dissipate instantly, turning into smoke. I turn on her, ready to explode in her face, but Hypnos steps between us, grabbing my arm.

"You know this was not the time for a direct conflict; we are outmatched, Hermes. Don't let your temper get in the way." We stare at each other, daring the other with our glare as Hypnos' creamy white eyes hold my stern gaze.

After a moment, the fog of Rhea's nearness clears, and my pulse begins to slow. The ache in my body caused by her close proximity calms, returning to the back of my mind, burning like an eternal flame of blue light and waiting for her.

I am nearly suffocating with the selfish need to be near her and lost all sense of tactical planning. Ares may have any measure of wards or precautions in place preventing us from rescuing her. And if the God of War is here, so is his army. We will need more Immortals on our side before we can retrieve her and Demeter.

"You're right. Thank you." I nod at Mor.

Hecate suspected Demeter was being held captive by Ares' forces. Based on the comfort Demeter exhibited just now and her presence at the attack causes me to doubt the claim.

Perhaps Demeter is here willingly, even helping Ares. And if she is, Hecate could be working as their ally as well, hiding a true allegiance to the God of War.

I have always mistrusted Hecate. My mother blamed it on the clash between our elements. Light and Dark rarely work well together as each is a direct antithesis of the other.

Since my mother was killed four hundred years ago, the bond of the triple moon goddesses has been severed, and perhaps so has their oath.

"We need to leave here. We are in the center of a large pyramid, and it is even larger underground." Mor keeps her undulating shadows searching the area as her eyes flick from feature to feature, taking in the space.

I step out, and recognition hits me. We're in Mexico at the top of the Pyramid of Kukulkan.

When Damien, an author and outcast Shifter, risked his life to meet with me the day I first saw Rhea in that bookstore in Atlanta, he was trying to solve the mystery of the Lycan, the Shifters who cannot transform. The information he collected, passed on to us when he was murdered, led us to three temples where the upcoming Mabon ceremony may be held.

This ceremony had significance with the constellation Orion and three temples placed across the realm in alignment with the star formation's infamous belt. Learning about the upcoming alignment of the triple moons, starting with Avalon and Gaea, things are beginning to make sense.

We debated whether Kukulkan could be one of the three locations, and Ares' presence, along with his army, tells me this is where the Mabon ritual will be performed.

"Let's go." I return to my companions, and my newly returned power of Light senses my need, and it begins to spark within me. Smirking, an idea forms in my mind, and my power responds by casting an orb of blue light around us.

This is going to be great.

⚜

My Light ability opens a portal, and we appear in an instant inside Medusa's office.

"What the fuck, Hermes?" Medusa yells out as our arrival has the effect I hoped it would. Startled by our sudden appearance, she jumps from her seat at her desk. A flush fills her dark skin, and her braids are poised for an attack.

"Where in the blazes have you been, and who in the goddess's name are they?" Medusa asks, looking Hypnos and Mor up and down like they have three heads as several strands of her braids snap out and push my shoulders.

"What in the twelve realms, H?" Achilles stands protectively in front of my sister, wearing a white tank top, making the colors of his tattoos brighten against the daylight streaming in through the windows.

Callie stands behind him with her arms folded over her chest, the whips of her Winds blowing her hair and narrowing her seething blue eyes at me. *She is livid.*

"We have a lot to talk about," I say.

"Understatement of the year." Medusa retorts.

Everyone is silent while I talk of Avalon.

The realm we thought was lost is very much alive but possibly starving. I fill them in on the hidden ties to my mother's family, the grail, and my returned teleportation ability.

Testing the threads of the realms as I did on Avalon, there is no trace of the linkage to the other lands of the Titans now that we have returned to Gaea.

I sense the realm encased in a protective shield, thick and powerful, preventing me from grasping into the fibers of another realm and transporting myself there.

These are the guards erected after the refugees fled from Tartarus and the other realms destroyed in the Titan Wars. Gaea became the last sanctuary for those displaced by the enormous gods that decimated planets as they fought.

The strongest of the Elementals that sought refuge here erected the wards, hoping to save the realm from Chaos when he came for Gaea. As I test the barrier, my mind stills as I pick up the presence of my father. Apollo's radiant yellow Light, brighter than the sun, forms some of the protective threads woven into the massive shield.

Warmth flows through me, as if I'm suddenly surrounded by the aura of my dad. He was always larger than life to me. Greater than the dragon Titan of Light as he served by Theia's side, her faithful apprentice.

The residue of his golden light mingles with mine, and the feeling of his power eases the tension in my shoulders, making me feel as if everything will be okay. I pass the lingering essence of his power to my sister.

Closing her eyes, Callie welcomes the strength and reassurance it offers her, though it does nothing to quell her temper with me.

Medusa flicks her evergreen eyes at Mor as I talk.

Mor picks at her nails, bored. Hypnos looms over the room with his arms crossed over his chest, his pearlescent eyes bounce over the space, and I contemplate his power, enabling him to see while his eyes have no vision.

The ancient attire of our two new friends from Avalon makes them stand out as clear outsiders. The leather and tunics are more reminiscent of medieval England than modern-day anything.

"It's been two days, H." Callie still has her arms crossed, an angry glare beginning to soften as I finish the account. Cold fingers run a chill up my scalp in alarm at the large pass of time that I missed being away.

"We only had dinner." I look to Mor and Hypnos; my brows furrowed at the time lost. Thinking back to the expanse of time Rhea and I went missing, it seemed like a few minutes passed, but it had been several hours. Now, my latest off-realm excursion put me out two days. "Wait, that means Mabon is tomorrow."

"What it means is, I'm tired of everyone I care about vanishing. Flora, then Rhea, and now you." Callie's pale complexion burns with her anger as she glares at me. Callie's red-rimmed eyes flood with tears, and she buries her face in her hands.

I hug my sister into me, and her shoulders shake through her tears. Something else is bothering her to be so upset.

"What is it Calla Lilly?" I use the name my mother affectionately called her.

I feel Callie holding back her answer as she cries. Fear tickles my spine as the prospect of how much could have occurred in two days' runs through my worry.

"Tell me?"

"It was so fast." She chokes out.

My face heats with guilt and anger. Something happened, and I wasn't here.

I pull her away and place my hands on her shoulders, bending several inches to meet her eyes.

"What?"

"The Sirens; Ares' Wind Sirens. I didn't know until it happened. They must have picked a time in advance because there was no warning."

"There was a mass assassination yesterday of fifteen world leaders." Achilles takes over the explanation as Callie bursts into another fit of crying. Dropping my shoulders, I pull her back into my hug, and she lets me hold her while she cries. "Wind Sirens used Piercing Wind and executed the American President, the Prime Ministers of the United Kingdom and France, and a dozen other countries.

My friend pauses, and the weight of what he doesn't say hangs heavy like a grey thundercloud too full of water, refusing to drop its rain.

"What else?" I wait for Achilles to answer as he looks out of the large windows that make up one of the walls of Medusa's office. With his arms folded over his chest, his tattoos seem to darken as if they know the gloom that is stretching across the realm.

"Hecate reached out to Medusa right after." He pauses, looking at me with an apology coating his eyes. "She had sensed something just before the assassinations happened and found Rhea in Washington DC." His tongue runs across his bottom lip, delaying a second longer before he finally tells me the heaviest truth that burdens my sister and makes her weep so harshly. "Rhea killed President Sims herself."

The realm slips away from me as my stomach surges through my throat. My grasp on Callie hardens because she is the only thing keeping me affixed to this office.

"I didn't know." She whispers into my shirt as she clutches me. Her tears slow as she sniffles and looks up at me with soggy eyes. "I would have gone to her if I knew."

I take a steadying breath as I fight to relax my muscles that have pulled tight with the information.

I remember when Callie was younger, and her older half-sister was trying to teach her to hear the news of the realm by the voices that carry on the winds. Callie got so upset with herself when she didn't hear a tsunami approaching the small Mariana Islands after an earthquake in the middle of the western Pacific Ocean.

Thousands died, and Callie cried for hours. Our father went to her, stroking her hair as it glowed like the sun. I watched from the doorway while he spoke to her in low tones, trying to comfort her. I repeat his words to her again, reassuring her now as he did back then.

"Didn't Dad tell you to stop being so much like Atlas? You can't carry the world's weight on your shoulders and blame yourself for everything no more than you can stop the winds from blowing around the globe."

"But I can stop the winds if I wanted to and I'm mad at Atlas for letting them take Flora." She sniffles, and it makes me chuckle. She won't stay angry at him for long, or me for that matter.

The assassinations couldn't have been done by Rhea.

She would never harm the mortals. Ares has to be forcing her, controlling her actions somehow. He's done it before; used her as a weapon to take out entire continents with her power, charging her like a battery until he can finally consume her power.

I shake my head in disbelief as I struggle to focus on the words pinging around the room.

"Not to be insensitive, but we have a lot to figure out." Medusa pulls me back to the present with a smack to my shoulder as she stands from her desk and begins pacing her office.

"The world is already tipping into a state of turmoil with so many leaders taken out at once. Countries are trying to shift to new power, pointing the finger at each other all while Ares gathers his armies underground."

Deuce walks the length of her office, her forehead tight in the center. Her braids, half pulled back and tied together, stay out of her face and hang low by her side. The tendrils of her long hair sway in agitation as her emotions fill up the stone beads.

"My two most trusted warriors betrayed me, let the enemy into our camps, and one of them is dead. The other is in cuffs in the mountain." Medusa pauses and runs her hand down her face. "Ares was holding and torturing their sister. He sent them pieces of her until they agreed to do what he wanted."

I recognize this frustrated side of Medusa. She's always too hard on herself for not being in a dozen places at once, and the first person she wants to blame in any situation is herself. But the blame I'm carrying for hurling my sword at my mate, even if it was unknowing, is driving me to the cusp of insanity.

Gods, why did I throw my sword?

My mind races with a dozen murderous thoughts to rip this realm to shreds to find Rhea, to remove her from Ares' claws, and to ensure she is safe. "Can you blame them, Deuce? What would you have done for Athena?"

She looks at me, and a dark shade crosses over her eyes. I know what she did in those centuries after she lost Athena. The myth of the monster queen terrified everyone who dared cross her path until she was able to find her way out of the darkness and give herself a new purpose.

"You know that answer."

Callie moves away from me and meets her mate by the window. Achilles places his arm around her waist and pulls her to him with a kiss to her temple.

"So, let's move forward to the next problem. We need to make Rhea drink the waters of Avalon from this chalice." I nod to Mor, and the box materializes out from a cloud of shadow.

"By the goddess, I never thought I'd see the Grail again." Achilles approaches the cup, looking around the goblet that is floating on a small cloud of dark shadows from Mors powers. "Do you remember we took this blasted cup on a chase from Arthur and his decrepit Mind Mage, Merlin, all over England?"

"I don't think it was Arthur and Merlin." The room looks at me as fractured memories become clearer in my mind. "It was Ares and Moros, hunting the artifacts that hold the power of Nyx."

Like pieces of a scattered puzzle are slowly putting themselves in order, the chaotic memories scattered within my mind are slowly stitching themselves together. Frustration pulls at my patience.

I want to use my speed to put everything in order, so I know the clear answer to help Rhea, to break this spell and prevent another cycle of reincarnation from starting again.

I teleport myself to the cottage, snag the four tarot cards still sitting on the table where I left them, and shoot myself back to Deuce's office with a flash of light.

"I will damn you to the shadows of Elysium if you do that again without warning." Medusa snaps at me, startled by my sudden reappearance. With a smirking grin, I wink at her and then lay the cards on her desk in the same order I found them inside the book.

"I think they have to be released sequentially. My sword was the first." The dark memory of Nyx's death rolls through my mind slowly, and, again, I watch her Ichor as it flows out of her, running through four grooves in the ground toward these four objects.

The sword, the chalice, the pendant, and the staff.

Everyone crowds around the desk, taking in the images on the cards. I hold my breath eagerly, desperate to see a spark of recognition light on one of their faces. Perhaps the new information and closely inspecting the clues within the cards will help recover something buried under the heavy weight of Nyx's spell.

"Your Caduceus," Callie exclaims, pointing at my staff painted on the final card. "I haven't seen this in ages. I nearly forgot about it."

"I haven't seen it since we evacuated Tartarus." My mind replays a dozen memories at once of that horrible day. The screams of so many inhabitants echoed through the dry desert air as the Titan's war raged on.

Hyperion, a mountain himself, stood fifty feet in height and wore stone armor as the Titan of Earth's elemental power and guardian of Tartarus. He drew up an extensive mountain range to separate his people from the fighting. His Cyclopes, stone giants standing twenty feet tall, held dozens of people in their vast hands, carrying them carefully to the portals, allowing as many to flee as possible.

A nebula cloud of Death rolled in from the distance as Chaos approached. White lightning shot out of the cloud of darkness, and one of the bolts of his power struck a mountaintop. It fractured, raining large boulders upon the fleeing people of Tartarus. Medusa and her two sisters quickly drew up a wide rocky cover to protect the people from the crumbling mountain, but it was too much.

Straining under the impacts of the falling rock, they struggled. I only had time to get Medusa out before it came crashing down. Her scream echoes across the returning memories as the scene replays itself in my mind.

That is when I teleported her and a small group of others to Gaea, directly to Oceanus Palace at Atlantis.

"Chaos has come for Tartarus." My voice rings through the halls of his abalone castle as I run to the end of the great ballroom and step onto the vast balcony that overlooks the sea. My Caduceus, tight within my grasp, flares to life as the beacon of Light projects the message of Theia's Herald across the realm. "Hyperion needs your aid."

Gaea groans as Oceanus draws himself from the sea. The great water giant rises, draining the Mediterranean as his Titan form takes solid shape. Torrents of water crash into the exposed sea floor.

Standing fully, the clear blue waters of Gaea that swirl within him must reach sixty feet in height. Looking to the blue skies above, the man, formed of water, becomes a column of white-capped rapids as he surges into the atmosphere, transporting himself to Tartarus.

"Stay here." I rush back to Medusa, who collapsed on the floor, made of smooth shells, polished to perfect reflected tiles. Breathing heavily, her forest eyes stare at her reflection on the floor, unblinking. I grab her shoulders with both hands. "I'm going back to get them. I'll bring your sisters."

❧ ❧

The memory frees me, and my shoulders drop as I release a pent-up breath. My aura filled the space with blue, and the receding Mirage fades with a dissolving image of Athena rushing toward us. Looking at my companions, they stare at me with wide eyes, their chests rising and falling with gasping breaths.

"Can you try to control your memories, H?" Medusa's complexion pales as she speaks to me with a break in her voice, still staring at the place where the memory of Athena faded away. "We all saw that memory. We felt it, too."

I hold her stare as heat rushes to my face. I hadn't intentionally broadcast the memory; it just flooded me. I hadn't even recognized I was sharing it with the others.

"I did not realize the Titans were so large." Hypnos's deep voice fills the stifling silence. "The Goddess of the Hunt was not nearly so huge in stature."

I never met the Titan Artemis, who held dominion over Avalon and the power of Sensory. She was the first Titan that was slain in the Cannibal Wars. The first domino that was pushed over in a long line of events bringing us to this current moment.

Silence commands the room as the heavy memory clears itself from everyone's minds.

"All right, retrieve Rhea, give her the waters of Avalon, stop the mortals from starting another world war, and stop Ares from doubling his army all by tomorrow night," Callie says with a huff. "Sounds easy."

"Sounds impossible," Mor adds.

"Sounds like we need help," Medusa mumbles.

The room becomes suffocatingly small as the fate of the realm hangs within our discussion. The next moves we make will play a part in the survival or decimation of mortals, the preservation or restarting of civilizations.

Everyone falls silent with either vacant stares or worried glances.

"I think there is something we need to see first," Achilles says, a slight grin on his face as he cuts his eyes to me. An obvious break in the tension building within the room. "Do you want to test those restored powers of yours before we go kick Ares' ass?"

I smirk, knowing where this is going. He wants to race.

"Oh no. Seriously, you two?" Medusa interjects, putting her arms between us like a referee.

Mor stands, her shadows whipping around her protectively, watching us intently.

"Want to take this outside?" I cock my eyebrow at Achilles.

"You bet your ass I do."

"What is about to happen? Will they kill each other?" Mor asks Medusa in hushed tones. A faint smile flits across Medusa's face, but she corrects it before answering.

"No, they want to race each other to see who is faster."

"Is this important, given the situation?" She asks Medusa.

"Hey, sometimes you have to stop and smell the roses, you know?"

Mor studies Deuce with her head tilted to the side in confusion, looking very much like a bird. "No, we don't know to stop and smell roses."

My friend and I take off with a flash, literally, as both of our Elemental abilities flare to life. Smoke and flames billow from Achilles as starlight illuminates me. Nearly evenly matched, we push and prod each other as we dart through Medusa's Commune and surge down the mountain.

Like two streaks of bronze and blue light, we are a blur as we descend to the plain below.

Reaching the grassy field simultaneously, we rest our hands on our knees, our chests pumping hard as we smile. The intrusion was a welcome break to force us out of the stifling room and into the open air and sunlight.

The teleportation pad on the plain flares to life as Callie, Medusa, Mor, and Hypnos join us.

"Look," Callie calls out, pointing to the tree line.

Our heads snap to the other side of the plain as two figures emerge from the foliage.

"The Zeta King," I announce through clinched teeth.

"Take these to Triton," Demeter instructs Terra before washing her hands at her sink. Demeter found me in a state of sweaty panic, having discovered the Dark Shield. I played off my excuses like I was just walking around, trying to calm down after a bad dream, which is mostly true, before I heard the wails of pain and desperation emanating beyond the shield.

Taking me up to the surface for air, she prodded me further, pressing hard to know why I was so upset.

I can't possibly reveal what I found.

It would surely be an instant death sentence to admit I had pried around Ares' fortress and discovered the place where he hides his secrets. The feeling of someone beaconing me within that darkness was so powerful I could barely resist it.

These could be echoes of the past, but the feeling that they are whispers from the present sends a chilling grasp up my spine.

My mind is a reeling vortex of tangled cobwebs and shadows. I'm heavy and light all at once. Steady but shaky, focused but scattered.

There are blank spots in my mind when I try to think about certain things, like what happened on the plain before Flint and Terra came for me. There is a gap between feeling strong hands on my hips as I swayed to the beat of loud music and a hard grip on my neck as I watched Hermes' sword soar into me.

I'm usually better than this. I sit in the dark corners of rooms and see the small details that everyone else misses. I use them as an assassin to take out my targets with silent efficiency. But I've been a strewn mess these past few days since I was injured.

I should tell Demeter but don't want to worry her, thinking something is wrong when it's just me who needs to get over the fact we were ambushed, Immortals died, and I was severely wounded. It's guilt I carry that others died, and I did not, but also a lingering thought that I was the cause of the fight.

Ares took Beta and Cappa with him, telling Demeter to meet him in five minutes.

Within her greenhouse, tucked away in the Underworld, she sends her daughter off with a set of syringes filled with liquids in various shades of dark green, pale yellow, and black as coal before cupping a vial of milky white liquid and stuffing it into the pocket of her jean coveralls.

"Follow me."

Demeter walks through the tall corn with green stalks holding their pockets of gold within their leaves. They bend away from Demeter as she passes through, but I push the blades aside to avoid them.

Within the field of crops is a small portal platform that I never knew was here, and stepping atop it, a purple haze of elemental light delivers us to a room that covers me in an icy layer of fear.

This is Ares' room for *reconditioning*. The room he brings his soldiers to when they perform poorly or question his authority. Dread and trepidation accompany the unfortunate souls that are walked into this room. When they leave, vacant expressions and blind obedience are their companions.

"Why am I here?" I ask with a slight pitch to my voice as my chest rises heavily.

Demeter stands next to a chair wrapped in camel-brown leather. It reminds me of a dentist chair with a high back and seat. It's reclined back with an extended leg and footrest, ready for an occupant.

Metal restraints affixed periodically pull the echo of a memory forward. I recall Lucas, bound with a wooden bar clutched between his teeth. His neck was bulged with veins, his face blistered red, and his back was painfully bowed.

"To prepare you for the ceremony." Demeter motions to the chair expectantly, and I sit despite the tremor that comes to my fingertips as I grasp the arm of the chair. Demeter works to clasp my right arm, and I feel the power drain from me as the Thaumium clasp encircles my wrist.

Ice washes over my body as my Elemental power fades away out of my reach and leaves me feeling hollow. Before I can interject, a pierce on my neck stings like a dozen wasps have stung me at once.

Turning my head to the left, Demeter's barb retracts inside the bottoms of her cuffed jeans. Like someone has placed molten embers on my neck, the burn sears its way through my veins as a toxin enters my bloodstream.

She sticks my arm with the syringe of milky liquid, and my mind melts away as warm goo slides over my skull while she presses the plunger.

My body is heavy, weighing a thousand pounds. I can't hold myself up anymore and drop back onto the chair. Demeter continues to clasp the other cuffs, further suffocating my powers until nothing is left of my Elemental magic.

The poison acts quickly and strips me of my ability to move, starting first with my hands and feet. It rolls up my limbs as they drop with a thud to the chair, resting loosely on the soft leather.

I only had a second to turn my head back to center before I was fully incapacitated. Something within me keeps me breathing, but I presume that is the design of the toxin.

I'm wholly and utterly empty inside.

Ares enters my view as Demeter affixes the last of the cuffs around my ankle. Fully restrained, the metal suffocates my power, and the poison keeps me immobile; I'm helpless against whatever will occur.

The thoughts in my mind that would thunder through my brain like galloping horses are now trudging through the muck of a thick swamp.

This is not preparation for tomorrow.

How blindly and faithfully I walked into the web of deceit. Even though I knew, as I struggled across the thin silk strings that provide a shaky woven walkway, that I should have turned back.

This is my fault.

Ares must know I found his dark shield. He knows I was prying in the depths of his secrets and everything that happens to me now is to reinforce the lack of control I have over my impulses.

I focus all my thoughts on the Dark Shield and urge them to gather in the center of my mind. Thanks to the toxins running within me, they unhurriedly obey. Darkness, secret, shadow. I repeat the words until I hope that I have contained the thoughts into a dark vault of my own.

Imagining layers and layers of an intricate labyrinth, I move further and further away from the ideas conjured when I located the shield and my plans to return there. Finally, at the edge of my mind, I believe I have safeguarded the finding enough that Ares won't be able to locate my thoughts about it.

He will likely break through the meager barriers I erected as a flimsy fortress and when he discovers my lies, surely that is when my real punishment will begin.

From my peripherals, I sense Demeter stepping away. Hearing a stool drag across the floor, she sits. The noise of a food wrapper and the familiar sound of her phone unlocking blaze loudly in my ear. It gives me a sense of hope that I'm only exaggerating my unease at the situation.

"I need to save my strength for tomorrow, so make sure I only have to revive her once at the end." Her statement is a tidal wave that washes away my last fleeting hope for salvation. Deep down, I knew it was a pointless likelihood.

Despite my wish, I deserve this. I should have a clear mind and the ability to drive to the perfect conclusion in every scenario. Ares expects greatness and I must give it to him or else I'm no better than a new recruit, fresh into their training.

Ares looks over the chair into my eyes. Unable to move, I have no choice but to focus on him. "You know why you're in my chair today, don't you?"

I swallow, thankful I won't choke to death on my saliva but cursing the fact I can still speak. My eyes dart around the room, searching for the right answer but there is nothing.

Ares grabs my face, pushing my cheeks into my teeth with his firm grip. His eyes bounce between mine and I focus on the blazing orange ring that rims the black center.

"No." My voice is no louder than a mouse's squeak.

"You hesitated yesterday." Releasing my face, he looks behind him at the clock as the small hand strikes the nine. "Just before the assassination, I felt your hesitation as the Winds of the realm paused for a beat. The entirety of the world's Sirens felt it as well. We can't have that kind of disloyalty."

I did hesitate before I blew the head off President Sims because I didn't truly want to take that man's life. Despite my brief stall, I fulfilled my mission, but Ares still found out. Now, I'll be strapped to his table to be tortured until he feels he has driven his message of my halfling inadequacies into me.

Part of me is relieved he hasn't mentioned the shield, but knowing Ares, he could be working his way around his methodical routine of pain and will simply be waiting to get to it later.

"After this, you will never question me again, and if you do, you had better take your own Immortal life. It pains me to hurt you. You know this. Do not force my hand again." Ares rolls up the crisp white sleeves of his button-down shirt.

The heavy disappointment on his brow pushes against the indifferent barrier I try to hold around myself, pretending I'm not affected by his approval of me.

"I'm going to punish you for one hour."

Orange and black flames engulf his hands with Soul Fire. My eyes widen knowing he is going to sear the essence of my aura to begin my punishment.

Placing both hands on each side of my temple, the Fire begins in my brain. The jetstream of flames race down my body to my legs. It's like being dunked into a volcano, except the flames don't leave any burns on my skin.

I close my eyes to the pain, trying to squint and squeeze away the agony.

Screaming my stupidity in my mind, I wish I could slap myself across the face for bringing this upon myself. Despite the blazing pain, my body doesn't react. I feel every flame that bites at my body and tugs on every nerve ending. The heat makes me feel like my brain is boiling and my eyes will explode.

And yet, I remain still as a corpse.

Fighting against the pain to focus on the ticking hands of the clock, I try to sever ties with each of my nerve endings. As if I could pluck them out like weeds, I try to put a barrier between my mind and my body but it's pointless.

The fire within me is too much and I yell out. Finally breaking my silence the pleas flow from my mouth, begging the God of War to stop, telling him it's too much. It only prompts him to turn up his blazes along with the menace in his scowl as he watches my suffering.

The fire licks at my chin and I try to turn my head away before the flames can reach up to my neck but it's meaningless. The flames made of his aura, orange with a tinge of black, dance across me, searing my mistake into my soul.

As minutes pass, the pain evolves into a relentless throbbing and aching. It is as if a thousand needles stab my skin, each one sending waves of agony through my body with every heartbeat. Even the gentlest breeze or the lightest touch feels like a cruel and torturous assault on my damaged hide.

Black and orange flames of the Soul Fire dance seductively along my body. Everywhere except my head. The fire burning inside my skull, crawling through every crevice of my brain, brands Ares' intentions into me.

I can't escape it; the pain that I fully deserve is always there, an uninvited and unwavering companion with each tick of the clock.

Removing his hands from my body, my chest heaves and my eyes go wide having gotten through the blaze without losing consciousness. Spit flies from my mouth and lands on my face as I try to catch my breath.

Inhaling the fumes of my burned soul, it turns rancid in my mouth.

Ares pushes a button on the side of the chair, and it comes alive and whirs as a metal arm raises the seat. Lengthening so it appears as if I'm standing, Ares approaches the front of me.

"Twelve." His calm face with leathered skin appraises me as I remain confined within the poison. "Twelve seconds you stalled and let your allegiance waiver. Let's count them together."

Ares loves to let us know our pain or the reason for it as he punishes us. He feeds off the fear he incites by talking us through our punishment with his calming voice and the sureness of his steady tone.

Balling up his fist, he rears back and launches his arm forward, striking me in the ribs.

"One." His tone is calm as he recites the first of my twelve strikes and looks at me expectantly.

The pain is so overwhelming, it drowns out everything else, and I'm choking on it. The smell of my fried soul stings my nostrils, and bile threatens my throat.

Again, he hits me, using his other fist on the opposite side of my ribs. "One."

I open my mouth, trying to take in a gulp of air but I choke, despite myself.

As Ares pulls back again, I gasp, finally pushing beyond the tightness in my lungs.

"One" I barely manage to cough the word out.

Satisfied, Ares nods his approval before launching into a back-handed slap that rings across my cheek. Flinging my head to the side, my chin nearly meets my shoulder with the force of his blow. Waiting again, Ares holds only a second before grabbing my face and centering me before slapping again.

A third time he strikes me, this time splitting my lip until I count again for him.

"T-two." A line of spit falls from my mouth, unable to bring my jaws together.

Demeter crumples up the wrapper that contained her food, now eaten, and it pains me more knowing she is causally sitting by, scrolling on her phone and snacking while Ares burns his will into my mind and beats his corrections into my body.

Red crowds my vision from the blistering heat within my skull. I'm certain it will blind me as my eyes will surely pop like the cherries Demeter used to prepare for her fall pies, bubbling in thick syrup and ready to be poured into a browned pie crust for baking.

"Th-three."

Vomit wants to rise to the surface, but the venom keeps my body locked in stillness.

"F-f..." My body is spasming from the impact my torso. Each strike has to be delivered several times before I'm able to count the number finally. "..f-four."

I finally reach the end. Ares' breathing is winded from dealing out the punishment I forced him to deliver, when I say the final number.

Each hit forced the air from my lungs, and my whole world wanted to zero in on that one spot, throbbing in agony and begging to curl in on myself.

Ares positions the chair back to recline, and I can see the clock again.

My gaze fixates on the minute hand as it moves agonizingly slow. *Twenty minutes.*

It's only been twenty minutes.

Time itself has taken on a cruel personality, taunting me with its lethargy. Each tick is an eternity, and I can't help but resent that clock for its indifference to my situation. Every second drags across its face like a two-ton boulder, and I can't shake the hopelessness that washes over me.

I asked for this when I hesitated. I chose this. And if it keeps Ares from finding out my treachery of locating the Dark Shield, I can endure this.

Ares lays the chair flat, and a mirror on the ceiling forces me to face myself. A tear rolls down my temple and is welcomed into my hair. The only sign of unrelenting agony my body is allowed to show.

As the minutes stretch into what feels like hours, my desperation grows. I can't see the clock anymore, but the ticking echoes through my mind, roaring above the flames that sear me. I know it's irrational to blame an inanimate object for the passage of time. But the clock has become a symbol of my torture, the reason for my pain. I hate that clock for trapping me in a never-ending cycle. Each dragging second mocks my hope for this to end.

Ares stands tall, leaning over me to ensure I can see him.

Releasing a latch on the underside of the chair, Ares moves my cuffed right arm, still affixed to the armrest. My trembling fingers now lie limp on the leather-wrapped board as the poison forces me to lay here, pliable and complicit.

"Four minutes you stood there after the assassination when you were supposed to return immediately." *The four minutes Flint was whining to me.* Ares places his hands firmly on my bicep and forearm. "Let's count them."

I didn't hear the crack of my bone. Perhaps my mind broke at the same time, and the noises canceled each other out. I only felt the shoot of pain that crashed through me like lightning. The clock stopped ticking, and I think even time abandoned me.

He waits, only a second before driving his burning fingers into the break point. The surge of searing agony rips a scream from my throat, and he squeezes harder.

"ONE!" He screams in my face. The color of his skin turns nearly purple with his anger and his slicked-back hair falls in my face.

Sucking in a loud gasp of air, I scream the number back at him.

Ares moves around the chair to my other side, releasing a latch under my left arm. He runs his fingers through his hair, putting the strands back in their perfect place. My breathing rises fast with the successive rising and falling of my chest. Breathing through my nose, I try to prepare for the next arm.

In the mirror, my right arm, bent unnaturally, throbs in a relentless ache that beats in time with my heart.

My body jostles and my bone gives a sickening crunch as it buckles and breaks. I feel the sharp point of my humerus rip through my flesh as Ares tears my limbs with his Immortal strength.

This scream is silent. Trapped under the weighted pain of my punishment.

An angry growl is my only warning before Ares raises his fist in the air and brings it down on my hand. Two fingers are crushed under his power.

"TWO!" I finally bawl the answer he is becoming impatient to receive. My sobs tacked on to the end of number steal my breath and it demands to be released from my body.

The white bone gleams at me oddly, and the thrumming pain dissolves. Taking a deep breath inward, I focus on it. Insanely, I can't look away. I should watch Ares for his next move, but the bone holds me, transfixed.

My body is giving up. It's ready to die. The person reflected in the mirror doesn't seem to be me. My misshapen limbs and shriveled soul seem to belong to someone else.

To break my legs, Ares must first strap leather belts to each of my knees. The latches of the chair are quite inventive as they pivot downward when he pushes on my knee. The board splits in the center of my femur, and the bones easily snap in two.

Ares barely has to emit any force.

My eyes are blinded. White has taken over my vision as the pain washes over my mind. Still unblinking and fixed at the ceiling, I see myself. Legs and arms are oddly still attached to me but at unnatural angles.

The relentless burning and misery of my pain drown out my cries of the last two numbers. The scratch of my throat is the only evidence of my wailing.

You will not disobey him again. Is a mantra repeating in my mind with a voice that is not my own. *You brought this upon yourself, selfishly. Look how you upset him. Look how exhausted you have made him.*

The shadows of my despair show in the dark circles that form under my eyes. The world around me moves forward while I'm stuck in this relentless and suffocating stillness.

Time was once a friend, a comforting constant in my life. But now, it's become a tormentor, an unrelenting force mocking my stagnation. Making me feel like I'm adrift in a sea of despair, with no land in sight and no guiding light to lead me out of this darkness.

Dripping fire like acid on my skin, he marks me. Carving my faults into my flesh and searing them into my soul with a sharp-tipped knife made of his Flames.

Traitor

Betrayal

Defector

Unfaithful

The smell of my singed skin engrains each signifier into my heart as he carves letters on my chest, and I know they are true. As he makes each turn and twists the letters, my will breaks. I feel my brain crack open like my bones and the truth of the words nestle into my mind.

When the last loop has been made, and he stands back admiring his marks, I feel the venom dissolve inside my bloodstream. My chest convulses, and my muscles spasm. I blink for the first time in minutes, and it burns. Everything burns.

My head falls to the side, and another tear runs down my cheek. Spit collected in my mouth drips from the corner of my lips as my body twitches.

"At least you didn't kill her this time," Demeter says with a bored tone. She wipes her hands, freeing them of crumbs, and reaches over her head, stretching as the hour is up.

"Get the healers and then send her to lunch." He commands Demeter without another look, and the God of War walks out of my vision.

It's ten o'clock in the morning.

⚜ ⚜

Cappa and Delta are waiting outside the doors of the reconditioning room. They refuse to meet my eyes, and the tension in their shoulders pulls mine tight as three healers walk down the hall before us. Demeter hangs back, hesitating as I keep my eyes on the floor, exhaustion and humiliation holding my gaze there.

"Leave your escorts again, and you'll be made to watch what punishment they face for not being by your side every hour of the day." Her brown eyes darken as if they have filled with shadows, and her cold tone strikes me like a slap in the face.

The silence extends uncomfortably long, and with nothing more than a frigid roll of her eyes, Demeter leaves us.

I feel like I'm a youngling again begging for help from the monsters that lurk around the corners of the Underworld, not realizing until now my aunt was one of the monsters I should have been hiding from.

As I grew, a half-mortal with the Wind powers of a Fae, I learned how to stay quiet and dissolve into the shadows to disappear when the monsters were around. My feelings never mattered. The only thing that mattered was that I behaved, did my best to appear invisible, and kept Ares's secrets. Above all, the secrets were the most important thing.

As I got older, the threat was always there like thin lace in every word and glance. Ares, calm as ever, would never let on that I had disappointed him. But when he took me behind closed doors, the fire in his eyes could melt even the hardest stone in this world and was my warning of what comes next.

My handlers follow wordlessly behind me as I navigate the tunnels. My healing took only half an hour and I'm not yet ready to face the Underworlds residence in the larger kitchen. I need to eat something, but I don't think my stomach can handle much right now.

I opt for one of the smaller kitchens on the lower residence levels and begin making my way there.

Fractured memories of being here as a child clash against the fear that I caused someone to be punished because I snuck out of my room. I wonder if the Shifter that I left asleep at my door is still alive. Hopefully, Ares felt generous with having two souls to torture today and only scolded him.

Guilt is a heavy chain that bears down on my shoulders as I add another link with the thoughts I may have cost that man his life.

I shouldn't have been so mindless to think there would be no repercussions for hesitating during the assassination or slipping my patrols, but the dream I had confused me, and Flint didn't care that I had woken up so suddenly, gasping for air. I just wanted a break for a moment. It was selfish.

"I'm sorry I got your friend in trouble." I turn my head behind me, addressing Cappa and Delta.

"We know the risk," Cappa answers.

"We volunteered to monitor the goddess. It's our honor." Delta adds, stopping so I'm forced to turn and look at him. "No matter what happens, it's *our* honor."

He holds a stern and steady look in his eye, not moving until I do.

The guilt that overwhelmed me fades with each step we take away from Ares' room of torture and anger rises within me. Too many times, I've been made to think it was my actions that caused the punishments. If I were somehow better, stronger, or less annoying, Demeter would love me. Ares would respect me; care for me even, like a father.

I understand now, no measure of perfection will ever satisfy the God of War.

He starves us until we beg for the crumbs of his meager praises while he feasts on the anguish of our punishments. Setting impossible standards, he waits for us to fail the slightest offence.

And Demeter is no better. Sitting idly by, inflicting her own pain with a tongue made of knives. She cuts almost as deep as Ares most of the time.

Straightening my spine, I square my shoulders and resolve to keep myself in the shadows. Sulking back to the corners until I can understand the calls I hear from the Dark Shield. Then, with that mystery solved, I'll leave the Underworld and find a life for myself above the surface.

As we enter the kitchen, a small boy, around eight years old, sits at a metal workstation. Mussy brown hair sits ragged on his head, a bit too long in the front and slightly covering his brown eyes. A bowl of fruity cereal, all colors of the rainbow, fills a large bowl, topped nearly to the brim with milk. His feet swing happily as he sits atop the tall barstool, bringing a smile to my face.

I feel drawn to him, a wisp of nostalgia brushing against memories buried deep within my mind that push away the lingering drain of the punishment I just experienced. Seeing this young boy sitting so innocently within in the kitchen of the Underworld, makes me want to take him in my arms and rush him out of these tunnels.

I don't want the monsters that prowl here to leave shadows on his life as they have mine.

"Well, hello there," I announce our arrival and sit next to him, grabbing a bowl and pouring myself a helping of the fruity rings. He never looks up but nods his head once as he shovels another spoonful into his mouth. My guards round the other side of the preparation table, leaning against it on their elbows.

The heavy expressions they carried during our trek here lift instantly when they spot the boy. They smile and stand slightly taller with raised eyebrows and genuine excitement to see him.

"What's going on, Ted?" Cappa holds his large fist out to the boy. Dropping his spoon, Ted bumps fists with Cappa before they launch into a complicated series of handshakes. A ritual they must have performed countless times before.

"Ted, huh? That's a very grown-up name." I pause to take a bite of cereal. I can sense Ted is a Shifter, and it's as if I can see a faint barrier around him, telling me he is a Lycan, unable to call out his wolf.

"I'm pretty grown up, so it suits me." The boy says, very matter of fact.

"Is that so?" I chuckle.

"Ted here is a spy," Delta says, giving me a subtle wink. "One of our best informants."

"What have you been working on, Teddy?" Cappa leans in closer, lowering his tone and turning serious. The quiver of his lips is the only giveaway of the teasing question.

Ted looks to the kitchen entrance as if ensuring no one is listening. Ducking his head, he leans into the two Shifters and lowers his tone.

"Well, the word is, we've all been brought here for a ceremony. There is a powerful goddess, and she will make our wolves come out." He leans back and reaches into the pocket of his worn blue jeans; the knees faded and ready to rip at any moment. He pulls out a folded five-dollar bill. "I have a small reward for anyone who knows who she is." And with a serious look at each of us, he returns to his giant bowl, filling his cheeks with another large bite.

I nearly blow bubbles into my spoon of cereal, and Cappa can't help the smile that forms on his face, though to his credit, he quickly straightens himself out.

"See there, top-notch informant if I ever saw one."

"I can fit into the vents." He looks at me through his shaggy brown hair that rustles when he blinks.

"You be careful in those vents," I tell him with genuine concern.

He takes another bite, studying me as he chews.

"You're pretty. I'm going to be your friend." He declares before turning his bowl, empty of cereal with only the milk remaining, and drains it with loud gulps. He hops off the stool, wiping his mouth on the sleeve of his flannel shirt. "See ya around."

My smile washes away with each step he takes as the darkness of my morning with Ares looms over my mind again. It's as if his innocence stripped away the pain and burning and sound of my bones snapping. But now that he is leaving, it's all rushing back to me.

He is older than his years because of the prejudice he faces as a Lycan. If he could shift into his wolf, I wonder what kind of child would have been sitting on that barstool today, instead of the grown-up boy that fits into vents and eats breakfast alone in a world of darkness.

I beg the Fates that I can help him tomorrow so he can return to the world of the Shifters and hold his head higher.

"See ya around," I answer too late for him to hear.

11

Hermes

"You're smaller than I thought you'd be."** I taunt the Zeta wolf as we stand on the battle plain. After Calypso pointed out the pair of Shifters standing at the tree line, Lucas and a woman accompanying him approached us. We stood in a deadlock for several seconds, evaluating each other while I scanned the area for more wolves hiding within the bush. They came alone.

"Maybe I've heard the same thing about you, *Ferryman*." He replies, making me scoff.

"Not likely. What do you want?"

Several inches shorter than I am, Lucas is still a large man, but the size of his wolf is beyond comparison to every other Shifter within this realm.

The scent of pine sap and fog that covers a forest at dawn hangs on his dark grey t-shirt stretched tight across his shoulders. Clearly a man more accustomed to hard work outside than his fallen brother, Lupo, who spent his days in a three-piece suit behind a desk.

A woman stands stoically next to him. Her tan skin with warm undertones gives her a bronze glow under the Kenyan sun. Jet black hair that is long and straight billows in the wind. Her hair is the only thing moving as she waits observantly beside her Alpha.

The Zeta takes a measurable pause, taking each of us in with his hazel eyes before he begins.

"You killed my brothers." He nods at Medusa, and I take a step toward my friend. The Beta shifts her eyes to me in warning, but Medusa puts her hand on my arm, pushing me aside and stepping before me. I know she can handle herself and is a more than capable warrior. But I also won't stand by and let someone I care about get threatened.

"I've killed many wolves, but you need to explain why you are showing up at my Commune again after the ground you stand on still reeks of the Ichor that your packs spilled?"

"I want to talk about a truce." Lucas steps forward, his hands resting casually at his sides, but his eyes snap to Achilles briefly before settling on me. "I'm the one that sent Damien to seek you out, Hermes."

"Why?"

"He told you. The wolves are dying, and we need to understand why. The Shifters have been submissive to Ares since he created us in the belly of the Underworld because he forces us. I intend to free them of his control."

"You seemed quite submissive when you tried to attack my mate as Moros tore the mind of my other mate to shreds." Achilles's voice is coated in the anger of his loss from the day of the Trojan War when we lost Pat.

I'm surprised Achilles didn't charge Lucas on sight, but my friend is showing great restraint as he speaks to the man who has caused him so much pain. "When you murdered my sisters Commune and had her throat dangling from your fangs."

Lucas flinches with Achilles's reminder of past brutalities.

"There were mortals in there. Children."

"Why should we work with you?" I interject before Achilles's temper makes this a more difficult conversation than it already has to be.

"Because I know where they took your mate. And I know exactly what they did to her. And I know what they plan to use her for."

I eat up the distance between us in a heartbeat and take his shirt in my fists, pulling him into me. His Beta takes a step, but Lucas puts his hand up to stop her.

"I already know where she is. Tell me the rest." I talk through my teeth. My patience before was barely hanging on by a thread, and it's about to snap now.

"She is being guarded by two of my pack. She's currently eating a bowl of cereal. You get nothing else until you agree." We stare each other down, neither willing to break contact until Medusa interjects.

"Step away, H, and let him talk. We need to hear him out." Medusa tries to be the voice of reason. I hold the glare a moment longer before releasing him.

"There is a truth about the raid on the Viking Commune, and Achilles deserves an explanation. My pack lives with the memories of that day and what we did, and I can't change the past. But we can decide to fight Ares alone or together. It's up to you."

It's my turn to pause before answering. I study him with my aura and glance at Hypnos.

Like is eyes, Hypnos' aura is like the pearly inside of seashells and he sends it out, wrapping his power around Lucas as if he is feeling the Shifter King out. I realize what Hypnos' ability is; he is a Sensor.

My mother was also a Sensor, able to detect the residue of emotions of a soul, it made her skilled hunter, able to see the trails of animals left behind as they meandered through the forest.

Hypnos is inspecting the rise and fall of Lucas' feelings and should be able to detect signs of lying or deceit. I'm curious if he senses Lucas is telling the truth or not.

As if knowing my unspoken question, he nods once at me, confirming the Zeta King is telling the truth.

There have been thousands of years of prejudices between the Shifters and Elementals. Eons of fighting and bloodshed and it won't be easy to overcome our long and tumultuous history quickly. But I can give him five minutes.

Achilles steps forward, and I know that look in his eye. "You wanted to eat my mate. You killed my sister." This is not going over well. "Fuck your truce."

As soon as he gets within ten feet of Lucas, Achilles erupts a ball of fire and holds it in his hand, reared back, and ready to launch. Without hesitation, the woman jumps in front of her Alpha, no longer in human form. As quickly as it takes her to land on her feet before him, she shifts into a large wolf, bearing her teeth. The bronze skin and black hair are replaced by brown and black fur with patches of grey.

She lunges for Achilles, still threatening Lucas with his fire blast, but Callie is quick. She flicks her hand, and a vortex of wind shoots the wolf into the air and back to her position behind Lucas. The wolf lands gracefully on her four paws, snarling at the offense.

"I don't think so, honey," Callie warns the wolf with her tone.

"Kai, it's okay," Lucas calls back to the wolf, keeping his eyes on Achilles.

"This realm is interesting," Mor whispers to Hypnos, who nods in agreement.

"Who is she?" Medusa asks as she puts her arm out to pause Achilles forward path.

"My Beta."

"Nice. A chick Beta, eh? How progressive of you, Lucas." She nods her head approvingly. Medusa has always been a greater proponent of women's leadership than men. Even in this tense situation, it would seem.

"She's the right wolf for the job, trust me. My packs don't prohibit our women from challenging as other packs do. She completed all the challenges, just like any other Beta."

"I can respect that." Medusa gives the Beta a bow of appreciation, and the wolf dips her large head in answer.

"Let's hear him out," I stand by my friend of many years and encourage him quietly. The subject of his history with Lucas has always been hard for him to confront as it was never directly with Achilles but the people he loves.

"We all know what happened at the Viking Commune, but some aspects have been kept a secret." Lucas begins. "Other aspects have been removed from our memories. Until two days ago."

Yeah, there's a lot of that going around these days.

"You have never known what we were sent there for and Ares's role in the attack."

"Do you think any of that will help the fact you had my sister's life dangling between your bloody jaws?" Ash and smoke billow off Achilles as his temper rises.

"No. Nothing will ever absolve me of that." Lucas waits, holding Achilles's stare as he did mine.

This wolf has a set of balls on him; I'll give him that.

Callie relaxes the small vortex she's been holding, and the release of wind rustles against all of us. Achilles's shoulders drop as soon as her power caresses him, and she strides next to her mate, grasping his free hand in hers. The other still holds a ball of Helfire.

"Achilles, let's listen." Her tender voice pulls him from his tense standoff, and the fire in his palm dies. He lowers his hand, but fury is still hot in his gaze.

"Talk."

"Kai, go ahead and get changed. I'll start with the story." The Beta follows her orders and stalks away into the line of trees as Lucas talks. "Ares works with a powerful Life mage, Demeter."

Hypnos and Mor shift at the mention of their queen, but they remain silent as he continues.

"She would restrain me in her dungeons for hours, injecting me with the poisons from her plants and testing me to see which would effectively gain control over me. Finally, she figured out the solution was Wolfsbane. So, Ares had us all injected and set us on a mission for the Viking Commune. The poison took away all our control until the fever burned through us, and the toxin passed. But we remember everything we did. Demeter made sure her cocktail would leave us with the memories of that day."

Kai returns from the shelter of the trees with a new set of clothes and joins her Alpha as he continues. "Believe me, I felt every person as my fangs and talons took their lives. And I could do nothing to stop myself or the pack."

The Beta takes a step forward, taking a breath to address us. "I am responsible for the lives of twelve children; two of them were still nursing babes. The only reason I didn't take my own life after the toxins wore off is because my Alpha commanded me to stop."

Lucas flexes his hands at his sides as he vocalizes the admissions. His face is relaxed as if he has come to terms long ago with the actions of that day and as he recounts the events, I send soft waves of my Light around him, searching for the dark shadows of deception but find none.

"Lupo and his bloodthirsty packs reveled in their murders and didn't need Demeter's toxins to happily wag after Ares orders. But my packs are not like them. You need to know; we have been working to fight against Ares, but he knows better than to expect loyalty. He ensures it."

"What does that mean?" I ask, checking on Achilles to see how he handles the story of his fallen commune from the pack leader who took it down.

"I can't answer, truly. If I could physically speak the words, I would." A stern gaze cuts into me, and I wonder if he is bound by the wards of a witch or perhaps a potion, ensuring his silence. "You must know, his Dark Mage is the most powerful I've ever known and lives exclusively in the lower levels of the Underworld."

"He works with mortals and their black markets to steal wolves for expensive entertainment. Ares will send a squad of mercenaries after a family if a man disobeys, like Damien. I saw the state of his wife when her body was returned to him, and I can assure you, horrific doesn't even begin to describe the agony she endured."

"Why did Ares want the Viking Commune?"

"It wasn't the Commune he was after. It was Freya's necklace."

Achilles and I share a confused look, our eyebrows knitted together in the center as we try to find the connection. Freya's necklace was an amber gem encased with a thick gold band. Much like the blue topaz stone on the hilt of my sword, Freya's amber gem channeled her Earth Elemental ability, and she would construct magnificent structures hewn from the rock and dirt.

Achilles recounted a time when his twin sister hid a mortal village with the power of the amber stone, effectively shielding the mortals from the Shifters and Ares's attacks.

Perhaps Ares wants the stone to expand the Underworld further, or maybe topple the mortal cities.

"Brísingamen? Why would Ares want that?" Achilles asks, perplexed and unable to connect the clues of the story.

"It's an artifact that holds a stone containing the power of Nyx." Lucas answers.

I **knew it was a risk coming here.** The Shifters and Elementals have been coerced into believing they are mortal enemies when we desire the same thing.

Absolution against Ares.

Only a few nights ago, when Ares' forces led an attack on this very plain, I held my packs back from the fight, pushing my power as Alpha to combat the Oleander toxins Demeter injected into us.

It took all my power to hold them back and attempt to exert my control over Lupo so he could do the same. He was never as strong as me, but at the same time, I've always felt restricted. Like more power was resting dormant within me, waiting to wake up and Demeter's drugs only intensified that feeling of restraint.

Ever since I first shifted, I knew I was different than the others. Not only as the first Shifter born of Gaea but the largest, the strongest. And different for the abilities I keep secret, hiding away parts of my power so Ares is not aware of my true potential.

Ever since I shook hands with Persephone at Lupo's funeral, I have awakened to my true purpose. I have been shown the reason for my existence, and it's time to share the truth.

It's time the Shifters and the Immortals stop acting like children and go after Ares together. So, I'll risk it. I'll pay whatever price the Elementals want me to pay to form this alliance.

Hermes and his friends talk in hushed tones while two other characters, straight out of the twilight zone, stare us down. The man is incredibly tall with white eyes. As he looks me and Kai over, I feel like he can sense everything about us, each secret we harbor, every insecurity we hide, and I feel totally exposed.

The short woman looks like darkness incarnate with her pale skin and raven hair. Leather clothes and metal weapons are strapped to their bodies everywhere. Her deep red eyes shift to pale yellow in a single unnerving blink.

The woman of darkness straightens her posture, seemingly growing another two inches in height. She cocks an eyebrow at us and turns to her giant companion, whispering something in his ear that makes him smirk. With another blink, her eyes return to their crimson color, and her posture returns to indifferent slouching.

I lean to my Beta and whisper, "You see that shit?"

"Sure did," she confirms quietly.

The woman's entire demeanor changed as if she embodied another personality and then shifted back.

The circle breaks, and Achilles approaches. My faithful Beta is tense, but I can tell the difference in Achilles' behavior now. While I know it's impossible for him to forgive the actions of my pack against him, his twin sister, and their Commune, even what happened under Demeter's control at Troy, he's willing to put his difference aside.

"You have your truce." He extends his hand, and I shake it firmly, careful to release a relieved sigh.

"So, spill it." The Ferryman tips his head at me. "If Ares made you, how can you go against him? Won't he just do something to control you again?"

I was waiting for this question, and I smirk before I deliver it. The truth revealed to me with the touch of Persephone's hand on mine two days ago. It opened up a slew of memories that were hidden within me.

Memories that begin with the true Persephone, the reincarnation of Nyx who lived in the Underworld thousands of years ago. Three nights ago, another woman, a new incarnation of Nyx had her chest cleaved open by her lovers sword and was stolen to the Underworld. She was given a false identity, and her mind was melted into a new one.

But as if Nyx foresaw these events long ago, she left herself a trail of breadcrumbs. A path of clues for herself and others to follow so that she can return and face her hunter again.

And I am one of those breadcrumbs.

"I can go against Ares because he didn't make me. Nyx did."

I hold my hand out to the Herald and share my newly released memories so that they may see. Hermes understands my gesture, and with a nod of approval, I place my hand on his shoulder, and with his power of Mirage, he shares the images that flood my mind.

The memory of Nyx, creating a Titan.

* * * * *

The hallway is stale and dank with moisture as we walk in silence with my hands in Thaumium cuffs. Everyone wears these at all times. The alloy metal has been perfectly blended with gold, silver, and mercury to block all power and strength of any immortal being.

Bare feet, dirty and scraped, pad on the rough floor. Ares walks in front, and a little girl with bright pink hair and pointed ears skips beside him, holding his hand. She looks back at me, and deep purple eyes take me curiously before she smiles. Ares pulls her back to the front with a scolding look.

The next memory flashes, and I'm lying on an examination table. Thaumium restraints firmly hold my ankles, wrists, and chest against the table. Demeter enters with the pink-haired girl, who is several years older now. Taking a seat behind me, Demeter's hands flex on each side of my head, and searing pain burns down the length of my body as if molten lava has been poured over me. It's blinding, consuming every sense as the breathtaking pain takes over.

The agony flutters away with the wash of a cool breeze, and my breathing returns to me.

"Better?" The pink-haired teen smiles at me so innocently.

"Why do you pity the beasts?" Demeter asks. "You know it won't save them."

"I can't stand to see them in pain."

The memory changes again; I'm in a drafty, mirrored room with a tall ceiling. The Thaumium collar is bothersome and chafes my raw skin. The pink-haired ray of sunshine bounds into the room as a young woman. Mature purple eyes are tight with worry, and she's out of breath. Shutting the room's doors, she ducks under the window, hiding from guards who run past. One pauses, looking around my room. I flip my middle finger at him, and he shakes his head before running after his companions.

"I don't have much time. Please listen, and hopefully, I can save you so that you can save the others." I nod, and she reaches forward to unlock the Thaumium collar, removing it from me. Her cool hands heal the wounded skin underneath, and I feel guilty for being so dirty. I never wanted the grime of this place to rub off on her innocent soul.

"These people are not my family. I know that now. They are bad, and they have bad things planned. They want me to collect items that I've hidden, but I've forgotten that I hid them. The items have a lot of power in them, and my father... Ares... wants them for himself. He can't have them. Do you understand? No matter what, he can't have the power inside them."

"How do you know all of this?" My raspy voice is hoarse. I've not had water or food for days. With another flourish of her hand, she raises it above my head, and a stream of water flows from it. I quickly move my mouth under the stream and drink from it greedily. The enchanted waters glow with pink and teal iridescence from her magic and not only does it quench my thirst but my hunger as well. The scrapes and bruises on my skin from the days of torture heal and fade away like they never existed. The torn tendons and ligaments from the stretching machines knit back together, and my dislocated shoulder pops back into place.

"Thank you." I wince against the healing sensations and finally release a deep sigh of relief.

"A woman with a dog found me in my dreams. She told me things, showed me things. They are terrible people. I have to get away from

here. But there are others in the above world that will help me. I just have to find them."

"Yes, go find them. I'll save as many as I can here."

"No, he has something bigger coming. Something no one knows about. I need to help you, or you'll die here."

"Why me?"

"Because you fight him. You have fought against what he is trying to do every step of the way. When others have broken or died, you haven't. You're a prisoner here, unlike the other one who wants to be made into a monster. You only want freedom."

She's right.

"I will give you the power he wants you to have. And then you can give it to others. The good ones, like you. But he can't know it came from me. He'll try to take it from you. He'll try and defile it to turn you into a monster."

"I understand."

"No, you don't. I'll have to hide your memories of this, and you won't remember. But I'll make sure you know that he can't be trusted. And that you know to keep your true powers a secret from him. Just make me a promise."

"Anything." And I mean it. The intensity in her violet eyes and the kindness she has always shown me and the others trapped here have already won my loyalty because she is a prisoner herself.

Delivered here like cattle for slaughter, Persephone has never been allowed to leave the hallowed tunnels within the earth. And despite never being able to set eyes on the setting sun or rising moon, she has remained pure and steadfast to those she encounters here.

"One day, you'll remember this. When you do, it will mean that I need your help. Promise me that you'll come to help me."

"I promise." She nods her head, and tears well in her eyes. I take her hand and hold it. "Thank you for showing me kindness. I'm sorry you had to grow up here. You deserved better than this." My words pull the tears from her eyes, but she wipes them and gathers herself quickly.

"Okay, now, you'll have to trust me. Please remove your clothes. I won't look." The inappropriateness of her request takes me aback. "Please. Before we run out of time." She turns her back to me, and I undress timidly.

"Kneel down." She calls over her shoulder, still refusing to see me in my state of undress. I do as she asks and kneel down, trying my best to keep myself covered. My mind is screaming a million thoughts of what will happen and my heart feels like it's going to explode out of my chest.

"This will feel strange, but please try to stay calm." My eyes are wide, scared but hopeful. She believes in me, and I won't let her down.

She places her hand on my chest, and it warms. An orange aura with speckles of starlight flows from her into me. I can feel it knitting into the fibers of my being. The strength and power that flows into my body is like trying to hold a mountain still during an earthquake. My very bones are shuddering under the pressure, and I feel like I may explode. She envelops me in a whirl of healing waters, and a burst of her aura fills the room with the colors of the rainbow as she intensifies what is happening. As rapidly as my body is tearing apart, she is healing it. The agony and instant relief are too much, and my vision is beginning to fade.

I tense and hold on tighter to my resolve. To the things that have gotten me through every beating, every cut, and every agonizing invasion of my mind over twenty years of my captivity. But my hold is slipping away. Fearful that I won't survive, I strain and scream into the water flooding around me. Then it stops.

I crash to the ground, dizzy and swaying. The water bubble evaporates into a fine mist that coats me in a calm sheen. The sounds of the caves and tunnels echo loudly in my ears. I feel like I'm dying. The scents of the cave and its occupants all heighten to a nauseating intensity. I may vomit from the overload of senses. My skin tingles with the power lurking under my flesh, prowling to be released.

"Let's just go kill him now," I say in a breathy voice that doesn't sound like mine. Sitting on my knees, with one palm on the ground to steady myself, the other wrapped around my stomach, trying to keep the overwhelming sensations from spewing out of me.

"We can't. He's too powerful. I need to do one more thing for you. Are you ready?" I nod my head, and she stands back from me. Holding her palm out, silver starlight pulses out of her hand and rushes through me.

"I hope this room is big enough." She says as she backs up to the wall.

An agony beyond description rolls through my body. Every bone breaks simultaneously, and I grit my teeth against the feel of my skeleton and muscles moving under my skin. It's quick because she wouldn't let me suffer. She's always blocked the pain for me because she is a good person. I blink, and the world changes.

No, the world didn't change. My eyes have changed.

She's much smaller now than she was before.

Wrong again.

She is the same size. I'm larger.

I turn my new body to the mirrors, and the great red wolf that looks back at me is enormous. Easily standing thirty feet tall, my giant head and muzzle could take the girl's entire body in one bite if I attacked her. But of course, I wouldn't do that. I turn back to her and look at her.

She smiles at me with pride, which swells in my heart. Thumping behind me makes her giggle, and I clumsily turn my large muzzle. A bushy tail is wagging back and forth against the wall as if it has a mind of its own. Turning back to her, she reaches her hand out to me, and I bend my head down to her. She closes her eyes, and a tear falls down her cheek as she hugs the furry snout of a giant wolf.

"I hope to see you again in this life, but if I don't, you deserved better than this too." A whimper escapes my muzzle, and I lower my head against her, rubbing my nose on her. It makes her laugh, and she tries to reach her arms around my nose to hug me again. "Okay, time to go back to being a human."

Another wave of her silver power washes over me, bringing a fresh roll of pain. The body of the great wolf shifts back to the human man. I fall to the ground, unsteady on my two human feet. She rushes to me, unbothered by my sweaty, dirty body, and hugs my human neck tightly.

"Goodbye." She whispers as a final rush of her power rolls through me.

13

Hermes

"The fuck, man?"** Medusa exclaims when the memory ends.

"Did you see the size of him?" Callie exclaims.

The vision Lucas shared and the extraordinary transformation seen through his perspective were remarkable. The sensation of the power pouring into his body, the burning of his bones and muscles tearing apart and being healed immediately, was unbearable. But Lucas held on through it all. His resolve was just as strong as the energy that flowed into him.

As captivating as that was, I could only fixate on the woman in the room with him.

Seeing the woman in that memory, even though I had never set eyes on her before, it was as if I had gazed at her beauty a million times before; it was Nyx. The pure silver starlight of her aura pulsed in time with the beats of my heart, and I wanted to fall into the vision to be closer to her.

She must have incarnated into the body of a Fae from Avalon, with thick hair, pink as orchids, and resting just below her shoulders in wide curls. Her pointed ears were elongated and reaching behind her, a trademark of the Fae, though it would have been easy enough to conceal with a glamour if she ventured out of the Underworld.

But everything else about her would have screamed ethereal and stolen the admiration of anyone who set eyes on her. Her skin was radiant, like a sheen of pearly moonlight constantly kissing her. Her high cheekbones, with their iridescent flourish at the peak, drew my gaze around the perfect lines on her sculpted face. Almond eyes, the color of violets at night, sparkled with silver flecks within them.

Kings would have given their kingdoms to her; mankind would have worshiped her, placing the realm at her feet.

I would move mountains for Nyx if that meant she could walk on smoother paths. I would challenge the twelve Titans and the armies of their realms if it meant protecting her from harm. For her, I would become a fortress, a safe haven, a steadfast rock upon which she can live unburdened.

Nyx is not just a woman to me; she is the very essence of love and grace, a beacon of light in the darkness. Nyx is the melody to my soul's song, the warmth on my coldest nights, and the inspiration behind every beat of my heart.

She is not just my mate; she is my purpose and guiding star in this vast universe.

A part of me rages at the thought of Lucas having the opportunity to know Nyx in that form. Persephone's voice in the memory was as light as a bell and wrapped around my soul in a satin caress. Gooseflesh swells along my skin, recalling it. But as he shared the vision with us, his every feeling and sentiment was also passed onto me.

He thought of her as one would a niece, watching her grow from young child to young woman just beginning to mature into her strength; he admired her and saw the compassion in her that survived the dark confinements of the Underworld.

The look on her face as she knelt down to help Lucas, the care swimming within the violet eyes as he transformed, and the controlled power radiating from her took my breath away.

"Demeter brought her here from Avalon, and Ares raised her as his daughter in the tunnels of the Underworld, and they never let her out."

"What happened to her after that moment?" My heart pauses a beat because I feel as if I know the answer.

"Her life ended a few minutes later. Ares and Demeter caught her trying to escape. She fought them, and Demeter killed her."

Mor releases a growl, and it sounds like a panther stalking prey in tall grass, salivating over the prospect of a meal. "Looks like we're not bringing back our queen anymore." She says to Hypnos.

"We're bringing a traitor back to Avalon." He adds, his eyes flaring white.

I try to reach Rhea through our broken and shattered bond, sending reassuring and calm pulses with a steady rhythm, hoping she is safe now. My soul craves her, and my body ignites with a need to race across the realm like a flash of Light until I find her.

My only hesitation is the greater need to make sure she survives this lifetime. She's given enough, and if one of us will not make it to the end of this trial, it will be me. I'll rip this god's damned realm into pieces and teleport her to Avalon before I watch her suffer another death.

Lucas continues, shoving his hands in his pockets and shifting on his feet. "I didn't remember the transformation, turning me into an Immortal and then making me a Titan until two nights ago when I shook her hand at Lupo's funeral. Our contact unlocked the recollections, and I had to leave the reception. I spent the rest of the night reliving memories and piecing them together with Kai."

My jaw clenches, and I grind my teeth in anger. They made her go to the funeral of the man who tortured her and beat my sister. Taking a steadying breath, I puff out my cheeks and run my hand through my hair.

"And you're here to keep your promise?" My eyes pierce him, looking for any sign of betrayal, but his loyalty to her is etched all over him.

"I am."

"You weren't that large during our battle, Zeta." Medusa has a devilish look in her eyes. She wants to see him shift into his Titan form.

"The Gorgon wants a demonstration, does she?" His tone lifts as he senses the teasing in her voice as he evokes the name of her tribe on Tartarus. Lucas takes several steps back as he pulls the t-shirt over his head and tosses it to the ground.

Shifters rarely wear clothes and mostly for the comfort of non-Shifters. Otherwise, they would ruin more wardrobes than it's worth. But we all look away respectfully when Lucas removes his clothes.

His muscular frame is laced with pale scars that gleam in the sun against his olive skin. The result of many pack fights of those who likely challenged the position of the Zeta hoping to dethrone him.

Kai stands next to Medusa as her Alpha shifts. The transformation seems impossible as his bones twist and crack under his skin. As the red fur sprouts and its length grows, we step back, putting more space between us and the emerging animal.

The ground quakes when four massive paws hit the earth. We turn our heads toward the sky as he towers over us. Lucas has to be thirty feet or more in height, soaring over the trees behind him and casting a large shadow over the land.

Kai beams at him, and the pride in being a part of his pack is glowing on her bronze skin.

"Hey, Hermes?" The wolf's rough voice echoes eerily in my mind as he speaks to me with telepathy. Shock pulls my eyebrows into my hairline as Shifters typically can't transmit thoughts with Elementals.

"Yeah?" I answer out loud, looking around to see if the others hear the snarling voice of the wolf as well.

A sly smile spreads across the muzzle of the great animal, if that is even possible. *"Am I still smaller than you thought?"*

Okay, point proven.

With a roll of my eyes, I cross my arms over my chest. The giant wolf sits casually, and the earth grumbles at the disruption. It's been ages since I looked upon the form of a Titan, and an odd mixture of disbelief and uncertainty circles my mind.

Pushing my hair out of my eyes, I consider what end Ares could be trying to reach with Rhea. We have always known he has wanted to consume her power, but armed with new information that she can create a Titan, I have to wonder.

Can she create more Titans and with other powers?

Perhaps Ares wants to be turned into a Titan himself or use her to create an army of Titans. Gods, if he has been working to control Lucas, it would make sense he knows her ability and worked to keep both her and Lucas within his reach, waiting for the day he can perfect his serum.

"We've got to talk to Atlas and see if there is anything in the archives about Titans being created or put under control."

"There is something else as well." The wolf growls and nods its huge head at Kai.

She eyes Medusa as she circles around her, looking her up and down, then takes a place next to my friend again. Running her hands over her face, through her hair, and down her chest, the movement causes a transformation. In a matter of seconds, we're looking at an exact copy of Medusa. Even Kai's clothing changed to match what Medusa is wearing.

"Goddess!" Medusa marvels at the duplicate of herself, walking around Kai and inspecting the metamorphosis.

"After Persephone made me a Shifter, Kai is the first that I turned into a Shifter like me, and then I turned several others. Ares and Demeter thought they had finally unlocked the key to turning us into Shifters.

"With samples to work from, Demeter could use our blood to make more. But something unique happened with Kai; she has always had this additional ability where others did not." Lucas explains.

Medusa inspects one of the replicated braids that hands around Kai's face between her fingers. "When a Titan declares an apprentice, they bestow a remarkable gift to them. A part of the Titan's power they share to signify the importance and authority of their apprentice to others. That is what you did for Kai."Lucas had been a mortal before he was captured and turned; he would have no awareness of our history, and I'm sure Ares didn't bother to teach it.

Kai stands a bit taller with Medusa's explanation. Being the Zeta Kings Beta was already an honor for her. You could see it all over her. But confirming Lucas is a Titan and knowing he blessed her with special power, satisfaction is overflowing in her expression.

"Alright." I clap my hands and turn to our new Shifter friends. "Let's go destroy the Underworld."

Commotion near the door grabs my attention. Goddess knows how long I have been sitting in the cafeteria of the Underworld, spaced out and holding my fork stuffed with a bite of salad and chicken without eating it. My unfocused eyes roam the space to get my bearings.

I don't even recall coming here, much less making my lunch selections, or sitting down.

I can't stop seeing myself with broken bones and hearing the cries of children within the inky darkness of the layer I found.

The culprit of the commotion is the Zeta and the new Alpha, Gabriel. The women filling the cafeteria buzz with excitement and the men sit taller and puff out their chests. I want to choke on the ridiculousness of it all.

Gabriele stalks around like he's newly won the lottery and doesn't realize everyone is only clamoring for his attention for selfish reasons. But he is not the one they are excited to see. Lucas pulls out the chair across from me and sits.

"By all means, take a seat." I look at him blandly as he invades my lunchtime.

His hazel eyes narrow at me as if he is thinking while he toys with a manilla folder in his hands. His aura ripples and thrashes like an agitated animal, mirroring the swirl of colors in his eyes. Hunter green blends with traces of sandy brown and sky blue, creating a beautiful effect.

Lucas is handsome, with a sharp jaw and dimple in the center of his chin. Tan, tall and muscular with wavy brown hair that reaches his shoulders. Any of these women would mate with him in a heartbeat, but he remains single. Fated mates are rare in the Shifter community but not unheard of; perhaps he is waiting for the Fates to present his partner to him.

Largest of all the Shifters and the first son of Ares, being his mate and producing his pups would be like royalty. The eyes burning into me from the nearby tables tell me the women of the packs are not very appreciative that Lucas joined my table.

"Is there something I can help you with?" I ask when he doesn't break the silence.

"Yes."

His answer catches me off-guard. Lucas and I have never traveled in the same circles here, and I didn't expect him to answer my snarky comment that way.

"What on Earth can I possibly help you with?"

"It's not something *on* the Earth I need help with. It's something *in* the earth."

This piques my curiosity, and I lean closer, tilting my head, wanting him to continue, but he doesn't.

"What is *in* the Earth that needs my help?"

"I can't tell you."

Confused, I lean back in my chair, dropping my fork into my bowl of Caesar salad and turning my palms up in irritation.

"What the fuck? So, why even mention it? What kind of game of charades is this?"

"Tell me what happened to you in the recalibration room this morning."

Venom runs down my throat that he would bring up my punishment. I figured his lackeys, Cappa and Delta, would tell him I was there since they were waiting for me outside the door as my escorts. But I didn't take him to be a giant asshole that would mention it.

"Fuck you."

"No, *try* to tell me what happened. You won't be able to." His sharp eyes burn a brighter shade of green among the tan and aqua swirls as he encourages me. The weight of a thousand unspoken words hangs within his stare.

The sound of my bone cracking echoes in my mind, and as I open my mouth to tell him how Ares broke my arm, my throat closes, blocking off my airway and gagging me. It's as if a large hand with sharp nails clutches my throat, and I'm suffocating, unable to speak the words.

Panic seizes me as I clutch the table, my eyes blowing wide as I look at Lucas. The feeling of warm goo slides over my skull again, just as it did when Demeter injected me with her milky toxin.

Lucas leans forward with a hard gaze on me. Placing his hand on mine, he squeezes.

"Let it go. Let the thought go." He speaks in hurried, hushed tones as I try to release the thought. It floats back into my mind like a balloon caught in the wind, and the grip on my throat eases.

Air returns to me, and the dark spots that formed around my vision ebb away.

"So, you see, I *can't* tell you," Lucas repeats himself, looking at the nearby tables of Shifters who noticed my quick moment of panic.

I play it off, coughing and drinking water like I choked on my food.

"Then how am I supposed to help you?" Leaning in, I whisper.

"Pay attention around here to what you *don't* see, and I'm confident you'll figure it out." He winks a hazel eye at me and stands. Before he leaves, he bends down to my ear and places the large envelope on the table with the word "Apprentices" written in large letters with black ink. "Look at this when you are alone." And then he covers it with my napkin and walks away.

❧❧❧❧❧ ❧❧❧❧❧

Tomorrow night is Mabon, and Shifters pile into the tunnels every hour. It's stifling, and the narrow passages with buzzing light bulbs get smaller and smaller with each passing minute.

My two shadows follow me as I wind through the maze of corridors. My entire body is sore, even my eyes feel like they have had a workout, and I'm not even sure how that could happen. I suppose it's the lingering effects of the Soul Fire that burned within my essence during my punishment.

Nodding politely as I pass Shifters and Elementals, a pair catches my attention, and a tickle of familiarity makes me stop.

Where every other being in this subterranean structure stares at me like I have ten heads, the man and woman walking toward me make every effort to look everywhere except me.

"I'm sorry, have we met before?" I ask the young woman around my age. With beautiful features and jewels for eyes, she looks like a gentle bird with the spirit of a deadly predator lurking within her. The man by her side is tall and bald. He looks up and down the tunnels as if paranoid someone will see our interaction.

"I–I don't believe so," she stammers.

"You've not met my sister before, and we must go." The tall man, with a gaze as dark as his complexion, answers for her with a thick African accent. "Let's go, Zara."

As he says her name, it echoes within my mind, and a vision of the pair flashes in my mind. Another flash of a memory presents a woman with green eyes and long braided hair. A sharp eyebrow raised confidently as she crosses her tattooed arms over her chest.

Then a final flash of Hermes with his brilliant blue eyes gleaming like the center of the hottest star that burns in the galaxy. He looks at me with such tenderness, and a warm, soothing wave flows over my skin.

Within three beats of my heart, the visions stop, but I recognize the grassy field shown as the location of our ambush when Hermes and his broad of Elementals attacked us. Was that perhaps the start of our battle that resulted in my chest being cracked open by Hermes's sword?

And why would he have looked at me with such fondness and affection?

I can't help but admit I wish Flint would look at me with eyes like that.

Not only the deep blue hues of the richest colors of the ocean but with the range of affections I felt in that quick flash of a memory. Love, adoration, and protectiveness are all encased in a single determined expression.

As the man pulls his sister along their previous course, Zara looks back at me as if to say she is sorry, and I can't rid myself of that sense of knowing. Perhaps she has one of those faces you think you've seen before.

Shaking the encounter from my mind, I keep the folder tucked protectively into the crook of my arm as I return to my assigned room. Cappa and Delta station on each side of the door when I close it behind me.

The lack of windows and stale air add to the drab atmosphere, and some time to relax in a bath is exactly what I need to unwind my exhausted brain.

I'm curious what happened to the sleeping guard that I slipped by in the wee hours of the morning, but I'm afraid to ask. The Shifters are already tense as we wait for the lunar alignment so we can bear witness to the ceremony's outcome. I feel the weight of their grief push down on me as I walk through the maze of the Underworld.

I wish I could just stay in my room and sleep away the next few days, but I know that can't be. Ares's missions are in constant movement, directing us from one point to another as we battle the Elementals to tip the scales of fate toward Ares's plans. There is no way to remove yourself from his army except death, so my choice for tomorrow's ceremony has been made for me.

After a nap and a few pills for my period pains, I run a hot bath. Bringing the manilla folder from Lucas, I sit it on the counter's edge, planning to look it over later. My aching limbs and throbbing back are screaming for me to dunk myself into a hot bath and more healing minerals.

The soothing waters immediately soften my tense muscles and ease my bloating as I rub my hands along my neck and shoulders, squeezing the stress away. Working my hands down my shoulders and arms, I continue to apply pressure, kneading the knots with minimal satisfaction.

What I really want is a pair of strong hands that cover my shoulders in their strong grip and work out the stiffness for me. As I keep kneading and rubbing my body, my hands roam to my breasts, my nipples tender because of my period.

Why do periods make you feel so miserable and horny at the same time?

It's not fair that I feel three pounds heavier and have a constant backache, but I want nothing more than to grind myself against the lean body of a man.

Eyeing the folder, I open it and find two papers, each with a picture clipped to the corners.

In the left hand, Apollo. His blonde hair and bright blue eyes shine even in the small watercolor painting. Ares painted the image himself and signed his name in the corner in neat script.

A preservation spell has been placed on the old paper, but it still shows wear and tear of being looked at often. There is a permanent imprint from the paperclip, and the corners have been worn down, giving me the impression Ares has looked at the picture of his old enemy many times.

In my right hand, I'm ensnared by the image of Hermes, and I can't look away from his picture. It is also a watercolor painted and signed by Ares, showing Hermes as a young boy. Behind this old picture is a modern image, snapped when Hermes was out in a bustling city, as depicted in the blurred background of cars, traffic lights, and tall buildings.

A grown man with the handsome features of his father and the dark hair of his mother, he is striking. Hermes' gaze is looking just off to the side of the camera, and his wide smile gleams with happiness. Pulling the clipped picture from the paper, I let the folder and stack of information fall to the bathroom floor.

Sinking back into the tub with the Herald of the Realms at the forefront of my mind, I stare at the image as I trace shapes on my skin with a featherlight touch of my finger.

I hope the picture will help me recall the fuel that ignited our battle three nights ago; the only thing I can recall is the look of pain and horror on Hermes' face as his sword ran through my sternum.

I don't want to remember that feeling, playing like a broken record in my mind, so I focus on the picture again, and a fantasy starts to form. I imagine I'm spending the day in the sprawling downtown, far above the dark underground prison that is my current home. We explore restaurants, and he pulls me around by my hand as we hop off subways and run into shops.

We laugh and flirt, and Hermes stands close to me as we wait at a red light to cross the street. He would run his hand up my arm and pull me into him for a kiss before the light turned green. I feel safe with him, happy, and like nothing in the world can touch me if he is near.

As I run my hand down my body, a water droplet races down my chest into the steaming pool of the bath, and I imagine it's Hermes running his finger down my body.

My body erupts in chills as I imagine him stroking my skin with his firm hands, and I run my fingers across my chest and down my stomach.

Thinking of my fantasy, Hermes would bring me back to a stylish downtown apartment at the end of our perfect date, eager to touch me in a way he resisted when we were in public.

He crawls over me as I lay sprawled across cool sheets on a large bed. He lavishes my neck and then my breasts before running a trail of kisses down my stomach until his tongue finds my wet center. Licking up my arousal, he pins my hips down with his strong grip and holds me still to relish in the slow, beautiful torture his mouth gives me.

My fingers find the point of my arousal, and I slowly circle my clit, abandoning the picture to the top of the pile on the floor. With closed eyes, I envision dark hair that tickles my skin as Hermes moves down my body, licking and kissing my exposed flesh as my hips tilt, eager to meet his touch. I swear I can almost feel his breath against me. Every inch of me is electric with the need to be caressed.

Kissing each side of my thighs, the fantasy is so close to giving me what I want as my fingers do the work that I'm imagining. A sigh escapes my mouth, and I tilt my head back against the cool tub. Steam rises off the surface of the bathwater, and my core tightens, longing to release my built-up tension.

I can see him so clearly in my mind as those sapphire eyes look at me, heavy and dark, with the desire to consume me, to pull my pleasure from me and feast on my orgasm. As the fantasy I see in my mind lowers his head with the promise to give me my release, three loud bangs on the bathroom door rip me from the vision, and the tension of my desire dissolves into nothing.

"Yes?" I call out with a frustrated huff.

"It's dinnertime, and Ares expects you to make an appearance in the cafeteria." Flint is not being forceful in his tone and is only relaying the message, but I can't help the irritation that washes over me, followed by the guilt of thinking of my enemy in such a manner as I was just now. I should be plotting Hermes' death, not wondering how his hair would feel through my fingers as I come on his tongue.

And it's only now that I realize my mind should have thought of Flint as I concocted a fantasy to get me off. I should have wanted to call him to me and get the satisfaction from a real person, not just my imagination and my own touch.

Covering my face with my hands, knots form in my stomach because I let myself romanticize someone who is not my partner but also someone who tried to kill me only a few nights ago.

Reluctantly pulling myself from the bath and deciding my punishment of remaining horny without satisfaction is appropriate for my actions, I quickly dress and find myself alone in the suite. I guess Flint didn't feel the need to wait for me, so I'll grab my two babysitters and head to dinner.

Opening the door and preparing myself for the crowded hamster tubes of the underground bunker, I'm surprised to see Cappa and Delta have been replaced by Lucas's Beta, though I can't recall her name. Cappa and Delta said they volunteered to guard me. Does that mean she did as well, or is she here on orders from Lucas to keep a closer eye on me?

"The boys are taking a break, and I'm covering the night shift," she answers a question I didn't ask. "I'm Kai." She holds out her hand.

"Persephone," I reply, shaking her hand.

"I know." She gives me a curt nod and then waits for me to pass.

The walk to the cafeteria is quiet, and it doesn't seem Kai is much of a conversationalist. Continuing my polite greetings as we pass people on the walkways, Kai remains stern and doesn't acknowledge anyone outside of a few who address her as their Beta.

The cafeteria is a cacophony of noise, all jumbled together. The number of Shifters squeezing into the tables has nearly tripled since lunchtime, and a constant stream of people pass in and out of the serving lines, full of a never-ending buffet of food.

Kai must sense my hesitation and waits with me as I pause at the doors. I feel her cool gaze on me as I look over the sea of people, casually eating and laughing. My eyes search for Flint but he's not here.

"A lot of good people are depending on you tomorrow for Mabon." She says to me.

"I know."

"And a lot of shitty ones too."

I swallow my surprise and look up at her as she stands several inches taller than me. Harsh brown eyes hold my look as a crimson aura, the color of oxblood swirls calmy around her. I nod as if understanding some hidden message, she can't say. Maybe I can talk to her when we return to my room and see if she can share more privately.

"Over here!" A little voice rings out from the crowded cafeteria, and the messy brown hair of a little boy bounds out of the masses toward us.

"Haiya, Kai!" Ted says with a grin and what seems to be a newly lost tooth. "I saved you a seat!" He grabs my hand and weaves us through a maze of tables. A young woman with two small children a few years younger than Ted, looks at us expectantly as we approach.

Open seats are waiting for Kai and me, and we take them. Reaching my hand out to the woman, I introduce myself.

"I'm Naomi." She looks at the two boys beside her, mirror images of each other. "These are my twins, Jayden and Jamal." Naomi is a young mother. She can't be more than twenty-eight years old and wears her hair in long braids with a colorful headband holding them out of her face. A golden septum piercing in her nose brings out the gold flecks in her brown eyes and sets nicely against her rich skin. Her boys have a much lighter complexion than she does, and their blue eyes are striking in their unique color, with light brown hair in tight coils on the top of their heads.

"Nice to meet you."

The boys are feasting on a plate of spaghetti as Naomi savors a helping of meatballs in a pomegranate red wine sauce. The twins erupt in quiet giggles when they slurp their noodles and splash sauce on their faces. Their mother takes a napkin to their mouths with a roll of her eyes.

"I'm adopted," Ted says frankly as he slurps his own noodle, focusing on working it through the new gap in his smile from the front tooth that is gone.

"You boys, go refill your cups," Naomi instructs, then watches them as they bounce away.

"Ted's parents were taken to the gladiator pits when he was four. I found him behind my café, eating out of the garbage," she explains when they are out of listening range.

"My gods, that is terrible." My heart dips in my chest with the explanation, and I find myself looking for him to ensure he is okay, even though I just met these people.

"My boys and I are Lycan, and so were Ted's parents. The poor thing walked alone from Newhalem to Seattle for days, scared out of his mind." Naomi's eyes drift away as if she can see the image of a younger Ted, dirtied and scared. "It's a miracle he ended up finding me. Seattle is a heavy Shifter region, and his fate could have turned out very different."

"You're welcome in the pack at any time. Lucas means it when he says he has kept a place for you whenever you're ready." Kai tells her.

It gives me reassurance knowing Lucas is aware of her situation and is trying to help her.

"Do you have a partner? I'm sorry if that is too invasive." My cheeks burn as I realize the impropriety of my question too late.

"I'm a widow. My husband was also Lycan, and we lived as Lone Wolves. He joined the human military and died overseas."

"I'm so sorry."

Naomi reaches over and puts her hand over mine. Years of hardship strain her young eyes, and it's impossible for me to understand her struggles. I can only tell they have been great.

"You have no idea what it means for us that you are here to help. I want to thank you. Even if the ritual doesn't work for us and we remain Lycan, we're grateful for the chance to try."

A gasp next to us draws our attention, and our heads snap in the same direction.

Ted has returned with the twins, staring at me with wide eyes. "It's you?" He holds my eyes, blinking with his round brown eyes.

Relieved, the two ladies accompanying me join me as we all relax our posture. Naomi pulls Ted into her arms and rests her cheek on his head.

"This is Persephone, and she is the Elemental that will try to help us tomorrow."

"Nay-Nay, I knew she was a good friend to have. I can always tell about these kinds of things." Ted smiles at Naomi with his holey grin and sits with his brothers.

"You sure do, Teddy bear."

Ted bounces in his seat again, trying to twirl too many noodles on his fork without success, and then turns to me with a very serious expression. "Will it hurt when you pull my wolf from me?"

His tiny voice pulls at something in my heart, and I want to protect him.

"I promise I'll do my best to make sure it doesn't hurt."

This is going to be the longest day of my life. Waiting until tomorrow, when I can pull Rhea out of Ares's clutches, will take every ounce of self-control possible. Lucas refused to tell us where the Underworld was and left with Kai to return there. His need to protect his people is understandable but clashes with my need to save my mate.

The day is wearing on my patience, and so is everyone else. The Kenya dining hall is solemn as the Commune filters in and out to eat their lunch. No one feels ready to laugh yet. They have dared only a few small smiles as the residents allow the dead the respect of passing onto the Void.

Callie is hovering around like I'm going to disappear again. I suppose I earned this by leaving without at least telling them what was happening, but no amount of worry is going to help us right now.

Since meeting Lucas, Achilles has been sulking over the memories of his sister's death. With his leg bouncing a million miles a minute and the brooding look on his face, everyone is giving him some distance.

Medusa is like a bag of cobra snakes, twisting and writhing in a burlap bag just waiting to be unleashed. The betrayal of Anahita and Avaley has her wound tight. Mainly because she didn't sense it, but she's restless putting up extra measures and wards around the Commune.

"Hypnos, what is your power?" I blurt out as we sit around eating our lunch in silence.

"I am a Sensor. But you figured that out on the plain below." He looks at me with his pearly stare, and the feeling of being completely unmasked washes over me as if his look can unearth every secret I have. He's correct, knowing I made my prediction as we spoke with Lucas and I'm glad to know I was right.

"Can you assess Medusa's prisoner and determine the extent of her betrayal? Help tell us if she is being truthful or holding anything back?"

"Of course." Hypnos stands. The serious expression never leaves his face, with his thick arms crossed over his chest. Mor remains at the end of the table, pushing more food into her mouth than should be possible.

"You have quite an appetite," Achilles says, impressed as he watches her eat four times the amount of food he puts down. As she did at Starfall, Mor abandons the plates and slides a platter of meats and rice directly in front of her.

"We get very hungry." She says with her puffed-out cheeks full of food.

Achilles twitches his head in confusion before deciding it's not worth probing into. Decidedly Mor has an odd way of referring to herself but not everyone can see the three souls living inside her body as I can.

I'll have to talk to Atlas about Mor and text on how the Titans were created. Decidedly, we are breeching into new territories every day it seems since meeting Rhea, and it gives me hope. An optimism that perhaps destiny is taking over in place of the Fates, and we'll finally defeat her hunter and rid her of this cursed spell.

Standing, I tug on one of Medusa's braids and snap her out of the fog within her thoughts. "Come on, Deuce. Stop torturing yourself, and let's get you some peace of mind."

And get me something else to think about.

Anahita is being kept in a cell with Thaumium bindings. Peering into the small window on the door, she is backed into the corner of the cell, sitting on her bottom with her knees pulled into her chest. She's been offered a change of clothes and food, but she is refusing until she can burn her sister's body properly.

The other sister, Aryana, was recovered on the battlefield and taken for healing. She is resting in the medical wards but is also in Thaumium bindings as a precaution.

Medusa and I enter the room first, followed by Hypnos.

Immediately upon passing into the room, a heavy curtain of dread takes our breath away.

"Tsssssssh!" Hypnos hisses. The force of his power washes over me as he widens his stance and bends his knees, lowering his large form and getting into an attack position.

Pushing one hand in front, the translucent surges of his intentions pulsate like a beam of concurrent waves, striking Ana in the chest. She cowers and grunts at the force, and Medusa tries to move toward him.

"Un....hand..... her," Medusa grunts against Hypnos. His power compels her to remain away.

"I need The Morrigan!" Hypnos' voice echoes and is amplified, as if he is speaking into a microphone.

The room's shadows darken and reach into the center of the cell, just in front of Hypnos. With a flourish of darkness, moving like smoke, she appears from within a portal of shadows.

"Take the lights, Herald." Mor's voice is a little more than a growl as she sneers at Ana. Hypnos and The Morrigan's reaction to Ana is so defensive and hostile. But she has always been faithful and loyal, until this incident that involved their sister being held in a ransom.

Hypnos' power eases, and I dim the lights, leaving the smallest amount. My eyes flick to Medusa, and she is enraged. Trembling in her frozen stance against the wall opposite me, with our position, we watch as Mor fixates her dark glare Ana.

The pupils of her eyes shift and split into three dark circles, as they begin to glow a fierce yellow. Even in the dim lighting, her yellowing skin seems to decay in front of us as her hair turns oily and hangs heavy around her face.

I witness the three balls of Light within her swirl and mingle with each other, as if the souls inside her are combining to transition the woman into the dark divinity that stands before us. The transformation of the pale woman into this creature of power freezes Medusa with shock locked on her face.

The Morrigan's aura explodes around her, and shadows whip and coil erratically. The sound that comes from her mouth jars

Medusa to her core as she hears the screaming whisper that takes over Mor's vocal cords. That sound of three voices fighting to speak at once crawls around the small room, commanding it to obedience.

"Show yourself, Lurker."

Pushing her hand at Ana, ribbons of shadows spew from her palm. My eyes follow the ribbons to the corner of the cell, expecting the shadows to encircle Ana. Remembering the feeling of those cold tendrils of slime that wrapped around me when I arrived at Avalon sends a shiver down the length of my body.

It's not Ana that becomes encased in The Morrigan's shadows but a massive black void directly behind her. Eight feet tall and hiding within the dark corner of the cell, the void takes shape as Mor's dark garlands restrain it.

It's impossible to describe the face of a shadow other than different levels of obscurity that show two voids for eyes and another for a mouth. The Morrigan is somehow able to keep the figure, made of nothing more than a viscous cloud of dark smoke, ensnared with her power.

"Lights." Mors gargled voice instructs me, and I feed my power back into the bulbs above us.

The creature opens its oversized mouth and, raising its head to the ceiling, releases a screech that pierces my very soul. It writhes and thrashes in the corner as shadows of the darkened room grow and reach for us.

Shuddering under the fear that snakes up my body, thoughts of terror pierce my mind. I see my parents withering away from the poisons Ares fed them, slowly rotting until their Immortal Ichor seeps out of their bodies and their ashes blow away. I drop to my knees and clasp the sides of my head with both hands. Screaming, I try to push the crushing misery from my mind.

I see Patroclus limping toward me with a hand outstretched, a wooden spear impaling his head through his temples as a slow stream of blood oozes from his mouth, nose, and ears. The jarring expression of the overly stretched smile and widened pale eyes that were forced onto his face haunts me.

"You could have helped me, H."

I hear my friend's long-dead voice right before his body burns from the inside out, turning into a blackened corpse. His eyes explode and black ooze drips down the withered face as he keeps staggering toward me.

"Help me, son." My father.

"Hermes, please, help us." My mother.

"Hermes, why can't you protect me? I don't want to die again." Rhea.

Hundreds of visions of my mates' deaths replay on a loop. Thousands of faces look at me at the moment she dies again and again with the same pained expression locked on each one.

"Don't you love me enough to save me?"

The raw hurt in her voice is brutal and so near; I look around, expecting to see her, but find only the darkened room with my current companions.

Bracing my hand on the ground, I push the essence of my aura out and encase myself in a Shield of Light, driving away the Darkness. The vice around my mind is released, and with gasping breaths, I look at Medusa. My unfocused eyes find her lying on the ground with tears streaming down her face.

"I'm sorry, I'm sorry." She keeps repeating, trapped in the same torture, and likely seeing the visions of her own terrors.

I project my Light Shield on her, and her body instantly relaxes, alleviated from the pain and whatever horrors she saw in her mind. Hypnos' waves of power are still assaulting Ana, and it seems she is not impacted by the scream of the shadow creature as Medusa and I were. The Morrigan keeps her hold on the figure and shows no sign of strain, though the shadow keeps up its relentless fighting and thrashing.

Approaching the being, Mor pulls one hand over the other and wrenches the whips of shadow that ensnare the beast. It dissolves as it passes through Ana and reforms in front of her. Mor takes a step toward the figure, then another as she pulls it close with her ribbons of dark aura. A yellow glow that matches her eyes flares from the center of her heart, and the being sizzles and hisses, exposed to the strange light she is producing.

Like water circling a drain, a vortex of yellow light swirls from Mor's chest, and the shadow creature is trapped within it. Pulled slowly, it disappears into her body. The screeching and thrashing instantly stop. The shadows of the room soften, and Mor's appearance transforms back to the pale woman with crimson eyes and raven hair.

Turning to her companion, Mor nods once at Hypnos, and he releases Ana of his power beam. She collapses to the ground, twitching and convulsing. Her eyes stare blankly at nothing as she lies expressionless on the floor. Medusa rushes to her, cradling Ana in her arms as she cries over her friend.

"What the fuck was that?" I ask Hypnos as I stand and brush the dirt from my pants. Sweat has formed on my brow and runs down the side of my face.

"A Shadow Lurker," Hypnos answers as Mor leans casually against the doorframe, picking her molars with her nail as if she didn't just ingest a being of darkness while the rest of us relived the most traumatizing moments of our immortal lives.

"What is a Shadow Lurker?"

"It's a being of Elysium, the Shadow Realm." Mor answers, her voice back to normal as she speaks with her melancholy tone. "It latches onto a living thing and feeds off its fear. Based on the size of it, it's probably been latched onto her for at least three moons."

If the moon cycles are anything like those on Tartarus or Hel, that is likely around a year, here on Gaea.

"What would something like that do to a person?" Medusa asks, still holding Ana, who has turned her face into Medusa and is sobbing quietly.

"It starts off small with nightmares and feeds at night but then would attach itself permanently and feed continuously as it grows. Always sending invasive thoughts of harm or destruction, it would find a person's greatest loves and their greatest fears, then use them to conjure images that would torture their host and consume the fear they release. Eventually, their mind would break, and the Lurker would find a new host."

If Hypnos is a Sensor, this Shadow Lurker would be his antithesis. A Sensor can detect and interpret emotions discharged by living beings. If the Lurker was siphoning Ana's fear, it makes sense that Hypnos could detect it.

"Thank you for removing it." Ana's tiny voice filters up from Medusa's embrace. She finally sits up, wiping her eyes.

"Did you know it was attached to you?" Medusa asks her friend. Ana shakes her head no.

"I've been wracked with anxiety and having the most disturbing dreams. Avaley was as well." Her voice hitches as she takes in a shaky breath. "We were seeing images of our sister's torture, terrible things. We heard Aryana calling us for help constantly. All day, screaming in our minds."

Ana continues telling the story of what she and Avaley experienced for the past year before they were finally approached and offered a deal. A month before I arrived with Rhea, asking for Medusa's help, a cloaked Dark Mage delivered their sister's finger with a ring of their family crest still around the severed digit. They were promised the return of their sister if they would disable the commune portal. They were told to wait for the signal, which came on the night we left for the club.

"You should have told me." Medusa's sorrow filled eyes take in Ana but a fact of her account hold me in thought.

How could someone know we would end up with Medusa? Ana and Ava have been feeding this thing for a year and were approached a month before our arrival. We hadn't even met Rhea at that time.

The meeting at the bookstore wouldn't have taken place for two weeks when they were petitioned a month ahead of us.

Does someone have a gift of foresight, or perhaps there is someone pulling the strings behind the curtain and steering us all into their trap?

"She is being truthful. Someone placed the Shadow Lurker with them. It fed them fears of their sister until they broke and agreed to betray you." Hypnos provides his evaluation of the situation.

Medusa cradles Ana as she weeps, whispering apologies to her Headmistress.

✦✦✧✦✦ ✦✦✦✦✦

Sitting on top of Kenya mountain, the pyre of Avaley burns as Achilles sets the body of the fallen immortal ablaze. The warm sun begins to dip behind the horizon, and the anticipation of nightfall vibrates around me. It's as if this wise, old mountain knows the goddess of the night has returned and longs to welcome her darkness to the sky.

Or maybe those are just my thoughts.

A tension is within me, being away from Rhea, unable to feel her aura, and I feel as if the tightly wound band of my anxiety will snap at any moment. I search inside myself for that tether hanging limp inside me, and the bond to Rhea is there. The faint heartbeat of my mate on the other end is soothing, even if it's only a faint echo of what was once there.

The day was hot, but as night takes over the sky, it cools quickly. The chill in the night air does nothing to cool the burn of my anticipation, and I lay on my back, looking at the constellations as sweat runs down my sides.

I release my aura in a steady flow and my Light fills the night sky.

Ribbons of blue haze fills the darkness above me and stretches across the horizon.

Dancing with the atmosphere, green streams mingle within my blues, and I fill the realm with my power.

I need to find her.

My very essence feels like it's weighted down with thousands of years of sorrow and only her smile can alleviate the ache within me.

My pulse races and unease washes over me.

I try to calm myself with a steadying breath, but I'm only worsening.

My aura, extended around the world, warns of Hypnos' approach before I hear the pebbles bounce across the footpath as he joins me at the top of the mountain.

"This realm wears the deceptive mask of peace very well." His deep voice rumbles as he sits next to me on the ledge. "It's almost believable."

"Hmph." I snort a laugh through my nose. "It's never been believable. The mortals would rather turn their heads than know the truth."

After freeing Anahita of the Lurker, Mor, and Hypnos returned to their meal, and Medusa and I visited Aryana in the medical wing of the Commune. Missing a digit that healed naturally, the ring finger on her left hand was severed at the base of the joint.

The healers have worked to clean and heal her wounds, bathe her, and restore her energy with the healing Water and Life elements. She no longer looks like a skeleton form of an Elemental on the brink of eternal death as vitality has been returned to her.

Chocolate hair lays in tight coils around her face, and her eyes match those of her sisters, shining with green like the springtime and laced with sorrow. She survived captivity within the dungeons of the Underworld, knowing her sisters were being tortured with visions of what was happening to her. She nearly went mad herself, but she kept faith her sisters would come for her.

She never left the prison where she was kept, and her only visitors were Ares, Demeter, and a Dark Mage. Aryana never saw their face, kept under the cloak of darkness and shadow, but the Mage was the primary executioner of torture while Ares observed.

As I think over the shadow that has lurked in the dark corners of events since meeting Rhea, my heart nearly pounds out of my chest in a sudden burst of energy. I bolt upright, covering my heart with my hand, and attempt to take in a deep breath, but my throat seems to collapse inward.

Hypnos turns, attentively watching me.

"What is wrong with you?"

"This... this isn't me." I gasp out.

His white eyes brighten as he peers at me with his power. Sweat pours down my face and back as my hands shake and my vision begins to spot.

"It is the goddess, your mate." He says to me calmly. "She is in distress."

Trying to get my feet under me, I lose my balance and fall back on my haunches. I need to get to her. I need to teleport to her.

"She... having a... panic... attack." The words trickle out of my mouth as my throat continues to close, preventing my lungs from taking the air I need. I've seen her in the throes of her panic, and so has Callie, and it overwhelms all of her as her fear chokes her.

Hypnos places his hand on my chest, and the gentle pulses of his power flow into me.

"You are in luck." He smiles. "She is sleeping." He stands and pulls me up with him, wrapping one of my arms around his neck.

"Dreams are nothing more than our emotions, playing out in our minds as we sleep. I am the god of dreams on Avalon. I can send you into her dream."

The vibrations of his power increase and the sensations of Rhea's panic leave me. My blurred vision clears, and I cough out a lung full of stifled air that was blocked in my chest.

"Is she better now?" I stand fully on my own and clutch my chest as my heart returns to its normal pace.

"No, I simply blocked you from feeling it. Teleport us to your room; you need to lie down for this next part."

Laying on my bed, Hypnos releases the leather tie of a dark brown sack fixed to his belt. Opening the small parcel, it's filled with black and emerald sands from Avalon. He pours a small amount into the palm of his hand.

"You taught me this trick, young Herald, when you celebrated your eleventh Great Year." He pours the sand from one hand to the next, and I'm transfixed by the glimmer of the emeralds within the fine grains of dark sand. "Mirages and Empathic Echoes greatly mimic the dreams or nightmares of our minds. "

"You can see Empathic Echoes?" I ask him, sitting up on my elbows only to be pushed down again with Hypnos' hand on my forehead.

Empathic Echoes are the residue of emotions left behind at a location by living beings. They dissolve quickly and are difficult to detect, nearly impossible to interpret.

"You frequently would help cure your sister of her nightmares when you were younger and moved on to more *formidable* minds as you crafted dreams for those who slept around you." Hypnos runs the obsidian sand into his palm once more before taking a pinch and holding it above my face. "The properties in the sand combine with my power and help me do the same."

Sprinkling the sand slowly over my closed eyes, my room melts away, and a new room takes shape. My body is replaced with an astral projection, matching the cobalt blue color of my aura.

"I will remain near to monitor you but will respect your privacy with your partner." Hypnos' voice becomes an echo in my mind as I drift into an induced state of sleep, and I melt into the dream of my mate.

These Thaumium cuffs are stifling inside this prison cell. *The sound of a crowd outside makes my heart thump in my chest. Why are humans so eager for an execution? They are always so hungry to watch the life of another fade away.*

It's a disease, and they love spreading it to each other.

"Let's go, Joan." My guard opens the cell door, and a nauseating wave of his body odor washes over me. "Unless you want to pledge loyalty to him?"

"I would rather die than do something which I know to be wrong or to be against the will of the Fates."

The walk to the pyre seems to last too long, and thoughts crowd my awareness. Breaking free of the darkness from the stone dungeon, the bright sunlight burns my eyes, and the man with blue eyes that fills my dreams floats across my mind.

I wish he were more than just a dream so I could finally put a person to the man who has filled my imagination these years. Something in his eyes has held me through each of these terrible days, and I'll fill my consciousness with him as I burn, even if we never had the chance to meet.

Scanning the crowd, I look for my friend with long raven hair. Hecate has been so nice to visit me each week and bring me extra comfort from outside the prison. Sneaking food and clothes and offering her companionship has been a welcome intrusion to prison life. She has told me this is not the end of my life but the start of a new one. She shared visions with me, memories of lifetimes we have lived before this one. She taught me about the voices I hear and others with powers like me.

The flapping wings and echoing caw of a crow guide my eyes to her, and she nods her cloaked head at me in solidarity.

"Go boldly." She told me last night. Her last visit before my death today. "Go boldly into your new life. I'll find you again."

My body is heating up, even before they ignite the flames that will chew through me. Climbing the steps of the wooden platform that will serve as my stage and my kindling, I keep my chin high as I turn and face the crowd. A few of my former soldiers are here with solemn faces, hiding under hoods, and I don't want to show them my fear.

It was never easy for them to agree to be led by a child of fourteen, much less a girl. Until they saw my powers, then they followed me with every ounce of loyalty into war. But when we were seized by others with powers like mine, my mortal soldiers didn't stand a chance.

Most of my troops were killed on the spot, and others were taken to prison. They have likely already met their executioners. The few that had a chance to escape will do well to remain in hiding. The lies these heretics spread about me are vile. To think I would ever sit by as a talisman while my men go off and die is offensive.

The pyre is lit behind me, and the white smoke wafts before me, blown by the wind.

"Go boldly," I repeat the phrase for courage as the heat and flames grow around me. As the fire begins to lick my fingers, I find her once more. A tear rolls down her cheek, and sorrow fills her eyes.

"Go boldly," I say aloud this time, and Hecate moves to the front of the cheering crowd directly before me. With a sweep of her cloak, she drops to one knee, and with closed eyes, she bows her head. My brave soldiers join her. Dropping their cloaks, they fall to their knees and bow their heads. These five people before me are the only ones who will likely remember my life.

I can't look at them as I die. I lift my eyes to the skies, but a glimmer on the second-story tavern beacons at me. Someone is flashing a piece of metal at me. As the shine burns my vision, a face, blurry at first, comes into view.

When I see him, the flames erupt around me like a fireball, and my scream rips from my throat. The agony is beyond description as my entire body is consumed by fire. My lungs stop working because of the searing pain and clouds of smoke that work to choke me from within as the blaze around me eats me from the outside.

⊱ ⊰

"Wake up." Someone is shaking me, but my body feels like I'm a million miles away.

Pressure on my shoulders weighs down on me, and a warm blue light surrounds me. It covers me like a heavy blanket and relaxes my tense muscles.

The heat of another person lays envelops me. A pair of arms corded in muscle wrap me in their safety. My hair is stuck to the sides of my face, and my breaths come in rapid, short bursts, but I don't care as sobs wrack my body. I lean into the comfort of this embrace, and the dream melts away from me. Clutching the shirt of my rescuer, I pull my face into them and cry.

Ares burned me.

It seemed so real, like a memory. I could have pulled the burning of the flames and the smells of the old French town right out of my mind with how vivid it was. My flesh still feels like it's tingling from the heat of the flames.

My heart hammers against the chest of my savior and their arms pull me tighter into them.

"It's okay. Rhea, I'm here." The deep voice is low and breathy like its owner sprinted to get here.

"My name is not Rhea." My hoarse voice croaks out, bouncing around the room in an echo. My liberator only exhales loudly in response. It feels like I'm still dreaming, having awoken from one delusion and fallen directly into another.

This is not Flint.

I should be alarmed, but it feels so good, so familiar. My mind is still scattered from the trauma of the dream and the panic that washed over me as I couldn't wake up from the fire. However, my soul is telling me to stay here and rest in this embrace because I'm safe. Somehow, I know it's the truth.

The body of this man is much larger and stronger than Flint's. Where Flint is lean and slender like a runner, the hulking frame around me is all strength and muscle. This man's body closes over me, allowing me to hide within him. And I do. I could stay here as long as I wish and let the world drift away from me.

Inside this embrace, there are no thoughts of Shifters that are waiting for me to produce some miracle that will change their lives or the thoughts of revenge that circle my mind like buzzards over a kill.

The smell of this man intoxicates me, unlike the smell of embers and werewolf that surrounds Flint. I push my nose into the crevasse of his neck and pull his aroma into my mind to keep it with me forever. His deep voice resonates within the depths of my body as he grumbles at my action. I shift closer to him to feel more of him against me.

He feels perfect.

Like his body was made to wrap around mine, his arms snake around me, and he kisses my head and inhales me as deeply as I do him. With my body and mind calming down, I lean back and open my eyes to see my savior.

Hermes, the very man I aim to kill.

I should recoil away from him as my mind flashes an image of a dirt cell and a cave, but my body refuses to move. The thoughts of my bath and the books keep me here. The sense of calm and protective peace lock me in place.

"Are you really here?" My voice bounces around the room, and I know this is not real. There is a translucence to his form that glows with an unnatural sheen.

"No." He looks my face over like he needs to memorize it before I drift away.

"I'm still dreaming?"

"Mhm." He pulls me back in, and I sigh into him, melting into the warmth of his body. His large frame holds me in a perfect vice to calm the anxiety that was threatening to cascade over me only moments ago. "You were having a bad dream."

"Yeah."

We lay here together as he strokes my hair and lets me calm down. It's the exact comfort I wanted last night when I woke from the nightmare of the old woman. The dream that led me to the halls where I found the haunting Dark Shield and then was tortured for my earlier disobedience.

And Flint has never once sought me out today to ask where I've been or see how I'm doing. He's been fine to forget about me all day, as the sleepless night leads me down a day of decimation that I suffer alone.

How easily he forgets about me. Or perhaps he never even thinks of me.

But I'm accustomed to this. What other treatment can a half-Fae hybrid expect?

It doesn't stop me from longing, though. Too often, I'm the person that others easily forget. When people have no further need of me, the memory of my existence seeps out of their mind like I was never there.

Just once, I want to know what it feels like to be the one person that runs on a constant tether within someone's mind. I wish I knew what it was to be the person they look for in a crowded room, and when they don't find me, they are sad for it. Their shoulders slump, and they long for my presence.

This embrace makes me believe I could have it. Hermes' arms, even if they aren't real, are solid enough to let me pretend I'm important to someone else. That I'm desired for something more than a service I can offer.

"So, I don't have to worry about killing you at the moment?"

He chuckles, and the sound of it makes me smile.

"Not tonight." He whispers as he kisses the top of my neck, just below my ear. Chills surge from the point where his lips touch my skin, and heat drives into my core—the earlier frustration from my interrupted bath flares with renewed vigor.

"Do I have to worry about you killing me?" I ask as the darkness in my room deepens as if the moon were covered by clouds drifting across the sky. Many miles above me, I sense the Wind carrying the clouds across the sky and wish I could feel a fresh breeze on my hand.

"I would never hurt you, Rhea." He rubs his lips across my eyebrow before placing a tender kiss there and moving to my cheekbone.

Each touch heats my body, relaxing me from the nightmare and pulling me into the fantasy of Hermes embrace.

I work my top leg out from the weight of his body and throw it over his hip. Pulling him into me, he happily invades the empty space. I feel him smile against my skin before he places another kiss lower on my neck.

His hand travels down my back, over my bottom, and across my thigh. With his touch, I forget my next argument was going to be and I drift into the sensation of him.

Squeezing me, he pulls me into him more as if there is still too much space between us, even with our bodies flush against each other.

His soft lips kiss and nip at my neck until he reaches my collarbone. Hovering just above my skin, the promise of his caress brushes against my flesh, and goosebumps break out over my neck and arms. Continuing his tease, his lips barely touch me as he works his way up my neck, over my chin, until he pauses at my mouth.

With parted lips and heavy breaths, his touch has lit me on fire. These are not the flames that scared me in my dream of Ares or the heat I wish I would feel with Flint. This blaze ignites my passions, and his touch transforms my body into a vivid canvas painted with the hues of my emotions.

But he doesn't kiss me.

He withholds the caress of his mouth on mine, inflaming my desire by starving me of what I want.

The depth of his blue eyes are so deep in the dark of night as he consumes the sight of me. Anticipation tingles over my body, wanting him that my hips buck and my back arches, begging him to descend upon me.

"I don't know if I should kiss someone who is plotting my death."

Fisting his shirt with both hands, I pull him to me. "If you don't kiss me, I will plot your death." Pulling his shirt over his head, I throw it to the ground and hook my arms under his, scratching gently down his back as I pull him into me. Rippled with flexed muscles, he doesn't waste a second before his lips are on mine, parting my mouth with his eager tongue.

Shifting his weight fully, he covers me with his sculpted form, and I wrap my legs around his waist. Holding himself up on his forearm, his other hand runs down the length of my body, squeezing my ass into him as his hips pulse into me. I throw my head back, releasing a sign of satisfaction as the long length of his erection rubs against my sensitive clit.

I could come from this alone, and he's not even trying.

Breaking the assault his lips are waging on my neck, he frees my ass from his grip, takes the end of my shirt, and pulls it up slightly as he looks into my eyes.

"You know I'm a Light Bearer, correct?"

"I'm aware." I drive my hips into him again, and he groans with my movements. When he closes his eyes and pushes into me, allowing me to grind against him, it fuels my craving for more of him; my mouth waters with the need to taste him.

He takes his large hand and grabs my hip, holding me still as he releases a shuttered breath.

"I'm going to need you to focus here."

"Oh, I'm focused," I answer. My hands rub down his defined chest. I continue my trail downward, but he takes my left wrist, so small in his grasp, and stops me.

Bringing it up to his mouth, he kisses the inside of my wrist tenderly before pinning it over my head. Looking at me expectantly, he raises his eyebrows. "The other one, please."

With a huff and a roll of my eyes, I comply, secretly happy to give myself over to his mercy. "Only because you said 'please'." My snarky comment is rewarded with a mischievous smile, and I get the sense Hermes is letting me act like a brat because he likes being challenged.

Holding my wrists over my head, he pins me to the bed. Lifting the edge of my shirt more, he pushes the thin material but stops before exposing my breasts. Arching my back, I hope he relieves me of the article of clothing, but he doesn't. He's moving torturously slow as he draws circles gently on my stomach. Looking up at me through his lashes, the gleam of mischief burns in his expression.

"You're aware I can move at the speed of Light, then?" With his words, the tip of his finger begins to vibrate gently against me. My stomach drops at the sensation, and every nerve receptor in my body sings to feel him.

"Oh," Is all I can say.

Gods be dammed, he's a living vibrator.

"Would you like me to show you?" He leans down to me and asks in my ear.

Another wave of chills pebble my body with the promise of the pleasure he is offering me.

"Yes, but I'm on my period," My answer is full of breath and desire. Relaxing into the bed, my back arcs, and I squeeze him with my wrapped legs.

"Mmmm, I have made rivers swell with the blood of your enemies and used their bodies as a bridge to get to you. I'm not afraid of a little blood, goddess." His husky voice is heavy with need as he teases me with his lips again, then kisses me gently.

The word *goddess* out of his mouth fills me with satisfaction and my body warms with the feeling of my powers.

"You don't have to be embarrassed with me–ever." He cups the side of my face, and the look in his eyes flood me with sincerity, and if he were real, I would believe him. "Tell me what you want, and

I'll worship you with every breath." His breath against my lips, as he whispers, sends a roll of heat down my body.

"Make me feel alive."

Hermes frees my wrists and pushes himself up. A beam of light slices my top in two, and the thin fabric exposes my sternum; my breasts remain covered… for now. My mouth gapes open in shock, and Hermes laughs.

"Relax, beautiful. It's just a dream. No shirts will be harmed in the making of this orgasm." With a wink, his vibrating finger traces a line down my neck and the center of my chest. The sensation feels so amazing; it relaxes me and fills me with anticipation all at once.

"May I?" He asks, pausing at the center of my chest.

"Hermes, please." I'm nearly begging the man I plan to kill as this vision of him teases me in my dream. I must surely be in a state of trauma because I would do anything to remain right here, in this dream with the person I know I should stay away from.

The vibrations from his fingers pulsate rapidly as he makes a track to my left breast. The split shirt falling away exposes my pert nipple, standing fully and begging to be taken into his mouth.

"By the twelve realms, you are perfect."

Flicking his eyes to my face, he circles my nipple with his pulsating finger, and it works magic on me. Electricity jolts through my insides, straight to my throbbing pussy. I pull his hips into me with my legs and work my center on his hardness. He meets my thrusts, grinding against me with his cock, and warmth spreads from my core as my arousal builds. Not letting my other breast become envious, he takes my right breast with his mouth and lavishes my nipple with his skilled tongue.

Abandoning my breasts, he works his way down, kissing and licking every inch of my chest and stomach. Running my fingers through the soft tendrils of his dark hair, it's just as soft as I imagined earlier in the tub. As I give his hair a gentle tug as he ravishes my breasts, I'm rewarded by a throaty moan from Hermes. Splaying both of hands wide across my sides and stomach, all ten of his fingers come alive with vibrations.

The groan of satisfaction that escapes my mouth spurs him on, and Hermes moves lower on my body. Still ignoring my starving pussy that is begging for his attention, his mouth dives down and nibbles his way along the valley between my hip and leg. So close to the spot, I'm desperate to feel him but simultaneously miles away.

Every breath and touch he gives me ignites a new fire that burns my very soul. My body becomes a blazing furnace of passion, ignited in every corner by Hermes' touch. I barely register the creaking sound of a door opening as I writhe under Hermes until he freezes.

My body has never felt so alive with the rushing tingles that flow everywhere he has consumed me, but it all turns cold when I see his hard expression, looking off into the empty bedroom.

"Hypnos." He calls out to no one. "Is someone in the room with her?"

"Who are you talking to?"

His breathing is heavy through his nose, and his brow is stern. My pulse thunders as alarms spike around me in a warning."Som eone is in here with you." He stands, leaving me barren on the bed. "Wake up!"

Jolting awake, I sit up, my breathing ragged. The feeling of waking up from a dream and then waking up again makes my head throb. My eyes blink against the dark room as I orient myself. How do I tell if I'm *actually* awake now?

"Don't stop on my account, princess." Flint saunters into the room. The smell of sulfur and wolf washes away the memory of Hermes' scent, which irritates me. "That sounded like a delicious dream."

"Don't call me princess." Heat blazes my cheeks as I pull the covers around me. Shame has me checking that my sleeping shirt is still intact, and relief floods me when I find it whole and still on my body. "And I wasn't dreaming."

I turn on my side and pull the covers up to my chin.

"Where have you been all day, anyway?" I am still angry at his dismissal of my feelings about Lexi, but where has he been the past few days? Aside from sleeping here, he is rarely around and always returning reeking of Shifters.

I've practically been recovering and losing my mind all alone; I may as well be alone since I feel nothing when Flint is here. Certainly not the unbridled inferno I felt with just a dream of Hermes.

Gods, what would it be like if he were truly here to touch me?

My racing pulse beats against the chill that nears me as Flint approaches the bed. Crawling toward me, I squint my eyes shut, hoping he'll leave me for a shower, but he settles in behind me with one hand on my hip.

His semi-erect penis invades my back as he places a kiss on my shoulder.

"Flint, I'm on my period."

"Seriously?" He sighs with irritation as he attempts to move his kiss to my neck, and his hand migrates down my hip, heading between my legs; despite the tampon, my panties are soaked from the dream of Hermes and his delicious torment of my body. "I'd rather occupy that sweet mouth of yours anyhow. Daddy's had a long day at work."

I have to physically restrain myself from the baffling expression and acknowledgment that he just referred to himself as *'daddy'*.

And that figures. I'm the one that nearly died and feels like shit after *his* father tormented my body for punishment, and Flint wants me to end my day by sucking *him* off. *Asshole.*

Pulling his hand away, I turn my torso toward him. "Knock it off." Offense and finality ring in my tone. "You honestly think I want to even talk to you right now, much less touch you?"

Flint moves quickly, pushing my legs apart with this knee, and perches himself on top of me while he pins my arms over my head. The contrast between this and the dream of Hermes pulls a sense of dread and anger within me.

"Mmm...I love a little fight." He smirks with a dark gleam in his eyes as he dips down to my neck.

Rage and heat boil within me at his lack of consideration for my consent. *How fucking dare he?* Centering my power in my chest, I burst a gust of wind at him. Too angry for my own good, a flash of silver light also escapes from within me.

Well, that's new.

The gust of Wind and Light work together to send Flint soaring through the air and crashing through the door. With a reflex like lightning, Kai is there, saving Flint from flying over the railing as she holds him by his neck. His body dangles over the ledge of the three-story drop as he clutches her wrists with both hands, hanging on frantically.

In all fairness, the fall wouldn't kill him.

"Pull me up, you crazy-ass bitch!"

Flint looks ridiculous with his long legs flailing about and if I weren't fuming with anger, I would find this comical. His freckled skin turns as red as a tomato as Kai keeps her grip on him. Ignoring him as she holds him hostage over the side of the railing. Kai looks back at me with raised eyebrows.

"Everything okay in there?" She calls from the hallway with her hand around Flint's collar and throat.

My chest is thrumming, and I rip the cover off my body, standing to snatch the robe off the back of a chair next to my bed. If I answer *no* I wonder if she would drop him.

"It's fine. Just a little boy whose *daddy* did a shit job of telling him 'no' when he was little." Covering myself with the robe and pulling the belt too tight in my frustration, I slip on some sandals and storm out of the room.

"Let's go, Kai." I don't wait for her to join me, knowing she will.

17 *Hermes*

I could dunk myself in the Arctic Ocean, and it still wouldn't be cold enough to get rid of this erection. Twenty minutes in this cold shower, I'm still hard as a rock. My dick pulses, wanting a release as the thoughts of Rhea absorb every ounce of my attention.

The mounds of her soft breasts and the small noises of pleasure she was making nearly made me come in my pants. Gods, it would take me ages to recover from that embarrassment.

When she realized I was lying with her, I was prepared for her to attack me, but by the goddess, I love how easily her body knew me.

Leaving her in such a state of dissatisfaction was not my initial plan, but it may work to my advantage if she really plans on trying to kill me. When she woke up so unexpectedly, I was thrown out of the dream so fiercely that I flew across the room and slammed into the wall.

Whatever happened in those few moments after I left, she was pissed. I could feel her power surge and the anger she blasted out. I pray to the Fates she pummeled Flint and make a note to myself to practice moving into dreams.

Projecting a Mirage while someone sleeps is no great skill, but walking in the dream with them is more challenging than I would have thought.

During the shared dream, it is clear from her confusion around her name that something has been done to her mind. A poison, perhaps, or a Mind Mage could fabricate a new reality for her.

Now I have to make it through the rest of today until the Autumn Equinox ceremony, and we can rescue her.

Fuck me, this is going to be a long day.

Rhea

I've never been so angry that my powers rolled off of me, but when I left Flint, a cool black mist billowed in my wake as I stomped through the hallowed halls of the Underworld.

It's the morning of Mabon, and the Underworld is bursting with the beating hearts of Ares's army. The God of War has called an assembly in preparation, and every nerve in my body is on fire as the emotions filling the indoor amphitheater nearly suffocate me.

The half-circle stage set deep into the bedrock of the Underworld is lit with bright lights that burn overhead. I squint my eyes against their intensity as I take a moment to steady my breath.

Shifters and Elementals walk down wide, shallow steps to rows of stone benches, filing in with little space between each other.

Spectators would normally gather to watch plays or listen to the Sonus Elementals and Wind Sirens weave their spells into the air with their voices. But tonight, they listen to Ares as Demeter, and I stand to the side.

Thousands of Elemental men and women sit in rows and stand along the walls. With arms folded or shoved into pockets, they hang on his words. Behind him is a large screen playing clips from mortal news outlets of the aftermath of our mass assassination. Tonight will mark the second phase in Ares's plan.

"Three days ago, we started a campaign of truth. A campaign to shed light on the deception the Council has woven into the threads of the mortal hubris. Tonight, we will act again." Ares turns and indicates toward Demeter and me. The false smile plastered on his face is for appearance and doesn't reach his eyes.

Darkness resides there with a promise of punishment should tonight fail.

As he speaks, I find Lucas in the crowd, and my stomach clenches into a knot. He turns his head to the left, nodding toward Naomi and her sons. Teddy is looking at me and gives me a tiny wave, keeping his hand close to his side and trying to remain still.

I return the gesture with a small smile and raise my eyebrows once, making him shuffle back and forth on his feet.

Looking around the rows of Immortals and those crammed along the walls, I think about tonight's ritual and just how many are putting their hopes on Demeter and me to bring out their wolves and end their blight as Lycans. Shifters cluster together in packs or alone; some are with their partners, and, aside from Naomi's children, barely any are present at Ares' speech.

My armpits are sweating, and my hair is sticking to my neck with the heat of these lights. I swirl the cooling currents of my power around me and work to calm my nerves.

The faint glow of Immortal power hovers above the skin of the sea of bodies, and I study them. Somehow, within the swirl of magic, the essence of their power speaks to me, and I can tell what their element is just by looking at them. As a youngling in the Underworld, I often kept myself distracted with a little game of counting people, and I fall into that familiar activity now.

I spot several Sonus Elementals with their power over sound and look through the crowd, counting forty-seven of them. Then I see a cluster of Sensors and find sixty-three more as Ares drones on about duty and guidance for the mortals in the coming days.

Continuing to find a new element and counting the others, I recall what Lucas said in the cafeteria earlier. I need to pay attention to what I *don't* see.

"The mortals will yearn for guidance, for strength, and we will be the answer they seek. Our rule will be the balm to their disarray as we impose a new order upon their fractured minds." Ares emphasizes certain words and pauses on others for dramatic effect, but it rambles together in my ears as I'm not listening.

I run my gaze over the top of the crowd, running through the Elemental powers present, and one obvious group stands out, largely absent from the throngs. The manilla folder Lucas handed me suddenly flares into my awareness. I should have looked at the papers closer instead of getting distracted by Hermes.

"There are no Light Elementals in the Underworld." I am careful to speak only to Lucas through telepathy.

Breaking his stare on Ares, Lucas cuts his eyes to me, and a faint trace of a smile is briefly seen on his face before he looks back to the stage as Ares concludes his speech.

"To arms, my brethren! Let us harness the winds of change and ride them to ultimate victory. The realm of mortals awaits our rule, and their fate is ours to decree."

As the crowd cheers at the conclusion of Ares's speech, I mindless clap my hands along with them. My mind racing with the thoughts of Ares' collection of Elementals and those he leaves out of his army. There are no Light Mages because they could be a threat to what Ares is keeping hidden in the darkness.

I need to get back to that Dark Shield.

"Hermes, I love you, but if you don't find something to do, I'm going to petrify you."** Medusa rests her elbows on the counter of Lucas's packhouse in Mexico, pinching the bridge of her nose.

The packhouse would normally be teaming with wolves, but everyone has been called to the Underworld. Ares is taking no chances with missing his opportunity to use Rhea's power tonight.

The colorful tiles that line the counter and kitchen contrast the white walls of the hacienda, and I've been staring at the pattern as I spin Rhea's daggers for the past few minutes, mindlessly lost in thought. The square building has an open courtyard in the center, and bedrooms line the two upper levels. This main floor has most of the shared communal areas and four large bedrooms.

I stop spinning Rhea's daggers and return them to their new scabbards strapped to my thighs.

"Fine. I'm going to snoop around in Lucas's things."

"The food in this realm is delicious," Mor says to no one as she eats her fourth plate of enchiladas. I have no idea where she puts all this food. She eats enough for three people. Medusa chuckles as she shakes her head in disbelief. Callie and Achilles are relaxing in the courtyard and enjoying the sunshine. Hypnos remains close to his friend, standing in the kitchen with his arms crossed over his chest.

"Wonderful." Medusa answers. "I'm going to check in with Atlas and see what luck he is having with Eris."

I roll my eyes at the mention of the former Headmistress as I leave and make my way around the square home.

Checking out the rooms on the lower floor, I find the one that belongs to Lucas. He has a four-poster bed that is obnoxiously large and made of a rich wood that matches the reddish-brown fur of his wolf. Animals of all kinds are carved into the posts and headboard. Sea animals are etched and polished into the bottoms of the posts, while birds are carved at the top. All manner of land animals are sprawled in between. The detail and craftsmanship are amazing.

A table sitting in front of a window holds dozens of picture frames. Looking at the images, they are pictures through time of Lucas and his pack. I recognize Kai in many of them; his Beta declared early after his own transformation, as she seems to be with him in all of these. Some of the pictures are yellowing with age, and others appear to be taken on pieces of tin.

Lucas must have images taken on every type of camera that has been invented from the looks of it. Picking up several of the pictures and inspecting them, something in the background begins to stand out.

One of the images shows Lucas and several other people, likely Shifters, standing in a line with their arms around each other. Behind them, small round windows in a straight line show a deep blue color through their glass.

Rushing out of his room with the picture in hand, Medusa slams her hand down on the counter.

"By the goddess, Hermes. Can you give us more than ten minutes of peace?"

"The fucking Underworld is underwater."

<hr>

I'm livid. Outraged doesn't even begin to explain how I'm feeling right now. I have searched and scoured this realm for the Underworld inside the bowels of mountains and cave systems, and it has been sitting at the bottom of the gods' damned ocean the entire time.

It's the simplest thing I have ever encountered. A world, under the world. It's so elementary. It worked for ages to hide Ares' secret realm within Gaea. Callie burst into a fit of laughter when she saw my flustered expression.

Sitting in the sky, high above the step pyramid, we wait for the ceremony as I shake my head for the millionth time since figuring it out. Callie has collected a cluster of clouds for us to sit on, and we're waiting for the sun to set. My Mirage keeps us hidden from view, and Mor will take over when it is dark out and shield us with her shadows.

"I bet you Triton built it." Medusa tosses an empty sunflower seed shell into the air as she and Mor snack on them. Mor spews shells from her mouth with a slobbery ejection to the applause of Achilles, who is teaching her to spit. "He has Aquatic Adaptation, you know."

"Probably." I flick a beam of Light with my finger it bounces across the blue sky like a skipping stone on a lake. I watch until it disappears across the horizon. "What did Atlas have to say?" Excited and defeated about figuring out where the Underworld has been hiding, I forgot to ask earlier.

"The Mortal Council called an emergency meeting with the heads of the Communes." Medusa declined to join because her Commune needed her to recover from Ares' attack. "The Commune heads are being assigned to the countries that are turning over new leaders due to the mass assassination. Odysseus and Penelope split up to help with more coverage. Atlas was heading to South America while Eris was assigned to North America."

My attention trails off as I keep thinking of Rhea, hoping she is okay, and that Flint has not touched her. My jaw tightens as I think about his clammy hands on her soft skin. My Immortal Ichor begins to boil when I can't get the image out of my mind of him between her legs with her head thrown back in ecstasy.

"Why don't you go walk around the vendors and buy a fake obsidian blade or a Mayan Calendar? Otherwise, I may push you off this cloud." Callie teases me as she bumps me with her shoulder.

With a heavy sign, I work to release the strain of my jealousy. I wrap my arm around my sister, and she leans against my chest.

"We'll have her back in no time." She reassures me.

"And why don't you," Achilles stands, holding his hand out to Callie to help her up, "join me for a dance. It's too beautiful a day to waste, don't you think?"

Callie smiles at him as if he put the clouds in the sky just for her.

I expand my Light Shield beyond this perch in the clouds and raise it upward to keep them concealed. Callie creates a thin sheet of Wind that serves as their dancefloor, and Achilles twirls her around the clouds. I can see the beam of her smile from here as her hair fans with the movements of the dance. Achilles looks down at her like he's thanking her for providing the very air that he breaths.

She brings the clouds with them. Her Winds bend and shape them, creating thin sheets that act like glass and reflect a dozen prisms as they dance within the rainbows. The mortals below can't see the two Elementals enjoying themselves in the clouds because of our shields, but they notice the striking display of colors and stare at the sky in awe.

My mind carries me back to the age when my sister met her mates, and the day Patroclus took her dancing in the clouds. The small moments Calypso and Achilles take to remain close to the memory of their slain mate always tighten the tendons around my heart with fond sadness.

The thoughts of Rhea that race through my mind aren't helping anything. I know I'm being pathetic. But the uneasy feeling of my mate being in the lair of my enemy is eating me alive from the inside with each passing moment.

I recall lifetimes where I searched for the essence of a soul that called out to me, never finding her. My Lights would stretch across the sky every day until one day, I stopped sensing the pull. Eventually, I came to realize she was gone, and I mourned the loss of her each time.

With every death, Nyx's spell would reset the realm and hide our memories until her next life, when they would begin to unravel again.

As I replay our rescue plan in my mind, I keep my resolve firm that this life is going to be the one that changes everything. It's in this life that we will break this curse. And if we don't, it will be my soul ushered into the Void, instead of hers.

We knew the tunnels under the pyramid would be too heavily fortified to attempt a rescue before the ceremony. And Lucas is anxious to help free the Lycans of the curse that afflicts them. He's certain the call of the Titan will convert their loyalty and begged us to wait to pull Rhea out until just after she releases those that can be helped.

I'll wait as long as I can, but I didn't make him any promises. If things turn bad, our best bet is for Mor to cause a diversion with her shadow beings so I can teleport to Rhea and get her out of here.

The shadow creatures of Gaea are isolated to the Labyrinth, except for the Lurker Mor took care of. I would be surprised if any of these Shifters have ever seen the creatures of darkness, so the initial shock will give me all the time I need.

With a flash of my light power, I emerge on the ground below and walk among the hundreds of locals and tourists converging to watch the sunset at the great pyramid of Kukulcan. As the sun sets, the shadows will appear to move down the steps, giving the appearance of the great serpent descending the temple.

The mortals don't remember that this temple was built for the goddess. One of the fractured memories returned to me with the release from Rhea's power and the puzzle pieces begin to fit together as I walk the site.

She is rebirth and renewal, the great serpent representing the cycle of life and death.

Born into Mayan royalty on the Spring Equinox in one of her lives, her people saw a time of peace and prosperity when she was their queen. But Ares came for her, and the mortal Mayan were no match for the forces of his armies. We gave her people time to flee as we held Ares back, but she died on this land on the Autumn Equinox.

The surviving Mayan built the pyramid to honor their fallen queen, and El Castillo stands tall, waiting for the day twice a year when she descends the stairs of the monument to be worshiped by her people on the days of her birth and death.

Walking through the ancient buildings and the restoration of the mortals, some of the ancient carvings have been replaced. The revered queen of the Mayans has been replaced with kings and warriors of men. Time has forgotten the sacrifice of the goddess and the generations of Mayans that lived on after her death.

Wandering the paths and following the flow of the mortals with my Mirage making me invisible, I find myself among the hundreds of columns erected to honor the fallen warriors of the great battle of Ares. Walking down the rows, a prickle in the back of my neck gets my attention, and I know she is near.

Turning, I see her.

Fifteen columns away from me, the setting sun shines in her honey hair, and she glows like the dawn. My heart bursts in my chest as if it's been silently waiting for the moment of being near her to pump blood through my veins. Her sweet berry scent invades my every sense and lights all my nerve endings on fire.

Everything in me begs to go to her, but she is surrounded by a flock of guards.

Running her hand up one of the columns, she looks at it with wonder and amazement. I'm curious if she has any memories of this place, if being here sparks anything, or if Demeter's poison effectively blocks everything out.

Folding my arms over my chest, I lean a shoulder against the column to my side. I take in every particle of light that shimmers in her aura and obsess over each strand of golden hair that dances in the breeze of the oncoming evening.

A small smile remains on my face at the sight of her and the memories of sharing her dream last night.

Gods, she was beautiful.

The feel of her body, perfectly molded to mine, and grinding against me to demand her pleasure. And goddess save me, those moans escaping her gorgeous mouth. I wanted nothing more than to watch her let go and taste her as she came undone around my tongue. To have her squeeze her thighs around me while I worked her sopping pussy with my fingers would have only been made better if it was real and not within a dream.

My eyes consume the sight of her as she wanders the columns, unaware that I'm watching her. Using my Mirage, I project an image into her mind and her hand pauses its track up the carved pillar.

In the vision, I pull back on her honey hair, and drive into her from behind as she uses the pillar to brace herself. With my finger circling her clit, I stop the fantasy just before she comes. Released from my power, a red hue fills her cheeks. She bites her lip, looking around as if checking to make sure no one else could see what flashed in her mind.

I push off the column and take a step toward her.

"Hermes," Medusa chuckles into my mind. *"Mor says stop fucking around and get back here, or 'they're' coming down to get you."* I can tell she would prefer to see the latter. *"There are a dozen Shifters watching her right now, and we can't move with all these mortals in the way so, don't be stupid and get up here."*

I cock a sly smile and take another step toward my mate regardless, but Medusa locks me with her power. The rigid petrification of my joints freezes me, and I shoot her a frustrated glare. She elbows Mor and nods in my direction, making Mor chuckle at my expense.

With a sigh of restlessness and a roll of my eyes, I teleport myself back to the cloud and cast them both a displeased glare that has zero effect on them.

Sitting to attention, with one leg folded under, Mor rests both hands on the edge of the cloud. Her eyes quickly dart between the crowds of spectators, and her shadows chaotically thrash around her.

"I sense something," Mor warns. Her eyes have shifted from red to grey with a silver sheen like granite. Medusa watches her, amazed by the transformation once I explained the three souls residing within Mor.

"What do you feel?" I ask her, looking attentively at the field below.

"I'm not sure yet."

Lucas and his pack emerge from the top of the pyramid first. Lucas is in human form, wearing a pair of ivory linen pants, as are the rest of the Lycan men waiting on the field below the pyramid. Kai wears a long ivory linen dress like the Lycan women. The clothes are specifically chosen to allow for an easy shift for those who will have their animal pulled from them tonight.

I appreciate the solidarity Lucas and Kai show to the Shifters who cannot call their wolves. The King and his Beta could have joined the ceremony in wolf form, as the new Alpha and his pack have.

But remaining human and donning the clothing of the ceremony, shows sympathy and support of the Lycans.

The rest of Lucas' pack are shifted into the forms of their wolves. Giant canines with red, brown, and cream color fur march down the large steps of the pyramid with a pack of wolves with obsidian pelts.

This would be the pack that used to belong to Lupo, until he lost his head on the sharp edge of my sword.

The deceased Onyx Alpha, with all black fur, was menacing and imposing in size over his pack. But Lucas's pack has the clear size advantage over the other wolves. Even his Cappa and Delta wolves are larger than the new Alpha.

Demeter and Flint arrive next, and finally, Ares.

With a growl escaping my chest, the crowd below us cheers as he raises his hands, waving at the sea of Lycan below. It's an even mixture of men and women, with only a handful of children mingled among them. A Lycan mother holds her daughter on her hip, swaying back and forth as she kisses the girl's head tenderly.

"My faithful family." Ares begins. "Twenty-four years ago, I promised you a cure. The return of the goddess was written in the stars, and we searched the realm until we found her." He pauses for a cheer from the gathering, but as Lucas remains still and somber, so does the crowd.

My blood begins to boil, referring to my mate as a *cure*.

"With the return of the Maiden tonight, many of you will have your retribution. Those worthy will be made whole under this Equinox night."

The crowd parts, and the bright moon casts a glow on Rhea at the far end of the courtyard below the great pyramid. Clasping her hands in front of her, she slowly walks toward the monument. As she passes, the Shifters populating the grassy field resting in El Castille's shadow bow their heads.

Mor stands to attention on our cloud, still concealed with my Mirage. Her tight shoulders are pulled back, and there is a sharpness in her tense brow. I follow the path of her eyes but see only a deep well of shadows beneath a patch of trees below us.

"The Titan of the Shadow Realm is here."

19

I feel like I'm going to vomit. It is incredibly hot, and thousands of people are here tonight. Families and Lone Wolves from around the globe have arrived. Dozens of pairs of eyes close as the owners bow their heads at me while I pass down the aisle they have created.

My white stola is at least light and airy as the draped dress blows in the gentle breeze circulating the air. A silver crescent moon pin sits on my shoulder, fastening the two pieces of the garment, and the silver links of my belt clink gently as I walk.

I look at the moon high in the sky, and it hangs above me like an ominous weight that is about to drop on me. I'm afraid I won't be strong enough to hold it up. The faintest whisper of daylight remains on the farthest edges of the horizon, and Ares will rouse the crowd until darkness falls and the alignment has been made.

I beg the Fates that I don't have another vision like I did at the monument of the columns. Allowed to catch my breath and get some air, familiarity kept picking at the back of my mind and as I touched the stone.

I hoped for a revelation to my awareness of this place. Instead, my pent-up arousal flared, and my mind gave me a vision of being ravaged against the pillar by Hermes.

The fact he is consuming more and more of my thoughts, with such ease is going to make killing him more difficult. Aside from the fact, he is the most powerful Light Bearer the realm has.

His deceased father, Apollo, would have been his only predecessor and I wouldn't be surprised to know Hermes' power would one day have outmatched his infamous father.

The giant pyramid steps open up as if welcoming me home, but it's an ominous greeting given my task tonight. Silence falls over the land; even the Wind pauses its track around the globe as if to stop and watch.

Goddess, please help me tonight.

On one side of the aisle, the familiar man with a shining bald head from the tunnels, stands with his hands on his sister's shoulders. They nod at me in reverence along with everyone else. The level of appreciation and respect the Shifters give me feels out of place. I'm an imposter walking down this path, an assassin who takes down the elitist who attempt to betray the God of War. I'm not the goddess of the moon with long flowing hair and grace they expect.

On the opposite side of the aisle is Naomi. One of her twins stands before her, and she holds him in place with her hand across his chest. The other twin hugs her hip tightly, and Ted is the strong big brother with them hiding his nervousness. His hands are shoved down in the pockets of his blue jeans, and his little shoulders are pushed back tall. A wide, toothy smile has the smallest falter as I look at him, the only crack in his brave armor.

Remembering my promise, I wink at him. He chuckles as Naomi looks down at him lovingly, and their exchanged look warms my heart.

They give me the courage I need to push forward. Little Ted is an orphan in this world because his parents couldn't shift into their wolves. Saved only by the graces of another who is also suffering but keeps him safe with a mother's love. If I can help them and something I do tonight can improve their lives, I'll try it with everything I have. Not everyone here deserves this chance, but Naomi and her children do.

As I climb the tall steps of the pyramid, Ares keeps his stern and expectant eyes on me. I know what he's conveying and understand the weight of tonight. Failing is not an option; death is my outcome if I don't give him what he wants. I look to the mass of Shifters as their aura's pulse at me. I search for the strongest of them. Perhaps I can predict how many we will be able to turn into their wolf forms, hoping it will be enough to save my life tonight.

Demeter and I take our places on each side of Ares, and he looks at us both. With nods in agreement from Demeter and me, he looks over the crowd, and something passes over his eyes.

If you don't know him, it would be easy to think it was love or appreciation for his faithful troops of Shifters. But it's not. It's arrogance that all these people are here because of their loyalty to him. But desperation has drawn them here.

An errant thought passes my mind of an army of Shifters who are strong enough to break their allegiance with Ares and oppose him. With Lucas, they could win, and I may just be brave enough to fight along with them.

He rambles on about pride and duty, and I can't help the uneasy feeling of a pillar of coldness standing behind me. Flint hovers beyond my vision, but I sense him leaning forward ever so slightly, hoping to get my attention. I work to keep my attention trained forward, not giving him any acknowledgment.

I didn't get much sleep last night, and when I did, Hermes joined me again. He wrapped me in his arms and held me, but there was no scent or warmth like there had been before. I swear I could feel every sense of his presence the first time when he was driving me mad with his lips and fingers.

When I envision Flint doing those things to me, there is nothing: no warm butterflies, no jolts of excitement, and no heat. Only endless cold, like a barren desert in the dark of night, and I wonder what ever attracted me to him to begin with.

As I lay in Kai's room on the floor, tossing and turning, I kept trying to get back to the beginning of our relationship, when we met and what drove us to together, but darkness is all I conjured with the thoughts.

Shadows stretch over the flat land, and it's as if the pyramid is growing with the rising moon. Like a curtain opening and letting light enter a dark room, something changes, and a veil is lifted over the night. The moon's light shines brightly, and cool tingles cover my skin. A current of static electricity can be felt around me, and I check to ensure my hair is not standing on end.

Looking past Ares, Demeter has her face lifted to the dark sky, her hands are at her sides with her palms facing outward, and she breathes in the night as deeply as she can. The alignment of Gaea and Avalon has begun. Like Demeter, I close my eyes to the shared power of the twin realms. A flash of a castle and a lake with dozens of shooting stars racing across the sky like jewels pass behind my eyelids.

Reminding me of my dream and the warning of the arrival of the Herald. I've lost count of how many times Hermes has entered my mind today., His burning blue eyes sear into my soul, making me waiver in my mission to end his immortal life.

"Ah-hum." Demeter and Ares are both looking down at me. Apparently, I missed my cue. A flash of anger passes over Ares's face, and a wave of heat burns my cheeks. Closing my eyes and taking a steadying breath, I look over the crowd. The directions from Demeter have left me, and my mind is surprisingly blank.

Great.

Buying myself a second's delay, I walk down two steps to put some distance between Ares and me. His very presence is suffocating as he looms over me, larger than this great pyramid. An endless sea of faces look up at me, blinking their expectations. Murmurs float across the Shifters, and the intensity of their doubt grows inside me.

The ceremony is centered around the moonlight. The moon of Gaea is made stronger by the alignment of Avalon's moon, and the power of their forces flows between the two realms for a month until they will be joined by the eclipse of Tartarus that occurs on the final night of their alignment.

The brief period when all three realms align causing an enormous swell of power.

Looking up at the moon, a beam of light catches my eye, and I follow it down as it casts itself over Zara. The familiar young lady from the tunnels whose brother is hovering over her like the world's most imposing security guard. He shuffles on his feet and flexes his fingers, still holding onto her shoulders like she's a balloon that will drift away without his help.

Keeping focused on the moonlight, I see the particles that glisten within it. Like billions of pieces of holographic glitter have been poured into a glass of swirling water, I focus on them. Watching them dance in the air, they look like pixies that have come alive under the light of the moon. My eyes glaze over, and I'm fixated on the specks of Lumos within the moonbeam as a sharp pain stings my calf.

Nyx

Opening my eyes for the first time in ages is always an adjustment. The light of the moon is bright, and I hold my hand up to it, shielding my eyes. Inspecting the unfamiliar limb that moves with my will, it feels odd, new. I turn over my hands, examining both sides before holding them out before me.

My eyes run up the length of my body before I feel the weighted gaze of a crowd and take them in with bewilderment. It's always the clothing that is my first sign of the time that has passed since my celestial sight has looked upon this realm.

At the last awakening, ladies wore exquisitely detailed gowns and corsets on a night with a gathering like this.

How quickly it changes.

My spirit thrums with power, but I can feel the mortal feebleness of this body, so I must be careful. I can't damage it, and I'll need to return to my slumber soon until my mate awakens me. He searches for me. His desperation to reunite with me, to heal me, fills the realm with his longing, and I bathe in it.

Soon, my love.

A beast rages in the sky above me, and a strange contraption soars high within the clouds, lights blinking as it arcs through the sky like a large steel bird. So many changes occur while I rest, and I always wish for more time to explore them. My curiosity is always ravenous.

But something has called me out of my chamber early. I rummage through the broken and scattered mind of the mortal shell I occupy for this incarnation.

Until the entirety of my power is returned, so much mortality of the previous life remains, and this period of imbalance is always the hardest.

But I sense the strong-willed spirit that inhabited this body before me, and I sense the darkness that has been implanted in her mind. There is too much of obscurity coating this mind. I can burn away the poisons that lock her under Demeter's spell with nothing more than a thought. While I can't do much more than that, it will help her when she wakes.

The pierce of a barb in my calf burns, and I know Demeter is here—the *traitor queen.*

Turning my eyes to meet hers, I understand what is happening. She is passing her power to me, begging a favor of the goddess.

"Why should I help you?" The voice of my new body is odd inside my mind as I speak to Demeter.

"It's not for me." She answers. *"It's for them. They are suffering."* She leeches herself, feeding the power of Life into me, waking me up, and disturbing my rest.

The Shifters before me could flood this grassy plain with the tears of their suffering. It secretes out of them in endless flows, and the discarded energy soils the earth with their pain.

"They are suffering because of you, trapping them in false forms." I argue.

"These forms are best for this realm. You would not understand. Please, goddess?"

Demeter has lost control of her own spell and wants me to clean it up for her.

One particularly fragile-looking Shifter is quite deceptive. Everything, from her posture and bone structure to the delicate arch in her eyebrows, gives the appearance of a soft female. Dainty, reserved, submissive. But the beast within is thirsty for revenge, waiting for the moment to prowl on her massive paws with a fire burning inside her emerald and carnelian-speckled eyes.

I step down, and she stands tall as I gaze hard on her. She doesn't back down or flinch as I tuck my finger under her chin and rotate her head from side to side, inspecting her.

"What is your name, child?" My voice echoes across this plain and heads crane, vying for a view.

"Zara." The soft voice adds to the feminine allure, and the corner of my mouth ticks up as I fight back the smile.

Zara: *Radiant blooming flower.*

What a deadly thing she would be if it weren't for the spell coating her like the muck at the bottom of a bog. I can see it like sludge, coating the auras of these magnificent beings. There is a tremor to her chin as she fights back tears.

"Why do you weep, beautiful flower?"

She holds her answer, rolling it over within her mouth before responding. Her pale pink lips purse together, and her nostrils flare as she cools her hot tears. She allows her shame pull her eyes to the ground.

"The journey has been hard." The strength she has carried for so long has made her tired, and she whispers her response.

Ducking my head to meet her eyes, I bring her gaze back to mine. Some of the light has dimmed within them as she allows herself a moment of weakness. I drop my voice to match her own. "It often is when the calling is higher."

She understands, and the fires of determination blaze again, returning a gleam in her dark pupils as resolve flashes across her face.

"Tell me what you want, flower."

"I want to meet my wolf." The tender voice of the young woman answers me with surety.

"And why would you want to wear the coat of a fraud?" I cock my head with amusement, enjoying drawing out the revelation to come, soaking in an extra moment of consciousness before I return to my slumber.

She twists her head at me in confusion. Her protector takes an instinctual step toward her with concern etched on his furrowed brow. The crowd draws in a sharp breath at once. A part of me would like to extend out the dramatics further, but I'm on borrowed time.

"You are no wolf." I turn on my heel and climb two large steps. "But I'm happy to introduce you to your beast, all the same."

We'll need a bit more room for this. There are so many suffering here. And so many more suffering that are *not* here.

With a wave of my hand, I guide the beam of moonlight, and it eagerly obeys. Like a domesticated canine, happily wagging after its master, the Lumos swirls, and my powers reel within me, happy to be useful after all this time at rest. Even if they are muted and only a fraction of my true strength.

Zara is confused but patient.

I can feel her tenacity. Nothing means more to her than this; she is willing to remain calm despite my toying, and hope pours out of her. She knows something more awaits her. She has always known she was more than the claims made by those who would try to crush her. Those who have tried and failed.

The diamond light of the moon encases her, and the dark spell melts away, fizzing and dissolving with the cleansing light of Theia. The great Titan of Hel and Realm of Light that bends at my command.

Zara's rich skin glows as the gold shimmer of her aura surrounds her. Like the burning beacon of Alexandria, guiding ships around the harbor of Pharos, Zara glistens, and the transformation begins. Within the human flesh, the bones of the beast take shape—fur sprouts as the skin retreats. The majesty of the Shifter's power is always a fascination to observe.

Her protector is concerned, and I send him reassurance with my aura. His tight brow relaxes, and he releases his hands to his sides, flexing his fingers before balling them into fists.

As the moonlight coats the Shifter, it cradles her in the air, and she gives herself over to the transformation. Curled upon herself, the animal within emerges, and I no longer hide the smile of pride as I look upon her true form. The many faces gasp and whisper in their awe as the moonlight delivers the beast to the ground.

As the massive paws touch the grass, it does so with the grace and elegance of a dancer. The claws, sharp and gleaming, stretch for the first time as a short golden pelt shines in the moonlight. Her eyes shimmer like emerald and carnelian jewels as the lioness looks at me.

With a bend at my waist, I bow to the Princess of the Pride. The noble bloodline of her ancestors sings to me from within her veins as a cousin of the great Titan Fenrir; she was not meant to serve within the low ranks of a pack. She is a queen, meant to rule and I hope I may return to see her reign.

She cranes her neck to the moon above, and the roar of the lioness dances freely for the first time. Her protector looks at her beautiful form in awe, and happiness weeps from his eyes.

My time is running short.

I feel the power of Demeter waning as she fights to feed me an adequate supply of Life.

"How weak you have let yourself become." I snarl at her, such a pitiful excuse for an Immortal and a queen. Demeter straightens

her shoulders, but I see the sting of my insult on her treacherous soul.

She sustained me for one. Thousands more need my help.

Turning back to the steps, I ascend to a higher vantage point. The expectant eyes of the Shifters below singe my back. They are fearful I will leave without helping them. I should leave them. So many of them are unworthy. But a feeling of pure innocence from within the hoard of entitlement gives me pause.

Such a tiny aura, tainted with so much pain, and yet it remains pure and full of hope. I hear his prayer for his mother and brothers but nothing for himself. Turning behind me, I find the little boy immediately within the crowd. Part of my consciousness feeds me a memory.

"The goddess made you a promise, Ted. And she will keep it."

The little shoulders of the cub drop as reassurance washes over him. He is only concerned for his family and would be happy knowing they were cured, even if there is no hope for him. He is such a sweet boy, and a rare spirit.

The Flame stampedes down the step and grabs my arm in his rage—smoke billows from his shoulders, angry with my action.

"What the fuck do you think you are doing?" Ares barks at me.

"Do not touch me, Flame." As I cock my eyebrow, my Wind flicks him backward as if he is nothing more than a flea in the palm of my hand. Turning to the crowd, tired from their travels and strained under the weight of a curse that is keeping them bound, they hold their breath in wait for me.

I will perform this favor for them, knowing many will repay the gesture by joining the army of the goddess. When return from the dark caverns of my slumber to face my hunter once more, I will see many of these faces by my side.

"So many of you are trapped, wearing the cursed fur of an imposter and wondering why it doesn't fit." They glance between themselves as I stretch my voice across their gathered masses. "We'll set this right."

The Titan is behind me.

The Titan Shifter I made so long ago in that moment of despair. His iron heart still beats with righteousness. Lucas was the right choice then and remains their best chance now. Raising my arms to the moonlight, I look back at him. His expectant eyes were staring harshly, hoping for my recognition. His shoulders relax in relief and he nods once. He was always intuitive; even now, he knows I need help, and like before, he is ready to give it to me.

Demeter is borrowing the power of the alignment and giving too much of herself to fuel me. A strip of her hair bleaches as she continues to feed me. A sign she is nearing the end of what she can give. But the power of Fenrir, which now belongs to Lucas, will be enough.

I pluck the bard from my leg and toss it to her feet. The traitor queen drops to the stone steps, unable to carry herself a second more. Lucas widens his stance and prepares his body for my assault as I borrow from his aura and the power of the Titan within him.

Lucas is strength. He is what an Immortal should strive to be.

He accepted the burden of the Titan and has carried it for the people who need him. The hope of salvation to come fuels him; not choked by the prospect of power he could steal.

I detect the milky slime of Demeter's poison coating his insides just as they coated mine, and I remove her toxins from him.

"Thank you." He whispers in my mind.

The beams of moonlight expand around us both and are blasted across the field as I widen my arms, spreading the jeweled light of the moon. The bodies of the Shifters glow and gleam all the colors of the rainbow as I cleanse them of their curse.

The moon's white light burns across the realm, and the expense of power drains me. Darkness takes over my vision. As my body gives way to exhaustion, I drift back into the void of sleep, but my eyes meet his for a second. Standing on a cloud as if brought forth from my dreams, he is here, and comfort floods me as I collapse.

Hermes.

20

"What do you mean the Titan of the Shadow Realm is here?"** My Light bursts around me, creating a shield and exposing my sword in its newly fashioned scabbard.

"We cannot summon the shadows while the Titan of Elysium is near." Mors eyes bounce around the darkness as she searches for the being.

"We need to stick to the plan." I drop next to her and coat my eyes in my power, searching for the absence of Light to help find the darkness concealing whoever Mor is detecting.

Our entire strategy depends on her shadows for a distraction. Looking at the scene below, Ares is still speaking to the crowd. The shadows are crawling across the ground, with the sun nearly vanishing in the sky. In mere moments, the alignment will begin.

"The shadow realm walks with us, every step we take. It waits for our command and opens at our beckoning." Mor gestures to herself as she speaks. "Erebus is the embodiment of darkness, and the creatures of the shadow realm will go to their Titan if I bring them forth."

"How can Erebus be here? I saw Chaos and his cloud of death consume the Dark Titan." I continue my argument as I watch Ares continue his long-winded speech.

The battles we have faced on Gaea have been cataclysmic, but nothing can prepare you to witness the damage of scale of a battle between figures that are capable of ripping entire realms apart with only their might.

"That is not a question I can answer. I can only tell you that the Titan is here." Mor's tone is laced with offense.

The Fates always enjoy weaving obstacles into matters at the worst times. No sooner does the thought of the alignment cross my mind when I feel the electricity in the air ramp. Chills cascade down my body as the fine hairs at the nape of my neck pull at me in irritation with the surge of power. The alignment between Gaea and Avalon has snapped into place.

We're out of time.

I quickly look to the ground below and watch Rhea walk down the pyramid's steps and face Zara. In a second, Rhea transforms, just as Mor does, and something ethereal washes over Rhea, transforming her entire demeanor.

Her eyes turn black like The Void. The golden hue of her iris and the whites of her eyes are swallowed in nothingness. Her honey hair whips wildly about her as if powered by a current of wind that billows only for her—the silvery spindles of her starlight aura flex and pulse like a beacon. As if her hands have been dipped in tar, her black rolling mist covers her hands and climbs up her wrist as it bellows out of her.

Standing, my heart hammers in my chest as I watch her. It's as if she stepped out of the darkness and I'm taken back to the first moment my eyes first saw her. Rhea is still here but the essence of Nyx surrounds her.

I'm powerless to look away from her.

"You are no wolf." She says to Zara with a voice that doesn't belong to her. "But I'm happy to introduce you to your beast, all the same."

"Hermes, just hold your position." Lucas knows we're here, but Mor has taken over the shield and covers us in a cloak of darkness. *"Nyx is in control."*

I scoff, as if I need his guidance to recognize the soul my very essence was created to love.

Medusa is waiting on the edge of the cloud, her eyes tight, transfixed on the young woman she pulled out of the gladiator pits fifty years ago. Deuce has remained in Zara and Kellan's life ever since because she cares for the siblings, not because they owe her as they pretend.

The transformation Zara undertakes is breathtaking. We watch as the body of her human form melts away to an animal, and a lioness steps forth. Her roar is deep and full of relief, as if she is releasing decades of pent-up abuse and admonishment from her fellow Shifters.

"Yeah! Look at you." Medusa whispers as she pumps her fist in celebration, rooting for the young Shifter.

"Beautiful," Callie exclaims in low tones to Achilles, who agrees.

With a great blast of moonlight, searing across the field of Shifters like the mushroom cloud of a bomb, it spreads outward in all directions, beyond the horizon. I send the expanse of my Light chasing after it. My power longing to feel hers but also observe the majesty of her reach as Shifters across the realm transform.

The Shifters within the field have traveled here from every corner of Gaea, hoping to get help from the goddess tonight. One by one, they lift into the air, powered by the moonlight, and transformations occur by the dozens with flashes of aura cascading upward like rainbows.

After the moonlight is dispersed like a blast of Absolute Light, Rhea drops to the ground. As she spots me, a split second of recognition flashes in the deep abyss of her blackened eyes. I power my Light element to teleport to her and wrap her in my arms, but I'm stuck within Mor's Shield of Shadow.

I watch as Lucas dives down several steps, catching her head before it can bounce off the hard stone of the ancient pyramid.

"Release me!" I bellow at Mor. Anger sears my veins being locked in place.

"This isn't me." She sneers between her teeth as the transformation to The Morrigan takes over her flesh. The next sentence is said with her harrowing voice, strained with its screaming whisper. "The Titan has discovered us."

The scene below can only be described as pandemonium. The Lycan have been forced out of their human forms by Rhea's power and shifts of all manner are taking place below us. Ares kneels next to Rhea's unconscious body and yells behind him. Terra is quickly by his side, and the stone steps of the pyramid swirl with her quicksand power. Demeter and Flint reach them just in time to dissolve into nothing as they leave the mayhem unfolding.

Kellan only joined the field today to stand with his sister, hoping for her transformation. But as I watch his body, encased in gold aura, rise several feet off the ground, he shifts from a strong man with rich umber skin and firm expression to a mighty lion with golden fur and a black mane. And he is big. Not nearly as large as Lucas in his true form, but Kellan is a massive lion, ten feet standing on all fours with wide, muscled shoulders.

As the moonlight releases him, his enormous paws rest upon the grass, and his sister steps to him, still in her lioness form. They touch heads as a sign of affection before turning their attention to the beasts around them.

Lions, panthers, and leopards dot the mass of animals as other large feline species emerge. Three other male lions turn their heads to Kellan and Zara. Licking their snouts with firm gazes on Zara, they prowl toward the siblings. Brother and sister respond by taking a stance shoulder to shoulder. Their muzzles quiver as they growl a warning to the approaching cats. Kellan takes a step in front of his sister, a clear sign to the other Shifters to back away.

Now that these Shifters are no longer Lycan, the instinct to claim a mate and breed is going to be strong. This is going to be a bloodbath if Lucas can't regain control.

"We have to get down there." Medusa is a bundle of nerves as she keeps her eyes locked on Kellan and Zara.

An ink-like shadow reaches up from below, and the crawling dread of fear that Medusa and I felt back in the cell with Ana attempts to creep upon us again. The Morrigan combats the shadow with her own column of darkness. As shadow and shade collide and static roars around us, drowning out the growls and snarls of the animals below.

"Oh, my goddess, no." Callie stares wide eyes, and I follow her sight line to the field below. She is trying to use her Winds to propel us onto the ground, but we're immobilized on this cloud, trapped in a shield of darkness by the Titan, who keeps out of sight.

A large black bear stands on all fours with warnings of murder flashing in their eyes. Just behind the bear, three small cubs cower and quiver together. Two of the cubs appear identical in size and match the black coat of the adult bear protecting them. One of the cubs is only slightly larger with brown fur.

Descending upon them are six menacing bears of brown and black fur. All of them large males.

"Achilles, we have to do something. The male bears will kill the cubs, then they'll all breed with the mother." Callie's voice cracks with the urgency and desperate desire to help the bear-Shifter below. It must be a mother with three children.

Backed away from the larger pyramid, the mother bear tries to flee with the cubs but the males track her. With her back to a small temple, the cubs will have nowhere to go, and this single female won't be able to hold out against all these males.

"Lucas!" I bellow to him with telepathy. The strain and desperation in my voice pulls his attention as he yells out commandments, and his pack members dart out across the grassy field, but he can't find us within this Shield of Shadow.

"Where are you?"

"Not us, the bear!"

Lucas' eyes dart around the vast expanse of land, searching within the sea of fur and talons.

"To your right at the temple."

Lucas finds them. He could make it there in a single leap if he were shifted.

Tracking the bears, they are hunting the mother and her cubs. They have fanned out so they can descend upon the small family at once. Several will pull her away from the cubs and kill them. Their primal instinct to mate with her and impregnate her with their offspring is the male bears only goal; driving them to hunt after her and her cubs.

A guttural scream behind me, and a wave of dark shadow billows from The Morrigan's center. Her eyes are flaming yellow-orange, and she is directing her column of dark matter to a small cluster of trees. That must be where the Titan of Darkness and Ruler of the Shadow Realm is hiding.

The Morrigan has found Erebus and wastes no time beginning an assault in an attempt to free us of the Titans dark cage.

"Hermes." Her eerie voice, the whispered scream I first heard when I arrived at Avalon, struggles to speak my name as her endless array of Dark Matter batters against the shadows within the cluster of trees. "Help... Us."

Turning toward her aim, I hold out my hand and blast a beam of blue light, matching the trajectory of her dark column. My Light illuminates a cloaked figure, and dark shadows stretch toward us in retaliation.

A sphere of shade and depressing shadows forms around us, threatening to squeeze smaller and smaller until it bursts with us inside. I reach for the hilt of my sword, and my arm quakes, straining to grab it. The darkness is like a huge crushing hand, bearing down and restricting us.

Wielding my sword in one hand, it gleams to life with the enchanted runes, and I work to pull it in front of me. Still shooting my Light beam at the Titan, my other hand struggles against the pressure of the darkness.

"Hypnos," I grunt out as my teeth chatter with the strain. The Morrigan keeps up her beam as my Light collides with it in the center of the Titan's cloaked chest. "Put... the Titan... to... sleep."

"You want *me* to put a *Titan* to sleep?" He exclaims back to me. His pearly eyes begin to glow brighter in the shadows that are deepening around us.

"Y-y-yes." I stammer as I bend my knees and push against the Darkness with my left shoulder. Still pulling my sword with all of my might, I add a Light pulse behind my elbow to help me bring my arm around.

Focusing my radiance through the topaz stone at the hilt of my sword amplifies it. Pulling the sword in front of me, I can blast a stronger beam of Absolute Light directly at the Titan. I think the Titan knows this and is pushing against me, trying to hold me back from getting my sword in front of me.

"I can't hold a Titan in sleep. They are too powerful." He screams over the roar of the darkness and light colliding.

My arms burn from the effort to hold my stance and push against the darkness as I try to work my sword from its scabbard at my back. Wincing against the strain, I grit my teeth and widen my stance, bracing more against the Titans attack.

"We... only need... a second." The Morrigan's voice croaks out as she pushes hard. Her beam of dark matter billows a deafening roar.

Hypnos stands behind us as The Morrigan, and I are shoulder to shoulder against the Titan. Our beams of Light and Dark both reached a center point within the Titan's chest.

Hypnos's aura is as pearlescent as his eyes as it flares around us. The pulsating waves of his power ripple in the atmosphere between us. His element pierces the Titan in the same spot as our beams of light and dark, the shadows around us falter, and the hold against my sword arm weakens.

Straining and screaming against the remaining energy, I yank my sword in front of me and channel my full power through the topaz stone, expelling a beam of Absolute Light at the Titan. The Morrigan follows suit and clasps her hands together, roaring against the night as her column of Dark Matter becomes a Void Beam.

Like a tear through the very atmosphere, it is as if her Beam has ripped through the fabrics of this realm.

Hypnos adds his own vocals to our cacophony as his growl fuels his Sensory power, and he induces sleep against the Titan. The Shield of Shadow releases us with barely a whisper as it vanishes into the night.

❧ ❦

Freed from our shadow prison, perched on our cloud of Callie's power, we shift to the scene below. Callie and Achilles were ready to add their powers to our mix of light and dark, but the Titan vanished when the power ruptured around us. Achilles' Fire blast exploded against the space the Titan occupied as Callie hit it with a burst of Wind.

Lucas prepares to leap across the field. He is still human, but his beast is just below the surface as he poises himself on the corner of the step pyramid. The bears are about fifteen feet away from their targets as the cubs cower under the back haunches of their mother. Backing the younglings against the stone temple, she attempts to shield them with her massive body.

Lucas cracks the stone steps of the pyramid as he launches himself into the air. The transition happens in flight, and his bones crack and elongate instantly. Landing between the female bear and the male Shifters descending upon her, it seems to take minutes for the beast to stand to his full height.

As large as his natural form takes, the red fur of the great monster fully engulfs the female bear, her cubs, and the small temple they were using to cover their backs from attack. Moving my eye up the beast's great body, the growl of the man-turned-animal raises the hairs on our arms as it acts like a shockwave across the field.

Pulling the attention of every Shifter gathered at the ceremony's start, they turn to him. Raising on his hind legs, a massive Grizzly Bear stands before us, nearly half as tall as the great pyramid. Lifting his brown and red snout to the sky, the roar of the bear brings us to our knees, and we cover our ears against the deafening sound.

As the beast rests on his four large paws, the ground cracks under the weight of his massive body. The trees shake, and birds evacuate their homes, flying away from the field, cawing their complaints of the disturbance into the night.

Hazel eyes burn into the bear-Shifters that were descending upon the mother and her cubs as he watches them, begging them to move a muscle forward with his fiery stare. They cower and back away, keeping their eyes locked on his, in case the great beast decides against the mercy he is showing them.

The mother and her cubs emerge cautiously from under their Zeta King, with the threat of the bear-Shifters expelled in an instant. Lucas huffs as he surveys the field of his people, who watch him in awe.

From the crowd of frozen animals, the black-maned lion saunters toward Lucas, followed by the golden lioness. Stopping at the edge of the crowd, the lions lower their heads in respect to their king, their Titan.

One by one, the rest of the animals follow and bow in respect. As Lucas surveys his people, he finds us perched on our cloud. Finally freed of the veil that kept us obscured from view.

The Zeta nods in our direction, and we bow our heads in reverence of the Titan, presenting himself for the first time upon this realm.

"Oh, Lucas, I think you kept a secret from us." I send him my telepathic message, laced with sarcasm and a tone of teasing.

I don't think I'll ever get over seeing an animal smirk, but he does. Then that son of a bitch winks at me.

The scene below looks like a zoo exploded, and animals of all kinds are running loose. A great golden eagle circles overhead. This must be a Shifter. The wingspan is easily twice that of a typical eagle, nearly twelve or more feet in length. Its massive body carries beautiful black and brown feathers as deep eyes hold us while it circles the cloud we are sitting on.

With a caw that echoes across the sky, it flies down to the field below. Circling Lucas twice, the wings flap and rustle the long fur of the Titan's grizzly form as the bird takes a position to the right of the Zeta.

"It's Kai." Callie deduces. Only the Beta takes a position to the right of their Alpha. "She's beautiful."

"Hermes." The graveled voice of the Zeta calls to me. *"I need your help."*

In a flash of Light, we're teleported to his side, and the field bellows with growls of Shifters as they spot our arrival.

A howl from the pyramid raises the hairs on my left side, and I pivot my body to the wolf descending the stairs. Dark fur with brown patches and obsidian eyes track me. The wolf is stalking down the large stairs, his growl warning us to leave.

As his large paw thuds the grass and dirt of the field, other wolves from his pack join him. It's the Alpha that replaced Lupo. A small pack of hyenas and several bears join the wolf as his growls turn to a snarl.

Movement behind me warns of the Zeta as the gargantuan bear rises. His shadow is like night, covering us in instant darkness. He takes a step over us, standing with his two great front paws on each side of us. His tall body allows us to remain fully standing as his size looms high above us. The bear holds the locked gaze of the wolf approaching.

This is a big moment.

Lucas is showing his allegiance to the Elementals by protecting us.

If the Shifters are communicating with each other with their telepathy, we are not privy to the conversation, but the wolf's snarls turn to barks as the animals taking the new Alphas side growl or roar in response.

"Look at them all." Mor's casual voice is nearly a whisper as we wait for the resolution to the standoff. Lucas keeps his stare with the Shifters challenging him, and we take in the scene of animals.

Dispersed among the field are animals of all kinds. Not only predator species but more docile animals that would be considered prey. A pair of swans with white feathers are huddled around a trio of goslings. Their fluffy grey feathers tremble as they pivot their heads in all directions, taking in the large bodies of the beasts around them.

"Achilles, look." Callie points, and I track her path to two orca whales lying on their sides. Several Elementals from Ares forces are coating them with water.

Movement under a dark cluster of trees steals my attention, and I pull the moonlight carefully so I can see the disturbance in the dark night. An older man and woman remain in human form among the animals. Their eyes dart from beast to beast as they usher a Shifter away from the throngs of animals. Trying to remain quiet, their movements show their paranoia, and I quickly see why.

A woman transitions quickly between different forms of animals and her human body. With long black hair and fear in her eyes, she backs away with the older couple that must be her parents. In her early twenties and with rich brown skin, she could be native to the area.

The woman shifts to a jaguar, then back into a woman before the body of a long anaconda writhes on the ground, then shifts to a tall horse with a coat of midnight.

"Lucas, wrap this up," I tell him through telepathy.

"She is in pain." Hypnos' deep voice rumbles low as he and Mor break their observation of the shifting woman and exchange a knowing look.

A swirl of Shadow consumes them as Mor and Hypnos leave us within the protective underbelly of Lucas. They appear within the shade of the trees to the shock of the older couple, helping the strange woman. A ripple of Hypnos' power targets her.

The rapid shifting stops, and she collapses in his arms, uncon-scious.

As if a great spotlight is suddenly shown on the group huddled under the trees, Lucas' head snaps to them, and the beast trembles before he splits the silence of the night with a roar of anger, com-mand, and finality. Raising on his two hind legs, he towers over us all as his great snout rises to the air, and the roar of the Titan carries across the realm.

The old couple huddles close to Mor and Hypnos as shadows engulf them, and they are gone. The bear drops to his four legs, and the ground quakes under the force of his large body landing. He swings his massive head back to the oncoming wolves, ready to direct his anger at the vanished woman toward them.

The approaching pack of challengers rescinds their approach and runs up the temple's steps. The wolf transitions back to a man, and with a final glare at Lucas, he heads into the temple at the top of the pyramid. I know an elevator will take him to where Ares resides below.

"Shifters," Lucas includes the Elementals in his telepathic mes-sage to the Immortals before us. *"A plague has infected us far too long. Our true forms have been locked away from us, and we have suffered greatly."*

Mor and Hypnos return and give us a nod of acknowledgment as if letting us know the woman was delivered safely. I keep my attention on the mass of Shifters, taking inventory of those in distress and those whose allegiance is siding with Ares' forces.

"The goddess has given us a gift tonight. The gift of truth, if we are strong enough to realize the meaning of it."

Shifters sway uncomfortably as cubs and goslings draw closer to their families.

"We are no children of Ares," He pauses and lets the weight of his proclamation settle over the beasts before he continues. *"Ares has forced our allegiance through his cruelty. Stripped us of our right to stand as equals to the Immortals, and slain generations of our families. No longer will we be held under another's control. I stand before you, with the power of Fenrir, and ask your allegiance."*

From each side of the step pyramid, reflective eyes of wolves emerge, returning to challenge the Titan. In an instant, the brown fur of the Grizzly shifts as Lucas transforms from bear to wolf. He turns his head to each side. A growled warning thunders above us as Lucas remains our protective cover. His new allegiance is clear as he speaks again to his people.

Spinning my sword in a circle, I hold the hilt low to my side and turn my stance toward the pyramid. I'm in a wonderful mood to take out a few more Alphas tonight if Lucas can't get the packs under control.

"Go now to safety, but make no mistake, this is not the end of our struggles. Tonight, marks the beginning of our freedom."

Kellan and Zara remain in their lion forms and stand with Lucas. Birds fly into the sky while some shift back into human form and jog away from the site of the pyramid. Others appear to be stuck in their transitions.

"Hermes," Lucas steps back, and the night brightens as his shadow leaves us. *"Please transport the amphibious Shifters to water. They'll suffer out here until they can figure out how to shift back."*

The wolves from the dark side of the pyramid continue to creep closer as Lucas turns to face them. Medusa, Callie, and Achilles step between the wolves and other animals who have decided to stand with Lucas as they prepare to fight their fellow Shifters.

"Mor?" I turn to her. She nods, understanding my question. "We need to get them out of here before Ares' masses an attack."

She clasps her wrists with Hypnos. "Stay safe, my friend." She tells him before turning back to me. "Want to race?"

The gleam in her red eyes is quick before she dissolves into darkness, reappearing twenty feet away, placing her hands on the sides of two bull sharks, and disappearing again.

⁂

I return to the packhouse in Mexico, soaking wet. Seriously drenched from head to toe and sloshing water from my shoes on the tile floor.

"What happened to you?" Medusa is holding back a smirk while Callie's mouth gapes open.

"Those fucking dolphins, man. *Assholes*."

Achilles snorts a laugh next to Callie, who slaps him in the stomach while covering her smirk and trying to protect my ego. Medusa takes no such care and bursts into laughter, doubling over the counter and banging her fist.

"Oh, that's perfect. If I could only have seen *whatever* happened."

The packhouse is full of warm, yellow light, and the smell of food permeates the air. The muffled noises of many guests play in the background as others have joined us with the conclusion of the skirmish at the pyramid.

Mor and I flashed in and out of the field to deliver animals to different bodies of fresh and saltwater as the others fought in a short skirmish. It didn't last long, with most of the powerful Alpha's siding with Lucas. The new Alpha was no match, and the fight fizzled out quickly.

"You have no right!" Lucas' voice booms from the courtyard.

"What's going on out there?" I ask.

"Mor is irritating the Zeta," Medusa answers with a quiver of her lips, still humored by my soggy state.

"Glad it's someone other than me," I mumble as I join Lucas in the courtyard.

I'm exhausted, wearing wet clothes and smelling like any number of amphibious creatures as I stand here *without* my mate.

Crossing my arms over my chest, I lean against the open double door and rub my hand down my face.

Shifters line the railing above, looking down at the courtyard center. Lucas stands with his hands on his hips and fury in his eyes. Hypnos is stoic with his arms crossed over his chest, acting as a buffer between the Zeta and his friend. She keeps her air of indifference as she stands slouched like a pouting child being scolded by their father.

"She didn't want to be discovered."

"She is my mate," Lucas says quietly, stepping closer to Mor.

"Then it will make for a romantic story for your kids to tell them how you tracked down your one true love." And with that finality, Mor stalks inside, looking me up and down as she approaches.

"We won." She says with a low tone as she passes me, making me grin. She is weird, and I hate to admit it, but Orion was right. She is growing on me.

Lucas throws his hands up in frustration and looks at me expectantly as if I'm supposed to stop her and force her to answer his question.

I raise my hands in surrender, "What do you think I can do?"

Hypnos steps to the Zeta with raised eyebrows as if channeling a warning regarding his friend and follows Mors' path inside. Stopping when he is next to me, he says discretely, "Hermes, your clothes are wet."

A smile forces its way to my face, and I work to pull it back so I don't offend my new friend. "I happen to be aware of that."

With two pats on my shoulder, he tracks after Mor.

Lucas rubs his hand down his face, the exhaustion from the night showing in the tightness of his brow.

"I need a beer."

22 — Demeter

Ares' hand is hot on my throat as he slams me into the pyramid's wall. The ancient stones fracture and dust billows around me. I siphoned too much of myself to Nyx and left hardly anything for myself. My knees buckle under his assault, and he supports my weight with his grasp around my neck.

"What the fuck did you do?" His shoulders smoke and billow with his temper, and his hand morphs into a claw as his talons dig into my skin. "It was clear she was supposed to shift them to wolves. Not open up their true forms."

My mouth opens, but I can't respond aside from gargled noise that escapes the tight confines Ares has on me. Pushing me back into the stones once more for good measure before releasing me. I tumble to the hard stone ground, choking and gagging air back into my lungs. My shaking hands barely support my weight as I struggle to remain upright.

"Take care of her while I go fix this." He storms down the hall to the portal for the Underworld. "We've suppressed them for ages, and you two fuck it up in a single night." He calls over his shoulder as he stalks away.

Flint scoffs as he looks down his nose at me, disapproving. Gabriele emerges from the elevator. His skin prickles with the fur of his beast, and he's completely nude, sweating in the dim lighting of the inner temple.

"Lucas. Fuck man, did you see the size of him?" Gabriele is out of breath as his chest rises and falls quickly. "What do I do?"

Flint stomps to him, taking the distance with long strides. With a slap that rings across the rocky walls, he strikes Gabriele across his cheek, eliciting a growl from the Shifter.

"Go be an Alpha, dipshit, and handle it."

Grabbing a Shifter-guard's collar who is securing the elevator entrance, Flint pulls the man into him. "Go get her a Lycan to leech, quickly."

"There are no more Lycan," Gabriele reminds Flint as the men cut their murderous eyes at each other. Flint turns his attention back to the guard who snaps his mouth shut quickly.

"Go find her someone or let her leech you, but do it now."

23
Rhea

"Line up the pups in front of her."

We stand at the top of Mount Vesuvio, and I'm bound nearly head to toe in a metal net of Thaumium. Inside the mountain is a sleeping lake of lava that stirs, calling to me, wanting to stretch its tired legs that have rested too long within the hollowed peek.

I've been Ares' captive for ages, living my pitiful existence within a box lined with Thaumium metal bars and warded so heavily with enchantments that it takes four elementals to carry it.

"Ares, are you sure this is necessary?" Demeter asks Ares. He slaps her across the face with a flaming hand without answering her. The singe across her cheek and the pop of her flesh absorbing the power of the Flame makes me wince. She heals the burn immediately and stands to my side, clasping her hands before her and masking her burned pride.

I've come to expect certain things with these trials from Ares, but something is different today. His eerily calm demeanor is absent today, and instead, he flexes his hand into a fist at his side, and there is a tick at the back of his jaw. Today, he is agitated.

Perhaps it is the report I overheard from the Gulf of Malis and the fact that the Siren and her two Flames are still living and fighting after two days that has him riled. He's eager to break their bond because their strength scares him.

I remember her.

I watched her through the dark cracks of my stone enclosure at Troy and peered at her through the thin wooden slats as we marched to the mountains. The Wind Siren with long white hair that called a tornado to devour Ares' men that night at the valley.

The night Ares lured my mate to the other side of the canyon so he could watch me suffer as my fate unknowingly walked away from me.

The Siren survived her terrible captivity, and each day since I try to be like her, fighting Ares and waiting for the day I may call my own force upon him and his men.

"Will you do it, or will I have to make you, Danaë?" His brown eyes have a ring of red, and his temper is as hot as the magma within the volcano beneath us. I don't answer him and look beyond him to the valley below.

I hold back my smile at the thought of rebellion that wants to spread across my lips, and he gives me a smack that matches the one he just gave Demeter. I feel my cheek bust open as a warm line of blood runs down my face, cooled by the wind.

My eyes water at the familiar pain, but I can't heal myself with these cuffs around me.

Looking below the mountain, I can see for miles with my Immortal vision.

It's lunchtime, and the sprawling cities below hum with life. Pompei and Herculaneum are two sprawling metropolises teaming with large populations of Elementals living harmoniously with mortals. They are loyal to Athena and an annoyance to Ares.

They don't realize they live under a sleeping giant that lies within the rockface of this mountain, and its hungry to erupt and swallow them all.

It's been lifetimes since any mortal has seen the lava burst from Vesuvio, and the current inhabitants of the towns below have done nothing to earn the wrath of Ares. They'll never know what struck them. They'll die, suffering and scared, wondering what vengeful god they angered.

"They're just mortals." I finally look at him. "And they scare you so badly, the great God of War?" Sarcasm slides across the words of his title. He's nothing more than a coward who makes everyone do his bidding for him, and I wonder why he never acts on his own. He is forever the puppeteer behind the curtain, pulling strings and making his puppets dance.

I feel the power of Flame within him. Raging as fiercely as this great volcano, and yet he doesn't call the destruction himself. He is demanding I become the murderer he wants me to be.

My reward is another slam of the back of his hand across my cheekbones. His shoulders billow as his rage builds.

"It's not the mortals that scare me. It's your lack of regard for our cause." Ares spits at my feet, and Lupo leads a line of children up the mountain trail.

Orphans. Lycan pups.

Dirtied and scared, they follow directions and remain in their line. Walking to the end, where Lupo points to the first child, they all stop and face me. I can't look at them, but the blister of their eyes on me weighs on my shoulders and threatens to drive me to the ground.

Ares walks behind the first child. The eldest, only nine. Placing his hands on the child's shoulders, a single tear runs down his dirty cheek. A trail of dirt is cleared, leaving a streak of somewhat clean skin. I focus my eyes on a thin button of his tunic, fashioned from a gleaming white abalone shell.

"Release the volcano upon them."

My heart spikes, and my anger builds. Pressing my lips into a thin line, I work to control my breathing through my nose. My hands clasped behind my back conceal my strain to pull my hand through.

Ares knows how many chains he needs to bind me, but like the Wind Siren who was captive long ago, I'll always find a way to fight back, just as she did.

All I need is one sliver of control over my powers, and I can free them.

"No."

Ares cocks his head to the side and smiles faintly at me.

The child begins to stir under Ares' grasp, and then screams. His flesh turns red, and the veins under his skin glow as if lava flows through them.

"Stop it!" I scream. Tears streak down my face as my body trembles with anger. The pain is genuine, the emotion is raw, but I use it to pull my wrist against the unyielding metal cuff. My flesh burns as it grinds against the steel, but my hand remains locked inside.

The children begin to cry and shuffle away from the boy, but Lupo is there with a growl and a command. They stay put, trying to stifle their tears.

"No." Ares answers. "I will not stop."

The boy falls to the ground, and flames erupt from his chest as he convulses. Soul Fire eats him from within. Ares is making it slow. The child next to the burning boy vomits down his tunic as the rancid smell of scorching flesh wafts around us. The screams stop, and the body is a column of ash. As a breeze dances around the mountain, it blows away his Immortal body.

"Release the volcano upon them."

"They're innocent!" I choke out as Ares walks to the next child and places his hands on the boy's shoulders. He's slightly younger, but not much.

I position my hands lower on my hips and use my bottom to pull against the cuffs. My shoulders scream, and joints of my hand stretch but refuse to yield to the narrow channel of the metal cuffs.

"They captured you, trained you to be a killer, and held you in their gladiator pits like an animal for sport." The second child begins to scream. A little girl is next in line after this one. "But I freed you. I try to show you the potential for greatness within you."

Blood runs down my palm as my skin tears.

"Stop, please."

"Release the volcano upon them." He repeats, speaking of freedom when he traps me in a box like a mouse.

My powers thrum inside me, even in the cuffs I've lived in my entire life, designed to dampen and contain my powers within me. They are never removed and are as much a part of me as the clothes I wear daily. They are the biggest prison of my confinement.

"I can't kill all these people."

"You can. And you will be stronger for it."

The ashen body of the second child blows away as the first did, and Ares moves down the line to the little girl. She trembles at his touch, and I want to rip his arms off his body. But she doesn't make a sound. He leans over and looks down at her with a smile.

"Look how pretty you are." And then he locks eyes with me again. Without asking his question, she screams like the two boys before her.

She looks like me.

Dark hair with thick springing coils that form a halo around her brown face. She looks at me, pleading with tears welling in her umber eyes.

I can't do this. I can't murder the people of these cities. But I can't break free and save these children either. I'm going to fail them.

"Just kill me!" I scream at him as tears roll in steady streams down my face.

"You're far too valuable for death, Danaë. Release the volcano upon them."

The little girl falls to the ground and begs as Ares burns her slower than he did the boys. Dragging out her torture and causing the storm raging inside my body to build with each passing second.

The mountain below me trembles, and its growls overtake the little girl's screams. After a moment, her silence is as void as her vacant eyes, staring at nothing while her body convulses inside Ares' flames. Smoke billows from the top of the volcano as I watch smoke roll off her small body. She can't be more than six or seven.

My power is firing inside me like a million shooting stars colliding with each other in the night sky, and I want to use it to take my own immortal life.

If I can end myself, then I can save the cities; I can save the children.

I can save them all.

The volcano quakes, and the next child in line loses his footing and falls to his knees.

Ares stands behind the little boy who looks up at me with mussy brown hair that falls in front of his brown eyes. His gaze drives my eyes to his, and I can't tear them away. Tears fall down his cheeks as he chokes on a cough. The gaps in his teeth, recently lost, hold my eyes, and I can't look away from them.

Ted?

Why do I feel like I know this child? There are no children in Ares' camps, and yet, something within me knows this child.

"No," My voice is a whisper.

"Release the volcano upon them." Ares punches each word into the air as the veins in his forehead expand, and his face reddens in his anger.

The little boy screams, and it rips through me. I add my own bellow into the air as the top of the mountain explodes.

⁓⁓⁓⁂⁂⁂

"Teddy!" I'm ragged and shaking as sweat pours down my back. Shooting upright in the bed, the sheets are soaked.

"What the fuck, Rhea?" Flint's rough voice mumbles in the dark, disturbed by my sudden waking from the nightmare.

A surge of chills cascades down my body as he calls me the same name Hermes called me in my dream. "What did you call me?"

"What Pers? Why are you being so weird?" Flint sits up and turns on the bedside table lamp.

"That's not what you just called me."

"Are you feeling okay? Do I need to call Demi?"

"Forget it." I throw the covers off and put my robe on. My body screams at me, pain firing everywhere, begging me to keep resting. *But how can I rest now?*

The memories of the Mabon ritual flooded me, and it was as if I was watching from outside my body while some other force took over. The power that thrummed through me felt as if it belonged to me, but at the same time, it felt foreign. It felt like some higher being took control over me, and I lost all free will.

The other force in control was gentle and kind. I felt slender fingers rummage through my mind and dissolve Demeter's poison from my body. So much of it filled me; Demeter must have injected me dozens of times.

How many times have her vines pierced me and forced me to do her bidding only to erase my memory?

After the ceremony, whatever occurred has ramped up my senses a million-fold.

Particles of Light and Dark, Wind and Water, swirl in the air like a kaleidoscope as I stomp to the closet and quickly dress.

I hope I know what I'm doing.

"Gods dammit. Get back over here," Flint throws the covers off him and swings his feet to the side.

With a flick of my finger, my currents push him to the bed and restrain his hands above his head. With his ankles crossed and a rush of Winds keeping his mouth closed, I pull on some dark clothes and slip on my boots.

My eyes see with renewed clarity, and the details of the Underworld are sharp. Every shadow and secret are on display and suddenly, my understanding of the Dark Shield and its purpose slam into me.

Lucas' clue to pay attention to what I *don't* see; it's so obvious now.

Children.

There are no children in the Underworld.

In the disembodied memories from the ritual, I piece together what occurred as I scanned the field of Lycan with my power, cleared of Demeter's illusions by the powerful light of the moon.

She had locked them into a controlled state of shifting somehow. Perhaps by injections that ensure they transform exclusively into wolves. Last night, I cleared her spell from the realm, and Shifters across the globe took to their true forms. But what of the children?

I'm guessing the children are held within the Underworld until Ares and Demeter can control their shift.

Flinging open the door, I expect Kai to be standing guard and startle when a man is there. But the deep oxblood aura is unmistakable, no matter what form the Beta Shifter takes.

"I'm Foxtrot." He says.

"Kai, I know it's you. I can see your aura."

The Betas mouth drops open, speechless for a moment before she recovers, tipping toward me and dropping her voice.

"Don't tell anyone. I'm here to protect you."

Putting my hand on her forearm with a squeeze, we hold a look of understanding between us, and I know I can trust Kai, just as she knows she can trust me.

"I need to go somewhere dangerous. I can knock you out in case I get caught, and I'll take sole responsibility. Or you can come with me. But you need to know, we'll be killed if we're caught."

I'm going to the Dark Shield, and while I don't want to reveal too much in case Kai wants to opt out, I'm hoping my vague explanation will help protect her, should Ares question her.

"Well then let's make sure we don't get caught." Kai answers with a smirk.

We sneak further into the recesses of the Underworld where access is only by staircase. Down and down, we climb until we reach a viscous layer of Darkness at the top of the staircase that will lead to the Shield.

This must be the first barrier placed by a Dark Mage to ward people away.

Unless you are a Dark Mage, this blockage would be invisible, and as you near it, you would be compelled to turn around and leave. I'm not sure why I can see it but there is no time to question the mystery right now.

"So, this is why there are no Light Mages in the Underworld," I speak to myself more than Kai, but we step toward the landing of the stairs with caution.

"Yeah, Shifters aren't very effective at ripping out the throat of a shadow."

I feel the hairs on my arms stand to attention as chills clamp around my body, and I visibly shiver as Kai rubs her arms.

Channeling my aura, I work to recreate the beam of light that blasted Flint out of our room. I focus on the particles I see floating in the air, and the palms of my hands begin to glow.

The Dark barrier begins to burn away like silver flames are eating it from the middle, working to the edges. Elation within me diminishing in an instant when a wave of dark mist and smoke billows toward us from the bottom of the stairs.

The metal staircase quivers, and a bawl far beneath us shake our bones.

Propelled by a strong wind, the smoke careens toward us.

Abandoning the barrier, Kai and I run, sprinting away from the surge of Darkness. I'm not sure what would happen if the smoke touched us, and it's rapidly gaining distance on us. Within a matter of seconds, it will completely consume us.

Grabbing Kai's hand, I pull her along with me, hoping not to lose her when the darkness shrouds us.

I shouldn't have brought her with me. I should have just knocked her out and investigated on my own. It would have been safer for her. We need to push harder and run faster, but the Underworld's narrow corridors slow us down.

A whisp of shadow flicks at my ankle, and a barrage of screams, just like the ones I encountered at the shield, shriek in my ears with a deafening harshness.

From my chest, a surge of dark mist plows out of me, laced with silver starlight and flecked with deep purple. Pulled endlessly from my aura, a vaporous cloud of my darkness encircles us, drowning out the wails from below.

The sound of a large wave crashing over us pulls the wind around our bodies as my dark mist envelopes us, transporting us to Kai's bedroom and dissolving instantly.

My heart hammers in my chest as I stare at with wide eyes at Kai. She puts her hands on her knees, breathing deeply before tilting her head to look at me.

"Portal Wands don't work down here. Did you just use a Dark Portal?"

"I think so." I answer with a shaky breath.

****

"In an astonishing turn of events, the citizens of Anchorage, Alaska, witnessed its first documented sighting of a man undergoing a mind-boggling metamorphosis, shifting into a giant polar bear. Eyewitnesses were left awestruck as the extraordinary transformation unfolded, blurring the lines between reality and the extraordinary."

I flip to a new channel for another mortal news report giving another Breaking Report on the upheaval Ares is causing as I sit on the edge of Kai's bed. She morphed back into herself, her clothes shifting along with her form in a remarkable metamorphosis.

"Bystanders captured the spectacle on their smartphones as the man's body underwent a seemingly impossible change. Scientists and authorities are racing to investigate this unparalleled phenomenon, seeking answers to the extraordinary questions this unprecedented event raises. On the heels of the last few days, when most of the world's superpowers are struggling in the aftermath of the mass assassination, none of us can know what future awaits us."

The next channel plays a report of a leopard-Shifter in the middle of London.

France is reeling as one of their leaders was included in the assassination. The citizens are rebelling against their government's orders for lockdown and have stormed the streets. The Eiffel Tower has become the epicenter for their gathering as they set the city ablaze.

The next was a woman in China interviewed about a water buffalo turning up in her neighbor's home before it burst through the walls and ran off.

Russia, Germany, and most of the countries of the Middle East have gone radio silent. No communication is coming in or out of the countries, and allied forces begin lining the borders of the quiet countries.

The last image seen from Russia was of two giant bear-Shifters standing on each side of the Russian President as he steps up to a podium and prepares to make a speech to his nation. The satellites were shut off, and Russia closed its doors to the world.

Riots are breaking out in South America as a hoard of big cat Shifters of all breeds run at full speeds through glass windows of ransacked grocery stores.

Every channel is flooded with cell phone and security camera footage of people in city streets or sitting in restaurants Shifting into animals. Police and National Security teams have been dispatched everywhere. Many of the Shifters were shot so many times they were finally weakened enough to be taken into custody.

Ares' plan to upturn the realm into pandemonium is working perfectly. Timing the assassinations just before Mabon was to serve as a distraction from the few Lycan Shifters who may have risked exposure by not coming to the underworld.

What Ares didn't count on was my subconscious turning that plan on its end by uncovering Demeter's corruption of the Shifters and transforming thousands of them to their true form. And Lucas splitting with the Shifters loyal to him.

I stop on a channel and stare at the screen in awe of the videos playing from around the world. Amid the chaos, a beautiful weather phenomenon is bringing the northern lights to all corners of the globe.

"Scientists are baffled at this natural wonder, last recorded during the times of Ancient Greece by one of the world's most well-known philosophers, Plato. For over two decades, the Northern Lights were seen world-wide in the night sky, baffling the academic."

"Interesting fact, Diane." The camera cuts to a news anchor broadcasting outside. The amazing blue lights swaying in the sky above him. "Ancient cultures either saw the lights as a good omen, that Odin and his warriors were celebrating. Others however, warned the lights in the sky were a herald of pestilence and war. Often times, a fire in the sky, caused by a vengeful god."

As the news continues, I watch the lights and dream of a beacon from a lover, forever spending their lonely nights searching for their lost love. The notion is so ridiculously romantic, I blink and shake my head to rid myself of the fantasy.

My anxiety is edging me closer to the door as I move from sitting at the edge of Kai's bed, bouncing my knee to pacing the room and biting my nail until finally, I'm standing with my hand on the door before I realize it.

She stands, and the facade of Foxtrot, a low-level pack member of Gabriel's new pack, slides over her body.

"I can't bring you with me this time, Kai. It's too dangerous, and I can't have your life on my conscience too."

Without giving the Beta time to argue, I exit the door and begin down the hallway.

"Made quite a mess of things, huh?" Ares's smoky voice bellows into the empty hall. Only the glow of his fiery eyes light the corner of the tunnel he is occupying.

Ice melts from the crown of my head and rolls down my body.

Demeter

If I have to leech one more godsdamned pigeon-Shifter, I **will vomit.** Ares refuses to give me a stronger Shifter now that everything has turned to shit, blaming me for Nyx and her bleeding heart at the ceremony for the Lycan. Gods, she was powerful.

I wasn't strong enough to hold onto her this time.

I'm eager to replenish my power. I gave too much of myself to fuel Nyx, and as I stare at this strip of white hair in front of my raven locks, I curse my appearance for how much I favor my older sister, Hecate.

Reluctantly, I wrap my vines around the body of another pigeon-Shifter held within the cage and siphon its Immortal lifeforce into myself. My stomach convulses, and my throat quivers as I drop the withered body into the incinerator.

The dust that covers the shoot is the only remnant left of the other twenty that dropped in before this one. My strength is nearly full, but I'll work up a brine to restore myself entirely.

A bang of my metal door slamming shut is my warning of Ares' arrival.

Thick-soled leather boots stomp across the threshold of my door, and a cloud of soot arrives just ahead of the famed God of War.

Pulling Nyx by her hair, she's kicking her feet and grabbing onto Ares' wrists, fighting against his hold. Flinging her toward me, she sprawls across the floor, sliding three feet before coming to a halt.

My vines encircle her, running up her spine and around her neck, locking her hands behind her back and binding her feet together. Suspended above the rocky grey floor, she writhes within the grasp of my climbing plants to no avail.

The more she struggles, the tighter they wind themselves.

My thickest vine, starving from exerting my power, salivates acidic sap out of its three-inch spike, dripping down her cheek. The skin singes, and my vines stuff her mouth with Oleander petals to silence her screams.

Ares crowds her space, spreading his hands on each side of her head, his fingertips heat as his Soul Fire burns her mind.

Squeezing her eyes shut, Nyx cries, choking on the pain as tears leak out of her eyes.

"Why?" Ares demands. "Why did you break their binding spell?"

Nyx can only shake her head back and forth, trapped within the suffocating hold of my plants.

My barb maneuvers to the back of her neck and pierces her skin, digging all three inches of the large thorn into her skin and piercing her spine. It's acidic venom injecting into her, burning away her reality and forcing her to speak the truth.

The veins under her skin blacken as the poison spreads within her, and as it creeps up her face and spreads across her temples, Ares extinguishes his Fire and steps back, panting heavily.

"How did you break the binding spell?" I ask calmly. With his hands on his hips, Ares paces back and forth as Nyx fights against the sap, compelling her to answer truthfully.

My vines unstuff her mouth of petals, and she cries out, choking and gagging now that her mouth is free.

"It wasn't me." She wails. "I didn't do it."

"She's telling the truth." I cock an eyebrow at Ares, who storms up to her and grasps her cheeks between his fingers. He pinches so hard blood runs out of her mouth as her teeth cut the inside of her cheeks.

"I will have your cooperation." He releases her with an angry push of his hand and a final squeeze, making her yelp in pain.

His large hands strikes her across the face, and even I flinch. Again and again, he strikes her. Grunting his anger out with each hit. Five, six, seven times, his slaps turn to punches.

With a final growl, he delivers his strongest hit. His fist aided by his black and orange flames, and he knocks her out of my grasp. Her unconscious body rolls ridiculously to the floor before coming to a stop.

Ares retreats toward the metal door, turning and pointing at me as embers brighten his brown eyes around the iris.

"Turn her mind to mush and get her ready for the arena. Do what you must to control her and find the Caduceus." Ares flings the door open and exits, calling over his shoulder as he walks away. "That is the only relic that matters."

How much worse can things get? Maybe I shouldn't have asked that question when I woke up in the hammock of Lucas's hacienda courtyard. Sleeping outside is the only thing I can do right now to be close to Nyx.

Lucas and I nearly came to blows last night, screaming about ambushing the Underworld and breaking my mate out of there.

He has too much at risk and explains how Ares holds the children of Shifters hostage, forcing their allegiance. Lucas had been under a toxin that prevented him from discussing it previously until Nyx freed him of it during the ceremony.

"And you sent my partner on a wild goose chase around the Underworld to find them and free them?" I screamed into his face last night, slamming him against the wall of his own home by the collar of his shirt. "I swear to the Fates, if she gets hurt or killed because of you, I will incinerate every bone in your body and feed you your own ashes until you choke on them."

Kai returned to the Underworld wearing a disguise and I spent most of the night trying to get to her or connect in her dreams, as I did before.

The wards protecting the Underworld must have strengthened, or perhaps she didn't sleep, because I found no trace of her.

Exiting my room with my hair still damp from my shower and rubbing it vigorously with a towel, Achilles is leaning against a pillar with an arm crossed over his chest and sipping a cup of steaming coffee.

Tipping it to me with a raise of his eyebrows, he offers me a greeting, "We have guests."

"I don't care if this is your packhouse, Zeta, I have an order from the Mortal Counsel. You will turn over Hermes and your Beta for questions." The shrill voice of my former Headmistress filters in from the courtyard.

"Goddess, help us all," I mumble, turning to offer Lucas some backup from Eris.

"I don't have to do shit the Mortal Counsel orders."

Achilles and I grin at his response as we stalk through the home. *Lucas is going to get along just fine with us.*

"Well, good morning, Headmistress." I offer my former leader a far too cheerful tone and oozing with sarcasm. She presses her lips in a thin line of irritation, and her two guards immediately start for me with cuffs in hand.

A quick flare of my Light Shield pulses, and I raise my hand in warning at their approach. "We're not doing that again."

My Light radiates through them like a wave, and they pause, looking back at Eris for orders. Soundwaves of annoyance emit from her as she attempts to use her ability of Sonus to coax me into submission. Her tactics of persuasion at the Sonus elemental ability of sound have never been effective on me, so I cock my eyebrow at her and put my hands on my hips.

Feeling the immersive hold of Hypnos' Sonus element compared to hers is like comparing a child blowing out a candle to Callie's hurricanes. Chuckling to myself, I recall the day my mother beat Eris's challenge at Delphi and think the Council must have awarded her Headmistress from pity alone.

"Eris, I'm sure this is unnecessary." Atlas rises from the patio table, wiping his mouth with a tan cloth napkin and washing down the remnants of his breakfast with a gulp of coffee.

Relief bathes me in warmth, seeing my mentor here. It's only been a little over a week, but it feels like ages since I've really talked with him about what's been going on. His visit on the night Rhea was taken was brief, and I was in no state then.

Atlas nods at me, remaining a few feet away and standing next to Eris.

"We need to talk," I tell him in his mind as he turns to Lucas.

"Indeed, we do." He answers me before speaking to Lucas politely. "With the events of last night's ceremony and the news outlets going crazy, the Council just has questions. Is your Beta around?"

"Many of my pack have dispersed to help with Lycan that were caught off-guard by last night's *transformation*." Lucas is smart to keep the truth from Eris. "I'll be happy to go in her absence. Surely the answers from the King of the Shifters hold more weight than his trusted Beta."

"Of course. The Council presumed you would be busy helping your people." Atlas looked at Eris with raised eyebrows.

Exchanging looks with her guards, they nod once at her and resume their fixed stares on me. I assume she's given them a message through telepathy that the rest of us are not privy to. I'm prepared for any sudden action, in case they are planning to ambush me.

"Atlas, I'm needed in Washington, DC. I'll entrust you to get them to the Council." She gives Lucas a long look up and down his body with her cold eyes, her mouth turning to its perpetual frown. The frigid pillar of discontent walks out of the courtyard with her guards, and they teleport outside the front door. I release a held breath and my shoulders release their tension.

"Have I got some news for you?" I tell Atlas as soon as Eris vanishes, and we huddle together in the courtyard. Callie emerges from the hacienda, and stands with Achilles, her arms crossed over her chest.

Atlas notices her tension, but he would never call it out in front of others, but I can see it bothers him that she doesn't greet him.

He listens closely, pushing his gold glasses up on his nose with his middle finger as I report the visit to Avalon, the shadow being that attacked Ana and Ava, and the ceremony last night. Mor and Hypnos emerge as I reveal the presence of Erebus.

"Truly?" He rubs his chin between his thumb and forefinger as he raises his eyebrows that disappear beneath his messy brown hair. "A Titan."

His eyes glaze over as he loses himself in thought. Likely a million ideas and questions are running through his mind.

"I have news of my own." He shakes his head as if clearing his mind and looks cautiously to the second and third floors of the packhouse as Shifters go about their morning. "I talked to Hecate about Flora."

"Has *Michael* figured out there was a jailbreak yet?"

"He has, and he's *unhappy*." Atlas chuckles, and knowing how much Atlas despises the Council, I can only imagine what kind of exchange the Archangel had when it was discovered.

"I think Eris knows more about what happened the night Athena was killed than she is letting on," Atlas says in hushed tones.

"Why?" Callie asks, pain still in her eyes at what happened to her friend but curiosity piquing her interest. Atlas visibly relaxes now that my sister has acknowledged him, even if it is a cold greeting.

"Hecate asked a Sensor to check Flora out after you all left her cave. They found traces of Oleander and Wolfsbane, as well as the Hemlock potion Flora made for herself that wiped her memories."

Lucas steps forward, his face blazing at the mention of the two potions Demeter uses to control the Shifters. "That is Demeter's calling card."

"She could have been poisoned without knowing it." Callie's voice is nearly a whisper, and her large round eyes look off toward the tiles of the hacienda floor. "Could she have eaten it Lucas? If someone put it on her food, could she have ingested it that way?"

"Absolutely. It's tasteless and odorless. Demeter has perfected her recipe and it's streamed into the waters that feed the Underworld. It's in everything the Shifters consume. It's how she's kept us so pliant all these ages."

"Someone must have poisoned her dinner." Callie's face turns white as she thinks about the events of that night. "Zephyr and Flora get up early with the livestock and tend to the crops before it gets too hot. They would have eaten early so they could get to bed."

It makes perfect sense.

Achilles rubs Callie's back as she leans into him. Her eyes are back on the tiles as she keeps thinking.

"I'd bet a decade of night shifts that Flint was working the cafeteria line that night," he says.

Callie gasps, "No, he wasn't. But Terra was." Her eyes well with tears; Achilles pulls her into his chest. His large arms nearly engulf her as she releases her sorrow.

Callie and Terra were pulled out of the same dirt bunker the night we rescued Callie from Ares; the night she met Achilles. Callie has always had a soft spot for Terra, and Terra always kept her heart hardened. My sister never stopped trying to melt Terra's icy blockade and befriend her.

Flora's brief stay at the Labyrinth nearly killed her. Who knows how much longer she would have lasted if Hecate had not rescued her. To think of Terra staging this on someone as tender as Flora angers all of us.

"Hermes, Terra left us after helping me deliver the books for Rhea's surprise library." Callie's voice breaks as she sucks in a sob. "She left to go poison Flora."

"Did Terra leave your sight during the trip to the bookstore?" I ask her with urgency coursing through my voice. "No, not once."

"Then she either already had it on her or got it later that day," I conclude.

"I came to the same conclusion, Callie." Atlas flicks his eyes to hers and then back at the ground. She looks at him with a subtle squint.

"Why, Atlas?" Callie's asks quietly, and Achilles releases his embrace. She turns to face the man that is just as familiar to us as our own father, and the pain in her eyes pulls the regret from Atlas. His shoulders drop, and he relaxes his strained brow.

"It was an assembly line of interrogations." He tells us. "I was sharing the memories of a dozen elementals at a time while the Sensors looked them over. The Headmistress was present with her guards. As soon as the tower to the Coat was seen in her memories, the guards took her and Flora was walking into the Labyrinth within a minute."

"Who took her?" I ask. Something is not adding up. She should have been presented to the Council first and given a chance for innocence.

"Archangel Michael retrieved her himself."

"Why would Michael come for something like this?" Callie asks.

"And there is no way that pretty boy can get anywhere in a moment's notice. He takes ages to ready himself to go anywhere. Michael knew Eris would need him ahead of time or he was already there." I scoff.

"Exactly." Atlas points his finger at me as if I were still a student under his tutelage and have given him a correct answer in class. "Flora should have had representation and a petition in front of the Council before sentencing." Atlas pushes his glasses up on his nose. A habit more than anything else. "They hid her away in there as quickly as possible."

He turns back to Callie, who is still visibly upset. Tears flow down her cheeks, and she refuses to look at him. Atlas has always had a soft spot for Callie. Maybe he wanted a daughter of his own, but he has never been able to tell her no. Seeing her upset is always his breaking point.

"Who do you think told Hecate she was there?" Atlas takes her shoulders, turning her to him. She pinches her eyebrows together at his revelation.

"You sent Hecate to the Labyrinth for Flora?" Her shaky voice cracks with a ring of hope, raising the pitch at the end of her question. Atlas gives her a flat smile.

"Of course, I sent the very Architect of the immortal prison to find Flora. Who else could get her out quickly? Hecate knows every secret of every layer."

Callie's composure crumbles, and she covers her face as she sobs. Atlas wraps his arms around her, and her shoulders wrack as she cries. She's been so upset with Atlas for letting them take her friend away when we all know there is no possibility Flora could do such things.

I think back to the moment we learned of our father's death when he confronted Ares.

Atlas was the one who told us, and he held Callie just like this. It seemed to last for hours, and he never moved until she was ready. He's stayed by our sides ever since.

Callie sniffles and pulls away. The light returns to her blue eyes, and she gives him a small smile as Achilles hands her a handkerchief.

Shoving his hands in his pockets, Atlas shuffles on his feet. Public displays of affection tend to make him uncomfortable. He's not big on touching and prefers to be in the company of his books more than anything else. Only me, my sister, or a sense of duty can pull him out of his bookshelves.

"I can only determine Eris is working against us." He squares his shoulders as he confirms what I have long accused. He's always believed in the better side of people. Always felt anyone could be redeemed. Even as he flips through their memories and can see every true intention, he thinks there is good in everyone buried somewhere inside.

But I don't believe that. Some people are too far gone down paths of evil to be saved.

"She refuses to act against the coming tensions, and she leaves for days at a time." Atlas takes a fresh cup of coffee from Lucas, taking a loud sip of the black, steaming caffeine before continuing. "Shifters and mortals are going missing by the droves. Rival countries are testing weapons near the borders of their enemies as the panic to replace slain leaders, and fleets of naval vessels converge off coastlines. Ares is priming the realm for another war of the mortals." He concludes.

"How can we prove her loyalty is faulty? Get her striped of her position and sent to the Labyrinth?" I ask.

"We need to know how the attack on the Atlanta Commune happened and that she helped."

"How long ago did the attack happen?" Hypnos asks as Mor stands next to him with a large bowl of chopped fruit in her grasp. She pierces a bright orange cantaloup chunk, and it disappears into her mouth.

"Nearly two weeks." Callie answers.

Hypnos raises his eyes to the skies as if running calculations in his mind.

"I can trace it." He nods.

"How?" Atlas asks with intrigue, brightening his brown eyes.

"I have the power of Sensory and have watched the moon's cycles on this realm. Time moves faster here, but the Echoes should still linger another few weeks."

"You have Empathic Echoes? Amazing. That is quite powerful." Atlas' eyebrows disappear under his brunette hair.

"He's fucking powerful," Mor says, taking a break before popping a green grape into her mouth.

"Very good!" Achilles smiles. "See, *that* is the right way to use that word."

Callie chuckles and shakes her head back and forth.

"You're teaching her to cuss?" I huff.

My old friend looks at me plainly as if offended I would ask. "Yes." He answers me pointedly.

Atlas places the empty coffee cup on the metal table and claps his hands together. Either the caffeine has given him a spurt of energy, or an idea has.

"That settles it. Achilles and Calypso take them back to the Atlanta Commune and see what Hypnos can see from the night of the attack."

Hypnos nods, accepting his orders. Atlas turns to me with a twinkle adding a gleam to his brown eyes.

"Want to go piss off the Mortal Council?"

⁂

A lower-powered Immortal woman walks us through the marbled halls, and her heels click, bouncing off the flat surfaces. She eyes Lucas with fluttering lashes, but he is taking in the ornate artwork and intricate carvings that line our path with his hands in his pockets, his eyes darting from piece to piece while his mouth gapes in amazement.

The Council sits within the deep recesses of the Vatican. Their archives have always been a point of contention for Atlas, who has accused some of the surviving works from Alexandria are within their vaults. However, the Council has always denied it.

After the destruction of Alexandria, The Vatican collection was established to store the important writings and history of the world. Mortal and Immortal alike. The Immortal, Pan, is a powerful Sonus and Life Elemental.

He has watched over the archive entrance for so long that he eventually took root. Literally like a tree, Pan has remained affixed to a throne made of marble as he scans the realm and records the events his elemental powers detect.

Saint Peter's Basilica was built around him, then much later. They erected the walls around the Vatican City to fend off Aphrodite and her fleets of Water Elementals when she attempted a breach the archive.

The Mortal Council formed eons ago after the mortal race drowned in a flood. Determined never to let the mortals suffer extinction because of our battling, the Council sits in the center of the realm, and serves as the judge, jury, and executioners for Immortals that compromise the rules enacted. Any being called by the Council must meet here, since Pan is literally part of the foundation.

Except Ares, of course, who remains hidden away in his well-hidden commune under the realm's deep waters, refusing the call of any being in this realm.

Callie, Achilles, and Medusa should be well into their examination of the Atlanta Commune, and I'm anxious to hear what Hypnos finds.

The wards that surround Vatican City stifle your power and makes you feel a thousand pounds heavier. Goddess only knows what tragedies could occur while we are under their interrogation, and I would feel much more at ease if I could make a quick exit.

As we walk, I test my Light abilities by sending Atlas a sudden Mirage of the great dragon Titan of Light, with her mouth open wide and her gleaming gold teeth ready to take a bite out of him. To my amusement, he startles and casts me an irritated gaze before mouthing, *"Careful"*.

Using too much power will trip the wards. While breaking the Mortal Council's security alarm may not be enough for the Labyrinth, they could certainly restrain you for a month or two within the Vatican chambers.

The extravagance and grandeur of the Council chambers is more ostentatious than the long walk that delivers us to the interior where the Council meets.

Surrounded by white marble and gilded carvings, the Council room is cold and stark with incredibly high ceilings and tall marble carvings.

Along the Council table, Circe sits to the right of Pan as the Council member for the Witches and his mate. Her long arm is draped around his shoulder as she sets her martini glass down. Her brunette locks bounce across the middle of her back as she positions her body for the three of us entering the Council chamber.

A large amount of her porcelain skin is displayed as the red stola draping her plunges deeply between her sternum, and a slit in the front showcases her lean legs and part of her bare hip. Taking the skewer with a fat green olive, she makes a show of rolling it along her tongue before it dives into her mouth. She has her eyes pinned on me as Lucas, Atlas, and I are delivered to the opposite side of the table.

The lower-level Elemental clicks out of the room, closing two imposing double doors behind her. The bang echoes around the marbled chamber.

Pan is an odd-looking Elemental by the standards of Gaea, and its mortals. Nearing eight feet tall when standing, he now sits endlessly on a marble throne. His skin has turned a creamy white color that matches the tiles. All pigment has been leeched by the ages devoid of sunlight as he sits below the surface of the Vatican City, watching the entrance of the archives as its eternal sentry.

Gold covers the bark of his Ironwood Armor formed around his body. Once strong and nearly impenetrable, it now looks like the peeling white bark of a birch tree. The decorative armor twists into an intricate chest piece with forearm and shin coverings woven together like twisting vines. With a groin covering, the armor serves as *clothing* in the presence of the mortal.

His eyes are black voids, much like the eyes Rhea possessed during the ceremony when the dark abyss of her gaze fell upon me as she was losing consciousness. His Sonus Element constantly scans the realm, listening.

His Life Element flows from him, creating roots and vines, acting as scribes. Dozens of barbs secrete black ink from their tips like feathered quills onto a thin roll of parchment that seems to flow endlessly from Pan.

Gods knows where it begins, and frankly, I'm too afraid of the answer to inquire.

He took up the charge to replace the Library of Alexandria when it was destroyed. Or at least when we thought it was destroyed. Perhaps I should more accurately say since my mate protected it under a massive Mirage.

The pretentious Archangels of Hel can never be bothered to arrive on time, so Michaels's seat is empty until he sees fit to grace us with his presence. And, of course, there is no space given to a Shifter or Vampire on the Council. The Shifters being loyal to Ares is understandable, but there is no reason for the Vampires to be without a seat other than the fact their leader has no use for the politics of this realm.

The double doors behind us fling open with a bang. Lucas pivots in a blink as Archangel Michael stomps through the grand Council room toward the table. A cloak of golden thread is affixed across his shoulders, and it billows in the wake of his large steps. An all-white uniform with gold accents radiates with the pompous sense of entitlement the blonde Infernal carries into the room.

"Let's get this over with." Michael grumbles.

"Oh, thank the Titans, you're here. We can begin now." I attempt to put as much dreariness into my tone as my face washes over with contempt.

Michael glares at me as he continues his wide gait to his seat.

Atlas cuts me a side glance.

"Ah, ah, Atlas." Circe clicks her tongue at him. "You know telepathy is forbidden within the Council." The wards Circe weaves around the Vatican trigger her when one is attempting to be broken. I'm curious if she caught my small Mirage in the hallway.

She stands, pulling the red stola of draped fabric up as she steps around the table. With bare feet and red-manicured toes, she pads across the marble floor. Thin gold bangles clink as she sways her arm. Reaching Atlas, she rubs her hand up his chest and grasps his chin. Her deep red nails, filed to points, dig into his skin before she releases him with a jostle.

She sways to me next. Her breasts rub against my sternum as she steps into me, breathing in deeply as she takes her time trailing her eyes up my body to my face. I keep my eyes ahead, fixed on a carved marble pillar.

"How is your Uncle Odysseus?"

"Still happy with his partner. I know how that disappoints you," I answer her blandly. Her games are tiresome.

"I can share."

"Unfortunately, I don't think Penelope can. Least not with you, that is." I give her a curt not and expressionless smile to dismiss her.

She sets her path for Lucas, circling her prey, looking for the best place to strike.

"Mmmm, the King of the Shifters." She licks her lips, salivating as she looks him over, her eyes appreciating the view. Lucas tenses as his jaw muscles flex. "I've had many kings before, but never a Shifter, can you believe it?"

Lucas doesn't answer, knowing she is only goading him. Her overtly sexual advances are her ammunition with men to have them eating from the palm of her hand while she weaves her spells of obsession into them. Makes them fawn and lust after her so she can devour their attention and feast on the power of rejecting them. All while getting them to do her bidding with the promise of tasting her fruits and false promises.

"Tell me," Her hand begins at the top of his shoulder and slowly trails down his chest, heading toward his stomach. "Is it true Shifters can *partially* transform? At will?"

He still ignores her, but she is treading close to the end of his patience.

"Even *certain* body parts?" Her hand continues down his abdomen. She turns her palm as her clawed fingers near his waistband.

Lucas snaps his grasp around Circe's wrist and twists it away.

"I'm spoken for." He growls.

Circe's cackle bounces around the room as she steps into him.

"No, you're not." She smells him by lifting on the balls of her feet and taking a deep breath close to his neck. She arches her back as she elongates her neck as if trying to tempt him. "But I'm more than happy to be mounted, your highness."

I can't help but snort a laugh through my nose—your *highness.*

Lucas is finding it less amusing than I am as he cuts a glare at me. "No, thanks."

"Sit down, Circe." Michael removes white gloves one finger at a time and discards them to the marble table with a plop. "Some of us have actual work to get back to. The Labyrinth requires constant supervision."

She lets her heavy-lidded eyes linger on Lucas as she turns and returns to her place. Sitting on the armrest of Pan's chair, he places a hand on her leg and strokes the skin of her inner thigh.

"Constant supervision, you say?" I look blandly at the angel, and his thick brow carries his contempt for my lack of regard for his position on the Council.

"Yes."

"Who supervised it when you left to retrieve a Life Elemental a few weeks ago?"

"I believe you are the one under inquiry today." He smiles. "You know I've always saved room for you, H. I'm hoping I'll be bringing you for a stay in my Labyrinth today."

Pan's eyes shift from all-black to all-white, and the barbs stop their scribing. With his attention fully on us, he finally speaks. "Quiet." His booming voice echoes through the marbled walls and crawls up the carved pillars as he glares at Michael. "My questions were for the Herald but there is something unique about you, Zeta."

Pan tilts his head back and forth, appearing very bird-like as he studies Lucas. One of his vines delivered a rolled-up parchment from within the archives that sit behind him. Unrolling it, Pan looks over the words scribed as he addresses Lucas.

"You were a mortal, turned Shifter, but I sense the long-dead essence of Fenrir within you. How is this possible?"

Michael's spine stiffens, and he lays a heavy glare at Lucas. I sense his Light aura passing over Lucas like an X-Ray. The judgment passing over his eyes pisses me off, like he finds Lucas undeserving of the power. Perhaps he would have liked it for himself.

I make a point to turn my attention to Michael fully. He meets my stare with one of his own before cocking an eyebrow and turning back to Pan, feigning boredom.

Michael and I come from the same realm, loyal to the same great Titan of Light. During the battle of Hel, the Archangels aligned with Chaos and helped him defeat the great cosmic dragon Theia, consuming her power, except Michael. He was one of the few Archangels that didn't fight with Chaos, but he also didn't protect Theia.

As Chaos and the Angels scorched the realm, the dragons fled, scattering to Tartarus, and Michael fled with them. In the aftermath, he rounded up most of the Angels, and imprisoned them within the Labyrinth of Gaea, where he serves today as its overseer.

His desire for power and self-preservation makes him untrustworthy.

"It occurred many years ago. The memory of my transformation was blocked until a few nights ago."

"How can a mortal survive absorbing the power of a Titan and keep it hidden from my Sonus?" Pan's eyes turn black again, and the barbs resume their vigorous scratches across the endless stream of parchment.

"Maybe the Immortal who transferred the power kept you from hearing it." I offer. My stomach begins twisting in knots.

"Impossible. Nothing can be kept from my knowledge."

"Except this, apparently," I smile politely. "And everything that Ares has been doing to sabotage the peace of this realm for—oh, I don't know, how many Great Years?"

"You will mind your tone with me. I was the apprentice of the Titan Themis, Lady Justice."

"That explains a lot, actually, and yet, at the same time, nothing at all." I drop as much sarcasm into my reply as possible.

A sheen of sweat forms on my brow as the knots in my stomach flare. I clench my abdomen and tighten my jaw.

"Did you sense the Titan of the Shadow realm lurking around Gaea also, or did that slip through your branches as well?" I growl, my voice barely above a whisper over the rush of pain waving over me. My body is aching with an undulating muscle spasms.

"There are no Titans residing on Gaea." Pan snaps. The barbs of his vines stop their unremitting scribing and flare toward us in a warning.

"Is that so? What am I, then? A giant piece of cow shit?" Lucas steps once toward the table.

In less than a blink, Michael lashes out with a gold chain of Light, intending to ensnare Lucas and restrain him. My own blue whip flicks his away, and I tilt my head. With raised eyebrows, I scold him like a child.

"Now, kids, let's play nice." I look at each of the Council members in turn. My eyes set to take in each of their positions, should I need to act.

"A Lurker was taken off the back of one of Medusa's generals." Atlas chimes in with his even voice and calm presence. "Surely that was transcribed, Pan? I was not present and would like to review the report."

"The Archives are confidential." Pan and Atlas share the same look of contempt as their cool expression do little to hide their irritation with one another.

"And the record of Flora's trial. May we petition to see that?"

"The actions of the Council do not require a full trial for each infraction." Pan counters.

"And how *just* would Themis find that? To throw an innocent Elemental into the pits of despair without a single question."

Pan narrows his dark gaze, and Circe smiles wickedly with a Cheshire grin. "State your inquiry, Mage."

"Who was in the room with Athena when you listened to her choke on her own soul burning inside her body?" Atlas turns into the calculating Mage that sets up a careful chess game to lead his opponent into defeat.

He turns to Circe. "I recall your Greek Fire burns an Immortal very similarly to a Flames Soul Fire, Circe."

"What are you accusing?" Pan spits as the barbs from his vines grow into eight-inch thorns of death—black poison leaks from their tips in anticipation of secreting within our skins.

"Where is the transcription of the Goddess of War's murder, Pan?" Atlas says each word slowly.

Circe leans further against Pan with a devilish gleam in her dark eyes and a wide smile like the cat that got the cream. Pans deep set eyes cut hard at Atlas as he returns the sentiment, anger and distrust etched on both faces.

"Either Circe killed Athena, and you are protecting your mate, or Ares killed her, and you are protecting him."

"Bold claim, but how far did you have to leap to come to those conclusions, Mage?"

"No leap at all when the Minister of the Labyrinth comes to retrieve someone for disabling a shield within a second's notice when the brutal murder of someone we all respected went ignored."

Pan doesn't answer, and their stand-off continues as Michael looks at his filed fingernails as if bored.

"You valued her strategy and cunning at one time." Atlas' voice lowers and a frown pulls the corners of his mouth downward. "Did you even feel a hint of sorrow as you listened?" Atlas' brown eyes narrow as he keeps them trained tightly on the Sonus who can't deny the claims Atlas is making. "Listened, and did nothing.'

A powerful Mind Mage, only Atlas's sense of morality and Circe's strong wards keep him from diving into their minds and unfolding every secret. Should Pan ever venture out of his marble tomb of archives, I'd be first in line to watch their challenge.

My stomach jolts, and I double over, wrapping my arm around my abdomen, hoping to alleviate the pain. A sense of dread washes over me as I begin to feel as though I haven't the will to move, or think, or feel. My mind feels like it's been drowned in a vat of inky darkness, and it clouds my vision.

My sword necklace dangles on its silver chain, swinging back and forth, and I clutch it tight within my hand to keep me centered.

Where is this coming from?

Lucas turns back to me, concern showing on his pinched brow at my state of discomfort. I try to stand again from my hunched position as I understand the source of my pain and grimace as I speak through clinched teeth.

"Rhea has left the Underworld."

I **feel like I'm dead inside.** Nothing more than a hollow ghost animating a body.

I'm standing in front of a metal reflective wall within an expansive greenhouse. A thorn, brown and several inches in length with a wide base, is buried in the side of my neck. The green vine connected to it undulates as it pumps me full of noxious venom.

I feel the point of entry boiling as thick sap coats the inside of my body. I try to lift my arm and pull it out, but my arm doesn't move. My heart doesn't even react by beating faster at the discovery as I wake from an apparent slumber.

My mind is empty, an expansive void where the beginning of time meets the end of time and becomes nothing.

I am nothing.

I have no other option but to stare at myself.

Like a puppet placed in a chair and waiting for its master, my head lolls to the side as my eyes stay open, unable to blink. Drool streams slowly out of my partially open mouth as a woman with short dark curls dresses me.

Putting me in a deep purple dress, like the color of plums, she pulls my hair from under the garment, letting my long locks fall behind me.

I see tall stalks of corn behind me and hanging baskets above my head with all manner of flowers growing within them. Small carnivorous flytraps rear back and flail toward me, snapping their jaws with poisonous spikes, missing me by inches.

Demeter.

Aunt. Avalon. Trustworthy.

The words float into my head with my voice, but I didn't think them.

As I search the empty cavern of my memory on where I am or how I got here, I realize I don't even know my name. As the realization enters my mind, a name filters through the air to me: *Persephone.*

While some part of me connects with this name, it's as if the relationship to this identity is foreign to me. As if Persephone is a stranger like someone I used to know intimately but lost touch with.

Putting her hands on each side of my shoulders, Demeter turns me to lace up the sandals that run midway up my calf.

When she pivots me, a vision flashes within my blank mind of myself opening a door and seeing a pair of glowing orange eyes in a tunnel. A sense of repetition heats me as flashes of that same event occur repeatedly like a strobe light behind my eyelids.

I'm seemingly stuck on a loop, playing through the broken fragment of an event that has occurred many times before.

Searching my mind for the answers to what pulled me into the greenhouse, each moment I come close to, runs away from me.

With another flash, I feel a great pain at the crown of my head as a firm hand holds my hair tightly and pulls me along a stone ground. I see my feet scraping the floor, trying to add resistance, and I feel my nails digging into the wrist of the person dragging me.

In the present moment, Demeter stands with her hands on her hips, wearing a deep navy stola cinched at her waist with a silver belt. "Ares is busy dealing with the mortal President of Russia tonight. So, you will appear at the Arena in his absence."

Memories of past exhibitions in the ancient gladiator rings flash like turning channels of a television.

I can clench my jaw at the needless violence but otherwise my body remains unable to move. I suspect this venom has removed my thoughts and memories, replacing them with the will of Demeter.

The blue dress brings another flash into my mind as a pair of sapphire eyes gaze into mine. They belong to a handsome man, and a name echoes within my brain.

Hermes.

The name enters my mind and is instantly pushed out the side as the toxin runs across my mind, coating it in a cool, thick gel until I can no longer remember it anymore.

Demeter squints her dark eyes at me. "You'll do as your partner tells you and will not cause any scenes tonight. You nearly tore society apart, so this is the least you can do."

I'm curious about who my partner is as my mind has trouble forming even a simple thought until the images are forced behind my eyes.

A red-haired man, tall and of average appearance, looks at me in my mind.

Flint.

An eerie chill runs up my body when I see wisps of darkness mingle with his indistinct orange aura. Some innate power within me assesses his abilities and knows he is a low-powered Fire Mage. That part of me also knows he is *not* my partner.

At least no partner determined by fate so perhaps we entered a partnership willingly. Though, based on the way he carries himself and the cruel look in his eyes, I can't imagine that would be the case.

Demeter's barb extracts itself from my neck, and the fire running down my spine's length steals all the air in my lungs. She turns and heads toward the thick metal door with the end of her blue stola waving after her.

I have a strong and uncontrollable urge to follow her, and my body robotically walks after her. My spine is abnormally straight, and my arms hang still at my side. It is as if her retreating form is a magnet pulling me along with her and I have no say in the matter.

After a few minutes of mechanical walking through the turns and tunnels of this underground cavern, more recollections seep into my mind. Some memories feel as involuntary as my forced gait, following after Demeter, and others enter my mind as a soft caress of wind that runs like fingers through my hair.

I catalog which voice gives me the answers. The mechanical answers are likely lies and those gentle responses are the truth.

This internal knowing will help break me from the custody of this poison.

Demeter stops in front of a door, rapping her knuckles three times. Flint emerges, just as I saw him in my mind, wearing a deep green button-down and adjusting the sleeves to fold them partially up his arm.

You love him. You love him. You love him.

It's like a broken record playing, but I'm not the one who dropped the needle to the vinyl to play the track. While the internal voice repeats the phrase, my soul feels no connection to it, as if it were a thought inserted inside me and foreign.

"So, she'll do anything I want?" He asks as he looks me up and down. An heir of superiority and hatred coats his cold eyes.

"Yes." Demeter answers dryly as she resumes her walk, heading toward a portal at the end of the hall.

Flint pulls my face to him, pinching my chin between his fingers. Craning his neck down, he whispers, "You shouldn't have left me chained to the bed with your power. We're going to have so much fun later." Then he kisses me, shoving his cold tongue in my mouth, and it writhes around like a worm partially exposed from the soil.

Nothing, I feel nothing.

The poison has numbed my body and dulled my mind, and every moment before seeing my reflection is gone. If this is my partner, I should rejoice at his presence; I should melt under his touch, and his kiss should revive my soul.

This man is not mine, and I am not his.

It's as if I just popped into existence within the last few moments. I try to push my mind back further, before my hand turned a doorknob, before I was pulled down a hall by my hair. The only thing there is a bleak, foggy ravine of emptiness.

"I do love this mouth." He purrs at me as he brushes his thumb across my bottom lip. "We have a few minutes before the Arena, right Demeter?"

Over my dead body.

Perhaps I am in no state to defend myself, but I will find a way to break through this spell and regain my freedom from the poisonous chains encasing me.

"Don't start your shit with me, and let's go."

As we near a dark portal at the end of the hall, a man stands, eyeing me with grave concern, hiding carefully within the tight lines of his creased forehead. His oxblood aura swirling in constant fluctuation.

"Trust the Chameleon." The Wind whispers into my mind.

❧ ☙

Under the great pyramid of Kukulkan, hollowed out from long dried cenotes, Earth Elementals have excavated and shaped a vast underground arena for spectating the brutal and deadly gladiator fights of Ancient Rome.

A dark portal delivers us to the underground arena, and the crowd's cheers create a low roar that is so loud it seems quiet.

Wide limestone steps lead up to an observation booth like you would see at a sporting arena. Packed with people, food, and liquor, a large glass window shows the fighting arena.

Flint walked ahead and is already inside. When our eyes meet, a fleeting darkness coats his face quickly as he tilts his head back and swallows an amber liquor in a single gulp from a simple crystal glass. The look is a reminder of his plans to take advantage of my incapacitation, however, I will not be giving him the satisfaction.

The index finger on my left-hand moves slightly through an exhaustive effort and insurmountable concentration. I barely graze the hand of the chameleon and they hide their reaction well.

"What happened to you?" He asks in my mind, though the voice is that of a woman. I understand the reference of the chameleon now. This person can morph into other forms and is wearing a disguise.

I'm unable to respond as my thoughts seem to push against a dark barrier at the crown of my head, acting like a ceiling and keeping everything in.

As with the answers to my own questions that seemed to float into my mind from the Wind, I focus on the tendrils of air that surround us and sweat forms on my brow as I work against the toxins within me.

Like silver satin ribbons, I see the current of Wind meandering around us.

A man stands with a woman, wearing all red. The couple stares at me with hate in their heated gaze. As they walk toward Flint, their bodies push through the silver ribbons of shining air.

Gabriel, asshole. Lexi, bigger asshole.

The currents of air swirl and spiral out of the couple's path, and I beacon the Wind toward me. As if my words were spelled out on my hands, I pass the Wind from myself and envision it traveling into the chameleon's ear, whispering my reply.

"They've poisoned me. I can't remember anything. I don't even know who you are."

"Fuck." The chameleon wipes their hand down their face as they blow out their cheeks in a huff. *"I'm Kai. I shapeshifted into a man as a disguise."*

As I roll their name around my mind, the vision of a woman, with long raven hair and tawny skin appears from the dark fog of my mind.

I'm here to protect you. I recall them saying as their appearance morphs between the man next to me and the woman from my memory.

"Do you know what you were poisoned with? Maybe I can find the antidote."

"It was a large thorn from a vine that grows out of Demeter." I respond on the Wind.

"Double fuck. That is a venom unique to her, and no remedy exists." Kai answers as we keep communicating between her telepathy and my messages on the Wind. *"You'll just have to wait until it runs it's coarse."*

Like hell I will wait around for that. Goddess knows that could take hours or days. I have no intentions of waiting around to be a puppet on their string, a victim to the wills of Demeter and Flint.

I begin to think of this poison like a virus, trapped inside my body as a foreign contaminant, and maybe heating it like a fever will make it run through faster.

I sift through the Winds and summon the warm currents that run toward the top of the Cenote, hundreds of feet above us. Gliding them around my body and combining them with the exertion of my efforts to work against the paralysis, I sweat.

The size of the fighting arena before us is absolutely gargantuan. The stone-carved stands are full of mortals and immortals alike.

Elite men from the populations are here in their finery, with women stuffed full of plastics. They balance on platform heels that are unforgiving against the uneven floors hewn from the limestone cenotes. Serving as trophies for a night of being showcased, they suck themselves in and elongate their frames while they give each other fake smiles that conceal daggers.

Four circular teleportation pads blend in with the tan sand that covers the Arena floor. Large bolts affixed within thick walls made from dark stone await large beasts to be chained to them.

Demeter walks before me, pausing and leaning toward me to whisper.

"Tonight's fight is your punishment. The next time you get an urge to go against Ares' plan or go snooping around in dark places, just remember he has an endless supply to fuel this arena." She runs her eyes down me, and the animosity practically drips from the scowl on her mouth. "The blood spilled tonight is on your hands."

As she takes her seat, images begin flashing in my mind. Like the words, brought to me on the Winds, I feel the tender caress of them as they rush through my mind, and I believe they are genuine.

I see a field of people, turning to all forms of animals under the white opaline glow of moonlight. I see my outstretched hands, roiling with a powerful black mist that flows endlessly around me. The white moonlight explodes and propels across the globe and the vision stops.

Another image is only a large round vault like one would see in an old bank fashioned out of thick steel a hundred years ago. Only this vault is formed of darkness and obscurity. It pulsates with a heartbeat, like a beacon that begs me to enter and explore it.

Flint sits beside me and puts his calmy hand on my thigh, rubbing high and grazing his finger along my panties. The intrusion makes me grit my teeth, and my blood begins to boil.

When I free myself of this trap, I'm breaking his hand for touching me.

Next to Flint is Gabriel and then Lexi. The lipstick she wears is a slightly less obnoxious shade of red than her stola. Her velvety black hair is nearly purple when the light hits it correctly, and her tan skin shines like she has lathered herself in baby oil.

Leaning forward, she grabs Flint's attention. "Did your little muse blow your mind before the fight?"

Mentally, I roll my eyes at her attempt to irritate me.

Flint chuckles under his breath. "I wish." He mumbles.

"Aw, I didn't know you picked a prude to be your mate. Pity." She smiles at me, showing too many teeth in an obvious ploy to goad me, but she only comes off looking like a baboon more than the viper I think she may be going for.

"My girl can't keep her hands off me." Gabriel croons as he wraps his hand around the back of Lexi's neck and brings her in for a chaste kiss. Her red lipstick smeared around her lips and his. "Swallowed me whole on the way here and took it up against a wall once we arrived."

Her lips curl into a smile and she winks nearly imperceptibly at Flint.

"She'll be full of my pups in no time." Gabriel brags.

Flint shifts in his seat and Lexi pushes her tits out with pride at Gabriel's praise of her.

Looking at me with a serious expression, Flint says loudly, "You should take some notes and learn a thing or two about how to care for your man." Leaning closer, he says the next part loud enough for me alone. "Don't worry; I'll give you a *good* lesson after the fight." He rubs two fingers against my center, the friction stinging me.

I feel my face heat with anger, but I'm locked with the bindings of the poison and can't snap back at Flint or Lexi. The provocation is only helping to burn off the poison, as I can move several fingers on my left hand and my thumb on my right hand.

"GO fuck yourself, Flame?" Kai leans forward and comes to my defense. Pushing Flints hand away from me.

"You can watch how you speak to the son of Ares, *Foxtrot*," Gabriel warns Kai, and the chameleon growls turning back to watch the crowd. Foxtrot must be the identity of her morphed form.

The lights around the Arena dim, and three portals give off a deep purple glow of the Dark power that allows us to Shadow Walk from place to place. The antithesis of the Light portals the other Elementals use.

The crowd quiets, and the lights raise, giving us the first glimpse of tonight's starting fight. An old woman with thin lips and white hair pulled back into a tight bun stands in the center of the Arena.

Eris. Traitor.

She welcomes the spectators of the fight and introduces herself as the sister of Ares. Flint stands and my body moves with him. Like a puppet on a string, something guides me to stay with him and we step to the front of the box.

A bright spotlight shines on us and as the light burns my eyes, the toxin makes me bear it, without squinting or being able to shield myself. A forced grin is plastered on my face as if two phantom fingers pulled my smile open for me.

With one hand around my waist, Flint raises his other hand and waves like a politician, receiving a polite response from the crowd below.

Eris speaks of the games and congratulates us for setting the Shifters free of Lucas's curse, branding him a traitor and fugitive from the God of Wars army.

"That's a lie." Kai sneers in my mind.

Calling a start to the games, Flint looks at me. The control of the toxins within me, turn my head toward his and wrap my arm around his waist. Forced to raise on the tips of my toes, he holds the back of my neck and pulls me into a kiss.

Turning his head and letting his tongue explore my mouth again, the puppeteer controlling my actions makes me return the fervor of his kiss as we appear to be a happy couple.

My stomach turns to knots and ignites a flame within my body. I feel the poison inside me begin to roil with the heat as I decimate myself from the inside. The pain is incredible, but somehow, I've sparked a hidden and deeper power, and I intend to use it.

As Flint's spit dries on my mouth, unable to wipe the disgust he coats me in, I'm forced back to my seat. My eyes alight with my rage as I make eye contact with Kai. Her irritation matches my own.

The arena turns to darkness, lit only by the teleportation pads as they flair to life, bringing several living beings to fight before us.

It takes my eyes a moment to absorb the entirety of the scene that is intended to play out because of the sheer size of the arena.

The four platforms hold bears, easily dwarfing the size of a typical bear. These are Shifters, brought here to fight against each other.

Divided between two platforms, the four bears step down. The thud of their large paws beats over the roar of the spectators. Slowly, they stalk toward the two center platforms.

One, holds a large bear with black fur. Two thick chains and metal cuffs around the bear's hind legs keep it affixed to that side of the arena.

Kai rises from her seat, and while I can't turn my head and face her, I feel the waves of emotion surging off her. Shock, anguish, and anger spill out from within her.

When my eyes land on the final platform, the sight sends a surge of freezing chills rushing through me as if I were plunged into the arctic waters of the northern seas.

Teddy.

27

Hermes

The look on Circe's face when I teleported, whisking Atlas, Lucas, and me away from the Council chambers, was nothing short of priceless. Her meticulously woven wards, designed to negate Elemental powers within the confines of the Vatican walls, had proven effective against everyone for ages. But it seems they are powerless against my unique gift, newly returned to me thanks to my trip to Avalon.

Knowledge of this newfound advantage is a comforting thought, albeit small in the grand scheme of the turmoil we face.

I was a messenger of Light, trapped in the darkness, without a voice. Spending ages stretching and reaching for the Light but only able to grasp a fleeting whisper of it. Now that the power has returned to me, the heavy burden of my confinement lifts from me.

The surge of my powers stretches across my body, like the wings of a great dragon, unfurling after centuries of imprisonment and starving to consume the Light. I'm eager to unfurl my own wings and finally fly again.

I want to wrap my Light around Rhea and free her from Ares, bringing her to the farthest reaches of the realms and exploring them together. I long to watch her golden eyes come alive, gazing at the beauty of the other lands without the weight of her curse or the dread that she may suffer another death.

Something within me stirs, and a vision of Nyx, standing on the horizon of a dark realm creeps into my mind like fog rolling across a still lake.

Lifetimes ago, I recall the first time I ever saw her.

It was nighttime, and the sky glinted with billions of stars as if a dozen galaxies collided and cast the jewels of all the realms across the atmosphere just so she could admire them.

She held a sapphire star within her hand, like the color of my aura, A song, her song, echoed across the fabrics of the realms, calling me to her.

She looked at me as if she had never seen another being before. With wonder affixed on her face, she cast the star upward, and it drifted back into the night sky. I fell into the depths of her eyes, never wanting to leave.

The memory fades as my blue light wraps around Atlas, Lucas, and me in the underground archives of the Council.

A burning promise of retribution seethes in my eyes as I exchange a fleeting look with Pan, deciding he and the Council had a hand in the attack that had led to Athena's untimely death.

Then, with a gesture, I tauntingly flip Circe the middle finger, deliberately delaying the flash of teleportation, I savor the brewing storm of anger in her gaze.

Black veins surge like ominous rivers up her pale neck and flushed cheeks, while her once-brown eyes blaze a fiery crimson. Her ordinary teeth grotesquely morph into sharp fangs. Their malevolence evident as she crushes the fragile martini glass in her trembling hand.

As I sense the portal of Light open on both ends, a ready servant of my command, my heart aches with a deep yearning, for it knows exactly whose presence I long to find.

Michael stands with the rise of his golden aura, an expletive hanging precariously on the edge of his lips. The power of starlight crackles and hums, enveloping us like a protective cocoon, and whisking us away from this chamber of lies.

In the blink of an eye, we traversed the realm, descending to a dark location. Our eyes swiftly adapt to the darkness that shrouds us, and the stagnant air hints that we are now deep underground.

The subterranean caves stretch far beyond the confines of the ones where I had first rescued Rhea from her metal prison. An overwhelming roar fills our ears, reverberating through the hollow expanse, as Lucas, Atlas, and I crouch within the recesses of rough-hewn rock walls.

My Light Shield and Mirage are woven together, concealing us within the cloak of shadows that cling to the uneven surfaces as several shadowy figures amble towards arched openings.

Before us lay the infamous Gladiator Arenas of the Underworld. A place where mortal heroes had once battled against supernatural beings for the amusement of the others. I shudder at the memory of these gruesome spectacles, and a gnawing sense of unease washes over me.

These games were outlawed long ago, for obvious reasons.

Medusa and the others remain at the Atlanta Commune, out of reach of my telepathic connection. Their absence gnaws at my soul, leaving me feeling vulnerable. I wish we had more time, but the tipping balance of power within the realm demand we move with haste.

I beg a favor of the Winds and ask them to send a message to my sister. If they deem it worth their time, the currents of the realm may carry my request to Callie. Though I've never been as adept at negotiating with the fickle element of my sister as Achilles is but it's worth a shot.

"Kai is with her in the VIP box," Lucas reports, breaking the oppressive silence and then he simply vanishes into thin air.

"What the hell?" I exclaim, my voice echoing softly through the cavernous space as the pain I sensed persists within me. It's like fire is coursing through the inside of my body, and I can do nothing to move against it.

"Stay put," Lucas's voice resonates within my mind.

"Where are you?" I grit between my teeth, extending my Light energy with care, wary of any lurking Sensors or Dark Mages. A dragonfly flits before my face, and I absentmindedly swat it away with my hand.

"Watch it," Lucas warns.

I chuckle with understanding and clutch my stomach with a surge of throbbing. *"Are you the dragonfly? I could totally squish you right now."*

In my mind, I sense Lucas taking a deep breath, a sigh of frustration escaping him. *"I'm beginning to think I hate you."*

I can't help but play along with the banter despite the sensations flowing through me. *"Just imagine it: The Herald squashes the Titan of the Shifters. You'd never live it down. How do you think Pan would document that?"*

"Just keep an eye out for your girl. I'm going to sneak into the VIP box and secure Kai's portal wand. We're going to need reinforcements."

While we do need the help, I can't resist a final jab. *"How do you plan on carrying a portal wand with your tiny dragonfly arms?"*

"Goddess, help me," he retorts before vanishing into the shadows.

As my Light flows through the dark crevasse of the Arena and sneaks around the forms gathered to watch the event, I detect many Shifters and Elementals alike, along with hundreds of mortals.

Peering into the secluded room, that must be the box Lucas spoke of, my resolve wavers as I catch sight of her.

She is here, within a dozen steps of me.

Stunning, like a celestial being depicted in the painting of mortals and their former fascination with our ancient selves. Her milky skin radiates an ethereal luminance against the deep purple stola that rests just above her knees. The golden-brown strands of her hair dance with a life of their own, shimmering in the ambient light. It was as if the very stars in the heavens had bestowed their fiery brilliance upon her, and no force, not even the combined might of the twelve Titans, can tear my gaze away from her.

A torrent of emotions surges through me - joy, relief, and an overwhelming anticipation of holding her in my arms once more.

The vision of her etches itself into my mind, an indelible memory that I will carry with me for eternity.

She follows Flint, her expression solemn, and a searing heat courses through my Immortal essence with longing to reach her. However, my heart freezes when she lovingly wraps her arms around his waist.

Her tender touch on his body and the affection in her eyes tear at my very soul, threatening to render it in two. I feel the tattered and frayed bond that had once destined us together. It pulses and throbs in agony as I witness the completion of my soul embracing another. Regret, despair, and an unending loneliness cascade from her like a waterfall plunging over the precipice of a cliff.

I know, deep down, that this is not her choice. Demeter's potent and long-perfected venom is likely acting as an evil puppeteer, manipulating Rhea's mind and heart. But the pain of watching her in this embrace equals the anguish of feeling my sword pierce her chest.

In my memories, dozens of versions of her eyes stare back at me, each one a wellspring of pain as death tore her away from me, again and again. I can't help but wonder if she had been disappointed in those final moments, saddened by my inability to save her. I question whether the relentless cycles of loss have carved into the very fibers of her soul, leaving her hollow and broken. If I left her hollow and broken.

Do these feelings of remorse and desolation haunting her now stem from my failures?

A burning ache seizes my chest as I feel the phantom sensation of her healed wound, an intensity that threatens to consume me. My fingers clench around the rock wall; the pain so vivid. The severed bond between Rhea and me, that desperately longs to reunite, claws at my very essence.

My Light filling the underground pit is my silent spy and shows me her face. And then, the world around me explodes in a blinding burst of light as she lifts her face, and Flint's lips meet hers. The ground around me quakes and I struggle to keep my powers from rupturing out of me, decimating this entire arena.

My ragged breathing threatens to consume me, my trembling form collapsing to my knees. I struggle to keep my Shield of Light extended around Atlas and me, my vision blurred by unshed tears, my heart heavy with despair.

"What happened?" Atlas inquires, his eyes reflecting genuine concern as he drops to the ground beside me, his brow furrows in worry.

"I... I saw her with Flint," I whisper, the words laden with anguish.

"I'm so sorry," Atlas murmurs, his voice filled with empathy as he places a reassuring hand on my shoulder. "But I need you to focus if we're going to make it out of here alive."

The trembling ground continues, no longer shaking from my quivering power but with the roar of a great beast. Pebbles and dust rain from the ceiling, sprinkling our shoulders as we cower under the deafening cacophony of the creature.

And then, as if the world itself has erupted into chaos, mayhem unfurls around us.

28

Rhea

It's a cub. A child, shifted into a small brown bear. Standing alone on the platform opposite the other chained bear. The cub is affixed with a collar around its neck, leading to a chain in the wall behind him. The young Shifter cries out a small roar as it looks across the arena.

The adult bear begins to trot toward the scared cub, and the chains allow it twenty paces before reaching the line's end. The cub hurries to meet its parent, but the short restraint yanks it down when the youngling reaches the end of it. The cuff around his neck holds fast, and the cub is thrown to the ground by his momentum.

As the large bear shifts toward the lone cub, another shocking sight pulls the breath from my body, leaving my locked limbs tense with the need to act.

Quivering together on the platform, two more cubs, small in size, watch the large bear retreat away from them, headed toward the other youngling. Their snouts sniff the arena air and take in the surroundings where they are meant die.

Kai grabs the railing with white knuckles and clenched teeth. Turning to me with rage burning against brown eyes, the Chameleon grumbles, "It's Naomi and the boys."

Naomi. Jayden and Jamal, twins. And Teddy.

Teddy. My friend.

I see them in my mind. Chatting with Teddy over a bowl of cereal and meeting Nomi and the twins at dinner.

A chasm breaks within me as light, and fire collide inside my aura. Smoke rolls off my shoulders, and black mist leaks from beneath me. As my anger surges up my body at the sight of the family, lead like sheep for slaughter, my power vaporizes Demeter's poison.

My hand moves first, as Flint turns toward me. His eyes bulge and he takes a step back, surprised by the elements spilling off me. In a flash of power, using the Wind to help propel me, my hand snaps to his neck and I lock my fingers around his esophagus.

My legs are stiff as the poison works itself out of my joints and ligaments but again, I summon the Wind to my aid.

With a gale behind me, I surge forward. Flint slides back on his heels, his arms pinwheeling to keep his balance and grasps at nothing to try and stop me. Chairs and Elementals go soaring, pushed out of my path by the currents, until I slam Flint into the rock wall behind us, and it crumbles.

With my nails digging into the meat within, I feel him swallow against my grasp.

"Stop this right now!" I grit my teeth as my cracked voice speaks for the first time in goddess knows how long.

"It's too late for that." Flint sneers back at me. "The little cub should learn not to be so nosey and crawl through the vents."

Looking to the Arena, one of the large bears tracks Teddy while the other three head toward Naomi and the twins. Raising her large muzzle to the cave ceiling, her roar warns them of her rage before she sets off on a path for the closest bear approaching her. The rock walls vibrate under the power of her growl and the crowd cheers.

Flint raises his hand with a ball of Flame within is palm, aiming to blast me in the face.

My air currents make quick work of pinning his arm to the wall, and puffing out my cheeks, I extinguish his fire as if I were blowing out a candle.

His face turns from red to purple as his damaged pride and anger fight each other within his expressions. "Ares will kill you."

"He can fucking try."

As the toxins leaves my body, more recollections seep into my mind. As if I'm traveling backward in time, I've been able to recount the last few days but there is so much sluggish darkness to work through.

I can't focus on the memories right now, while Naomi and her children need help.

Slamming Flint further into the rock once more for good measure, I glare into his eyes before releasing him and turning to Kai. Wild desperation is on the cusp of spilling over into uncontrolled rage as she awaits my next move.

"Are you with me?" I ask her pointedly.

"To the end."

With two running steps, we grab the railing and vault ourselves over. The ground is thirty feet below, and I use my Wind Element to control my descent at the last moment to land carefully. Kai is a Shifter, and the distance is nothing for the beast within her Immortal form, except Kai doesn't land next to me.

The shriek of a giant eagle with great golden wings spread wide pierces the Arena, and every pair of spectating eyes turn upward. The large bird sweeps in an arc, and I'm amazed by the beauty of the animal.

The crowd roars, believing this to be an added element of the performance for tonight, and they make my stomach curdle. The excitement at the prospect of watching this family's murder should be the forfeit of all their lives.

Circling behind me, the eagle heads toward the left of the Arena on a path to the platform where Naomi and the twins wait. Lifting my Winds, the currents wrap around my body like ribbons of cool satin, and I go right, heading toward Teddy.

We surge away from each other like speeding bullets as Kai, and I come to the aid of the woman and her cubs.

Shadows darken the left side of the Arena as the sound of static overtakes the snarls of the bears. A column of darkness hits Kai, and her winged form is thrust upward, slamming into the ceiling high above us.

Darkness hurls toward me, and as I wrap myself in my Winds, forming a tunnel that will propel me out of its path. But a blazing blue light surrounds me, forming a protective wall.

My trajectory is thrown off, and the Arena is too small for the speed I'm traveling. I tumble to the rows of rock-carved seats and spectators below.

Crashing into a dozen bystanders, and rolling over the tops of them, humans and Immortals dive out of my way. I watch just in time to see Kai's unconscious body, still in bird form, slam to the ground, unmoving.

The thump on the hard rock matches the thump of my heart pounding in my chest while I watch the body of a woman take shape as the bones and feathers of the bird retreat. Kai no longer holds the shape of her animal or the man she impersonated.

Arms push and shove at me, forcing me back on my feet as the crowd runs away, dispersing from another column of darkness that comes for me.

Something pulls at me, wanting me to turn around despite the second attack approaching. I know I should defend against the obscurity, but I can't resist the sensation tugging at me from within. Turning behind me, I see the unmistakable blue glow of sapphire eyes that have been flashing in my mind since I woke up, mindless and full of poison.

Hermes.

His name envelopes my mind and travels into my heart. Something within my core recognizes him, and a dozen emotions pull at me so suddenly they steal my breath and pull tears from my eyes.

It's as if my very soul has searched for this man endlessly and can't believe he is finally standing before me. My heart wants to follow the feelings but my mind pulls me back.

His aura ripples and flexes around him as blue light fills the entire Arena. Concentrating his power behind me, he forms a protective wall, gleaming like the center of a star has exploded.

With hands outstretched and strained, pushing the angular features of his face into a grimace, he holds the wall of blue light steady as columns of darkness pound against it from the other side.

A man with gold-rimmed glasses touches Hermes' shoulder and points across the Arena.

Atlas.

A shout forms in his mouth, and I can barely make out the words. I grab the sound waves as he speaks and carry them to me on my Wind. *"The Titan."*

I follow the line of his finger across the vast arena. In a dark recess, deep within the caves, the shadows consume a cloaked figure. As it slowly emerges, I see the darkness emerging from the being. Spilling outward like tar and soot, carrying obscurity in their wake.

Trapped between Light and Dark powers that collide and consume each other, the bear-Shifters descend upon the lone mother and her cubs.

I don't know why Hermes protected me from the column of darkness, and every fiber of my body begs and screams at me to run to him. But right now, Teddy needs me first. And I'll trust the waves of knowing and reassurance that abound within me at the sight of Hermes that I can trust him.

As if he knows the battle I'm fighting, deciding against the urge to rush to him and instead, needing to help the cub, Hermes' bright eyes lock on mine, with a single nod of his head, his baritone voice caresses me, wrapping me in a seductive reassurance as he speaks into my mind.

"Go."

Ignoring the urges to be near him, I point both hands together and blast a series of Wind Bursts in a steady percussion at the large male bear stalking the lone cub. My Wind travels through the Light Shield and knocks the bear to the ground.

Teddy looks at me, and his large brown eyes gleam with hope as his ears turn on the top of his head and point toward me. My heart breaks, wanting to teleport him out of here, but the Thaumium cuff around his neck prevents him from Shifting back to his human form and teleportation.

I don't even have a portal wand on me. *Damn.*

My best bet is to take down the attacking bears and free Naomi. Together we can protect the cubs, and perhaps Hermes will come help us get them out.

Working through the crowd that is still fleeing from the arena, I hurl myself over the last two rows of patrons. But as they panic to abandon the arena, they trample my path, and I fight against them.

A large man with a very round belly rams into me as he runs from the arena. I bounce off him and run into someone else behind me. They push at my back, and I stumble forward, hurling my arms in front of me and using my Winds to keep me from falling on my face.

Frustration and irritation burn the last remnants of my patience, and I blast a jetstream of Cutting Wind through them. As if giant arms have pushed through the crowd, my Winds surge against them, and the divided people are thrown to each side, clearing an aisle for me.

Sprinting the remaining distance, I vault to the arena floor and land on the dirt ground with one knee, placing my palm down to steady myself.

Ribbons of shadow and a cloud of darkness engulf the entire arena, rendering me blind by the murkiness of the shadows. I part the darkness just as I parted the crowd, and gaze into the black hood of a Titan.

I can't hold this shield much longer against the Titan. the darkness batters my element, blocking the attacks from hitting Rhea–for now.

The first column had already hit Kai before I could cast it, but I can detect the life within her thrumming aura. She's alive, and my Light covers her like a blanket, incinerating the small pebbles that fell around her when she slammed into the ceiling.

"We need the others," I grunt and strain against the force of the Titan's dark attack on Rhea. "Mor has the chalice." The words are broken as I widen my stance and lean into my power.

Rhea hurls herself into the Arena after casting me a look that broke my heart. It was as if her eyes set their sight on me for the first time and her soul called out to me. Wrestling with herself, turning back to the Shifters, and with pleading eyes, she looks back at me.

"Go," I call to her through our minds, and her silvery aura sways in time with her honey hair as she moves.

Gods, she's amazing.

As I prepare to teleport to her side, a dome of darkness covers the arena floor, swallowing Rhea, the Shifters, within the deep power of the Dark Titan. I can't penetrate it, and I can't sense anyone trapped within it. The shimmer of Rhea's silver aura, muddy and diluted but still shining like a torch burns brightly within the dark fog. It is a beacon I can track as I look for a way to get past the barrier.

Sensing movement behind me, I turn as quick as lightning and find Flint behind me. A Flaming Blade is in his hand stretched above his, aiming to bring it down my back. Grabbing his forearm, I easily hold him back, cocking an eyebrow and enjoying the surprise on his face when he realizes I stopped his surprise attack.

"I warned you about putting your hands on *my* goddess." I sneer at him.

My Light glides through the meat and thin bones of his forearm, severing part of his limb from his body. At first, he doesn't register that his hand is no longer attached and now belongs to me.

Leaning to the side, I put the full weight of my strength into my movement. Swinging my arm across, I slap him in the face with his own hand. His blood sprays across his shirt, and the impact sends him stumbling to the side, tripping over his feet.

Tossing his severed hand down the steps toward the arena, it bounces on the top of one of the stone benches. The noise of his lifeless appendage smacking the stone carries into the open arena. It skips across the bench twice more before thudding to the ground and leaking the remaining blood.

Clutching his arm, he screams as the pain races to his dim brain.

Extending my aura outward, I locate the retreating forms of several pieces of shit I would gladly send to Elysium.

"Eris is getting away with Demeter."

Atlas uses a nearby wand to portal to the corridor, forming a barrier between the two Elementals and the portals they were heading for. Atlas is more of a scholar than a fighter, though he used to be a skilled warrior long ago, before he vowed to never use his powers for violence.

The hairs on the back of my neck warn me of an approaching attacker only a second before the muzzle of a wolf is wrapped around my forearm, wrenching me away from Flint before I can sever his other hand.

Blazing my aura in a wave of Pure Light, the wolf incinerates into ash, but not before the momentum of his oversized form sends me tumbling through the wall of the VIP box that held the important spectators of the event. The wolf's fangs punctured my arm, and warm blood drips down my forearm, dripping onto the stone floor as I search for Flint again.

He took the momentary break to flee. Holding his arm against his chest, he pulls a portal wand from his pocket and pushes the button. He smiles a crooked grin as a purple wave of light swallows him.

A pack of Shifters takes up the space he occupies, snarling and creeping toward Atlas and me.

I try every burst and beam of Light power within my ability in hopes of breaking open the darkness covering Rhea, but the Titan shield holds fast.

I need my sword.

"We can't hold back the Titan on our own," I call out to Atlas through our minds.

Atlas returns in a flash with Demeter and fends off a carnivorous barb, holding it back with two hands around a thick green stem as it tries to push closer to his eye.

The darkness encompassing the vast space flares as silver starlight bursts and explodes within the dome. The silhouette of two bears, raised on hind legs and grappling with each other is the only glimpse of what is happening inside.

Rhea is fighting the Titan.

A dozen vines shoot out from Demeter's back with four-inch barbs. Milky sap oozes from the sharpened tips as if the carnivorous plant is drooling at the prospect of delivering its toxin within Atlas and sucking out his Immortality.

Using my Light like a lasso, I wrap my power around her ankles and fling her from the VIP box. She flails through the space, sending her vines out in all directions, catching herself before she collides with the ground thirty feet below us.

Like a wave of water rolling onto a sandy beach, green and brown vines spread outward from her position in all directions.

I pull Kai's unconscious form through a tunnel of Light to the spectator's box, out of Demeter's reach. Placing my finger at the temple of her head, I send a gentle beam of my element within to wake her.

Atlas focuses his ability on Demeter, attempting to shut her down.

"I can't–control her." He grunts as he strains to take over her Mind. She is the queen of Avalon, and her powers would have been amplified when she was crowned but the alignment between the realms is boosting her. But I don't think it's her strength keeping Atlas from her mind.

Since Patroclus was killed, Atlas refused to use his ability in battle for harm, feeling responsible for what happened. He's never been in a skirmish since the Battle of Troy, leaving the fighting to us and helping with planning or intelligence gathering.

With fluttering lashes, Kai wakes, wincing and covering the back of her head with her hand. Pulling away, blood covers her palm, but she sits up.

"Can you connect with Lucas from here?" The desperation in my voice must match the intensity in my eyes because awareness takes her over. The Beta of the Great Shifter rightens herself with a nod.

"What do you need?"

"The cup. And help."

A dull bellow of static thrums from within the darkness. Squinting into the obscuring cover that blocks our sight from witnessing the batting within, bright starlight collides with a dark beam.

"I'm coming for you." I send my promise down the severed mating bond and feel it warm within me. A thought slams into me like a freight train and I clutch my chest. The mating bond is still there, alive and responsive. I can feel it thrumming with the need to connect with her. It's not gone; it's only disconnected.

Medusa spoke once of her severed bond with Athena, which was hollow, cold, and vacant. Like it had been physically removed from within her, and she could feel its absence. She could feel the place where it used to be and felt the empty chamber. My heart races, and my face heats with the prospect this brings.

We can fix it.

Demeter cackles, and it bounces around the hollowed cenote.

"Do you honestly think Ares was unprepared for your power, Atlas?" She calls out through the empty arena. "Are you so foolish to think he would not ensure you had no way to enter our minds?"

Three barbs shoot inside the large window like vipers, ready to attack. My Light blazes and burns them before they strike Atlas, Kai, or me. But thousands more are crawling through the opening on all sides, growing in thickness as they inch forward.

Peering over the railing, Demeter's Life element has flooded the interior of the arena and turned the hard rock into a jungle of hungry plants. Vines crawl along the floor and walls, making the arena floor come to life as they slither toward us.

White flowers grow out of the stems and bloom, their petals turning black and hissing at us as they shake in a predatory warning like snakes.

Afraid to blast a large wave of Absolut Light, for fear of hitting Atlas or Kai, I prepare to use smaller beams to take on the plants that swell in girth, preparing to attack again. Dozens of vines are ready their barbs to attack, and Atlas positions himself in front of Kai as her shield.

The rattling plants grow around us before they rear back. Poised to surge forward, I prepare to slice through them before they can strike, but a wave of heat surges behind me. Blasting a torch between Atlas and me like a flamethrower, Achilles incinerates the plants.

Conjuring a Fire Bow and nocking an arrow in place, he pulls back on the flaming string and releases it. The arrow made of Fire arcs toward the ceiling with a hiss. Three feet in length, the arrow reaches the apex of its arc; it splits into five flaming arrows. As they descend, the tips point to the ground, and they drop like bombs.

Striking the rock below, fire blazes outward and cremates the hungry plants. The roar of Achilles' flames drowns out the howl from Demeter as his Fire swallows the ground and walls.

"Perfect timing, brother." I nod at my oldest friend.

"Yeah, anytime." He pats my shoulder as he passes and leaps over the railing. Smoke billows off his shoulders, and he jumps across the open space toward Demeter.

Smoke and soot fill the area as the last of the plants smolder into ash. Callie joins me at the opening of the spectator's box. Her winds blow a cool breeze until the air is clear and the smell of sulfur is gone. The tendrils of her bright blonde hair settle as the Wind dies. Her eyes focus across the arena, and she nudges me with her elbow.

I track her gaze and see what stole her attention.

Ares stands at the opposite side of the Arena as Shifters run past him. Keeping to the sides, they gallop along the edges of the darkness that still contains a battle between Rhea and Erebus. Eris, stands by his side.

"Atlas." My calm voice alerts him that the situation has grown to anything but calm. He joins us at the window and looks across the distance into the dark eyes of someone he's not seen in hundreds of years.

Ares nods once and turns his back, walking into the black tunnel behind him with Eris following. She must have gotten to a portal and alerted Ares to our attack.

Looking at my mentor, Atlas takes a steadying breath and pushes his gold glasses up on his nose with his middle finger.

"Let's get Rhea." He clasps my shoulder, just as Achilles did, and we descend into the lower level of the arena.

The Shifters, led by the new Alpha form a line and crawl toward us. Movement along the cenote wall begins to swirl into a vortex as Terra steps out of it, entering the vast cavern and standing next to Demeter.

She wears black tactical gear, as she did when she was a part of our team. Her short auburn hair with a slight curl bounces as she walks toward Demeter.

"Mother." Terra greets Demeter, to our shock.

Callie takes a sharp breath, and her bright eyes darken as she narrows in on Terra. Terra played us this entire time. A mole, planted by Ares and Demeter, apparently her mother, into the cave where Callie was captive for over twenty years.

"Get to the goddess," Demeter says to her quietly.

Achilles stands with his weight on one leg and his arms crossed. The colorful tattoos on his arms are on display as he cast his shirt to the floor. Atlas and I stand on each side of my friend, and the unmistakable quiver of power behind me tells me The Morrigan is here.

Her compact form radiating dark energy stands on the other side of me with her faithful companion, Hypnos. Medusa takes up the space next to Callie and Achilles. A growl from the tunnel behind us crawls across the walls of the cenote, letting the Shifters know their Titan has arrived.

Lucas, in his wolf form, the size he was the night Rhea fell on my sword, stalks into the arena with his troops of Shifters.

"Get rid of the Darkness. I'll keep them from attacking." His deep voice rumbles in my mind. Still sounding like Lucas, but with the growl of his wolf trailing on the ends of his words.

Lightning stretches within the dark dome and arcs across the interior of the shadows, and Rhea and the Titan battle within.

"Now," I call to the companions that have joined Atlas and me to help save Rhea.

Callie surges us upward with her Winds as we leave the Shifters to Lucas and Demeter to Medusa.

Like a rainbow of powers, our elements collide—a dark beam from The Morrigan, pulsating waves of power from Hypnos, and, similarly, Atlas. My blue Light collides with Achilles' stream of flames as Callie's cutting Wind whistles through the air like a white mist.

Growling below us pulls my eye across the line of animals at the floor of the empty stands that held the cheering bodies of the crowd only a few moments ago.

Gabriel and his loyal Shifters are yapping, roaring, and barking as their bodies quiver and tremble; they remain fixed on their locations. Lucas keeps his head lowered, and his hazel eyes firmly locked. The power of the Titan is holding them in place, under his will as the Alpha of them all.

Medusa and Demeter head for each other. The vines of Demeter's Life element are crushed within Medusa's Earthen petrification.

The combined elements firing into a center point of the dark dome begins to ripple and wave as if weakening the forcefield. We only need an opening to get Rhea out, and we can give her the waters from Avalon. Sensing the bubble of protection is weakening, the fight inside the dome increases.

Darkness and starlight collide while a field of static electricity builds along the dome. Like webs of lightning crawling across storm clouds, the energy of the Titan is building. Erebus is preparing to attack Rhea with a large burst of Absolute Night. The antithesis of my Absolute Light, the wave of super-cold dark energy that would annihilate us all.

The cold fingers of dread coat my body, dripping down my spine and covering me in chills.

Everyone senses the same ending approaching and pushes more aura into their Elementals powers. The dome begins to crack, and as the spot of our attack weakens. My Light begins to eat away, widening a crevasse as Callie releases a roar, surging more of her Winds into the opening.

A small view of the scene within the dome reveals itself like a curtain opening to reveal the stage while a play is already in progress. We get our first glimpse of the warzone inside.

Two male bear-Shifters are dead as they were struck down on their way to attack the female and her two cubs. The female still fights a surviving bear while her two cubs cower by the wall behind them. Blood darkens her muzzle and fur, dripping off her snout from a deep gash along her face.

Columns of shadow and ribbons of Light swirl and collide with each other inside the open space as Rhea combats the Titan. Sweat covers her brow, and her hair whips wildly about her as the powers surge around her. A blackened gash reaches across her brow and left eye, with red seeping down her cheek and smeared into her golden hair.

Kai has recovered enough to shift into her eagle, and she soars toward the dome. A tendril of shadow wraps around her and slams her down to the ground as the crack of lightning echoes within the rocky arena.

Shadows take the forms of faceless children that claw at Rhea's arms and legs, and darkness snakes around her body, suffocating her. Bolts of dark lightning crack and shoot into her, causing her spine to stiffen, and a pained expression takes hold of her face. The impact surges between Rhea and me. It singes my heart and pushes me back, making me unsteady on Callie's winds.

She recovers me, but the disruption causes the darkness to begin swallowing the small opening we have made. My power roars out of me, seeing my mate under attack, and a bright wave of my power surges toward the dome. The inside of the cave is bathed in blue as my power fills the space.

Countering my oncoming assault, a wall of darkness is thrust upward from the ground, devouring the wave of my power.

"Atlas," I grunt as I resume casting my Light beam to the opening. "Can you—get into her—mind?" The words are a struggle as I push more force into the beam of Light, eating away the shadows.

"I can't. She's blocking me." Atlas strains through his teeth.

"We can't hold this, H," Callie yells over the roar of powers beating against the dome and the swell of energy happening within.

Black lightning cracks louder than before, and Rhea is wrapped in whips of darkness, buzzing against her body. She stiffens, and the jolt surges within me as I feel the pain the Titan inflicts.

"I can bring her into *my* mind." Atlas's voice rings with hope. "I can bring her into my mind." He repeats louder.

I can't walk out of this cenote without my partner. I've come so close, and within this dome, she is still miles away from me. With Ares aware of our alliance with Lucas, he could very well decide to kill Rhea and wait for her next reincarnation to try again.

The pain surges between Rhea and me, but instead of Absolute Night, a siphon of darkness forms like a funnel directed at Rhea's chest and connects the Titan to her. The black cloak conceals a woman's body made entirely of swirling shadows. Erebus is trying to consume the power from Rhea.

"Atlas, now!" Desperation surges as I blast another wave of Light, beams and whips of my power flail erratically, trying anything to strike the Titan and stop her from devouring Rhea.

Stopping his assault on the dome, Atlas lifts his head to the ceiling and closes his eyes, I feel the second he invites the goddess into his mind. I feel her enter his memories, and the anguish she carries with her makes my heart falter.

Alone, terrified of failing, and suffocated by chains that encase her, she feels imprisoned, choking on a boulder of doubt that sits heavily on her chest.

I pass my warming Light into Atlas, wrapping her fears with my aura and surging my love for her through the connection. I feel the dark poison coating her mind. Shadows inch along her brain like maggots, eating away at the truth and memories, leaving behind a sludge of their contamination and deception.

The Titan has submerged her mind in a deep ocean of endless nothing. Atlas feels her despair, too, and responds in turn, filling the dark waters with the memories he saw when he first met her.

Thousands of happy smiles and the laughter of a small boy dance in my mind as I see what he is sharing with her. Warmth blooms when sunshine blazes through a canopy of trees as dandelion seeds float through the air, disturbed when a happy woman spins in fast circles, holding the hands of a younger Rhea.

The Titan counters our attempt to free her of the darkness, but my Light serves as a shield. Atlas's brown eyes turn to white voids as he pushes himself to the end of his limits, attempting to hold Rhea inside and together, we keep the Titan at bay.

In the next memory, an old man pushes Rhea down a hill as she learns to ride her bike, and two parents stand on their porch waving as she walks onto a school bus. These are the mortal memories of the young girl that occupied the vessel before Nyx took it over.

Atlas avoids the visions of the car crash and anything to do with Demeter, so he moves on to his own. Showing Rhea a dozen memories he has of Athena, watching over her when she had no idea.

The night Rhea arrived battered when we rescued her, Athena sat with her for hours, watching over her. Atlas peered through the doorway, and Athena looked up at him, offering a reassuring smile as she kept her hand gently on Rhea's forearm.

Athena, watching the moment Rhea showed me her powers and produced the tiny stone. She was on the second-level balcony, and Atlas joined her. Resting his forearms on the railing, he observed alongside her.

"Amazing, isn't she?" The voice of the Goddess of War rings like a bell, and the soft pitch of her words triggers a reaction within Rhea.

The silver starlight of her aura collects and builds within her center as her body turns inward. Exploding in all directions, Rhea's powers discharge. Spreading outward from her epicenter, a wave of Elements hurls toward us. The ground beneath her bucks and surges away from her. A cloud of fire and wind billows toward us as the darkened columns of shadow and light ricochet out of the dome of confinement.

Callie and I hold our powers like wide protective shields against the elements of Rhea's spent energy propelling toward us. Callie's Winds work to dispel most of the fire and combat the chunks of the cenote tumbling across the ground. My Light consumes the darkness and starlight bouncing across the surfaces, and we brace against the barrage of elements that make it past our defense.

The floor of the cenote is crumbling into the levels of darkness below. Gabriel's Shifters fall into the opening cavern below as the ground around them disappears.

Medusa covers Kai with her body, and a rock wall pulled up from the broken cenote protects them from the barrage of elements. Lucas and his Shifters back up into the tunnels behind them, away from the crumbling ground and avoiding being swallowed within the dark pit.

A scream sounds around us as Demeter falls with the Shifters. Her vines stretch out with desperation, elongating frantically toward Terra, who lunges to the ground, reaching a moment too late. Demeter, breaking her fingernails as she claws against the stone ground, slips and is consumed within the deep recess waiting below. Only the trailing echo of her receding scream lingers behind.

Atlas is locked in his trance, still holding Rhea within his memories, and I feel him fighting to release her. Dark and Light tendrils of Rhea's power have woven a net around his mind, and as she squeezes him. He brought her into his head, but it's him that is trapped within her grasp.

A dark column of power bounces off the cenote wall behind us, heading directly toward Callie. She has her eyes squeezed tightly as she exerts every ounce of force into her Wind Shield. She has no idea; the unleashed power of the Titan is bounding toward her.

I blast a beam of Light, and while the powers of Dark and Light can counter each other, the darkness is closer and just as fast as my Light as it consumes the small distance to Callie's chest.

Still connected to Atlas, I feel him let go. I feel his surrender, and he disappears. A portal flashes above us as he arrives in the space between Callie and the darkness. Suspended momentarily before gravity pulls him down, she turns to him as the portal wand drops from his hand.

Freed from the Titan, Rhea looks at him, and I hear her project a single word into his mind. *"Out."*

The white voids of Atlas's eyes dim as I sense his soul leave his body. The dark column invades an empty shell, and he seems to float into the sunken ground beneath us.

Rhea turns to the Titan and with both hands cast wide, Light and Dark energy surge in powerful columns, raging as they roar across the space. The whipping shadows that make up the essence of Erebus grins, and like a puff of smoke after a candle has been blown out, the Titan is gone.

Callie screams as she watches Atlas, and my heart drops into the void with him. Empty brown eyes stare back at her, and Achilles wraps her in his arms as she tries to go to him. Her Winds search for Atlas within the dark hole he enters, missing him as her blinding tears chase after him.

The last remaining memories of our father that lived within Atlas plunges into the darkness with his limp body.

Looking back to my mate, she drops into the earth within a swirl of Terra's quicksand as a loud crack surrounds us.

A mighty shift above us causes the walls of the cenote to buckle. The rocky ceiling plunges downward several feet before it stops. Quivering rocks and boulders the size of the Shifted wolves are frozen high above us, pausing their inevitable descent upon us.

"Hermes," Medusa calls out with strain in her voice. The dark tattoos that paint her deep skin dance along her toned arms as she strains, holding the ceiling in place with her Earth element. "Get them out."

Sweat forms along her brow, and her knee shakes before it drops hard to the rocky floor under the tremendous weight she is bearing with her powers. The cavern groans as more cracks form along the walls and particles of dust and rock rain down.

The battle of the Titan depleted all our powers but watching my friend fight to hold back the earth bursts through the frustration of the battle we just lost. Rhea is gone, and Atlas is dead.

My anger rages forward like a tsunami, unapologetic as it builds to a peak before devouring anything that dares to remain in its path. Blue Light hurdles out of me with a high-pitched ring that strains the ears of everyone remaining in the cenote.

The four bears, remaining inside the Arena, a few of Gabriel's shifters, Lucas, Kai and his pack, Achilles, and a sobbing Callie with the stoic duo from Avalon are wrapped in my Light. Roaring against the straining boulders that beg for release, Medusa drops to both knees as I propel my aura to her, wrapping my power around her; I descend to her as I teleport my companions to the bright daylight far above us.

The earth complains as it groans and shakes. Medusa releases her hold and the ground around the great Temple of Kukulkan disappears in a cloud of grey ash and crumbling rock. Consumed within the earth, the large monument to the ancient princess, long forgotten, disappears.

Shock and confusion give everyone pause. We blink against the bright sunlight and clear air as we watch the ancient temple disappear into the earth. A gasp pulls our heads toward Kai as her lip quivers violently.

"No," Lucas whispers a regretful denial of what his eyes observe.

Still bound in their cuffs, two small bears clutch to the leg of a large black bear. Unmoving, it seems like a statue. Following the track of its large dark eyes, the body of a small brown bear lays motionless on the green grass. The reddish fur with small patches of orange gleam in the sunlight as birds chirp happily in the trees above us.

A shadow cast over the cub conceals the deep wound in the bears throat as the last of the immortal blood stops seeping out of the small body.

Callie turns into Achilles' arms, her shoulders bouncing with her sobs. Lucas drops to his knees, and his own eyes well with sorrow as the great Zeta mourns the life of the child.

"Teddy," he whispers as Kai covers her mouth to stifle her gargled intake of air.

The large black bear turns its large head and looks across all of us as we stand inert. Heavy breaths from the fierce battle fought grumble from the chest of the beast as she surveys us. Raising her giant head to the blue, cloudless sky, the bear roars through the realm and into the void. Amplified by her sorrow and propelled by her pain, the long roar grows into a mighty bellow as the cry of an Alpha escapes her throat.

I can see the blast of power hurl toward us as the bear closes her large muzzle and stands protectively over the body of her child. The flood of a mother's sorrow careens into us as if begging us to mourn with her. The scene breaks my already crumbling heart further, and I can't help the tears that drift down my cheeks as I watch the pain-filled ascension of the first woman Alpha.

Teddy is dead. Terra stole me from him. She ripped me away as I was trying to crawl to him so he wouldn't be alone as his small body drained its blood on the dirt of the arena floor.

I couldn't save him.

"Where is Ares?" The fire running through my veins is enough to burn through every Immortal in these tunnels. My Wind whips around me in a current of heated fury, and my hair floats on its ends as I stomp through the hewn walkways of the Underworld.

Echoing as a warning before my arrival, my voice travels down the darkened channels. The turns and corners shift and take me to unfamiliar locations. The recognizable doors and rooms I'm expecting are gone, and pausing my pursuit, I listen.

Terra delivered me back to the Underworld and dissolved into her whirlpool, likely to find her mother. My entire body is electrified with vengeful anger at what just occurred. Flashes of my battle with the Dark Mage and the fight of the Shifters that took place around us make me flinch. That was no ordinary Dark Mage, and I want answers.

I want someone to pay for this.

I'm unfamiliar with this level, and it seems like an empty and endless parade of turning passages that lead to dead ends.

With long strides, my panting breath and draining energy from the battle burn my chest and throat. Still screaming Ares' name, I turn my head down each of the cross-sections of the dimly lit corridors. Passing the third tunnel, I look right, expecting to see another empty corridor, but a figure deep within the darkness stops me.

Like shadows moving underwater, the darkened figure takes form. My adjusting eyes squint as my powers flare around me, my Winds circling and ready to shield me.

Either the moving darkness tricks me, or my eyes are playing a confusing game as I see a person form out of the shadows.

A memory rushes forward from the deep recesses of my broken mind, pulled by a tendril of darkness. Unleashing a sleeping giant of lava and fire upon a valley of innocents, my Immortal eyes saw across the great distance as a small girl catches fire.

Mahogany eyes sear into me with betrayal, and my skin sizzles with a building heat that rushes in from behind her.

"You didn't save me." Her young voice booms through the tunnel, carried to me by a rush of ashen clouds as the fiery breath of the great volcano consumes her. Her body turns to calcified ash; she remains locked with her hands in front of her, with the pained expression of her death immortalized on her face for eternity.

The cloud of fire and ash barrels through the tunnel toward me, and I throw my hand up to cover my face. My Winds surge out of me and fight against the coming force. Dropping to my knees, I cover my head with my arms and brace for the impact of the flames to consume me. Holding my breath, I prepare for the final moment of my life, but the fire and ash never reach me.

With the cool air from the tunnels kissing my skin, I open my eyes and turn carefully, seeing a dark and barren passageway. The image of the long-dead child from the volcano is gone, replaced by the rock-carved walls with metal grates along the floor.

Pushing myself up, I run.

Sweat drips down my back, and my hands shake with the coming panic that wants to wash over me. The sides of my vision crackle with white and black static, and I try to blink away the adrenaline building within me.

I need to stay focused so I can get out of these tunnels. I need to get to the surface.

Not stopping to look, I run down the long and straight corridor that dissolves to pitch black shadow. A set of stairs should be at the end, and I can climb up to the tunnels I'm familiar with.

It's clear that no one has used this part of the Underworld in a long time.

"G–G–Goddess–s–s–s?" A small voice floats toward me, hitting the nape of my neck and sending a rush of shivers down my spine.

"Teddy?" I stop running and turn around, looking and listening for him again.

The Underworld is still while I wait for his call again. The shadows dance and crawl along the walls, eating any light that tries to reach the ceiling. Backtracking, I walk with wide steps, determined to find him. He can't be alone down here.

"I'm s–s–scared." Teddy calls back. His voice seems to sing on the darkness, coming from behind me again. Turning, confused, I head back in the other direction, my head on a pivot, looking down each crossing passage as I jog back the way I was initially going.

Finally, I find him as I turn and look down the walkway to the left of me. Sliding to a stop, I grab the cold stone corner of the wall and pull myself back, centering my position in the opening.

His red flannel shirt billows with a current I can't feel, and the front of his light grey shirt is wet with a growing pool of deep crimson blood that is flowing from a gaping wound at his neck. Torn flesh rests on his collarbone as the ligaments within his neck move while he cries.

My hands fly to my mouth and cover my scream as I take a step toward him.

"You didn't save me." His pained voice, so tiny within this large cave, is no more than a whisper as I watch the blood soak his front. It's so much blood.

A growl from behind him is the only warning I have before the muzzle of a giant brown bear melts out of the shadows, clamping around his neck and yanking him into the dark. His legs and arms flail forward as he's ripped away from my sight.

"No!" I call out as I race after him, careening into the darkness and hitting a stone wall at the end of the corridor. My fists beat against the immovable wall as my ragged cries choke me. "Give him back!"

My hiccup echoes through the empty air, and I stumble back to the intersection and see three figures standing about thirty feet down the darkened alley. I don't recognize them, but something in my mind creeps forward. A broken vision crawls to the front of my mind of a car and three people wrapped in shadows and smoke.

A small boy, very similar to Teddy, stands in the front with two parents behind him, their hands resting on his shoulders. Their eyes are coated in white film as thick black tar oozes down their cheeks. Vines and shadows creep along their legs, winding up their bodies.

The shifting darkness tricks my eyes, and the still figures seem to slide along the ground, growing closer to me, all the while remaining in their fixed position.

As the boy opens his mouth, hundreds of flies pour out of him, and the flesh of the trio dries, shriveling and decaying before me, rotting as it pulls tight across their bones.

"You didn't save us." He reaches his hand toward me, and I run.

I hurl myself down the hall with gargled pleas, begging this to stop. Sobbing and blinded by my tears, I trip on my fear and slide across the floor. A chuckle creeps out of the darkness as an old woman, nearly bald with age, clutches an obsidian dagger in her hand.

The same dark tar oozes from her mouth as she widens her sinister grin, opening her mouth to cackle. The shadows roil around her while a raindrop splatters on my face. Thunder rolls in the distance, confusing me within the deep caverns of the Underworld.

It's not possible for the weather above the surface to reach the far depths of the trench. The deepest chasms of the realm have long hidden Ares's underground world, and there is no sunlight here. But the familiarity of this scene tugs at me as if it's supposed to be a memory.

More rain paints my face, and I look up for the source of the shower. Above me, the old hag stands with her gaping mouth and sunken lips cast open wide. Her hands are raised above her head with the shining obsidian blade gleaming like a dark beacon.

As she plummets the blade downward, her cackle bounces between the rocky walls, and my Wind Shield responds on instinct. Like the ashen column of the small girl a moment ago, the old woman's flesh disintegrates into ash. The tip of the obsidian blade, frozen in place only an inch from my eye, blows away first, followed by her hands. As her arms and shoulders deteriorate with my Winds, her laughter booms around me, and I clamp my hands over my ears to stifle it out.

"You didn't save me." The little girls voice joins the cacophony of the old woman's laughter.

"You didn't save me." Teddy's voice filters in bouncing off the walls with the others.

"You didn't save us."

"You didn't save us."

"You didn't save us." The family of three says as the voices of these ghosts jump around me in a haunting echo.

"STOP!" I yell as I scoot back on my butt, pushing myself with the heels of my feet and the palms of my hands. My face is wet and sticky with my tears, sweat, and blood. My chest spasms as my crying turns to wails, and I beg for the end of this torment.

Backing away into one of the darkened tunnels, the old woman's voices and laughter continue to float along the bumpy walls of the underground passageways. Pushing hard against the stone wall, I cover my ears and squeeze my eyes closed tight.

Maybe I'm dreaming.

Gods, let this be a dream. Teddy is dead even though the thought feels foreign in my mind; too newly dead. Trying to drown out the reverberations of the phantom figures, I take deep, steadying breaths, centering myself and feeling within for the chasm that holds my power.

Resting against the stone wall with my knees hugging my chest, it's so cold, and I begin to shiver.

I stare down the empty passage, and the swirl of Elemental power is a thick Mirage hanging over the space. I keep my aura around me and expel my Winds. The Mirage clears, like smoke blown away by the breeze, and the reality of my situation becomes clear.

I'm in a cell and staring down a long, dark corridor that leads to the great Dark Shield. Instead of standing in the hall looking at the shield, I'm locked behind it.

The pitch of the wails ringing in my ears comes from the impenetrable wall of obscurity. The undulating faces of wraiths swim to the surface with gaping mouths hyper-extended open in a silent plea for help as their skeletal hands push against the barricade, trying to reach beyond their casing but cannot.

Closing my eyes, tears fall, and desperation clings to me as harshly as the frigid temperature. My mind wants to break into two halves if it will stop the sounds emitted from the shield. Gods, I would give anything to go back a few moments ago to the arena. Just long enough to save Teddy.

The vision of Hermes' face is there, blocking me from the attack of the Dark beam, bearing the assault himself. He saved me. Maybe I shouldn't have run away from him. Perhaps together, we could have saved the little boy that became my friend.

My heart roars at the thought of Hermes, and a second power inside my chest hammers within me, and I let it surge through me. Like the sunrise after a cold night, it fills me with warmth.

The exhaustion of the battle and the terror of the abandoned halls pull my eyes closed as I work to calm myself. Drifting between that place of awake and sleep, the horrors of the fight against the Dark Mage play like a movie behind my eyelids.

The shadows and darkness seemed alive with the screams and cries of a thousand souls, and I felt helpless to free them, just like this shield crying at me from the end of the tunnel. My attention was divided between the Mage and the family of Shifters who desperately needed help, making it impossible to keep the creeping dark away from me. The touch of obscurity was like the cold fingers of death and left a chill on my skin even now as a shiver runs along my arms.

I don't want to be alone.

Warmth radiates against my back like the cold stone wall is heating with the presence of another. Heavy lids refuse to open, but I recall this feeling from my dreams. Only two nights have passed since I dreamt of Hermes, but the familiarity of his soothing aura wraps around me as if we've done this for thousands of years.

"I've got you, my goddess." A deep-timbered voice full of reassurance sends a new wave of icy bumps trailing down my skin, but the sensation of warmth chasing away the cold leaves me with gooseflesh.

"Why are you here again?" My mind speaks through my grogginess.

"I'll always be here."

The hard and cutting stone is replaced with Hermes's lean lines and curves as if I'm resting against him, and his corded arms wrap around me, pulling me into the safe harbor of his embrace.

My mind is at war with my body, which has given up the fight and falls freely into him. Thoughts of how he captured me, beat me to extract my powers, and laughed in my face push against my mind. The torture and prying my eyes open to make me a witness to the pain inflicted on others until Flint came for me.

It feels forced. Like the thoughts pushed into my mind when I was filled with Demeter's toxic venom. These images ram into me, beating the feelings of fear into me.

"I've been searching for you, but you summoned me here. You brought us together."

"I didn't." My sleepy mind argues, and he chuckles in return.

The feeling of a phantom hand, which I know is not real, presses against the center of my chest, just above my heart, and heat flows into me, chasing away the chill of the Dark Mage and the linger of her aura.

Opening my eyes, he is not here in solid form but shaped in the blue light of his astral projection. The essence of his Immortal power is an ocean of blue light, flickering and exploding in billions of bursts of starlight, and it's beautiful.

A sapphire hue glows around the rocky walls and metal bars, confining me to this cell.

His large palm, nearly covering my entire chest, rubs up the column of my throat, and tenderly tilts my head to the side. The faint trail of magic skims my neck with a whisper of a kiss, and I relax into the feeling.

I just want to feel alive after so long of feeling trapped on the edge of the Void, looking out into nothingness. Utter loneliness is my primary companion, and Flint's vacant chill of emotion when he looks at me has been my other acquaintance.

Hermes feels like peace. It's hard to think these words and believe them when I feel as if I have never known a moment of peace in my life. I don't understand the concept of harmony within my soul, nor do I understand this connection to him. The instant feeling of security, like my soul has finally arrived at the end of a journey after wandering for hundreds of ages, is one I want to fall into. I'm terrified it will disappear as soon as I do.

"You battled a Titan and lived to tell about it." The sensation of fingertips trailing up my arm relaxes me as I lean into the feeling of more kisses along my neck.

A Titan.

I close my eyes again, pain pulling at my heart for the fear Teddy must have felt within the arena as I fought to help him. Fought–but failed.

"Take my power and heal yourself." Hermes says to me.

"Why would you lend me your power?"

"I would give everything I am for you." Hermes' voice vibrates through me, and I exhale into him.

Hermes surrounds me. Closing my eyes again, I take in the light that forms his body around me. Two long legs with muscled thighs bracket me, and the aura of his arms encase me. His power increases while he waits for me to siphon it, but I hesitate.

Running my hands down his thighs, the feel of caressing his aura electrifies me. I'm scared that when I absorb it, the light will fade away, and safety of this warmth will disappear. I don't want to be alone down here.

"Tell me what you want." He whispers. Taking my jaw and moving my head to the side to resume peppering kisses down my neck.

"I just don't want to be cold." Even in my mind, the response is breathy with longing.

His aura skims down my torso toward my leg where the tattered plum stola is raised, showing the apex of my right thigh and the bend of my hip. I huff in irritation when he fixes it, covering me like he's a gentleman. Hermes' chuckle rumbles through me as I shift my legs, making the end of the dress raise again.

"Are you sure that is what you want?" The question drips with seduction and promise, and I'm not sure how I should answer it.

I want to tell him something else. Goddess knows how I want to tell him so many things but fear of watching this form of warm light disappear scares me into silence.

Placing my hand over his, I guide him around my leg, pushing the dress up and exposing myself. A tendril of blue light rubs my skin before dipping inward and squeezing my inner thigh, so close to where I want him now.

Parting my legs slightly and letting my mouth fall open, I sink back into him as his power becomes a furnace around me. Continuing his trek along my neck, while one hand massages my thigh, he reaches beneath the folded fabric of the stola as he takes my nipple, raised and begging for attention, I come alive between two fingers made of Light from his astral projection.

"Gods, I miss you." He takes my neck between his teeth with a gentle bite that ignites a fire within my body as he pinches and rolls my nipple. His fingertip trails up the fabric of my panties.

My arousal dampens the material and pulls an approving grumble from his throat. *"Tell me if you want this."*

His mouth works down my neck to my collarbone, and another scrape of his teeth is joined by two fingers, trailing up the center of my panties. I widen my legs, giving him more access as my breath escapes me, the desire to pour out of me.

"Tell me." He repeats.

My cheeks flame. He wants me to say it. Pausing, he holds himself patient, the promise of his touch so near but holding himself back until I demand he give me pleasure, insist he pulls me back from death by his touch.

"I want this. I want you." My back arches, and I roll my hips as he rubs his palms along my legs, but self-doubt makes me pause. Embarrassed to say what I truly want, my desire holds on the tip of my tongue, wanting to dive off into oblivion with Hermes. With my heart racing and my face burning from the heat of my shame, I tell him what I truthfully want from him in this moment. *"Make me come."*

He stops teasing the lace edging of my panties and slides his fingers inside them, immediately ready to give in to my demand, and his willingness reassures me. The callused tips of his fingers scorch my skin as he explores me with practiced sincerity, a moan escaping him when he feels how wet I am, and it stabs my core with yearning. His two fingers slide easily along my arousal before he circles my clit.

"So fucking wet for me."

Every nerve in my body flares to life as Hermes kisses and nips at my neck, joining the pinching of my nipple as he works the sensations together. I bow into him and roll my head to the side as he gives my other breast his attention, and an orgasm collects quickly within me.

"I want to hear how beautiful you sound when you come."

His words wash over me, cascading chills down my neck. With nowhere to brace myself except against my thighs, I push the palms of my hands into my legs as my hips circle along with Hermes' fingers. His focus on my clit is bringing me to the peak I desperately seek.

Warmth and currents of Light encase me as Hermes brings me to the brink of pleasure.

I take a deep breath and hold it as my clit throbs in time with the beat of my heart. I pull in another breath, still holding the first one as my orgasm builds, ready to rupture and send me into my release.

"Let me hear you." The rumble of his baritone voice ignites me as vibration begins at the tips of his fingers. My legs jolt, and I fight to hold my breath when a gasp escapes. Hermes presses harder against my sensitive center as he works his fingers against me, demanding the orgasm surge through me. *"I said, let me hear you come, goddess."*

My climax ruptures through me as he applies more pressure on my throbbing clit. I release the breath I was holding as a wave of pleasure rolls from my core through my entire body. I push my feet against the stone floor to keep myself up as my hips work in time with the circles of Hermes and his skillful fingers.

I throw my head against him with an arched back, and he pinches my nipple as the orgasm reaches its apex. My groans echo through the empty halls, and he holds me in place, keeping his rhythm while the vibration at the tips of his fingers increases.

I writhe and hold on to his thighs as my voice bounces around the dark stone halls, releasing my ecstasy as the peek carries on, powered by Hermes' Elemental power. Slumping into him like a puddle of jelly, the orgasm dissipates as the remaining air in my lungs escapes in ragged breaths.

He abandons the sensitive bundle of nerves and spreads his two fingers, rubbing them down my center. I'm already longing for more. I reach my right hand behind me to grasp around his neck, but I'm met with bumpy stone.

I want to run my fingers through his velvety soft hair and grip something real. I want the feeling of fullness inside me while the body of a strong, warm man presses upon me; this man.

Hermes.

Gods, my mind is truly broken.

Longing with desperation, nearly salivating at the thought of a figment of my imagination driving into me as I come around him lets me know how incredibly terrible I am. I don't deserve goodness or care. The fractured mind that drives my thoughts only deserves torment and pain.

"I've waited four hundred years to hear that again." The phantom touch of lips along my neck is gentle, seemingly rewarding. *"But I think you are a greedy goddess."*

Hermes' left hand escapes the folds of my stola and runs down my stomach, heading downward to meet his other hand, still rubbing along my slit.

"Yes." My agreement is a panted whisper as my hips squirm with the receding waves of the first orgasm. Goddess, yes, I want to feel him again. I want to awaken from an eternity asleep and allow

myself to dive into the fantasies that fuel my passion, the desire for happiness and security.

Hermes rubs down the length of me before dipping his other hand below the band of my panties, he spreads me as two fingers dive inside me.

I clench, immediately wishing he were real and filling me with the fullness of his erection instead of an elemental projection of his aura. I want him to turn me around on his lap and drive me down on his cock and make me scream my pleasure into this darkened cell until it explodes around me.

This phantom touch of his aura is still amazing, but I wish it were more. His right fingers circle my clit again, and his left fingers plunge inside me. Pulsating his power into his fingertips, he curls them inside me, stroking and pulling another orgasm from me.

"Wake up, baby." I can feel the ghost of his breath on my neck, and shivers cascade down my sensitive skin. Everything is alive and tingling with the buildup of another climax as he works my pussy and clit together. *"Wake up and come back to me, my goddess."*

"I am awake." My mind can somehow string the words together as I drop my mouth open, thrusting my hips in large circles as my core tightens, promising a larger release than a moment ago.

"They're in your head, Rhea." His raspy voice is full of desire and breathy longing. A vision of Hermes, muscled and naked, resting his left hand above his head on the shower wall, flips into my mind. Steam rises off his wide shoulders as water beats upon his skin.

He's stroking himself, a slight part to his full lips as dark lashes brush the tops of his high cheeks; he breathes the name. "Rhea."

As if chiseled to perfection from the strongest granite, every curve of him is beautiful.

Is this real? Is he letting me see what he is doing to himself as his power pleasures me within the deep recesses of this dungeon? The thought of it tugs at my arousal and I moan. Wanting to feel him, taste him, and my mouth waters at the thought of taking him deep into my throat.

"I already told you my name is not Rhea." Is my breathy reply.

He presses firmly upon my clit, the pulsating quickens along with his diving fingers as he works to build my orgasm. My body is quaking with the feeling of him deftly plunging and curling as he swirls around my clit. Warmth cascades around me and through me, as my own powers swirl together with his.

"Heal yourself, baby, and I'll let you come." His kisses trail down my neck again to my collarbone, and it's like fire racing down my flesh. *"Let me give you what you need."* He breathes against me, and I want nothing more than to surround myself in the feeling of him for the rest of eternity.

I widen my legs, bracing my hands against my inner thighs, and he responds immediately, increasing his stroking and driving up the vibrations of his fingertips. His aura pushes against me, begging me to siphon it. As my orgasm tightens in the deepest recess of my belly, I pull his power into myself with deep breaths and hold them. Collecting the air in my lungs as the pressure builds within me.

With each inhale, I take him in. His power lights me from the inside and brings a silver glow to my skin. The gash at the top of my head stitches together, and the throbbing stops. Like I'm struck by the seductive lightning colliding within his aura, energy surges through my veins while he pumps his fingers into me.

The pressure of my release builds and nears its tipping point as I rub myself against the essence of Hermes' projection, writhing along with his movements to bring another release. With a gaping mouth, my spine is a dramatic curve as the orgasm is on the cusp of freedom.

Then abruptly, he stops.

With an immediate departure, the feeling of Hermes dissolves away, like smoke on the wind, and with it, the build of the orgasm withers, leaving me panting and bereft. *"No. "* The absence of warmth and light contrasts the stark, cold darkness of the tunnels.

Anger is a surging wave, replacing the fleeting lust that was choking me only a second ago. As if carried on a current of wind, Hermes' voice drifts away from me, chuckling like he's enjoying my irritation, knowing he left me on the edge of orgasm that would shake the very walls of this facility.

"Mmmmm, what a good goddess you are. " His voice wraps around my mind and floats across my back like a smooth silk ribbon. *"But you didn't think I was going to make it that easy, did you?"*

"Ugh, you've got to be kidding me!" I spit the words at him through my mind and stand, righting my stola and pressing my knees together to try and quell the throbbing between my legs.

He chuckles at my answer, seething into my boiling blood.

"I don't think so, baby. But come find me, and I'll give you another reward. "

"The only reward I'll take is your head on my blade. "

"You're welcome to try. " The faint trickle of his voice disappears and carries away from me.

Pulling in a deep breath through my nose, I push my shoulders down and twist my neck from side to side. Replenished and no longer exhausted, I refuse to be thankful to that asshole for letting me pull his aura.

I'm seething with annoyance, and my rage against him and Ares flares to new life. I need to get out of here. I close my eyes, and with renewed strength, I think back to the night I woke up from the nightmare and went for a walk.

I wanted to search for hidden levels of the Underworld where rumors of prisoners and torture circulate. A flash behind my eyes makes me flinch.

Fleeting recollections of pain and immobility are a strobe behind my eyes.

It was only a night ago.

Why can't I remember?

The memories have been taken from my mind, leaving only soiled residue lingering on my brain. It feels like waking up from a dream and slowly forgetting it and gods, it infuriates me.

The stale air and dank surroundings confirm this cell has been long vacant, and who knows how much time could pass before someone living comes in here? I need to summon some help, just like I accidentally summoned the vision of Hermes.

The Dark Shield is a viscous swirl of black shadow. Perhaps Hermes' Light could have countered it, but a thought twitching like a nerve in the back of my mind is warning me not to meddle with the shield.

I recall running from thick, dark fog when I last meddled down here, so it's best not to risk it again.

As I'm considering what elemental powers would be best, an idea forms. Darkness can slip through obscurity, hiding within the absence of light without detection.

Closing my eyes and rolling my neck, I think of a spinning eddy of obscurity. A dark portal or someone with the ability to Shadow Walk. But who can be trusted?

A sound pulls on my attention, like the echo of a pebble disturbed pings across the quiet space. I strain my hearing as the sound of footsteps approaching pulls the entirety of my senses.

Someone is here.

The footsteps quicken their pace, heading down the long corridor beyond my cell and out of my visibility, growing louder as they near. The hall's shadows deepen, sensing the newcomer and welcoming it into my torment.

Not someone, something.

The sounds of a beast, their claws clicking on the stone floor with each step, draws closer.

Adrenaline surges down my body, and I'm thankful for the bars of the cage that will separate me from the animal; at least, I hope. My fingers tremble with the sudden surge of energy as I prepare to fight in case they don't.

Walking down the middle of the wide corridor, the shadowed head of a large dog emerges as a dark paw hits the stone. A small flame blazes momentarily with each of the dogs' steps. Lifting its snout into the air, it sniffs and looks at me with burning orange eyes. Like embers of fire resting within its skull, they blaze as they observe me within the cell.

I know this dog. I recall seeing it resting in front of a fireplace with long logs inside a woman's cave.

Cerberus.

The shadows and smoke that make up the dog's form roll constantly and begin undulating faster. The dog splits, and three Dobermans with pointed ears look at me with stoic expressions.

As I wonder if the dog is here to help me or eat me, one of the three dogs shrinks down on itself and shifts into a puppy. Pointed ears are replaced with floppy ones, and the cropped tail sprouts a longer, more excited one.

I smile instantly with a sad chuckle. In a high-sounding voice, I make kissing noises and pat the ground. The small puppy excitedly dances toward me. Slow in its pace, as if trying to get inexperienced legs and its long tail working in time together.

Dissolving through the cage's bars, the young dog joins me inside before dipping to the floor and rolling on its back. The floppy ears of swirling shadows smack against the hard floor, and I can't hold back the smile on my face.

As if the brown smoke and black shadow make up the markings of a Doberman, I notice the coloring of the puppy's coat forms a heart over its chest, and I rub my hand on it.

I pull the pup into my lap, and he curls within my arms. His excited tail hits against my hip as he rubs his head around my hand and chin. A cold tongue licks my cheeks happily before he rests his head on my shoulder.

"How did you get in here?" I ask, knowing the dogs can't respond, yet the thought enters my mind as if they answered.

A Shadow Portal.

The pup in my lap tilts his head at me, and I feel as if he is asking if I'm ready to leave.

The two sentries on the other side of the bars turn to look at me. The burning embers for eyes studying me, and all three wait for the answer to a question that was never asked.

"Let's go find Hermes," I tell them as the short nubs of their tails wiggle back and forth with approval.

The two large Dobermans walk into the cell bars, pausing halfway through. The bars of the cell shift from metal to smoke, and I can walk through them.

I'm so angry Hermes left me. I know he was never really present, but I didn't want him to leave. I wanted to feel more of his soul pull me out of this cold darkness. I can't decide if I want to slap him or fuck him, maybe both, but I'll decide when I get there.

31

Rhea

Three shadow dogs escort me up a long walkway that angles upward. Their twelve padded paws dwindle to four as the shadows merge back into a single animal. Small puffs of fire and smoke are left in its wake as we walk.

Down the tunnel behind me, the darkness continues onward seemingly forever. I push a gentle current of Wind down the path. Nothing more than could be disturbed by the flapping wings of a housefly in case the Dark Mage that placed the shield has another waiting for me further down.

Deeper and deeper into the darkness, my Wind travels. It seems as if I stand there several minutes before the familiar chill of another shield is a warning for me to pull back. There is more lying in wait beneath the Underworld. This tunnel runs deep. So deep I feel the distant heartbeat of the realm, a quiet pulse resonating within the earth's center.

Our track up the tunnel takes five minutes before it levels out and opens up to a large space. Memories of my goal become clearer with each step. The longing to solve Lucas's clue, realizing he was trying to tell me about captive children, hidden away in the shadows of the Underworld.

Finally, I find the entrance. The imposing round Shield of Darkness traps me behind its barrier.

I want to turn around and go back down. The missing Shifter children could be held within the level below, but the faint sound of someone breathing and a gentle trickle of water causes my hearing to spike, working to home in on the noise source.

An outcropping within the rock walls, no larger than a coat closet, creates a makeshift cell. It spans no wider than six bars, and anyone crammed inside would surely suffer in the incredibly small space if confined for a long amount of time.

It's dark within the small closet of a cell, and my eyes try to focus on the mass of brown rock, shadow, and glistening water that trickles slowly down the wall.

Something breaks up the thin stream of water, and as my eyes move toward the rock floor, I gasp, jumping back when I realize it's a pair of men's legs.

Resting against the wall with the feet elevated at the top, the legs crumple and bend at odd angles, leading to a pair of hips tilted dramatically and a torso in the opposite direction.

The man's head is crammed against the rock with his chin tucked into his chest like he was a ragdoll, and someone chunked him into the closet and shut the door, forgetting about him.

It's difficult to tell his former appearance as most of his skin looks like rough sandstone, pale yellow, and rigid as it blends with the hard stone that has grown over him with time. Tens of thousands of years, he must have laid within this small cell, stuck in this position as the minerals of the water dripping over him have calcified as stalagmites.

His light-colored tunic is worn and shredded. Only faintly can I make out intricate embroidered designs that form the body of an owl in gold thread.

My gaze carries up the arm where the tunic is mostly intact, trying to make out more of the design when I see a pair of brown eyes staring back at me. I scramble backward, falling onto my bottom and scooting away.

A wave of heat followed by a cascade of chills swallows my body as I didn't expect the man to be alive in this state. I was certain he was long dead and slowly being ingested by the Underworld.

Minutes seem to pass when I hear another shallow breath and watch the man struggle to breathe. His aura is so dim I can no longer tell what color it used to be, but I sense the element of Water within his Immortal Soul.

I slowly crawl toward him, careful not to startle him as I fear any slight movement may cause him to die.

As I approach, I notice the water runs into a set of three slits in the side of his neck and trickles out the other side, like the gills of a fish. One of them is partially closed with a heap of barnacles taking up residence on the man's skin.

"What happened to you?" I ask as tears begin to well in my eyes.

I feel the man's suffering as constant and tremendous waves of pain flow off of him. Even if the rocks grew into his heart, it would still beat with eternal life. Unless someone helps him, this man will remain here until the end of time.

"I tried to free them." His weary and cracked voice is barely a whisper in my mind. His lips have turned to stone, and he can no longer open them. *"The children."*

His eyes flutter closed, and it seems to take forever for them to open again. His breathing is also incredibly measured like his body has slowed down.

"What is your name?" I lower my voice, and a tear rolls down my cheek.

My heart breaks at the sight of this Elemental, left here like trash to suffer a long death, and I look around the stone formed around his body for a way to free him, but I fear I would only bring him more pain.

"Triton."

I gasp, covering my mouth with my hand as my eyes flare wide.

Memories of a man, a great sailor, and Water Elemental, challenging Ares in front of everyone flash in my mind. He was so vivacious and passionate as he argued with the God of War.

Able to live underwater with his Aquatic Adaptation ability, the gills on the side of his neck and the shallow pool of water he has lived in all these ages, became his prison.

Rumor spread that he was allowed to live and work in the belly of the Underworld, but this was his true fate.

I recall Demeter handing several vials to her daughter, Terra, two days ago.

Take these to Triton. Were her words, and several vials were exchanged. They've been injecting him, drawing out his pain, and making sure he doesn't die.

"Can I help you?" My throat nearly closes with the sorrow of understanding what this man has endured, trapped in the darkness and frozen, having to watch new children be led into the under-belly of Ares's fortress when he first tried to save them.

"You can kill me, but you are not ready yet."

I break out into a sob, crying into my hands. "I can't do that."

"It's okay. I can wait a bit longer, goddess."

"I'm no goddess; I'm only a halfling."

Triton takes another labored breath. *"All of their might com-bined could never amount to the greatness within you."*

Cerberus walks up to me, whimpering and nudging me with his cold nose made of shadows. He passes the information to me that it's time for us to move and my heart rips in two as I stand.

"Ares' office." Triton chokes out. *"The relics he searches for are the key. He must not find the caduceus, but it is imperative you find the pendant."*

I watch him close his eyes and take another labored breath. When he doesn't open them again, I step back once, then twice.

I kneel down to my canine companion, unsure if what Triton said is true but ready to try anything to get out of this cave and find something that can help him. The Underworld will no longer be my home when I leave this room.

I need supplies and a plan.

"I need to get to my room to get my things. Can you take us there?"

As I rub my hand down his head, between his pointed ears, a swirl of darkness revolves around us and up our bodies. Cool and thick, the darkness encases us and like a shadow crawling upon a wall as the sun moves across the sky. We appear within a dark room.

Cerberus teleported us into the walk-in closet of my shared room with Flint.

Upon our silent arrival, Cerberus locks his eyes through a small crack of the closet door, resting slightly ajar. The dog remains on alert and the noises coming from within the room tell me Flint has a woman with him. My hands shake with a combination of nerves and adrenaline at the prospect of getting caught.

The woman moans, sounding as if she is enjoying whatever is occurring and I think back to the whispered promise of assault and the invasion of his hand on my underwear at the arena. I can't help my curiosity and wondering if Flint has trapped another woman here and is forcing himself upon her.

Peeking through the opening of the door, dark hair covers Flint's lap like a curtain while he rests back on one palm. His head is thrown back with his eyes closed. Deep breaths and sounds of pleasure escape his throat as Lexi works him with her mouth. She lavishes his crotch while making sounds like it's the most delicious thing she's ever tasted.

"That explains why he smelled like dog all the time." I blandly communicate with Cerberus through my mind.

Flint's dark tactical pants are a puddle around his booted feet, and she runs a hand up his bare torso, pushing him back onto the bed without finishing him off in her mouth.

My eyes blow wide when I notice his left arm is strapped to his chest in a sling; gauze is wrapped around part of his forearm and wrist. Capped off where his hand has been severed. The very hand that was groping me in the arena.

I had plans to break his hand myself, but it looks like I have someone to thank for taking the entire thing for me.

"Lex, that mouth is a wonder of the modern world." He praises her as she stands. Lifting her red halter dress, she climbs on top of him. "You are going to have Gabriel fuming when he smells my dick on your breath."

I roll my eyes at the smug satisfaction in his tone and want to vomit at the idea of being romantic with him. I can't believe there is a poison strong enough in the world to make a woman fall for Flint.

"What Gabriel doesn't know, won't kill him." She answers in a husky, breathy voice and I roll my eyes even harder. She is acting up the sultry attitude of a vixen and Flint is too much of a horny moron to know she's only playing him. "Am I hurting you baby? You're so brave, defending Demeter and Eris against Hermes. I'm so sorry he cut off your hand."

A smile slides across my face, hearing the information. My stomach flips, knowing Hermes is the one who injured Flint in such a way. Some twisted part of me wishes he had done it on my behalf.

Lexi keeps riding him, playing up the porn-star look on her face, and Flint lavishes it.

"When *you* steal the power from the goddess, you'll finally get the respect you deserve." She leans back, bracing herself with one palm on Flint's thigh and the other around his neck as she rotates her hips back and forth. He releases more throaty grunts as she works him.

My blood runs cold. Was that what he was trying to do with me?

My mind races at the prospect of Elementals stealing power from others. I believed only the Titans could siphon power from each other.

Triton's words a few moments ago, the importance of keeping the relics from Ares, could these be linked to the goddess and the power he wants to steal from her?

"Ares doesn't deserve you as a son." She pants as she quickens her movements, bringing him closer to his climax. "And when you are in control, I'll be your queen. This realm will be ours."

She loosens the tie of her halter top, letting it fall and exposing her breasts. Flint sits up, taking a mouthful and palming her ass with his only hand. She throws her head back and makes all the right noises. She grips the back of his neck, but joyless eyes stare with boredom at the ceiling. She turns her head behind her and locks eyes with mine as I watch from the closet.

Heated and guilty, caught watching the Shifter-mate of the new Alpha fuck my *former* fiancé, I can't move. I freeze while I wait for her to announce me.

Still watching me with her dull eyes, an evil smile curls on her lips. "Does your prude, little *goddess* ride you like this, baby?"

I squint my eyes and tilt my head at her comment.

Am *I* the goddess they are referring to?

Flint removes his mouth from her breast and looks up at her as she bounces on his dick. Not giving him time to answer, she ravages his mouth with hers, swiping her tongue with vigor as he kisses her back.

He breaks the kiss, dropping his mouth open in a gape as he comes. His breathy grunts are matched with fake sounds akin to a cheap porno from Lexi, as Flint releases his climax into her.

"Gods no, she could never ride me like you do." He leans up and kisses her harshly, winded from his orgasm. "You came too, right?"

"Of course I did, baby." She lies. "You always make me come so easy." She looks back to the closet again when he buries his face in her cleavage, still recovering his breathing.

I fake a gagging motion to Cerberus, and I swear the dog shakes his head in response before turning back and watching through the small opening.

Lexi dismounts his lap. I step back from the opening of the closet as Flint rises. Lexi helps him pull his pants up and tugs his shirt back on due to his newly severed hand.

"Demeter has been pumping her mind so full of confusing bullshit she doesn't even know who she is anymore. *Persephone* will be nothing more than an ancient myth when I suck her powers dry." He calls to her from the bedroom as Lexi enters the bathroom for a quick cleanup.

Murderous red clouds haze my vision. They *are* planning on killing me.

A dozen flashes stream through my mind like a reel of pictures.

Silver power from my hands flowing into Lucas as he grows into a monstrous wolf.

Looking at my broken body from a mirror as Ares looks down at me.

Demeter's thick barb, piercing my eye like the fastest cobra and digging deep into my brain.

I am the goddess they were referring to a moment ago. Flint plans to consume *my* powers and take down his father, killing me in the process. But what power could a Wind Siren halfling give to Fire Mages that would be so important?

Wind and Fire aid each other but there is no great tactical advantage.

My mind races, trying to complete a puzzle when I know I only have half the pieces.

Reappearing with her halter back in place and covering the crack of the closet with her body, Lexi holds her hand out to Flint, who entwines his fingers with hers. "Let's go to Ares' office, and you can eat me out on his desk. He won't be back until tomorrow."

They leave the room with a slam of the door, and Lexi giggles like a teenager.

My shallow breaths settle as my heart stops pounding in my chest. The sheen of sweat that collected around my hairline cools as I fan my face with my hand. Looking down at my shadowed companion, Cerberus waits with expectant cinder eyes.

"Do you want to kill them as much as I do?"

He snorts, which I take as a confirmation we agree.

Changing my clothes into black tactical gear and boots, I pack a small bag. Thank the goddess I'm over my period, but I'm not coming back here, so I load a few provisions into the sack and place my arms through the straps.

I can't go to Ares' office if Flint and Lexi are there, so I resolve to break into Demeter's greenhouse and see if I can find anything to help Triton. With another swirl of shadows, Cerberus delivers us to the back of the dark greenhouse. Crouched, we listen, waiting to see if anyone is here.

Two voices trail out of the distance, and I wait to hear the metal door bang shut before I move.

"The Dark Mage is on a mission in East Africa, so she'll be gone for a while."

"Thank Ares' for that. She gives me the creeps."

Sending my Winds gently around the space, I'm certain no one else is here, and Cerberus trots ahead of me to Demeter's workbench. A single bulb hanging from the stone ceiling casts a yellow glow over the area where Demeter does most of her work.

The light fades off into the darkness behind me, swallowed within the tall rows of corn and twisting vines of pumpkins growing in the dark soil.

I search quickly through cabinets and drawers, finding no vials or elixirs that I can use to work Triton out of the rock or ease him on to the next life. He's already suffered so much; I can't think of a way to free him from the rocks growing into him, but I also can't bear the thought of hurting him as he dies.

Triton has earned the right to a peaceful passing as his soul moves on to the Void.

Journals and parchment scatter the desk with Demeter's notes, and they may have something about the potions she's been using that will be helpful.

Black soil has collected in her workbench's cracks as empty pots sit among potted plants. I look to the cluster of journals, sitting open, one in the crease of another, where her red ink pen lays crooked across the open page. The name scribed across the top of a page dated ten years ago grabs my focus.

Subject: Rhea

This name has been haunting me during small moments the past several days, repeated almost by accident by Demeter and Flint, but spoken with conviction by Hermes as he visits my dreams, my very own Sandman.

The journal entry details Demeter injecting Rhea with poisons made from her vines, blended with power from the Dark Mage. She made Rhea believe she killed a family in a car crash, and Rhea suffered terrible side effects such as night terrors and panic attacks.

Flipping through the pages, there are dozens of these notations. Mentions from Demeter of experimenting on the "subject" as the person slept. She fed them potions and concoctions hidden in their food and drink to mute their powers and wove her vines in their mind to ensure fake memories Demeter planted tortured Rhea's thoughts.

As I continue to flip through the old pages, Cerberus turns his head back and forth on a pivot, raising his snout to the air sniffing, and as I read on, the *subject* was plagued with panic attacks, suffering much like my own.

"... she doesn't even know who she is anymore."

The dreams that haunt my sleep feel very familiar to the notes in Demeter's journals, and my chest tightens with the prospect of truth that rang out in Flint's admission.

Rhea is the goddess whose name has followed me like a whisper fading down a dark tunnel for days. She is the knowing look in people's eyes as they avoid my gaze because I am her.

I am Rhea.

My fists clench in anger, and black mist swirls at my feet as the truth breaks over me like a ruptured dam.

Terra stole me from the arena and locked me inside the Dark Titans' den. Ares is gone, searching for lost relics he will use to consume my power. Lucas begged for my help, pleading with words he could not speak to help the Shifter children locked in the darkness. And Hermes–it all begins with Hermes. The earliest memory I can pull is from a few days ago, as his sword rushed into my chest.

I remember the look on his face as it drove into me. It's not a look of satisfaction or accomplishment one would expect to see if he had impaled his enemy. It's a memory of agony and dread.

The expression of someone who is witnessing something terrible happening to a person they care about.

Hermes is an enigma that pulls at my every thought and longing. I feel like he is the missing piece of a puzzle that I need to solve the mysteries clouding my mind. But I can't focus on him right now.

If the Dark Titan will be gone for some time, now is my chance to free the children and Triton locked in the deep recesses of the Underworld, but I'll need help. I need Lucas and Kai.

Grabbing a portal wand from one of the workbench drawers, I return to the dark corner of the greenhouse, and Cerberus pads along beside me. Kneeling to him, I ask him to stay hidden and make sure it's clear when I return.

Pushing the button, the wand flares to life, and purple light encases me. My thoughts are crowded with the vision of Hermes blue light as I think of my destination and those who can help me free the Shifters.

Goddess, I hope I'm right about Hermes. If not, it's not only my life at risk, but the kids locked in the darkness below.

Hermes

Every attempt we make to free Rhea only results in **disaster.** This time, it cost two lives that are tearing at the emotions of our little group of allies. Back at Lucas's packhouse in Mexico, I sit with my elbows on my knees, lost in thought, as I try to devise a plan to get my mate back.

Each moment without her, I feel the world tipping further on its end, and I'm struggling to hold onto my control. My hands shake with the need to do something and know she is safe.

We helped with the pyre of the small boy, the bear-Shifter, whose name I learned was Ted. His mother couldn't find him in the hours before the gladiator event was set to begin. She was looking to leave with her three sons, and Demeter offered to help her search for him.

Naomi and her twins were dosed with Demeter's toxins, and when she awoke, they were in cells. Ted was separated in his own cell. Another round of injections forced them to shift into their bear forms just before the event began.

She recounted the battle within the arena, the attempts the Dark Titan made to capture Rhea, ensnaring her in shadows and trying to affix a dark hood over her face. I can't be sure if the Titan was trying to siphon Rhea's power there or only incapacitate her to devour her later.

Calypso wailed over Atlas for hours as Achilles held her. Each time she cried out, I kept seeing Atlas's body fall into the dark pit with nothing but colorless voids for eyes.

Hypnos offered to help her sleep, asking what she would like to fill her dreams.

"I'd like to dream of Patroclus." She answered with red eyes full of sorrow.

I walked away before my tears had a chance to fall.

I searched the realm with my Light again for Rhea until I heard her call for help. Like a faint whisper in the Wind, a small tendril of her power leaked out from the wards of the Underworld and wrapped around a ribbon my Light. I held onto it tightly and projected my aura where it led me. Her power pulled mine through the protective wards, letting me be with her and syphon myself to rejuvenate her.

She was locked in a cell in the darkness underground, and I nearly fell out of the shower when I realized it. Pushing past the wards was no use and my frustration is mounting to an impending explosion if I don't do something soon.

Rushing to dry off and put on some clothes, I stormed through the hacienda looking for Lucas. I may have taunted her, trying to lure her out, but I have no intention of sitting around and waiting to see.

I'm going to the Underworld and getting her the fuck out of there.

Finding him at a grill, flipping hamburgers, Achilles and Mor watch me as I grab his collar and push him against the wall. Achilles has taken quite a fondness for showing Mor some of his favorite things of this realm, and I suppose burgers are today's lesson.

My right fist connects with Lucas' face, and blood splatters on the wall.

"What the fuck, Hermes?" He growls as his hand rises to his mouth.

"I told you, if she gets hurt, that's it." I push against his throat with my forearm and hold a blade made of Light to his skin, the tip drawing a faint drop of blood. "You're taking me to the Underworld, and I'm getting her out of there, now."

My blood boils, and my face heats with irritation, mostly at myself, for agreeing to this truce to begin with. Lucas will only ever think of the Shifters first and is willing to risk Rhea for them.

"You don't understand everything that happens down there." Lucas bites back, but he doesn't fight against my hold. "The Dark Titan helps Ares ward off the Underworld, and Shifters are nearly powerless against smoke and shadow."

"Thankfully, I'm a Light Bearer and have plans to rip out every shadow I see without question." Pushing against him again for good measure, I release my hold and step back two steps.

The courtyard and upper levels of the hacienda are filled with spectators watching the tension unfold.

"He has our children held hostage, Hermes," Lucas yells, and it bounces around the courtyard. Knowing children are at risk cools some of the burn from my temper, but not much.

"So, we'll get them out, too," I say through clenched teeth. "But she's not staying down there another day. You saw how doped up they had her. She's an empty shell down there, and she is alone, and I'm not waiting another second."

Hypnos approaches, standing in the middle of Lucas and me, forcing us further apart.

"We learned much while we were visiting the Atlanta Commune, Hermes. You must take a moment to see, and it will help as you plan to breach the God of Wars fortress." Hypnos' calming tones and raised hands force me to take several breaths.

Blowing my cheeks and running my hand through my hair in frustration, I concede.

"Fine. Let's see it and get going."

The pearly whites of his eyes fill with grey as he calls upon a higher form of his power.

Waving his arm as if clearing a haze, the ripples of his power obscure the space before us and turn the courtyard into an endless field of white fog. The blue sky above us disappears, and all that remains is ourselves and the metal table and chairs we are sitting in.

"Allow me to interpret the residues of emotion and paint the pictures for you." Hypnos' baritone bellow surrounds us like he is speaking into a microphone as the interior of the Atlanta Commune takes shape.

A firm hand grasps my bicep. My shoulders jump as Medusa emerges from the fog, joining us. "Gods be damned to Elysium, I couldn't see a thing."

"Dammit Deuce. You scared the shit out of me."

She stands next to me as Achilles and Mor both join us with a burger. They tap the sides together as if toasting a glass of champagne before both taking large bites. Ketchup falls from Mors as a glob of bright yellow mustard remains on the sides of her mouth. Both cheeks are full of food as she chews happily.

"I will start with the goddess's entry to the grounds."

The most beautiful vision of Rhea walks through the double doors of the Commune, and her eyebrows shoot into the waves of her honey hair as she takes in the grandeur of the building with wide eyes of wonder.

I fall in love with her all over again as her mouth drops open, and a child-like curiosity washes over her face.

Faint brown freckles dance across her nose, and a blush comes to her face when she takes the portrait of The School of Athens. Callie watches her appreciatively with her hands folded in front of her.

As they walked the halls, Callie started to grab Rhea's hand several times but stopped herself. Perhaps not wanting to offend Rhea, unknowing at the time, they are as close as sisters.

"The goddess strongly reacts to this woman in the red stola." Hypnos motions to the devil herself as Circe struts down the stairs. Her eyes burn through Rhea, who looks away. "Inadequacy and self-loathing radiates from the goddess while jealousy and sinister hate exude off this woman."

"Son of a bitch." Lucas mutters while I seethe with silent rage. "What is up there, H?"

"It's Eris' private quarters and her office." I release a deep breath through my nose, attempting to cool the burn coursing through my blood. "So, Circe recognized Rhea then?"

"I cannot determine that from these emotions. But it is curious someone could react so strongly to a stranger, don't you agree?" Hypnos' vision continues as we whisper of the implications of Circe visiting Eris on the day Rhea arrived at the Commune.

The fog shifts to a new Mirage, and the Dark Titan stand with Lupo, watching the Commune on the night we rescued Rhea and Calypso from Lupo's hold.

"The Herald holds her release within his Light. She is no good to me until she unlocks her powers." The Titan strokes Lupo's ear, and he actually whimpers as he leans into her touch. I wouldn't be surprised if he started thumping his leg like a dog getting its belly scratched. *"When I drink her powers, you can feast on her flesh."* The Titan promises.

Over my Immortal body.

"I visited the office of your mentor, I apologize if this seems an intrusion, given he lost his life tonight, but it is important." Hypnos waves his arm across in a sweeping motion and the fog rolls, revealing Atlas's office, stuffed with books and his brown leather couch that many times served as my bed.

My heart rips in my chest as I see a vision of Rhea lying on Atlas' couch, Athena on one side and Atlas on the other. Both of these great Immortals are now dead and my mate is missing from my side.

The emptiness inside me could swallow the oceans of the realm in a single gulp.

"Immense guilt, confusion, a manipulated mind that is locked within a tight cage." This was the memory of Rhea's car accident, and in a few moments, she'll disappear.

"Did you inspect the portal?" I ask with eagerness.

"I did, young Bearer."

Atlas reaches into the portal and inputs the code. Then darkness swallows the memory.

"The great Titan had been lying in wait within the portal. A strong mirage, a Dark Oasis, deeply concealed her presence."

"Could you tell what happened?"

"The Titan attempted to steal the goddess with a Dark Portal, but Rhea conjured a doorway of her own nearly instantly. I doubt she even realized she did it. One darkness overtook the other, and she escaped through it. The Titan could only send a sliver of shadow along with the goddess as she made her escape."

While the fog disappears, I watch my two teachers fixate on the screen in Athena's hands as she points excitedly at something. Atlas pushes his glasses up on his nose as he leans down to watch. I've seen the gesture billions of times, and in this moment, I wish for a second more to watch them a bit longer.

A sniff beside me pulls my head as a tear drops from Medusa's eye and lands on a leather journal. Athena's name is etched on the cover. Atlas gifted it to her during the Age of Oceanus once. Sticking out of the journal are two jade hair pins with small snakes carved into them.

"You went to her office?" My tone is hushed as I ask the question that needs no answer.

"Of course, I did." She whispers back before she turns and walks away.

"Did you go to Rhea's room?" I ask Hypnos. The fog rolls to show us Rhea's studio. The room she first stayed in until it was violated.

We watch more visions shift, seeing Flint break into Rhea's room scaring her, standing with the shadow of the Titan around him as he waited in a portlet. The shadow surrounding him held him back from violating her, demanding he wait until I unlocked her power.

The shadow encased Terra, following her as she poisoned Flora's dinner and then clung to Flora's back as she disabled the shield, letting the wolves into the Commune.

The fog lifts and I process how far the Darkness spread around the Commune, hiding in corners and surrounding those we know betrayed us.

"Is Erebus possessing them?" I ask.

"Not really," Mor says, still munching on a hamburger. "Shadow Observing is taking a piece of your aura and letting it hang out with someone else. You can go where they go, see what they see."

The Titan of Elysium was working in the background within our Commune, plotting with Eris, Flint, and Terra the entire time. The wolves were a distraction, and they were only waiting for me to free Rhea of her spell with my Light so Erebus could consume her power. Flora was set up with a poison so to other elementals, it would look like she acted on her own.

Atlas was right.

He was always right about these sorts of things. Always able to see around the obvious and find the angle no one else does. I'm just sorry it wasn't soon enough to save Flora from a week in the Labyrinth, enough to save Athena's life. Enough to save Rhea.

"Did you get anything the night–" I pause, looking back to Medusa, who is pretending she can't hear us. "– the night of the Commune attack?"

"Apologies, no. We received your call for help and left immediately."

Stroking the stubble on my chin, the short bristles of two days' growth scratch against my fingers.

Gods, I wish I had perceived this Dark Titan back at the Commune.

We knew the Sensors found the presence of Darkness in the ally when Rhea and Callie were abducted across the street from Once Upon a Spine bookstore. Erebus watched and plotted the entire time, playing people against us and waiting for the right moment to pull Rhea from my grasp.

No longer crying, Medusa joins me, the journal tucked under her arm. "I'm going back to my Commune to interview Ana's sister again. See if she can give us any information on Erebus and how she works."

With a nod of agreement, I clap my hands, looking to Lucas with a plan determined.

There is no way I can counter that level of Darkness alone and I need to get Rhea out of Ares' fortress. If Erebus has the entire Underground warded and is holding a group of children as hostages, we need to get everyone out at once.

That means we need help.

And I know one group of Immortals who hate the Elementals, but they despise Ares more.

"Where are you going?" Lucas asks me.

"You mean, we—where are *we* going." I correct him. "We're going to make a truce with the Vampires."

⚜

Lucas, Achilles, and I teleport to Venice to speak with the leader of the Vampires. Callie, Mor, and Hypnos accompany Medusa to her Kenya Commune to question Ana about the Dark Titan.

The sun is setting on the floating city, and we wait, sitting in chairs of an outdoor café finishing an espresso. Pigeons are swarming around tourists who get their pictures taken with flocks of the grey birds all over them.

Venice is, of course, beautiful and a place of curiosity for the mortals. Little do they know the floating city was built to be a sanctuary for the Vampires. The growing requirement to feed their bloodlust secretly and live in relative normalcy drove the need to create a haven of their own.

But now that Vampires can practically order a blood bag like takeout, they have moved into other areas of the world. Only a small presence remains here. The floating islands belong to the mortals now. Overbooked tourists hop out of water taxis with fanny packs and camera phones pointed at the Doge.

Two men in black suits and sunglasses walk in step with each other across the Plaza toward us.

Achilles and I share a knowing look.

"Vampires are so dramatic." Achilles rolls his eyes at me before tipping the end of his espresso cup, draining it.

"We have very good hearing, too." Vlad the Impaler, the first Vampire in history, startles us. My heart thunders in my chest. Achilles shoots back from his chair as Lucas spills dark brown expresso down his grey t-shirt.

"Dammit." He mutters as he brushes himself off.

Vlad sits with one ankle crossed over his knee. His modern black suit, tailor fit, is snug to his lean body. The black shirt is unbuttoned, showing his muscled chest and tan skin. Long brown hair rests in waves on his shoulders, and light blue eyes pierce me, even in the darkening sky, as he delicately picks up a small espresso cup and its tiny saucer. Silver rings reflect on several of his fingers while the end of his index finger holds a piercing ornament.

Shaped to look like a pointed fingernail, the silver piece of jewelry slides onto the tip of his finger so he can pierce the vein of his meal and feast on their blood.

The devil has always been described as one of the most beautiful angels, and it's easy to understand how Vlad combats his sinister reputation with seduction. The mortals of this realm would have no defense to deny a deal with this demon should he set his vampiric powers on them.

"Well, have a seat." Achilles jests with an eyebrow cocked.

"I own all of this. I'll sit where I please." Vlad sets the espresso down, and another is immediately provided to him. The mortal waitress gives a timid bow and keeps her terrified eyes on the ground.

Like a cobra lashing out at its victim, Vlad's hand snaps around the thin wrist of the woman, and he pulls it to his face. Running his nose along her wrist, she releases a quiet yelp when he drags the sharp-tipped end of his finger along her skin.

"Thank you, Giada." Vlad turns his icy eyes on her, and tears fall from her eyes as she darts away, clasping the small tray to her bosom as she runs inside. "Let's make this quick so I can tell you to fuck off and get on with my evening."

"Why agree to meet if you're not going to help?" Lucas growls. His irritation ripples off the surface of his skin.

Vlad seethes back at Lucas, running his eyes down the length of the Shifters body before finally answering. "Down, boy."

"Okay, why don't we calm down and start over." I put my hands out at both of them, and Lucas sits back in his chair while Vlad takes another sip of espresso. How, in the shadow realm, did I decided to play peacemaker between the Shifters and Vampires is beyond me.

"I just find it funny how the Elementals are fine to leave the *bloodsuckers* out of their little parties until shit hits the proverbial fan and then come crawling to my doorstep. My very busy and lavish doorstep." He enunciates the syllables, speaking slowly as if he has nothing better to do with his day.

"What Ares is planning will not escape you, and the Council cannot be trusted. They are likely working together." I begin. I doubt we have time to get into any real detail, and I'm sure Vlad doesn't truly care. "Ares has abducted my mate and plans to use her to cause mass destruction of the mortal world before consumes her power."

"Perhaps you should learn to hold on to your mate better." He hits me with a low blow, but I keep my calm, tampering down the rage that wants to slice his tongue out of his mouth. He's part Fae, so it would grow back.

"The way you did?" I hit him lower.

It's a fraction of a second before I fly through the air and my back slams into the café wall. The crumbling plaster breaks around my frame as Vlad hisses at my neck with his long fangs exposed. His eyes turn black as if someone has dropped ink into crystal blue water.

The phantom outline of his large batlike wings glamoured out of view, flap in the shadows, and the wind rustles my hair. I keep my eyes fixed on his deep voids as darkness takes over his veins.

"I have long tamed my demons, Herald, but I'm happy to bring them out and teach you a lesson in humility."

"Ares will come for the Vampires to add to his army, or he will wipe your existence from this realm." I grimace as Vlad pushes his forearm further into my throat. "Join us, and let's end him."

Before he can answer, a bolt of lightning strikes nearby, and thunder grumbles as if complaining about our disagreement. As the wind picks up, the sky darkens, and my core vibrates with recognition.

The trusted sword charm on my necklace nearly dances, as if the pull within me wasn't enough to tell me Rhea is near.

Vlad and his men look up at the sky and then at each other. Immortals know the onset of ethereal power. We can feel it in the molecules of the air. A wicked grin slides across my face as the Vampires try to make sense of the being that is arriving.

The mortals begin running from the Plaza, heading for hotels or water taxis before the storm arrives, but as a black whirl of darkness swirls in the center of the Plaza, the storm that is my mate steps out of it.

Her honey hair whips about her, and the yellow of her eyes gleams like the most precious gold as she glares at Vlad, her gaze flicking down to his hold on me.

"Take your hands off him."

S eeing this man's hands on Hermes throws me into an immediate state of rage. I'm partly confused as to why my reaction is so intense, but I need his help. With the children, and to fill in the missing parts of my memory.

Something within me wants to cast aside all these excuses and just admit a plain truth.

I need him.

My powers seep out of my tight control, and a storm of my anger comes to my immediate beaconing as I get my bearings. I've seen Venice many times before to recognize the iconic bell tower and ancient palace, but I focus on the man holding Hermes against the wall.

I opened my mouth before I knew what words would come out of it, and as soon as I uttered the phrase, the dark Fae with shadows of a demon surged for me. Large wings unfurl from a glamor, and he is an arrow headed straight for me.

Hermes begins to turn to starlight as he evokes the powerful speed of his Light element.

But before either of them can take more than two steps toward me, I wrap my strong Winds like a net around the demon Fae's wings and pull him between the columns of the Palazzo Ducale. Slamming him into the wall, just as he had Hermes, my black mist anchors him in place, not allowing him to move.

I cut the man a daring glance as Hermes rushes me. Hope and relief wash off of him in torrents, and while I sense no bad intent from him, I cast a Wall of Currents to shield him from reaching me. He runs into it, as his hand presses against the shield like glass. His other hand holds the charm of a necklace.

I think I see a flash of pain cross his eyes, but he looks down quickly, blinking rapidly for a moment before returning his deep blue eyes to mine.

"I can't remember you." I begin, but my throat chokes out the rest of my words, almost as if they are too emotional for me to speak. Clearing my throat with a cough, I continue. "I can't remember you, but I want to."

Now, I'm certain I see the pain my words are inflicting on him. It is as if every syllable is a stab into his heart. While desperately wanting to take the shield down and touch him, I have to hold back. I can't trust myself or the thoughts I have.

These thoughts could be another layer of traps Demeter sets to ensure I remain ensnared by her and Ares' plan to consume me. With the children held within the Underworld, I have to ensure they are safe and keep myself from being tricked again.

I look beyond Hermes and find Lucas sitting with another man, both of them watch us closely. While they pretend to sit in relaxed positions, the tightness around their eyes gives away their attentiveness to the Plaza. I know they are poised to act should it be necessary.

"I found the children." I raise my voice and let it carry on the Wind to them.

Lucas stands and quickly joins Hermes, remaining out of reach by my shield.

"Can you get them out?" Lucas is almost begging with the strain in his question.

"With help, I believe I can." I try to keep my attention on Lucas, but my eyes keep finding their way back to Hermes.

The intensity of his gaze upon me pulls a blush to my cheeks. Then I think of the times I dreamed of him, of how I let him touch me in my fantasies, and I can't stop wondering if he knows.

It's written all over my face but I force a look if indifference as I speak to the men.

Being this close to Hermes is almost suffocating, and I take a few steps back, putting some distance between us and letting my Winds fill me with fresh air.

"I can get us behind the Dark Shield; I just need some help getting the children out." I stop fighting and let myself linger on Hermes and the handsome lines of his face. I work hard to keep eye contact and stop myself from looking at his lips and wondering about the way his stubble would feel against my face. "The Dark Mage went to East Africa, so she is not–"

Hermes' eyes flare at my comment, and he turns quickly back to the man still sitting at the table, then back at me. "What did you say?"

"East Africa," I repeat the words I heard as I snuck into the greenhouse.

"Achilles," Hermes calls out, and his companion is by his side with a flare of fire. "Medusa's Commune, the Titan went there."

Without further comments, Achilles dissolves into a whirl of blue light, activating a portal.

"Will you help me get the children from the Underworld?" I ask the pair of men remaining in front of me. Both of them look at me with pleading desperation, but I can't help but think they each have different reasons.

Hermes seems to be trapped, waiting for me to remove this Shield, and I wonder if he is fighting the compulsion to touch me as I am fighting to touch him. It's as if the proximity to him sets my skin on fire, and the only way to extinguish the flames is to get closer to him.

Lucas is a ready servant for his people, anxious to free them from harm.

As my Winds settle, a cold wave of darkness swells at my back with a building power behind me.

Shattering my Shield of Currents in an instant flash of cerulean Light, Hermes' arm wraps around my waist, and he turns me. My body is flush against his; my hands fly to his muscled chest to balance myself from the sudden exchange of positions.

The contact of my flesh, touching him directly, is like the birth of a universe, exploding into existence, and it steals my breath. The weight of a thousand words hangs heavy in his gaze, and it seems he has lost his ability to speak as I have.

Hermes' thick shield replaces mine, but instead of acting as a barrier between us, his shield is at his back, surrounding us in a wall of protection. The blue light crackles, and white smoke rises from the other side.

A column of darkness and shadow careens into him. The sound of darkness trying to split the light open is like a deep bass playing at a long and low frequency out of a speaker. It rattles your teeth and chest, making your vision shake.

I focus on him and steady myself against the constant blaze of his sapphire eyes as the Dark Titan attacks us.

Finally, *finally*, **Rhea is in my arms and my soul explodes.** I want to wrap her in my embrace and never let her go. I want to crash my lips upon her like waves crashing against a shore.

Moving with the Light, I can drag a second on for minutes. I take my time to study the gold flecks in her eyes and inspect every grain of golden brown, finding small hints of green, like emeralds dancing in a gilded river. I find a dozen constellations in the freckles that dot her cheeks and nose. One grouping even reminds me of the pair of lovers in the Summers Triangle. Vega and Altair, an old legend written in the cosmos of two lovers separated by a river of stars.

The Fates have destined Rhea and I to suffer, just as the lovers separated in the Milky Way, because each time we get close to our happy ending, it's ripped away into a torrent of agony. Even though she is only millimeters away from me, her mind, and her heart may as well be galaxies away and out of my reach.

I waited on the other side of her shield, knowing her power and the ability she has to make it impenetrable; however, it was a weak barrier. Lucas could have turned into a big bad wolf and blown it down without effort.

Rhea was not truly trying to keep me out, but the barrier made her feel comfortable and I was not going to risk her feeling of safety for the mere selfish need to touch her; the longing to reach out and entangle her fingers with mine and hold her hand was overwhelming.

But the Dark Titan left me no option.

I saw the swirl of her shadow portal, just as it flared when Erebus arrived at the arena. Thick, viscous grey and black smoke, spinning in a corkscrew with flashes of white lightning on the edges.

Before the Titan could walk through and throw her first attack, I was there.

Turning Rhea away from the danger and giving my Shield to protect her.

The action triggers a memory of Nyx, performing the same move on me during the battle that first took her life from me. The battlefield behind us is blurred in my mind as I can only see Nyx. Her skin was cracked like broken glass. Her silver aura shining from within her as something caused her power to break out of her.

A Dark Mage threw a spear, aiming for her.

I put myself in its path, but she spun us, taking the spear through her back; it skewered us together, impaling me through my chest.

I was happy with this outcome. Glad to die in each other's arms and join the Void together. But Nyx summoned a dark portal, and we burned through Avalon's skies before crashing into the lake. Nyx healed me, and I was forced to watch my mate slip away from me.

As I look at Rhea now, I renew the promise I've made myself. This lifetime will not kill her.

The look of confusion and lack of recognition in Rhea's eyes as she searches mine is enough to drag my soul to the depths of Elysium with the weight of my sorrow.

I wish to all the gods of all the heavens that she would know me.

That my touch alone would be enough to blast away the clouds that confuse her and bring her back to me.

"Will you do something for me?" Rhea's voice is barely above a whisper, but it rings as loudly in my mind as the seven trumpets of Hel.

I run my fingers through her hair, tucking a stray lock behind her ear and letting my hand linger on the side of her head. My stomach flips when she leans into my touch for the briefest moment.

It's over in a second before she composes herself, visibly shaking her head.

"I already told you, I would give everything I am for you."

She gasps, her mouth remaining open as her eyes widen.

It's the comment I made to her in the cell when the astral projection of myself pulled out wonderous sounds of pleasure from her throat. Rhea's freckled cheeks turn a blazing red, and I can't hold back the smile that leaks onto my face.

Her surprise makes me think she didn't believe it was real. Perhaps she thought it was truly a dream instead of a projection of my aura.

Rhea closes her eyes and takes a steadying breath before opening them again and letting me look into the golden sunset that lives in her eyes.

"Keep the Titan busy for me?" She asks.

A veil of mischief washes over her expression, telling me she is returning to the Titans layer to save the children. I will teleport this Titan all over the realm and run her ragged to give Rhea as much time as I can.

I pull her closer to me and touch my forehead to hers. My lips tingle wanting to kiss her before she leaves me again, but I won't until I know she wants it. Moving with the Light, I unhook the two thigh holsters that carry her blades and secure them to her legs.

She gasps and looks down at them with a deep crease between her eyebrows.

"Take these and go." I release my hold of her, and she readies her finger on a dark portal that will take her back to the Underworld. "Promise me, when you're done, you'll find me." I pour all the hope within my heart into the request and pray she can feel my sincerity.

"I promise." She answers. "I'll find you."

Before she can press the button, I turn to the Titan, and putting both hands against my Shield of Light, I turn up the intensity, pouring more of my aura until the light turns white, burning against the Titan's dark eyes.

Erebus casts her arm in front of her face to block the light, and it singes the shadows that form her cloak.

I mask myself and Lucas by refracting the light, rendering us invisible, and we run to a far corner of the plaza. Casting dozens of Mirages of myself and Lucas and projections of Rhea, the Titan's eyes dart between them all, trying to decipher which is our true form.

"Can you shift into other people like Kai can?" I call out over the sounds of the Dark Mage blasting beams of shadow at the Mirages I'm making.

"No, only animals. Big ones."

"Shit." That is not the answer I was hoping for. The Titan is here for Rhea; if Lucas could shift into her form, we could keep the Titan distracted more easily. "Okay, I'm going to piss off the Titan; you get the mortals out of here."

The Titan's frustration grows as she attacks my Mirages faster, grunting with each blast and turning quickly, searching for our true forms.

"And don't scare the mortals." I call back over my shoulder.

Lucas turns into a normal sized Australian Shepherd and begins running after mortals, barking and nipping at their feet to prod them toward the water taxis that are leaving the island.

With a surge of my aura, I project a tunnel of Light ahead of me and pull myself toward it. In a fraction of the time, it takes to blink, I'm in front of the Erebus, and my left-hand flashes a burning beam of light into her eyes while I punch her stomach with my right hand.

Darting away, she blasts dozens of dark knives in an arc away from her, hoping to hit me while she blinks quickly, recovering from my assault. One of the blades skims my forearm, splitting the skin, and beads of red blood form in a line.

I dance and dart around the Titan, drawing my sword from its sheath and blasting rays of blue light from the topaz stone.

Aiming away from Erebus, I teleport to the Light and refract it back to her. Like a grid formed with the rays of my power, it creates a confusing effect like a hall of mirrors.

The brightness singes the Dark Titan, hitting her shadows and eating them away as puffs of black smoke rise off her body.

Spreading my awareness to the rest of the island, Lucas is quickly sweeping through buildings, barking his warnings, and rushing the mortals toward the canals and docks for evacuation.

The Titan begins catching on to my charade of light and counters with her dark beams.

The shadows of the plaza reach for me when I stand too close, so I work to remain in the sun's light.

Catching me around the shoulder with a wisp of shadow, Erebus pulls me to her and rams my thigh with her knee before pushing off me, separating us and readying for another attack.

The ground becomes liquid under her power as it buckles and ripples. She steps down into it and braces against it to accelerate toward me again. Teleporting away, she rams into the crumbling wall with her shoulder, and the building quakes.

We take up the entire plaza with our battle. Erebus charges me. I keep her engaged, buying Rhea as much time as I can and hoping she works quickly to free the children.

Lucas's bark carries on the storm's winds as he yells orders at fleeing tourists, but Vlad and the Vampires have abandoned the floating city. *Asshole.* Water taxies and boats scream around the Venetian lagoon, carrying humans to safety.

High winds build around us, and the waters of the Adriatic Sea swell with the lingering anger of the goddess when she first arrived. Beating against the canals and splashing against the buildings, the Plaza is flooded in several inches of water as Rhea's Winds moan while they twist through the buildings.

Flipping out of Erebus' reach as she swipes the dark spears at me, her cheeks flare as anger rages over her emotions. She sheaths the obscurity within her cloak and flexes her shadowed hands at her sides.

Straining against her powers, a wide chunk of the plaza floor breaks apart. Dark ribbons spin rapidly around the mass as she hurls it at me. Dodging the boulder-sized block, it crashes through the corner of the island's iconic red bell tower. It breaks through one wall and exits the other.

The tall tower was a beacon to the mortals, ringing to let them know the palace was open for visitors. In truth, it was a dinner bell for Vampires, and called their meals to their front door.

Ceremoniously still ringing twice a day, the great bell gongs as the bell tower twists in the fluxing power of the Titan and the sway of the manmade island.

The ground below us snaps, and a fissure opens up the stone below our feet. Racing along the Venetian Island, the crevasse runs up the façade of the cathedral, shattering the elaborate glass dome.

A crack echoes into the roar of our elements colliding. The bell tower bucks, breaking under the force. Aiming toward Lucas, it hangs as if savoring the moment before freefall; then it surges toward the Shifter. Fixated on getting mortals off the island, Lucas doesn't notice the collapsing tower, hungry to crush him.

Erebus rips up two large sections of the ground and throws them at me.

Swaying between the blocks with my Light, I pull Lucas out of the way. The red bricks of the fallen bell tower are spread across the plaza and churned up a large cloud of dust that swirls in currents of the wind as I kneel next to his smaller canine form.

"She's going to sink all of Venice!" Lucas yells into my mind.

"So, shift into something bigger and help me out," I reply breathy. My chest rises quickly with my pounding heart. *"We need to give Rhea as much time as we can."*

Projecting more Mirages of our bodies and throwing images of long shadows onto the ground, Erebus' attacks are becoming erratic as dark beams shoot around all angles of the plaza.

"Is she a new Titan? She kind of sucks." I call to Lucas as I enter the fight again.

The Titans were there at the beginning of magic and were the birth of Immortality. Erebus is a pretty shitty fighter for someone who has lived across the birth and death of realms.

Unless Erebus truly died in the battle of the Titans and has reincarnated back to life. Perhaps she is getting accustomed to a new body, just as Rhea has done through her deaths and rebirths.

I watch the Titans counterattack and exploit her weaknesses. Pushing closer to her with a blinding light, I land hits and attacks, slashing at her with my sword.

As the Titan holds up her arm, blocking another ray of light, a gloved right hand, missing a ring finger, is splayed in front of her face. My attention narrows in on it, and my Shield of Light flares, snapping angrily around me and surging outward.

That's a very specific finger to be missing.

A Mirage.

The figure is inverted, nothing more than an obscure Mirage cast by the real Titan.

I sense her directly behind me and turn my body, hurling my aura in a circle, using it to propel myself; my hand grasps the throat of the Titan. The blast of my Light destroys her Mirage, revealing her true form before me. With an obsidian blade hanging high above her head, my power disintegrates the knife as I look into the face of Aryana, the sister of Medusa's generals, *rescued* from her captivity in the Underworld.

Her eyes are bottomless voids of darkness, and a menacing smile fills her face as the mask of shadows drops from her body.

With a burst of Darkness, she explodes away from me. Shadows propel her to the top of a crumbling building. Her black cape of obscurity whips around her, and the deep void eyes bounce between Lucas and me as if choosing which to devour first.

Having decided on Lucas, the Dark Titan pulls back, powering herself and then ejecting a Void Beam. Before the column of obscurity connects with Lucas, I shield him. Giving the Titan my back, I brace myself against the attack, bracketing Lucas around my power and taking the force of the Titan's attack.

Countering the darkness with my Light, I focus the entirety of my aura behind me, and my Shield absorbs the Titan's power. So cold it burns. I wince and grunt against the force and the pain of the darkness barreling into my back.

The island bucks and breaks beneath us. A quake throws us to the ground as the footings beneath Venice rupture, and the sea begins rushing in.

My power is building. I strengthen my aura behind me as my ability rises to meet the blue stone within the hilt of my sword. I sense the blue glow of starlight surge and hear a faint ringing of my power building to an apex.

I scream against the agony as Aryana increases her attack.

As if charged by the topaz secured within the hilt of my sword, my aura expels out of me in a blinding flash of blue light. The Titan's assault ends as a screech takes over the plaza.

Like a banshee screeching into the night, the Titan's mouth gapes open; the scream emitting from her forces my hands over my ears as I protect myself against the sound. It rattles my vision, and darkness crowds the edges of my eyes.

My light is burning a hole through the center of her chest, eating away at her shadowed form.

From her mouth, a plume of dark clouds races out of her. Wide and thick, it's like a stream of fast-moving smoke that transforms into thousands of black daggers. The swarm of shadowed weapons takes us over, obscuring the Titan from our view.

Lucas, still in the shifted form of a dog, jumps into the murky water through a large hole in the center of the plaza. I cast a wide shield and my light burns away the blades as they cross the threshold of my aura.

With an exclamation of anger, the Titan's roar bounces across the open space as her shadowed form folds in on itself until she disappears.

The ground below us buckles and groans before splitting. The crack within the great cathedral widens as the manmade island breaks apart. Running across the plaza, several mortals trip on a rising piece of stone and are swallowed within the fractured ground as the sea races upward.

"Think of something fast, Lucas." I scream out in my mind.

Erebus is gone and dozens of mortals still need to make it out of buildings and across the crumbling, sinking island. A building to my left fractures and plummets into the adjacent canal as the waves of the lagoon feast upon it.

Thrust out of the ground, a blur of something large and red surges from within the sea. Curling around the centuries-old cathedral and wrapping large chunks of the ground and buildings that remain, the tentacles of a great red squid hug the main island of Venice.

"Hurry." The strained voice of Lucas booms into my mind. Searching through the twists of arms, covered in suckers that slither along the crumbling island, it takes my mind a moment to process what is happening.

"This is what you come up with? Seriously?" I yell out across the plaza at the giant squid-Shifter. Lucas is holding up the largest pieces of the manmade island, but we likely only have a few precious seconds.

Expelling my Light, I find people trapped within buildings and teleport them to safety. My speed's building faster and faster until I eventually disappear. Only flickers of blue light flash in the places I pause long enough to secure the mortals. My power, charged by my need to get to Rhea, has never felt so strong, and I'm nearly drunk on it.

The wind and waves fight against Lucas as his giant Shifter form remains wrapped around the island. He's definitely larger in this form, but I can't tell if it's because of the animal he chose to shift into or if he is coming into his Titan power more.

Having cleared the buildings, I take to the plaza and stumble over the end of a bright red tentacle, catching myself before falling to the crumbling ground.

"Disgusting."

"Whatever. It worked, didn't it?" The long, slimy arms of the squid begin to retreat, and the waters of the Adriatic swell around us.

Teleporting myself, to the topmost part of the cathedral that is slowly being eaten by the water, the familiar propeller clip causes my shoulders to drop, and I rub my hand down my face.

"Oh, fuck me." I'm not a fan of flying with Medusa who makes every effort to dip and flip her plane until I'm as green as the algae that grows on the bottom of these upturned chunks of Venice.

Through the darkened clouds that begin to clear as the residues of my battle against the Titan dissipates, Medusa's plane, the *Serpetra,* screams past us. The amphibious white plane with dual propellers, circles the sinking island as we stand atop the remnants of the iconic dome.

With a final flash of power, I pull us inside the plane and feel the slither of the squid returning to Lucas' human form. Throwing our bodies into the few seats inside her small aircraft, Lucas and I melt into the soft leather cushions.

Lucas, naked but human again, is soaking wet, with pockets of slime covering him.

With deep breaths of exhaustion, we look at each other, unable to speak or form coherent thoughts about what just occurred.

He must realize the smart-ass comment that is on the cusp of my mind because he rolls his eyes and rests his head back against the chair. Closing his eyes and releasing a large exhale of relaxation, the tension of the past few minutes leaves him.

"Just shut up." He huffs, pulling a smile from my face.

I take a few steadying breaths and put my request in to the pilot. "To the Underworld."

Leaving Hermes and returning to the Underworld took all the strength of my Immortal soul. The way he looked at me; the way he held me, it was like I was something precious. As his touch left my body, I tried to freeze the moment to memorize the sensation of his skin on mine.

This feeling I've longed for but felt I could never have; felt I was never worthy of–I just felt it. Hermes makes me believe there could be a future waiting above the surface for me. A future of someone who may need me as much as I need them.

But the children locked in the Underworld need someone to save them, and I am their only chance. So, I have to push my wants aside, and give my focus to those who can't help themselves.

Ares has constructed a realm of darkness and shadow and packed Shifters into his armies, ensuring he had a way to keep them loyal and abiding.

But I will bring light to the darkness that holds them captive.

I'm going to free them and then free myself. I'll return them to their families, and I'll return to Hermes. I'll give my soul the freedom to search for happiness without guilt or the weight of feeling as if I only deserve suffering.

Teleporting back to the greenhouse, Cerberus rises from a nap on the dirt floor and sniffs me as if making sure I'm okay.

With a pet between his ears and a nod, I pass my intentions to return to the layer of the Dark Titan behind the shield so we can find the children locked away.

Cerberus' swirl of shadows envelops us, and we arrive at the layer where he first retrieved me. The empty cell beckons me as the place where Hermes restored my power, and my cheeks flame again when I hear him recite the line said to me twice today.

It was never just a dream. It was all real.

Suffocating down here in my loneliness, I realize hope was floating high above the crushing depths of the ocean where the moonlight kisses the waters. Hermes was searching for me.

I descend deeper into this level, beyond my cell and toward the Dark portal blocking the next passageway. My senses are attuned to the whispers of dark forces that swirl around me as the weight of the ocean bears down upon me.

I push on, driven by an urgency that tugs at my immortal essence and begs me to free the innocent souls trapped within this prison.

Once I set them free, the Underworld, a clandestine abyss hidden beneath the roiling waves, where shadows dance, and secrets whisper in the dark, will cease to exist. I'll crumble the foundations and tear out the pillars that hold up these oppressive walls.

As I move deeper toward the heart of the blockade, my determination swells. My purpose is clear and unyielding. The aura of malevolent energy grows palpable, throbbing against my skin like a warning to remain away from the dark shield.

The cold silence of these abandoned levels is broken by the distant echoes of lost souls that wail and beg from within the shield. With a flick of my hands, a brilliant luminance erupts, casting silver rays of starlight that slice through the undulating shield.

Beyond the pulsating barrier of this hidden trove of secrets, I sense them—the telltale presence of innocent souls, their essence obscured by a barrier of writhing, malevolent energy.

"Can you get us in there, boy?" I ask my smoky companion but feel I know the answer.

I approach the wall of elemental dark magic as Cerberus sits at my side, the tendrils of the shield wriggling and coiling in defiance as if daring me to challenge its authority. With a steady breath, I summon the extent of my aura, channeling the boundless power into a torrent that surges forward and collides with the unforgiving darkness.

The clash is cataclysmic, an explosion of raw energy as my Winds and aura assault the shield. I feel the strain on my essence, the push and pull of opposing forces threatening to overwhelm my very being as the darkness tries to pull me into its dark abyss.

Widening my stance and bearing against the obscurity, I refuse to yield. Not when the lives of the innocents hang in the balance, their faint cries urging me ever onward as they sense me here.

With each surge of power, the barrier weakens, its defenses crumbling under the relentless assault of my divine will. The cries of the children grow more fervent; their presence becomes the hope that fuels my resolve to shatter the chains of their captivity. Cerberus releases short huffs as if coaching me along to continue my attack.

I press on, my essence pulsating with the intensity of my mission, until the barrier finally shatters, dissipating into transient coils of shadow that fade into the abyss.

Looking beyond the large arched opening that leads into an expansive room, I see them.

There must be more than one hundred frightened children before me, their eyes wide with awe and fear, their fragile forms huddled together in terror, and my chest breaks open with both happiness and sorrow. Part of me hoped I could be wrong that perhaps children had once been kept here but were freed long ago.

I want to cry as I take in the dirt and ash coating their bodies and the thin, torn rags that hang loosely on their emaciated forms.

Older children protect younger children, using their bodies to cover them with their arms cast wide. The stain of trauma is familiar as I look upon them.

I know the pain that is etched into your soul as you endure torment and suffering inflicted by the hands of others. These children have suffered here, not only neglected by the lacking presence of caretakers but they have been abused.

Bruises and scars glimmer along their skin. The bends of their arms hold the lingering signs of multiple injections administered routinely and in the same spot.

In this moment, I vow to murder Ares, painfully and slowly. Not for the torture he inflicted on me, but for the pain he put these innocent souls through. He'll scream ten-fold at the agony I will inflict upon him before I snuff out his Immortal Flames. And if I could deliver him to the shadow realm myself, I would.

Dropping to my knees, I extend a hand, my Winds conjuring a warm breeze to fill the frigid space with a soothing warmth. I tilt my head and pray that my presence will envelop them in a cocoon of safety and reassurance.

"It's okay." My voice cracks as I speak, overcome with emotion. "I've come to take you out of here, to take you to your parents."

The kids exchange glances, and slowly, two or three of them begin to stir from their tense positions. They cast weary looks at Cerberus until he shrinks down to a puppy again and ignites a faint smile on several of the children. Cerberus wags his tail happily in response.

"I promise we'll protect you, but we must hurry." I try to urge them without upsetting them. Hermes and Lucas are delaying the Dark Titan, and I can only hope their attacks distract the Titan from sensing I have destroyed her barrier.

Looking at each other, they begin nodding and standing up, holding hands with each other and forcing their feet to move, one in front of the other, despite their fear of what could come next.

Together, we ascended through the swirling currents, leaving the oppressive darkness of the Underworld behind. Cerberus leads them and my heart crumbles as a sea of children cross before me. Ensuring everyone has left with us, finally, I walk with them.

We rise gradually with the tunnel; I am filled with a profound sense of fulfillment, watching as the children embrace each other quietly, with tearful eyes burning with the promise of rescue with each step we take.

Cerberus grows in size and is back to a full-grown Doberman as we reach the top of the tunnel, and I hesitate when I hear the faint trickle of water and the slow intake of breath.

I don't want to frighten them should they see Triton in his state of suffering.

Kneeling next to my new canine friend, I pass my instructions to him, and while I stare into his flaming eyes, I know he understands.

Cerberus splits into three Dobermans and circles the mass of kids. His forms each split into three more dogs, and he spreads himself around the large circle of rescued children. I urge them to pack in close around him and reassure them everything will be okay.

Some have become brave in the few minutes of our walk up the tunnel to put their small hands on his bodies made of rolling smoke.

With a nod, Cerberus engages his shadow portal, and a cloud of darkness engulfs them. Cerberus will locate Kai and deliver the children to her safely.

I know the Beta that risked her life to remain here with me will do the same for the children and protect them as they work to locate their families.

Giving me enough time to talk with Triton, Cerberus will return for me.

I may not be able to help him today, but I will return soon with someone who can.

Walking to his cramped cell, I kneel and wait for him to open his eyes. As if moving in slow motion, he finally does. I feel like I held my breath, waiting for the signs he is still alive.

"I freed them." I let him know.

It's important he knows the children he wanted to save, the reason he has been locked away in such terrible pain, are safe and okay. I want him to know his suffering will not be in vain.

As I begin to make my promise, the noise of a portal pulls my gaze.

Expecting Cerberus, I jump back as I see Terra soaring out of a vortex of swirling rock that has turned to liquid with her Earth element.

Two sharp barbs pierce each side of my neck, taking my breath as scorching lava runs down my spine, spreading out within me, clinging to my muscles, and weaving through ligaments.

With my hand moving fast to cover the wounds on each side of my neck, I remove the thick barbs. Black and curved, the three-inch monsters are like the angry thorns of a rose bush except much larger, and more hateful.

Turning to my right, Terra stands, her freckled face burning with anger as her body shakes. Her hands are clenched in fists at her sides, and her chin quivers with both pain and hate as her brown eyes pierce me.

Soundlessly, the rich purple swirl of Cerberus' portal brings him back, and he senses the attack immediately. Without hesitation, the shadow dog is a dark arc through the air with nothing more than a single growl.

Terra's face relaxes as if relief and recognition flow over her. Cerberus has opened her throat, and dark ichor of her immortal blood flows like a deep crimson river down her shirt.

The poisoned barbs do their job and leech their toxins into me. Rushing through my blood, they take over my will and turn my limbs into a state of catatonic rest, waiting for direction.

Terra drops slowly into her whirlpool of swirling rock as her skin pales. Cerberus' bite is turning black with decay as darkness spreads within her. The veins that run the length of her body darken and contrast her greying skin as she dies slowly.

I want to scream as the molten poison runs inside me like galloping stallions, but I can't. The poison has once against stollen my voice but much more so than before. I drop to my hands, banging my knees on the stone ground as my spine stiffens, forced to succumb to the control of the venomous barb.

"M–m–mother never loved y–y–you," Terra struggles to speak with her mind. Her voice brawling with the wound at her neck as the blood rushes out of her to drain along the floor. *"B–but she always p–p–picked you."* Her chest spasms, struggling to hold on longer as she sinks into the ground.

My hands and limbs lock, curling in on themselves as a seizure gripes me like a vice. I roll to the side, arms and legs stiff as they curl me into a ball, frozen.

"Kill him," Terra whispers, her voice deep and commanding, as if summoning some deeper power.

Cerberus growls a warning and steps between us as I remain locked in place, twitching as the poison coats my insides. Terra falls deeper into the pit of liquid rock that delivered her, but her whirlpool is slowing, the rock hardening again.

"Kill the messenger of the gods. Kill Hermes." Her voice is an echoing boom around me as all light is slammed out of my vision. The contagion coursing through me receives the command and a red haze replaces the darkness.

Cerberus whimpers as he watches me writhe on the floor before slipping into the shadows of the cave floor.

My body begins moving with the command given to me, the poison coursing through me, forcing me to comply as my mind repeats: *"Kill the messenger of the gods. Kill Hermes."*

We suck. We are the worst Immortals that have ever been blessed with power.

Hermes and Lucas are waterlogged and just sank an ancient city. Hermes is laying his head on the headrest in front of him, green in the face from using his powers to teleport us here, only to be rewarded with Medusa immediately putting the plane into a spin.

Mor loved it, but my brother is still a bit dizzy.

Achilles sits with me, drawing lazy circles on my palm as Mor and Hypnos stare out the plane's windows, taking in the scenery. Medusa is circling the Atlantic Ocean as we search for an ancient teleportation pad.

Powered by a large stone, encased with Elemental power and protective runes, the pad would have been used by the Titans to travel between realms.

The stone is likely powerful enough to transport us beyond the Dark Titans' wards and get us into the Underworld. The only problem is, we can't find it, and we've been circling the Atlantic for twenty minutes.

Medusa stares out the window, still shocked at what she found when she returned to the Kenya Commune.

Nothing remained but death and shadow.

She was seething as she walked her destroyed Commune, her emotions ripe with the demons of her past. She is working to regain her composure as we formulate our plan to recover Rhea.

At the Commune, Achilles arrived like a ball of fury. Rhea had mentioned '*East Africa,*' and they knew the Dark Titan was headed to Medusa's Commune in Kenya. But the damage had been done, and the threat was gone. We were searching for survivors, when Achilles arrived. He removed his shirt to staunch the bleeding of a Commune member, but they died within seconds.

Still shirtless, slouching in the chair with his jeans pulled low, his long legs are splayed wide, and the grooves of his pelvis are like a homing beacon, drawing my gaze downward. I allow myself a moment to feast on the sight of him. Carrying my eyes up his muscled torso, the tattoos that run up his arms and cover his chest depict the greatest hour and the worst moment of our lives.

The gruesome Battle of Troy is drawn onto his skin, and the tattoo ink is preserved with Elemental magic. On his left side, the war is raging with soldiers and Elementals battling. The mighty Trojan horses made from Cornel trees that stampeded the battlefield. On the other side, the barren ashes of war.

The only remnants left behind are those of scarred land and death. Even though he rests against the back of the chair, I know the portrait of Patroclus between his shoulder blades, as well as I know my reflection.

His seafoam eyes and the final tear that rolled down his cheek that was our last vision of him when he died on the Trojan battlefield.

Feeling the burn of my mate's gaze, I shift my eyes to his and find Achilles' heated expression, knowing he caught me so obviously ogling him.

"My, my, my. What on earth is the great Wind goddess thinking about, I wonder?" Achilles' teasing voice is a caress across my mind as he speaks directly to me and draws circles on the palm of my hand.

"Since you have no shirt, you may need to remove your jeans, as well."

"If you'll help me." He winks, making me grin.

As he opens his water bottle and takes a large swig of the clear beverage, I send him a mental projection of him sitting me on top of the flight controls and diving between my legs as I rest them on each side of his wide shoulders.

I can't help but giggle when he sputters, choking and coughing before shaking his head at me.

"What a voracious appetite my little Siren has. You know my favorite place in all the realms is between these two beautiful legs." He rubs my knee and squeezes my thigh, raising his scarred eyebrow into his hairline. *"It's a hard job for a single Flame to keep the temptress of Wind satisfied, but I will do my best."*

"I'm well acquainted with how–hard–it is." My grin is near sinister as he bites the inside of his cheek, fighting to keep his composure.

Hermes lifts his head, starting to speak before looking between Achilles and me. Recognition that we're heavily flirting with each other pushes his brows together, and he looks like he's going to be sick again.

"Ew. Really?" He asks aloud to his oldest friend. "That's my sister." He feigns disgust with his old joke, but he got over the bond his two best friends had with his sister a long time ago.

As we search the open ocean for the partially sunk portal, I think about Aryana, delivered to the battlefield, broken, beaten, and bleeding. Just like Terra.

We took her in and healed her. Everyone believed her to be a released captive, a bargaining chip against her sisters, forcing them to betray Medusa.

But it was her all along.

How many times can we fall for the same fucking tricks?

The medical room where Aryana had been recovering was destroyed in the powerful flare of the dark portal.

Every Elemental in the Commune had been decimated by darkness as the remnants of splattered shadows and immortal ichor stained the stone of the Kenya Mountain.

I recall the image of Damien's body when Achilles and Hermes found him in the darkness of his apartment. I found Anahita in the same condition. Her throat was ripped out by her own sister, decay already taking over her body as rigor mortis forever locked the pained expression and widened eyes on her deceased form.

In the end, she knew. Ana realized her sister severed her own finger and planted the Lurker on her and Avaley. Afflicting them with false Mirages of torture, Aryana forced them to go insane until she broke them enough to betray Medusa.

Aryana built a doorway to allow herself a way in and used her sister's terror to do it.

She had always been a Dark Mage, but, like Lucas, she was transformed into a higher power and took over the persona of Erebus, and formed the shadows around her to mimic the slain Titan's appearance.

We were all fooled, and the entirety of Medusa's Commune and the mortals they rescued paid the price for our blindness with their lives.

My brother sits up and points to the side of the plane where Achilles and I sit. "The portal is right down there." He tells Medusa, and she angles the plane in a turn and begins circling the space above the large teleportation pad.

As Hermes stands to take a look out of my window, he wrenches his face in a grimace and releases a scream of pain. His back bows dramatically as he falls to the floor.

I'm ripped out of my thoughts just as I rip my body out of my seat and rush to his side. He falls to the aisle between the seats and rolls on the ground, grasping at his neck.

I push his hands away, finding nothing, and Achilles forces Hermes onto his back, holding his head in place so we can try to talk to him.

"What is happening?" Achilles asks.

"It's Rhea." I gasp. "He's feeling what she feels." Heat rushes down my body at the prospect of my friend, my chosen sister, getting hurt as she returns to the Underworld to save the missing Shifter children.

"It–burns." Hermes chokes out.

A wind pushes into the plane, and Medusa fights the controls. I work my airstreams to keep the plane stable.

The currents of the realm scream at me as they warn me of the approaching goddess.

"Bring me the Herald, Siren." Rhea's voice travels on the Wind and dances through the cavity of the seaplane but it doesn't sound like her. Gone is the sweet tone laced with kindness. Replaced with a deep, emotionless command.

"She's coming." I breathe as my eyes widen, listening as Rhea and the airstreams speak to me simultaneously. "She's coming to kill him."

I push myself up and rush to the windows, looking out at each side.

In the far distance, a darkening sky with lightning crashing angrily to the ground gives me a good indicator of where Rhea is and how much time we have before she arrives.

A plan forms in my mind as I look at the horizon.

Rushing to Achilles' side, I pull my brother's arm and work to sit him upright.

"Help me get him up," I grunt, and my mate pulls Hermes' other arm.

"What are you doing?" He asks.

"I'm going to get my best friend." We move Hermes back to his seat, and I pull my hair into a ponytail at the top of my head. "And you're going to hide my brother."

Taking the few steps to the front of the plane, I relay my plan to Medusa as Hypnos and Mor listen closely.

"We'll need a shield around the islands," I inform my brother.

"Which islands?" Hermes answers, regaining his composure after the initial surge of pain either dissipates or he's working to get it under control. He's not happy about being left out of the plan, but he knows when I get stuck on an idea to step back and follow my lead.

"All of them," I answer as I push a portal wand into Achilles' pants pocket and raise on balls of my feet for a goodbye kiss.

He pulls me by the back of my neck, and with parted lips, he sweeps his tongue into my mouth. Closing my eyes, I savor the taste of him. Before he pulls back, Achilles rubs the tip of his nose across mine, making me smile.

"Be careful," Achilles says, and I give him another quick peck before I usher him toward my brother.

"You too," I answer with a wink. "You boys stay on the portal and retrieve the stone. The Light energy coming from the platform surrounds this entire area, and it should be too disbursed for Rhea to pinpoint Hermes."

"Gods, I love you and that genius mind of yours." Achilles grins at me as he and Hermes disappear on a wave of blue light, teleporting to the podium below of the broken teleportation pad.

With my hand wrapped around Rhea's necklace, I sent my message back to her on the Wind.

I haven't taken the necklace off since we checked on Hermes and found an empty potion bottle. It warms with my touch, as if reassuring me this plan will work. We'll have Rhea back and not just safe with us but free from the darkness that clouds her mind.

"Just circle this area." I have to yell at Medusa over the sound of the plane.

"I really hope this works!" Medusa calls back over her shoulder.

The memories of my last great battle here still send a shiver up my spine as I stand at the open door of the plan and look out over the angry waves of the Atlantic Ocean.

Six days of fighting against Aphrodite and her fleet of Sirens resulted in the deaths of over twenty thousand islanders. Penelope and I chased their ships north, where they finally scattered.

The mortals of the islands still speak of The Great Hurricane of 1780.

But today, there will be no lives lost. *I'll make sure of that.*

We make yet another pass, and in the distance, grey clouds reach down to kiss the horizon. A glimmer of silver flashes like the bright bulb of a lighthouse, illuminating dark waters on a stormy night.

"She's here."

Medusa continues her flight path, heading straight, and I glance at the sun, still about an hour before sunset. *I can work with this.* Grasping the headrests on each side of me, I peer through the windshield at the approaching storm.

"Damn," Medusa mutters an impressed curse as we watch Rhea advance.

Walking on a wave of water, her winds pull a tsunami nearly two hundred feet tall.

"I love a woman that makes an entrance." Medusa continues. "My baby could make the *sexiest* entrance." Medusa leans toward Mor slightly, complimenting her late partner, Athena. Mor nods in agreement, as if she knows what Medusa is talking about.

"Take us up a little higher, into the clouds." I pat Medusa twice on the shoulder and return to my position near the rear door of the seaplane.

Waiting until the plane is even with the sun and hopefully within a sun flair for Rhea, I open the door and drop myself into the open sky.

The breeze beats at my skin and feels like a thousand hands caressing me at once as I plummet to meet the ocean. Like a swan dive from a high platform, I hold my arms wide and push my feet together.

The fickle winds of the realm require some negotiation as they are conflicted on which goddess they should answer. The warm air of the North Equatorial Current is already a churning vortex of raging power, and it is begging to be unleashed, so we reach a swift alignment.

The winds that gather here are voracious and harbor the lingering cries of millions who prayed for salvation. Sometimes the answer only came from gluttonous waves that beat below the bows of death ships.

Medusa, having delivered her cargo, is pointed back toward the islands, and I help her along with a little push, eager to keep my friends safe while I wait to bring my chosen sister out of her haze.

"What are your terms, Siren?" Rhea calls out to me. I'll forgive her lack of recognition at our reunion, but I can't say I'm not disappointed. A small bit of me had hoped our friendship may be enough to spark something.

"Wind Element only."

She nods in agreement.

"Until death?" She calls back.

I lower my gaze at her, unamused. In her right mind that would have been a joke. In this clouded state of brainwashing, it's a very likely reality.

"Until yield. How can I deliver you to the Herald if I'm dead?"

"Fair point."

Her Winds grow and she lifts into the air, meeting me as I rest on a spinning vortex. The tsunami that carried her here is technically against the terms by using water. Now that she has agreed to the challenge, she releases it.

Wind Elementals are great partners with Flames and Water Sirens because our powers assist each other. I can bring my mate's Flames higher or create channels for rushing waters to surge at blinding speeds, but I have another objective today.

Just survive.

"Let's go." I sneer as the clouds behind me break, and the hurricane at my back engulfs us, swallowing Rhea and me in a raging maelstrom.

Come on, girl, all we have to do is survive.

37
Hermes

"**S**o, you have any ideas on shielding the islands?" Achilles asks as we watch the plane fly into the clouds. We pause as the Sirens call plays a haunting melody among the clouds.

"You know, more or less." I answer with a grin and a shrug. I have no clue how I'll generate a shield large enough, but I've got my sword and my power and we're going to take this stone from the defective portal.

Perhaps I can do something to use all three together, though I have to be careful with the stone. Its power is made for a Titan, not a Light Bearer, and I will burn myself out if I'm not careful.

"Looks like the challenge is on." Achilles nods his head at me once. I know he has faith in Callie and her plan. The mighty Calypso has never failed to bail us out of a lot of bad spots. But with Rhea's power out of control and her mind in a vice, I must admit, I'm worried, too.

I wish there were time to wait for Medusa, but I know that's a luxury we won't have. We're close enough to call to each other through telepathy, so I tell her my idea and ignore the laughter she sends back.

"It'll work," I promise Achilles, hoping to convince myself as well.

We stand on the portal in the middle of the Atlantic between Bermuda and the Caribbean islands. A disk of Light serves as our ground as we look across the angry waters. Tall waves reach upward like clawed hands of shadows trapped within Elysium's River Styx. The churn of the ocean mirrors the last few days of the realm as storm clouds crawl across the sky.

"Holy shit." Achilles exclaims with eyes wide and mouth gaping.

I can feel her before I see her. Closing my eyes, Rhea is radiant enough for me to observe with her aura alone. The atmosphere of her starlight churns far below the surface of the waves and rises again behind her.

Opening my eyes to take her in, she is a masterpiece. Art, created to be observed and amazed, intended to make you feel and rip emotion from you as you take in her magnificence.

The tsunami she walks on worships her. The element is all too eager to obey the whim of her needs and would happily flood a continent if she unleashed it on them.

Unbeknownst to her, she's helping me. The broken and busted teleportation pad that was exposed and functional in the time of the great Titan, Oceanus, now rests ten feet below the water's surface.

The mortals have named this place The Bermuda Triangle for the havoc this broken portal causes occasionally. Still emitting elemental Light energy, it's been known to sink ships and bring down planes as the mortal technology crosses into its field of disruption.

Someone should have taken care of this thing long ago, but it will serve to help my needs today, so I'm thankful for it.

As Rhea pulls the water with her, feeding it into her wave, it exposes the broken pad. I feel the power thrumming within the stone, and the intensity of it crackles along my skin.

Achilles and I climb down, hanging onto the sides as the choppy waters, which are lower than usual, beat against us.

After Callie's infamous battle against Aphrodite and the massive hurricane they caused, Callie moved to the islands for a few decades with Achilles. She wanted to help rebuild and rehabilitate the mortals who suffered under their power.

She couldn't bear it if something like that happened again, and neither would Rhea.

While Achilles or I would happily let this realm crumble for our mates, we know it's not what they would want.

Mirroring each other, Achilles and I are fixed on each side of the pad. Its tilted platform shields the runic stones containing the essence of Light. I feel it calling to me and hear the ancient voice of Theia, the great Light Titan of Hel, within its pulsating power.

"One, two, three." We count together and grunt, straining as we hold on to the portal with one hand and raise the platform with the other.

In perfect timing, the chopping propellers of Medusa's plane echo, and with her approach, she uses her Earth Element to retrieve the stone inside the portal. Lifting it with her ability, the stone levitates and travels out of the inner workings of the pad.

My hand reaches for the glowing blue stone on instinct, and I can't stop myself as I inch closer to it. Encased in sapphire light that matches my own, I want to be consumed by it. Something inside me, the immortal essence of my soul that bonds with particles of Light, longs to be infused with the stone.

A great boom in the distance sounds like a skyscraper collapsing upon itself, consuming floor after floor as it plummets to the ground. Wind rushes in, and static on the horizon warns of the approaching wave.

Rhea must have released her hold on the tsunami, and it will be upon us any moment.

Pulling ourselves back up to the crooked platform, I grasp the runic enchanted stone, and the surge of power into my arm courses through my body.

I feel like a bolt of lightning cracking endlessly through the sky.

My arm vibrates from the power within my hand, and a brilliant blue light glows within me, coursing through my veins as it radiates through my limbs. The world around me pulses with light, and it overwhelms my senses. Blinking my eyes against the increased luminescence around me, I see the oncoming wall of water as a solid block of light.

Teal, blue, and violet churn with yellow as the large body of water moves in a giant mass toward us. Within it, the residue of Rhea's silver aura swirls alongside the energies emitted by the life within the ocean. The amphibious creatures of the blue depths swim downward as the wave passes, otherwise undisturbed by the approaching havoc this will cause when it reaches land.

Pushing the stone in front of me and grasping it with both hands, the power regulates through me, and I serve as a conductor to channel the immense energy. It's a burn in my hands that feels good, and I can't let it go.

A bellow forms in my throat as I pull in the power and I feel it collide with my aura, merging within me to become one. My hands shake as the runes of the stone expend their energy into me. Gritting my teeth to stop them from chattering against the vibrations, I squint my eyes and bend my knees to brace myself further against the rush of power.

"Hermes?" Achilles' worried tone is distant, even though he stands right next to me.

I feel the water nearing, but the stone's power is still raging into me, and I'm helpless to wait until it's spent. A second ticking by feels like an eternity as I hold firm, shifting my feet to widen my stance and bracing further against it.

Building to an apex within me, I can't hold it back any longer, and I have to release it. I feel like I am the sun on the verge of exploding as it feels like molten lava has replaced my Immortal Ichor. The sounds around me turn to static, and my vision glows. Everything scorches so bright; the burning orange sky and the angry blue ocean blister white as the power takes over my vision.

⁂

"It's okay, son." *I look up and see the eyes of my father, and my heart breaks into a billion pieces. The sight of him surges through my conflicted heart like meteors burning through the atmosphere.*

I crash into him, hugging his waist and squeezing my eyes shut against the tears that fall, dampening his ceremonial tunic. It's scratchy against my face, but I like it.

It smells like him, like lemons and sunbeams that stream into my window and wake me up in the morning.

Pulling back, I strain my neck to look up at him. A child against a giant. At least that is how I saw him at this age, when I celebrated my eighth Great Year.

"I didn't mean to do it. I didn't know it was the Titan." More hot tears streak my face as they fall freely. My father kneels down to meet the level of my eyes. I sensed a terrible dream of someone nearby and sent them reassurance. I had no idea it was the mind of the great Titan.

His cloak with golden threads glistens as he moves, and it looks like melted gold resting upon his shoulders.

I miss him.

Cupping my cheek, his eyes relax, and sympathy fills them. A ring of humor hangs on the edge of his gaze that he is trying to hold back.

"Theia said it was the most beautiful dream she ever beheld." His eyebrows stitch together, and he cups my cheek. "Not just anyone can project a Mirage into the mind of a Titan. You're going to make an excellent apprentice to her."

"Please don't be mad, papa. I'll tell her I don't want it." I sob again and look down at my sandaled feet to avoid the disappointment that must be lingering in his thoughts. My father is the apprentice to Theia. I never wanted to unseat him.

"Hermes, a Titan never chooses an apprentice lightly. And never has a Titan chosen two." He cups my cheek and lifts my chin. Ducking his head and forcing me to meet his eyes.

Patient like horizon waiting for daylight, he doesn't judge my tears as he smiles.

His reassurance does little to quell my nerves. At least, I didn't cost his position, though I'm terrified to have to face the dragon.

"Theia will grant you a wonderous gift today, to celebrate you and announce to the realm her new apprentice. And I will be her Journeyman. One day, we will both be Masters of Light under her wing." He rubs his thumb across my cheek and wipes away a freshly fallen tear. "I would be honored to serve our Titan with my son by my side."

My mother kneels down next to him and takes my hand in hers. A dark blot of ink stains her left finger near the knuckle where she holds her quill. She smells of the forest and parchment as her dark hair blows in the soft breeze of the day.

"We're so proud of you, son. The moment we first looked at you and saw the power of starlight in your eyes, we knew you would be destined for something wonderous."

"What about Callie?"

"I'm already wond-rous!" She can't pronounce the word correctly through the two teeth she recently lost. "See! A witch gave me this."

She holds out a dandelion with fluffy white seeds while holding Atlas' hand with the other. He chuckles at her along with my mother and our father. Ares arrives and places his hand on Atlas' shoulder with an affectionate squeeze and gives my father a warm smile.

"My sister would not take kindly to being called a witch, little Cala Lilly." My mother nips at her nose and chuckles.

Taking a deep breath, Callie blows the frail white seeds, and they float in the air. Twirling her hand, she spins them into a ball above our heads and with a burst, they explode and rain over us like stars falling. "Now, any wish you make will come true."

"I'm afraid of her." My small voice quiets as I admit my fear of the great cosmic dragon, formed of pure light from the outermost reaches of the universe.

Atlas joins my parents and kneels next to me. "Then wish for bravery, my boy, and I believe it will come to you when you need it."

Next, I stand with my hand in my father's, and he leads me up the wide, pearly steps. At the top sits the Titan of Hel, Theia. Yellow and white light form her large, scaled body and wings, each tipped with a long talon. Curled around the circular temple, the wide set pillars are wrapped with green leafy vines and covered in flowers with petals so delicate; they blow off in the gentlest of winds.

With her mouth parted slightly, her teeth, made of pure gold, glint at me as they reflect the yellow aura of my father. Set within the rigid brows of her large skull are two carnelian stones for eyes, and I can sense her inspection of my soul. She knows everything. Every thought, every secret, and yet she allows me to continue my approach.

The realms have gathered to celebrate the passing of her house. Dignitaries and heralds have arrived for days and presented her with blessings and gifts. Now, they stand in quiet observation. My mother remains at the base of the monument with Calypso and stokes her platinum hair as Callie holds a fresh bundle of dandelion flowers. Mother gives me a reassuring smile.

Atlas and Ares stand on the other side, and each offers me a nod or a wink of encouragement. I take in a deep, steadying breath and walk up another step. Everyone is wearing the colors of my father with a sun crest on their tunics. My mother and Callie have a sun broach in their hair in his honor, and I'm scared of disappointing him. I'm *afraid I won't be able to carry the gift the great dragon will bestow upon me.*

My father releases my hand, takes his place to the right of the Titan, smiling brightly. His aura pulsates as it does when he is most happy. I remember the glow of his power for days after Calypso was brought to his door and warmth flows through my nervous limbs.

I take the final steps alone and stand waiting with my hands nervously clasped in front of me.

With a single flick of her stretched-out claw, a wave of cosmic light swells in all directions as the Titan declares me her new apprentice and Herald of Hel. She doesn't speak, but the pulse of power gongs like the purest bells sound. The Titan's power will reach all the realms, and every Titan will acknowledge her declaration.

She cocks her head to the side with curiosity before closing her eyes. Stretching her long neck toward me, she tilts her great dragon head down and waits.

Mustering every ounce of courage possible, I walk the final two steps. The breath from her large nostrils is hot against my sandaled feet, and my knees quiver. With a trembling hand, I place it between her eyes, and lower my head to hers just as Papa instructed me to do.

"Hmm." Her deep voice is a like an endless echo in my mind. "Bravery you already have my young apprentice. My gift will be an invaluable asset to your future as you are destined to build a bridge between the realms."

Behind the darkness of my closed eyes, a radiating light grows brighter as the power takes over my vision.

As if my back is ripped open, blue light is expelled from me like the beam from a pulsar star. I scream against the burst of light, and it expands, forming a massive shield that stretches hundreds of feet into the sky and rages down the length of ocean.

Guiding the light like a wall forming, it races against the wave as it surges away from Rhea. Hitting against my barrier, the large crash of water propels upward and slams down again, settling back into the angry ocean.

Reaching on farther than our Immortal eyes can see, the Shield of Light holds fast against the release of power from the goddess. The islands are protected and will be safe from the raging storm as the goddesses charge into their battle.

Medusa has landed her plane, and it nears the platform, bobbing in the rough waters as she opens her window and shouts across the screaming winds at us. "Let's go! I won't be able to take off pretty soon."

As Achilles and I climb into the plane, with the glowing stone safely in my trembling hand, my mind reels from the vision.

"I've never seen anything like that before. Ever." Achilles holds a look of shock with his hands stretched out as if in surrender. He takes in the sight of the great wall of light that fades beyond the clouds and stretches down the horizon. "How are you able to hold the power a Titan without it consuming you?"

"Because I'm the Apprentice of Hel."

Dark clouds loom ominously over the churning waters of the Atlantic Ocean. An irate sky mirrors the turmoil within my heart. Standing on a wisp of air at the forefront of the tempest, my platinum hair is glinting like a beacon amidst the chaos. Clinching my fists, I brace myself for the confrontation that my heart aches to avoid.

Across the furious sea, my best friend emerges from the depths of her wave and lets her own winds carry her into the sky. Once filled with warmth and laughter, her gilded eyes now radiate an eerie glow, a testament to the sinister enchantment that holds her mind tight within its vice. My heart twists as I see the transformation in my dear friend, my chosen sister.

"Rhea!" My voice carries across the raging wind, a plea laced with determination. "Don't you remember who we are, the bond we share?"

Rhea's laughter cuts through the storm, sharp and jarring. "You think me foolish, Calypso?" she spits back at me. "Regretting your challenge, knowing you have no power to match me? You should have thought of that before you hailed me with your offer. Now give me the Herald or give me your life."

Her words are a spike in my heart. She may as well have cast a narrow barb of Flaying Wind through my chest.

I knew it would likely come to this, and I'm ready for what I must do. Hope drowned inside me when I watched her approach, walking on the crest of a two-hundred-foot wave; I knew she came to battle. Perhaps I was naive to think something I could say would convince her to listen, but I had to try.

With a sorrowful resolve, I summon my Elemental magic, weaving currents of Air around me like a protective shroud. Rhea charges back both arms to her right side and surges them toward me, flinging a barrage of wind projectiles at cutting speeds. I deftly deflect them, my soul aching with each collision.

The swirl of our magic collides, and a churn begins to revolve around us. A barricade, caging us inside the winds of our conflict. Mine, with battling my dearest friend and hers, likely holding back just enough to keep from killing me, unknowing our true bond.

The moan and groan of our Winds pull the clouds to our epicenter and blocks the setting sun. Gloom coats the interior wall of the hurricane formed from our rage as the funnel grows in intensity and speed.

Opening my mind to the Winds, I bring the happiest memories of our lifetimes to my mind. The clouds swirl and form the faces of my friendship, a Mirage of our shared hugs, and secretive giggles crack across the sky as lightning streaks through the clouds.

The images and the sounds of our laughter distract Rhea. Thunder rumbles beyond the storm as confusion of the conjured faces crowds her mind. She hesitates, and the pause brings faith blooming to my aura and the images brighten. Inside, I know she can feel something conflicted within her. I'm certain of it, and while she is angry, she is scared, alone, and longing to wake up.

My gaze never wavers from my friend as my voice carries over the storm.

"Deep down, you know this isn't you. We've faced countless challenges together. We've laughed, cried, and shared dreams. Don't let poison and darkness steal this from us. Fight it!"

Across the waves that flail beneath us, I faintly see a clear glaze wash over her eyes. Gone in a blink, she furrows her brow and rearing back with both hands, Rhea surges toward me with a maelstrom of wind daggers, arrows, and spears.

As streams of supercharged wind shriek through the eye of the storm toward me, I twirl my body upward in a spiral, they follow me up the path of the hurricane. Colliding as the ribbons of my Currents guide them into each other, my aura bursts within them and yellow particles of my magic rain down on Rhea.

I have always been one with the Wind, a master of its tides and an embodiment of its capricious nature. It's followed my every step and been with me in the darkest pits of this realm. But godsdammit, so has she. And I'll make her see; I'll make her wake up from the slumber of this poison.

As the bursts of my aura rupture around her, the sounds of my memories dance within the storm. In whispered secrets and shared fears, we found a bond stronger than steel. During late-night talks and on starlit walks, we stitched our souls together with invisible threads and as her attacks attempt to cut each one, I hold onto threads of our friendship stronger and weave them tighter.

"Make a wish." My voice rings like a soft bell within the strong gales of our power as my memory bursts in the flashes of lightning behind the clouds.

Under an old oak tree thousands of years ago, we sat, shoulder to shoulder, as a rainstorm showered the land around us. We were exhausted after a long run through the countryside with Hermes and Achilles.

It was her idea, Nyx. But I'm betting she won't recognize herself through the brainwashing, so I only show myself. The memory sketched by the wind as if seeing through her eyes.

As the boys foraged for hares and berries and picked through the dampening brush to make a small fire, we regretted our choice to come along for their run. Dozens of miles we suffered, refusing to give up, knowing we would have to run dozens of miles back.

Picking two dandelions, I handed her one, and with my smallest finger linked with hers, we blew the delicate seeds. My Winds kept the white fluffy seeds dancing under the tree, tickling our noses and making us rupture with laughter as they clung to our lips and batted at our eyes.

Swatting them, she started a sentence, and I would finish it.

"May we weather all storms."

"And find the strength to overcome."

"And above all..." I started.

With a gleam in her eyes, we spoke the last words together, "...just survive."

In the memory, we burst into laughter, in this storm, it breaks into a thunderous boom as Rhea shatters the vision with a gale of wind. But her attacks are faltering, and her frustration is growing. I'm breaking through her stormy façade as I defend against her.

Our fight is a wager against which of us is more determined and I'm winning. The currents pick up and the speeds exceed that of the Great Hurricane when I battled Aphrodite, my sister by birth.

I couldn't save Aphrodite from her anger. Our relationship never stood a chance for that. But Rhea is my sister by choice, and I'll be damned to the shadows if I'm going to let her leave here without remembering me.

With another burst of my aura, like sunlight breaking through the clouds, I radiate everything. Closing my eyes and lifting my arms, I send out waves of my power and the images spin up the vortex of our conflict.

Weaving the scenes together like a tapestry of our friendship, the visions blanket us, and the winds carry the sounds in a melodic song. Tears, confessions, fears, and trust mingle together in a hypnotic melody that seduces her into a state of solace as she watches.

As my aura shines, filling the interior of the churning whirlwind, a slice of blue light cuts like a laser and I curse my impatient brother.

Fire ignites within Rhea's eyes as steam and smoke begin to roll off her shoulders. Narrowing her eyes at the cerulean aura of Hermes, she prepares to unleash her rage upon him. Flames and wind form a sphere between her hands as lightning arcs between her fingers.

Silver eats away the gold essence of my aura as her power swells.

"Now!" I cry out and reveal the small pocket of protection where I've been hiding Hypnos.

Patiently on my cloud with a cage of currents to keep him safe, he waited. Standing, with a pearlescent shine projecting from his eyes, his ability pulsates in fast-moving waves and strikes Rhea directly in the center of her forehead.

The Morrigan, hiding in another pocket adjacent to Rhea on the outskirts of our vortex, shadow jumps within the darkened interior of our hurricane, joining us in the eye of the storm.

My Winds compress around Rhea's body, and I hold her with everything I am. Hypnos pushes his might into his power, and The Morrigan is a loose shadow, riding the darkness within the currents.

Rhea pushes against us. Angered and confused, she wants to break free, and I'm losing my hold on her. I soar to her, my hair whipping upward as a brilliant burst of light surges from my chest, illuminating the storm again with a blinding radiance. Exhausted and weakened, I take Rhea's hands in mine, my voice gentle yet resolute.

"Rhea, let the light within me guide you back to who you truly are."

I send her the images of our captivity. Our shared promise through the cells, my worry while she was gone, and my terror when I saw how badly Lupo beat her. I send my anger and rage, wanting to consume Lupo with my currents for hurting her and my resolve to take each of his lashing without a sign of weakness.

I would be strong, for her, I would be an unmovable force of resolve, empowering her and fighting for her to be bold. Just as I learned to be with each of the days of my twenty-two years of captivity.

"Just survive." I send our promise into her mind, and she can no longer keep us out.

A momentary drop in her iron curtain and she finally succumbs to Hypnos Sensory beams of calmness and sleep. The Morrigan, ready with the grail of Starfall Castle, pours the waters into the mouth of the goddess and the ocean explodes around us.

"We have to get in there."** My voice shakes with the plane's turbulence as Medusa circles as close to the cyclone as she can safely fly.

"Trust Calypso," Medusa grunts as she fights the controls. "That is her best friend in there."

But it's also the mate I have watched suffer a thousand deaths, and I'm not keen on watching another.

My nerves are still alive with the throbbing power I absorbed from the teleportation stone. Looking back at the Shield, it's thick and impenetrable against the strong winds of the two goddesses. Storm clouds, black and swirling with their combined anger, are on one side of my shield, and clear blue skies with white billowing clouds rest undisturbed on the other side.

Lightning flares within the hurricane, and the clouds project large faces of Callie within their forms. She's trying to reach her.

She's trying to break through the fog and poison clouding Rhea's mind.

The storm is miles wide, and the wind speeds far exceed anything this realm has ever seen as the vortex sucks up the water, greedily drinking from the ocean as it spins, staying in a solitary position as they fight.

Yellow aura flares inside and I jerk toward the window for a better look. Rhea's form is silhouetted inside as lightning streaks behind her. Within the funnel, the winds must be singing Callie's memories, but outside, the haunting wails of the spent memories shoot out of the vortex and weep across the sky as if the Siren of the Wind is mourning the lives of her dearest friend.

A flash of silver eats the yellow power of Callie, and Achilles is the one that opens the seaplane door.

"Break open the clouds." He commands, scared for his mate as she battles mine.

My anxiety is not accustomed to waiting on the sidelines, and I'm all too eager for a glimpse of the temptresses of the Elements. Aiming to clear a small window, the flare of power from the stone surges out of me like a beam of Light cutting through the hurricane.

"Can't you see I'm working here?" Callie barks at us through her mind, and the winds howl around the seaplane.

Medusa strains against the plane as Callie loses some control of the funnel of Elemental Wind.

Desperation rocks Calypso as Rhea's focus diverts to me. Callie kicks her plan into motion, revealing pockets of clouds containing our Avalonia friends. The Morrigan causes the darkness within the shadowed fog of the storm to quiver as she darts from shade to shade.

The beat of Hypnos's power is a baritone thump as undulating waves of hypnosis fight to lull the great goddess to sleep, just as we did with the Titan of Darkness during the Mabon ceremony.

Rhea is on the cusp of pushing them back until Callie surges to her friend and grasps her hands. It's a fraction of a second but gives the trio the time they need to administer the Waters from the Grail.

As the enchanted waters pass to her lips, the explosion is like a mortal's nuclear weapon, discharged to end one of their catastrophic global wars. Like a mushroom cloud of water and power, a column of Rhea's starlight and aura bursts through Callie and consumes the massive hurricane, ingesting the currents of winds and surging into the sky. A plume of clouds forms a dome over the site and begins careening in all directions at great speeds.

The water of the ocean races away, revealing the seabed far below as the water rages and screams away from Rhea, and aura rushing out of her.

Hit directly by the force of Rhea's power, Calypso's unconscious body relaxes as her head lolls to the side. With eyes closed and arms lazily flailing above her head, the windswept ponytail drifts into the air as the propellers of Medusa's plane seem to slow their perpetual undulation.

Slowing down like the beat of a drum, time stills as my power flares. The swell of blue light around me competes with the raging orange flames of Achilles as he, too, powers his element.

Moving at once, we launch ourselves off the plane, each directing ourselves to our mates, both unconscious and falling.

Poised on the pontoon of the plane with a hand braced on the frame of the door, the thin metal crumples under his grip. My friend becomes a rocket as he pushes off the plane and his flames turn him into a streak of heat. Perfectly aiming his trajectory, he reaches Callie before she falls more than a few inches. The arc of his descent sends him skidding across the surface of the choppy ocean with my sister, unmoving, in his arms.

Medusa aims the plane downward as I turn to light and teleport to Rhea, plummeting toward the bare sea floor. As I move, challenging the swiftness of Light, I push my aura harder, faster.

With Callie no longer in control of the dissolving funnel, Hypnos' perch in the clouds drifts away, and he falls. Within the few remaining shadows, The Morrigan darts from shadow to shadow as Hypnos turns his body, putting his back to the quickly approaching ocean.

The Morrigan stretches her small frame and reaches for him as he casts his arms wide, ready to receive her. Upon contact, he encircles her in his arms, and they disappear, reemerging again within a dark corner of Medusa's plane as shadows swirl and her dark portal closes.

As Rhea descends to the blue ocean, it's expelled away from her. Like the parting of the Red Sea, the waters shoot away from the goddess. Starlight expels from the brass grail as it tumbles with her. The essence of her power returning to her soul as I chase after her falling body.

Medusa lowers the plane in a circular descent as Achilles' flames and speed carry him across the breaking water. As Medusa corkscrews downward, he lunges. Calypso remains unresponsive as he holds her head protectively against his chest, her body against his within his long arms.

With a jump and a turn of his body, he careens into the plane as Medusa pulls up on the controls, ascending into the skies. Traveling too fast and holding onto my sister, he can't slow his momentum. Crashing through the door on the other side of the plane, it bursts off its hinges and the pair of mates slide out the other side.

Achilles instinctively releases Callie's legs and tightens his hold around her torso. Reaching for the pontoon, there is no railing to grab, and his hand slides down the smooth float on the seaplane. As he turns his gaze to the choppy waters below, a firm hand grasps his forearm.

Closing his hand around his savior, he snaps his gaze upward and finds the three black pupils of The Morrigan looking back at him.

"We've got you, friend." Her eerie voice is swept away by the beat of the propellers as she pulls them inside.

Rhea is on a collision course with the seabed, which now lies barren before her, all the waters stripped away as if her aura is a forcefield keeping the great ocean at bay.

Like a shooting star she burns through the sky. A tail of silver following in her wake she descends like a ragdoll. Legs and arms flailing upward as gravity pulls her all too quickly to the earth.

The ocean stills as I barrel through time to reach her. Moving faster than the fabrics Immortal bodies can tolerate, the runic power I absorbed surges within me. Like the great cosmic dragon, my form turns to translucent light as I cast myself downward.

Meeting her before she strikes into the earth, I cradle her between my arms and slow my impact to soften our landing. The ground suffers under the force of my arrival, and a dent a quarter mile wide in circumference forms with the force of our touchdown.

As Rhea's power absorbs into her, the darkness and poison are extracted out. One propels into her while the other ejects out of her. The sound is a like a vacuum, sucking the atmosphere from around us, deafening me against the roar of the water, still pushing outward, held back by the force of Rhea's awakening.

Forged memories and fake alliances are broken as the light of her aura cleanses her mind. The shadows and darkness careening out of her is like acid, penetrating my astral form, eating me away. It burns and singes, but I push harder and harder against the cold shadows.

Refusing to lose her, I'll gladly let this be my end. Protecting my goddess as she repairs herself and ingests her immortality to continue the siege against her hunter.

Closing my eyes to the pain, I turn my face into her neck and hold her against me. The sweet berry scent of her hair warms me and chases away the biting cold of the darkness that stings like needles against my aura.

Holes ringed in white light form around my arms, where I hold my mate as the blackness weeps out of her. The dark is consuming me, and yet I embrace her firmly. Refusing to lose her to this power, I'll hold resolutely until I open my eyes again and see the vast expanse of The Void before me.

Touching my forehead to hers, I see it all. I witness the events of ten years ago as I see the newly returned goddess, confused and sleeping in the body of a fourteen-year-old girl during the first few nights of her new life. Demeter snuck into her room to weave nightmares and madness into her memories while smiling at her in the daylight and pretending to be a safe harbor for her mourning.

I see the visions of her deaths that Demeter orchestrated as she served Rhea up for slaughter to the constant presence of a moving shadow, a leech that clung to Rhea's lifetimes, waiting for the ripening of her power. Promising to return Demeter to Avalon as mates, to rule in darkness together, Demeter hung on the empty promises of the Titan Erebus.

Rhea witnessed more than she knew because Demeter was there to clear the memories and replace them with new horrors.

Movement against my cheek startles me, and I open my eyes to the sight of my mate. Pulsating silver starlight gleams; she cups my cheek as the last of the darkness dissipates. Her mind has been cleansed of the embedded poison, and she looks at me like it's the first time she's seen me in centuries.

Tears billow in her eyes as the cosmic rays of a thousand universes glow within the golden irises.

"You found me." Her voice breaks, and the tears spill from her eyes. Where we connect, our astral projections turn back to flesh, and we become solid form again. The holes in my aura are stitched back together by silver starlight as Rhea runs her fingers over the spots where the darkness was destroying me.

She knits my soul back together, and all I can do is stare at her; words escape me as hundreds of her deaths flare to the front of my mind. Guilt for selfishly living while she has suffered over and over again makes my face burn with shame.

As I gape at her, unable to speak, my silence pulls at her doubt and raises it to the surface. It shows on her face as her tight brow smooths as if a belief of her unimportance to me begins to war with her. Perhaps she thinks I've moved on from her after all these centuries alone, waiting for her.

"You could hide among a billion stars, and I would find you instantly." Raising my hand to sweep a lock of hair behind her ear, she tilts her head into my touch. "I'll always find you."

Pulling her into me, my lips on hers is like the first touch of warmth after the most brutal of winters. I am a frosted and barren forest, and she carries with her the rays of sunlight that spill orange fire over the horizon, chasing away the cold, dark winter.

She holds my wrist in her hand and clutches my shirt as I graze my lips over hers, expectant and longing for her kiss. I smile against her mouth as joy consumes me. Boundless happiness flows within me as my awakened goddess, knowing and cleansed of the poisons in her mind, rests within my embrace.

With parted lips, I sweep my tongue across hers, and four centuries of loneliness vanish. The gentle caress of her kiss against my lips heals me, and we surge into each other. I consume her, holding her tightly as she crowds me, wrapping her arms around my neck as if expecting a force to pull us apart.

My soul stretches within me for the first time in centuries, reaching out to wrap around my mate and shroud her in my love.

The trembling waters, still soaring high above us, begin to trickle inward. Slow at first, then rushing; the ground quakes as the ocean demands to reclaim its seabed.

Releasing a sigh, I want to curse the ocean as my Light begins to flare.

"I got this." She smiles against me as she raises her hand as if beaconing the sea to pause, and it does. With nothing more than a wave of her fingers, it waits. Water enough to drown a continent postpones its return because of the wish of the commanding goddess before me.

"Gods, I love you," I speak into her mouth, afraid to break our contact as I kiss her again. Raising herself on my lap, she presses her chest against mine as her arms encase me tighter. I clutch her hair in my hand, and as the silky ribbons entwine around my fingers, a sighing whimper escapes her throat until she finally breaks our embrace.

"Let's go find Callie."

40 Rhea

As soon as our feet hit the island, I knew something was **wrong.** The blue glow of Hermes's teleportation fades, and Achilles is bent over, kneeling on the sand.

Medusa is unsteady on her feet, one arm crossed over her chest, a glazed expression coating her eyes. Her other hand is mindlessly pulling at her bottom lip in worry as her braids stroke her arm reassuringly. A few nosey tendrils writhe above her head as if they were looking over the scene and trying to get a glimpse of what was happening.

Blocked by Achilles' body, the splayed ponytail across the sand makes my heart jump to my throat.

No.

Hermes's blue light has just delivered us here, but it's my own dark portal that brings me to her side. Kneeling, I place my hand on her forehead as tears warm my eyes and plop onto the sand below, darkening as my sorrow absorbs into the earth.

I can feel her fading away like a balloon caught on a breeze and drifting into the sky. My heart breaks for the millionth time and I wonder how it's able to keep beating through so much loss.

So many lifetimes of death and mourning have plagued my very existence but somehow I keep going. Just like now, I keep focused on my friend, my sister.

"Come back, Callie." I sniff as I place my hand on her chest. Closing my eyes, I search for her. "We promised. Above all, Callie, you promised me."

My power swirls within her, searching for the essence of her aura that commands the fickle Winds of the realm. The warmth of sunshine is fading as a cool shadow covers her like a sheet. Like the warm sun setting on the horizon, making way for the cool moon, her soul retreats within her.

The black veil of death taking the place of her bright spirit. *No.*

I'm not ready for this. I can't say goodbye to her yet. There is too much I haven't been able to share, too many memories locked away in the prison of my scattered mind.

I need my friend.

"No!" My voice is firm, and I pulse a wave of my aura into her. I refuse to accept this. "Don't you dare leave me when I just got back."

Another wave of my magic surges into her, and I find a retreating ribbon of her aura. Like a satin scarf floating in a pot of liquid gold, the essence of her immortality slowly retreats. I grab it within my power and hold her in place. "Say it with me, godsdammit. May we weather all storms and find the strength to overcome. And above all…"

I wait, my breath hitching in my throat.

Achilles weeps with quiet sorrow as he holds his hand across her brow.

"And above all…" I whisper it again.

My tears are a torrent that could refill a dry riverbed as silence stretches on too long. The memories she threw at me during our battle still swarm around my mind, meandering through the holes and cracks from my shattered lifetimes. The ribbon of yellow sunshine billows as I keep hold of it, wanting to leave this realm and join the Void.

Holding my breath for an eternity, I'm about to say our promise again until I feel her. Nothing more than a soft breath of air, the ribbon of her aura waves back at me. Then her voice is there, a faint whisper against my soul reaching back from the darkness.

"Just survive."

I chuckle and choke a cough as Callie's eyes flutter and then open. Her aura returns to her fully, and a radiant yellow glow illuminates her skin.

"Oh, my gods." Achilles leans down and places his forehead on hers, and then places a kiss there. "Never do that again, little Siren?"

"I can't promise that I won't go running into a hurricane again to save my sister." She says, looking at me as she sits up.

With sand stuck to her back and both of us soaking wet from the battle within our storm, we hug each other, and I don't want to let her go. Squeezing my arms around her, reunited after four hundred years of memories locked inside my mind, I have her back.

My friend, my sister.

"Thank you," I whisper my gratitude as my voice breaks.

It's all there. Like a movie playing in my head, I sit alone in a dark theatre as the reels of the last few days play at high speed. As if I had slept through it all, unable to wake, each time my mind tried to pull at reason, a dark tangle of twisted vines would pull me back into catatonic submission.

I remember it all; I feel it all.

Demeter pushing her vines into me and constructing terror, replacing the pain of Ares's torture with my blind submission to execute his command. The command to execute a mortal.

Gods, what have I done?

But Callie knew she could pull me out and came for me; even if it meant forfeiting her life, she did it anyway. I came so close to causing the death of another person I love, and I don't think I could bear it if it were her.

Looking beyond Callie, Hermes has both his hands on his knees and releases deep breaths as he stares at the sand. Two figures stand back, observing alongside Lucas. Medusa puffs out her cheeks as she releases her relief and wipes away worried tears with both hands.

I recognize them. Standing under a giant moon, Mor and Hypnos waved goodbye as Hermes and I left Avalon to return to Gaea. But there are too many twisting turns in the maze of my memories to form our history together.

Lucas nods at me, a crooked, knowing smile on his face, and I remember him too. I watched the fight he put up against Ares until

I made a Titan of him. *How many years have passed since that day?* Deep in the tunnels and torture chambers of the Underworld, I ended my life that night; knowing I placed another marker on the trail to my salvation, I knew I would return and find him again.

Collecting another soldier in the great war that will come to this realm.

Breaking my embrace with Callie, a force pulls at me. It's familiar, but I can't place the knowing. I can only say with certainty someone is approaching. Like the eerie sensation of knowing you're being watched, the hairs on the nape of my neck prickle and I turn behind me.

A mass of power builds ten feet away from us and I stand, my eyes fixed on the location. My action pulls everyone's defenses and Lucas flicks his right hand at his side. His hand swells and the claws of his wolf extend from his fingertips.

Hermes conjures a sword made of light as a ball of fire flares within Achilles' hand. He rises slowly, pulling Callie to stand with him and shielding her with his body. His long arm wraps around her waist as he holds her behind him.

The rattle of Medusa's braids warn of her readiness to petrify whatever should dare to step foot on her beach.

Mor and Hypnos don't seem phased as Mor, with her pale skin and dark hair inspects one of her nails.

"It's just a demon." She says blandly.

As she finishes her sentence, a familiar swirl of shadows rises in a twisted column within the shade of the bar we're standing next to. Recognition finally bringing me to understanding, I kneel and place my hand out, ready for the friendly greeting of Cerberus.

Wagging his tail and lopsidedly galloping to me, the shadow dog, in puppy form, clumsily approaches me. As I pet between his ears, the swirling shadow grows, and more figures emerge from within his portal.

Hecate, draped in the stola of ancient Greece, steps her sandaled feet onto the white sands. She looks as if she has just returned from battle as her stola is torn and singed. Dirt and soot are smudged on her exposed skin, and her lip is cut. With a gash over her eye and a bruise forming Hermes and I step toward her.

With a yank, a shadowed tendril that trails behind her surges forward, bringing with it, Demeter as she spills out of the portal. The shadowed whip wound tightly around her neck and running down her back, bind her hands behind her. She half crawls, half drags herself across the sand as Hecate's captive.

Bruises and cuts decorate her face and arms just as Hecate.

The dark-haired guest behind me hisses as realization hits everyone. My heavy heart, newly freed of her poison, is not angry, but sadness gripes me. This woman, the woman I trusted so much during each of my lifetimes, has done more harm to me, lacing her venomous torment and the weight of her own self-desolation into my mind than anyone.

She made me weak, made me question myself, and mistrust everyone. She calculated my deaths and resented my returns while feeding her toxins into me.

I wish I could feel anger, but aside from a longing to numb myself against the knowing of the suffering she created, there is only sorrow.

Flora and Zephyr exit the darkness next, with an odd log-shaped coffin floating between them. Flora looks as fresh as the night I left her in Hecate's cave and Zephyr is the ever-observant partner remaining close by Flora's side.

"Hey Callie!" Flora says with a wave. Her brown curls bounce as she pushes her round, silver glasses farther up on her freckled nose. Zephyr ducks their head in acknowledgment.

"What the fuck is happening?" Hermes says, casting the sword of light away as everyone else lowers their defenses.

"I believe this belongs to you," Hecate says coolly as she flicks the restraint made of shadow at Hypnos and Mor. The unsuspecting woman transitions to a ghastly being as her skin yellows and her eyes burn like yellow embers of a fire.

A hazy memory, glimpsing this ethereal being as the obscuring dome split during my battle with the Dark Titan, passes quickly in front of my eyes, and I glance at her comrade. His deep, pearlescent eyes take me in as if he can see the crimes I've committed, the countless I've taken, and the darkness that rests within my soul.

Teddy, lifeless as his immortal blood spilled onto the dirt and sand of the arena, clutches my guilt. As does the death of the Lycan children and the two cities I buried under tons of volcanic ash. The men and women around the world were assassinated only a few days ago.

I look at my hands and can almost see the chunks of skull and puddles of blood from assassinating the President of the United States with my Piercing Wind.

I shiver at the memories, and Hermes, attuned to the most subtle changes in my demeanor, rubs my arm as his warmth radiates into me. It chases away the cold but not the hate or the weakness I have for myself.

"Welcome back, traitor queen." The mealy voice of the woman is different from the voice that spoke a moment ago. Demeter spits a mixture of blood and saliva on the sand before her feet.

I stare at the log, and flashes of the Dark Titans fight are a strobe behind my blinking eyes.

It was horrible destitution as shadows tried to consume me while Shifters attacked Naomi and defenseless Teddy. I close my eyes and recall Atlas. He tried to save me.

Gods, no.

He tried to pull me out of the darkness, but I was so scared, so confused. My twisted mind was held in a vice of lies and betrayal. Everyone was an enemy. And I remember what I did. My chest begins to close and my breaths come ragged.

I killed him.

I felt the tendrils of his soul glowing green with the power of his aura. I gripped my hands around his spirit as I yanked his immortality away.

Hecate turns to me. Her eyes are tired, and her pupils are nearly blown black as she looks at me with understanding.

"It wasn't your fault."

The gravity of what I took away is too much, and her words crumble my resolve. My chest heaves, and my eyes burn. I want to stay in control of myself, but I can't. The weight of it all is too much. I drop to my knees, covering my face with my hands as I sob.

Hecate joins me, her tattered stola whipping in the ocean breeze; she wraps her arms around me and lets me cry. Resting her cheek on the top of my head, she weeps with me. I feel her tremble, trying to hold back her own emotions to let me pour mine out.

"I should have known. I should have protected you." She rocks me and strokes my hair as I cry.

I want to throw up. I want to walk back out across the ocean and sit at the bottom to let the weight of the world's water crush me. It would be lighter than the guilt I'm crushing myself with now.

I should have been able to fight against Demeter. I should have known she was an invasive weed, trying to suffocate me, but I believed she loved me. I cared for her and gave my trust blindly.

"No, I should have seen," Hecate whispers, regret a heavy blanket coating her words. With a sniff, she pulls back to look into my eyes. "I should have seen something wasn't right. I should have taken you with me. I should have saved you from her. And I'm sorry."

Holding her hand to me, she helps me up and wraps her arms around me again.

I can't look at Hermes or Callie.

I robbed them of someone important to them and I deserve their hate, but I know they won't give it to me. I know they will excuse me while the knowing of my murderous actions eats away at me like rust, slowly consuming metal until it's nothing.

"But I think you are holding on to something very important, and it's time you return it." She pulls back from hugging me; a sly knowing is a gleam in her dark eyes. "I will ask you trust me, though I have not earned your trust with my blindness."

She holds out her hand, and I stare at it.

Taking a deep breath, I take it as she guides me to the log. Enchanted and floating between the pair of mates, Flora carries a wary, sad smile as Zephyr eyes me with caution.

"This will be disturbing," Zephyr says as they reach across the log and pull back the top.

The sight will haunt me for all of eternity.

Ashen and grey, the body of Atlas rests within the log. Dead and white is his flesh, his lips are purple and match the coloring around his eye sockets.

I push out the sound of Callie as she takes in the sight of Atlas. I close my eyes, sorrow for the pain I have caused holds my throat in a vice, and I swallow hard against the tears. The deafening weight of Hermes' silence is like a slice into my heart.

Starting at the unanimated body of someone, knowing what it was like when life inhabited their vessel, it seems so odd to think this waxy-looking shell is all that remains. But knowing I'm the cause of making his life vacate his body sends a twist to my stomach.

"Atlas is suspended," Flora says. "He is not dead but is dying. I'm doing what I can, but I'll lose the body soon." Flora's high voice is like a bell that dings sweetly with the opening of a door.

"I don't understand what that means." My voice barely works, like I haven't used it in months as it breaks when I speak.

I grab the side of the log, and inches away, I can feel the chill radiating from his body.

"He is missing his soul." Flora's eyes are like deep chestnut, and I hold onto her gaze like it will keep me from drifting away into the dark recesses of my tattered mind.

"Close your eyes and search inside you." Hecate guides.

My chest rises swiftly as the words settle into me. *Suspended. Missing his soul.*

The fragments of what they have said are quiet, but the impact of the words they refuse to say are screaming at me in my mind.

Panic billows within my skull like an old enemy that won't stop resurfacing. But fingertips spread wide, applying pressure to the side of my head as Hermes runs his hand through my hair. Reaching the base of my skull, he squeezes gently. Warm blue light coats me like a warm bath and my body relaxes at his touch.

"Don't slip back into that void." His voice surrounds me, and I lean into his chest. His strength wraps around me as he encases me with his arm around my back, grabbing low on my hip and holding me against him. *"I've got you and I won't let go."*

I close my eyes and square my shoulders. I bite back the tightness that wants to choke me as I hold back the tears that beg to fall. "What can I do?" Trusting her tutorship, I follow Hecate, knowing she will help guide me as she always has.

"Find your power within you and follow it deeper inside yourself."

Brimming just under the surface is a coil of starlight, and I follow it within me like a spiral staircase leading downward. Broken and fragmented, I sense the missing pieces of my Immortality that wait patiently for the day I'll be made whole again.

Then, clustered at the base of silver is a small huddle of green energy. A foreign invader within my soul is the Immortality of Atlas.

"Out."

The word spoken in the arena when I yanked him away bounces around my insides, like the command is trapped along with his soul.

I stole his Immortality without even knowing and kept it self-ishly within me.

My hands shake, and my mind empties as I'm not sure what to do. Scared any movement will make it disappear, I try to remain frozen.

Thinking of my silver aura like a bowl, I surround the emerald power of Atlas and carefully raise it within me. Hermes' hold around my waist balances me while I focus, carefully and without moving too quickly, I shift the power down my arm.

"It's okay, Rhea." Hecate kept her tone even and calm, sensing the swell of my nervousness. She must know I found him. "You can do this."

I place my hand flat on his chest and transfer it back to him. Like a blanket laying over him, the green aura of his power covers his body. As if knowing what needs to come next, yellow, healing light blends with my silver aura and black mist as I restore him.

Dull hair turns lush, and the life returning to him chases away the purple rings around his eyes and mouth. His chest heaves, and his lashes flutter as his soul settles back into him. Brown eyes peer back at me, and a tear rolls down his cheek.

Hermes tightens his hold around my waist and squeezes my hip as Callie hiccups a cry next to Achilles.

"I–" Atlas pauses, flexing his fingers still placed over his chest. "I'm in a tree."

I can't help but snort a laugh as my hand flies to cover my dripping nose. Tears streak my face, and I hadn't even realized I had started crying. Hermes turns me toward him and wraps his other arm around me, engulfing me within his hulking frame. I release the tension of what seems like the last ten years and pent-up turmoil.

"You're amazing." He praises me quietly in my ear as I continue to cry. "You did so well, baby." He places a kiss on my temple and holds me securely within his arms.

Zephyr and Achilles hold their hands out to Atlas, and he clutches them. The power holding the log dips the end down, and Atlas stands. His grip on the two Elementals steadying him while he gets his balance back.

Callie gives him no time to regain himself before she surges into him. Hugging his waist, she buries her face into his chest, and he hugs her shoulders. Shushing her and letting her cry, as he gently strokes her hair. It's beautiful. Like a father comforting his daughter, he holds her as Hecate just held me in my own grief.

Guilt gnaws at me, and I close my eyes, trying to disappear within Hermes' hold on me.

"Hey." Atlas' voice rings behind me. Still as a leaf before it falls from a tree, I hold myself a moment before finally turning to him. "Thank you."

I dart my eyes away from his, hoping to hide my remorse, though I know it's pointless. The Elementals gathered here have the ability to see everything within me, no matter how hard I try to conceal it.

I know I'll have to face the truth of my past, the blood on my hands as Ares used me to murder millions. Echoes of their cries swim in the deep pools of my dark mind, and I hear them begging me to stop. As much as I wanted to, something else was there and in control. I can't help but think part of me is eternally broken and perhaps deep down, I wanted to kill.

Maybe one day I'll believe none of it was my fault, but not today. Just because I can erase this one tally mark from the death toll I have collected, the weight of millions of others will never leave me.

Releasing Callie, Atlas cups her face and smiles before turning fully to me. Shoving his hands in his pockets, he balances on the balls of his feet and looks to the ground. Taking in a deep breath through his nose, he meets my eye.

"I owe you an explanation." He tilts his head. "And an apology.

Sitting on the edge of the dock, the ocean laps at the wooden posts like they are reaching up to say hello to **me.** I feel the currents of water within the great blue deep, and I'm aware of all the forms of life within.

Just off the coast, a team of dolphins play together while a large sea turtle exits the waters, making way to the beach to lay her eggs. I sense the temperature changes within the sea as the ebbs and flows of the undercurrents dance around each other, just as I can feel the tugs and pulls of the wind in the air.

As I hear the Wind whisper of the Battle of the Sirens, the waters talk in hushed tones of the lover's reunion at the bottom of the ocean.

Atlas' footsteps meander down the dock, and he joins me.

The sky is a rich sheet of black velvet stretched above the silky surface of the ocean. The moon and a billion stars reflect in the cool waters as Atlas sets down a brown paper bag of steaming food.

"Cheeseburgers?" He says, handing me the bag. "Achilles is insisting Mor take home as many as Medusa can cook up."

Turning behind me, I see the stoic pair, Hypnos and Mor, standing on the beach, waiting. Hypnos holds four bags of food, and Mor holds a double cheeseburger in both hands. Her mouth is full of food as she chews, watching Medusa and her smoking flattop cook up more hamburgers.

I stare at them, taking in the details of their Avalonia apparel and thinking of past lives when I met them for the first time.

Mor radiates darkness, and it clings to her with admiration. Whipping at her ankles from the shadows of the ground, the obscurity worships her, just as I feel the willing waters of the ocean frolicking to gain my attention and the winds ready for my praise and my command.

"What *is* she?" I ask, as I watch the glow of three auras swirl carefully within her.

Atlas thinks for a moment, squinting his eyes as if examining her while he reaches to push up his gold-rimmed glasses, but they are not sitting on his nose. An endearing habit that makes me grin.

"Complex." Is the word he settles on.

Satisfied with a small grin, he settles in next to me, our feet hanging over the side.

I take a burger from the sack, and my mind settles on what could be a memory, but I feel like it's more of an understanding.

Trapped in Ares lair, remembering the folder containing Apollos picture, I consider the roles of three gods at the forefront of this conflict. The connection between them seems so clear now and I utter the statement as a fact.

"You were mates."

Atlas holds his gaze over the dark ocean, watching the moonlight bounce off the top of the waters. The look in his eye tells me his memories have taken him a million miles away, and I wait while I awkwardly hold the burger in my lap.

"Eat." He bumps me with his shoulder, taking a deep breath and lengthening his spine as he sits up taller. "I'm sure you're starving."

"You were dead, so I'm sure you are also starving." I keep my eyes on the dark waves as they slurp against the posts. "Hermes said you guys were like brothers, but that is not true, is it?"

"No, it's not true. And yes, we were mates." Atlas leans over and retrieves a small brown wallet from his back pocket.

I raise my eyebrows at the thought of gods, carrying wallets and he waves me off as a grin forms on my face.

"I started carrying one in the 1970's and just stuck with it." He pulls a small picture, sketched in fine detail with black ink and preserved with an old spell. It's a recreation of a larger version that hangs in Ares's office of the three young men.

They were all mates together.

"A Flame, a Light Bearer and a Mind Mage all fated together. It was unheard of but even more unique, we were all three apprentices to our Titans.

"It was during the Age of Artemis in the Realm of Avalon when we met. The Mind Titan, Coeus was fanatical about recording events and insisted on scribing the celebrations of the Titans himself. We arrived early, naturally, and I remember how itchy my robes were. Brown and simple, Coeus never made a fuss over extravagances, but the other Titans came to put on a spectacle.

"I saw Ares first, arriving through a portal of Fire with his Titan, Prometheus. They were magnificent. Hephaestus had forged many great weapons for the Titan Huntress, and Prometheus gifted her a Firebird, one of the rarest mythical creatures, even for Immortals.

"I remember Coeus leaning to me whispering, *'Time will tell if the bird brings her blessings or doom.'* Well, it brought her doom because Artemis was the first Titan that had their power consumed by Chaos.

"But Ares was the only one I saw. The Titan of Fire, a colossal volcano with flesh made of hardened lava, was not as compelling as Ares. I couldn't look away from him. Above the parade and spectacle, I watched the Flame, and I knew instantly, but–," Atlas shifts, uncomfortable to be opening up about his feelings, so I wait. "You know, I was a shrimp in an itchy brown robe with a drawn hood."

Atlas holds his hands out as if showing me the width of his hands helps emphasize his meaning. It makes me chuckle, and I wipe my mouth of the juicy hamburger. Atlas laughs with me and continues.

"Ares was so strong, wearing his Fire Armor and rams' helmet. He was confident and in command of himself, and I just stood, watching him with my mouth gaping open like an idiot.

"And then Apollo arrived, gleaming like the sun with his yellow aura and golden cape. He was such a good Herald of his realm. There was no mistaking the great cosmic dragon was arriving when you saw her apprentice. She seemed to form out of his light, and as her large, clawed limbs shook the ground with each step she took, everything stilled when Apollo looked at me with those deep blue eyes."

I'm so transfixed on this story; I haven't taken a bite in several minutes. Atlas prompts me with a pointed look that threatens he'll stop sharing unless I keep eating. With a roll of my eyes, I dive back into the burger as he dives back into the memories of meeting his mates.

"Apollo had made a name for himself within the Titans' Emissaries and Heralds, and Ares was quickly rising in the ranks of warriors. And for me, I was the youngest apprentice ever named by a Titan, taken in as a steward on my ninth Great Year; until Hermes broke my record and was named by Theia on his eighth.

"We were a threat. Three very young and powerful Elementals, whose powers only increased after they bonded. We would be a disturbance to the balance of power the Titans held. So, we lied. We hid our true relationship in public, something Ares always disagreed with.

"It took us a while, but we found our balance." Atlas pauses to make room for Callie, who joins us on the dock. She slips her arm through the crook of his elbow and lays her head on his shoulder. She has a content smile as she looks out across the dark water.

"We wanted a family, so Apollo had Hermes, and then little Cala Lily came along." Atlas jostles his shoulders and Callie snickers. "The conflicts with the Titans began, and Apollo and Ares were warriors. They were made for the front lines of war, and we knew it would separate our family as our Titans would need us. I helped with the refugee effort, and they went off to battle.

"When Tartarus was attacked, we barely arrived in just enough time to get a warning out, but we were not early enough. We only cared about getting to Hermes and Callie. They were refugees on Tartarus with Hermes' mother."

The heat at my back warns of Hermes' approach as he slides in behind me. Stretching one leg on each side of me, I lean into him. He trails his wide hands down my thighs as he nuzzles my neck, inhaling my fragrance deeply with a satisfied rumble in his chest and it sends jolts of excitement shooting down my limbs. Achilles joins Callie, sitting similarly.

Atlas continues his account. "We fled here, to Gaea, and the wards were put up around the realm. Ares was different, even more of a recluse to the family than he had been during the Titan Wars. His ranting became darker and power-obsessed, and a rift formed between him and Apollo. Their fight was monumental, and Ares's rage burned so hot, he incinerated two cities, turning them to stone.

"Apollo saw what took me a lot longer to see. He knew Ares could not be changed, but I thought he would see the light. I thought I could make him see."

"When did you know?" I ask, dread building in the pit of my stomach, knowing somehow I'm involved in the answer. "How did you know he couldn't be saved?"

Atlas looks at me pointedly for a moment, as if deciding his words. The first time he broke the news of my Immortality at his dining table, I didn't fare so well processing the information. Atlas lacked tact, but I was consumed by the thoughts of my power, and my panic suffocated me.

Perhaps it hadn't really been me, but Demeter's poison trained to trigger my anxiety and keep me in an induced state of weakness. I'm free of that toxin now and while I'm still shaky, I know I can handle it.

"Please just tell me. I'm trying to remember, but things are—confusing. Like everything is out of order and broken into pieces."

Atlas thins his lips, either at my confession or in deciding to tell me something he knows will be troubling.

"The first time he used you to wipe out the mortals. When he used you to flood the realm and drown the humans. Pockets of mortals took to boats or high ground to survive the initial tsunamis that circled the globe."

Instinctively, I look out at the water and feel it stretch before me, a waiting servant to my will. If I beckoned it, the seas would swell with pride and coat the land in their might for no other reason but to impress me. It feels intoxicating; it feels dangerous.

"But not many of them were able to survive," Atlas adds quietly.

In the distance of my mind, I can hear them. Screaming parents clutching children while they beat on vessels, begging for sanctuary. Eventually their screams turned to gargled agony and then silence.

"Hey." Hermes' deep voice in my ear coaxes me out of my haze. "Come back to me." With a kiss on my cheek, a gentle pulse of light soothes my mind, and I blink several times to focus my eyes.

I put my right hand over his and entwine our fingers as he wraps his arm around my waist, pulling me into him more. His left hand draws lazy circles around my thigh, and I watch the pattern of the waves, trying to slow my heartbeat to match them.

Atlas continues, rubbing his chin and taking a steadying breath. "When Apollo left, our bond was damaged. Ares became inconsolable and abusive. I tried to bridge them back together, but it only made things worse. And then I watched the joy in Ares's face when he realized he could evoke your power; I saw the wheels turning and knew there was nothing but a shell of the Immortal we once loved.

"It truly felt like I was carrying the weight of the world on my back because the next step I took would change the course of this realm forever. I left Ares, and the bond shattered." Atlas rubs his chest as if recalling the space their bond filled. "We had no idea bonds were so fragile, and it weakened us. It stripped away our bonded power and left us feeling diluted.

"Ares turned into something savage and began trying to rebuild his former strength. He learned how the Titan's power was consumed by Chaos, and he wanted that for himself. He wanted to feel the powers he had when we were mated again."

Atlas drops his head, nipping at the corner of his mouth as he refuses to look at anyone.

"If it weren't for me, none of this would have happened. He would have never known bonds could be removed." He pauses for a moment in the heavy silence.

No one tries to soothe him, perhaps because they have all tried before, and despite their reassurances, it's impossible for him to believe otherwise. Atlas takes a deep breath, straightening his posture and continuing.

"I went back once and tried to talk with him. His new Mind Mage met me at the door."

"Moros?" His name is slime on my tongue as if the essence of his power slithering around me lingers, even now.

Atlas nods in agreement as he looks down at his hands resting in his lap. A tear collects on his brown lashes and drops onto his pants.

"When Mind Mages battle, it's not physical, but it's a war of the consciousness with illusions cast within our minds."

Callie reaches over and grabs Atlas' forearm with an affectionate squeeze.

"I broke him." Atlas' chin quivers and two large drops of tears hang on the edges of his eyes, daring to drop at the ages old memory, but still pulls Atlas in opposing directions. "I was appalled at what I had done. I stopped before I killed him and just– I didn't know what to do, so I left him there." Atlas blinks quickly, clearing the tears and sniffling. "And Ares put him back together and then sent him after the one person in this realm that would hurt me the most."

"Who?" My eyes are wide as I stare at him, unblinking, even though I feel like I already know the answer.

"Calypso. He targeted her before, abducting her when Hermes and Achilles rescued her in the valley. And he targeted her mates, using them to tear each other apart." Tears continue to fall as Atlas fights to hold them back. After a moment, he looks at me with sorrow-filled eyes. "After Moros, I promised myself I would never invade a mind again, but I did it to you. I'm so sorry, but I had to know she wasn't in danger."

Callie's eyes are closed as she rests her head against Achilles's chest. He looks at the waves with unseeing eyes like he's lost in a memory of his own, and I understand.

I understand why Atlas feels a sense of responsibility and protection. He feels he put Ares on a path that intersected with Medusa and Athena, causing their ruin because Atlas walked away from his own bond and caused it to break. He feels accountable for what happened to Patroclus because of what he did to Moros.

Thinking back to the day I arrived at the Commune with Callie, beaten and a stranger, I can understand his eagerness to guard her. To know if I was a spy, planted by Ares to ruin the children he loves. The kids born from his mate that Atlas helped raise.

He knows Ares better than anyone in this realm, knows the depths he's capable of going for what he wants. And where lust for power fuels Ares, restraint and righteousness fuels Atlas.

While I was protective of myself and untrusting, Atlas was in a similar way. And despite his trepidation, he still tried to help me. Only because he saw someone broken that needed help. Perhaps some part of it was for Hermes and Callie, but I think he would have tried, regardless.

"I understand." I look at the burger in my lap, half eaten and unappetizing now that it sat cold. My mind is a puzzle, scattered on the table before someone takes the time to put it back together carefully.

I know I have a long way to restore what's broken, and a war is coming with Ares. As I shift through scrambled memories of my past lives, something feels different about this lifetime.

We've gotten this far before, but never have I felt so settled in my powers so quickly after restoring them. With the poison of Demeter's toxins cleared from my body, I can begin to heal my mind. I can stitch together the scattered memories, and with Atlas's help. I can uncover Ares' weaknesses and defeat him.

"Ares would have broken the bond himself if you hadn't walked away first." Callie nods in passionate agreement as I speak the words, as if she has tried to tell him this before. "He would have sent someone after Callie, even if you hadn't fought Moros before. You can't look back on the past and wish you had seen the future. There is no way you could have known the road he would have taken to get the power he craves."

"You sound like Hecate now." Hermes' dull voice is laced with humor as he teases me.

"Well then, she sounds like a genius," Hecate adds, joining us as Medusa sits beside us, a green leather journal in her lap.

"I can do this." I look at him firmly, and Atlas meets my eyes, pressing his lips in a frail grin. "I just need some help to sort out the mess up here, if you're willing?"

Atlas places his hand over his chest and bends in a slight bow. "I am your ward until the ends of the realm, goddess."

I feel my cheeks blaze with heat, and I'm thankful for the cover of night to conceal my embarrassment. Taking a deep breath and scanning my eyes to the farthest reaches of the horizon, my vision is sharper, my hearing extends farther, and I feel my power thrumming within me as if amplified by a thousand bolts of lightning.

But I also feel the holes within my soul. The gaps in the Immortal well of power that sit empty and waiting to be filled.

Hermes stands and holds his hand to me, helping me rise. Taking my hand, he leads me to the start of the dock, as the sand, pale blue under the light of the moon, creeps onto the wooden decking.

Turning to face me, he raises his hand and sweeps a lock of hair behind my ear. Eyes as deep as the ocean take me in as my neck cranes to look up at him. Turning my eyes to his booted feet with a smile, I step up on the steel toes of his shoes. Lifting myself onto the balls of my feet, I use him to give myself a few additional inches.

Wrapping my arms around his neck, he encircles me between two muscular arms, smiling at me. Placing a kiss on the tip of my nose, he dips down, taking my lips with his. Opening to him, our tongues meet as he squeezes me into him.

My heart soars as the Winds of the realm circle us. I hold him tighter and he follows, pulling me into him. Breaking the kiss, I smile, remembering my dream in the Underworld and his visit within the tunnels. Feigning a rush of irritation, I lean back and playfully smack his chest.

"What?" He chuckles, showcasing two dimples that drive a knot straight in my stomach.

"That is for your–dastardly visits while I was–out of my mind." I stammer, searching for the words as I tease him.

"Dastardly, huh?" He leans down, kissing me again as he lowers his grip around my waist and cups the base of my ass within his large palm. The tips of his fingers vibrate against my thick tactical pants and startles me, causing me to jump and squeal at the sensation. His crooked smile widens as he raises his left eyebrow. A sly gleam covers his eyes. "Baby, you just wait until I get you back home and I'll show you a new meaning to the word."

The promise of pleasure washes over me as he leans into my neck. I pull him tighter to me and arch my back into him. The scruff of his short growth is a pleasant scratch against my sensitive skin, and I suddenly feel like there are too many articles of clothing separating us.

Breaking away, he leans back and takes me in again. A stupid smile spreads across my face, and I know he can see the cherry red filling my cheeks.

"Want to go on a field trip?" Now we both have stupid smiles as we remember the quick visit to Angel Falls.

"Yes." I nearly bounce with excitement, but he turns serious suddenly, giving me pause.

"I'm going to *really* need you to trust me this time, though." His look is weary, and I narrow my eyes at him. "And no running off after."

Stepping down from my perch on the tops of his shoes, I return to my feet back to the sand.

"We'll see." I answer, a gleam in my own eye as I turn back to the dock to meet Callie.

Our new friends from Avalon stand at the beach, saying their parting words and with sacks full of cheeseburgers. In a few minutes, they will return to Avalon, and Demeter will face trial. Knowing the laws of the Unseelie Fae of Orion's Court, execution could be her only hope for a merciful ending.

Rhea called the Grail out of the depths of the oceans and Mor returned it to Pandoras Box. She'll return it to Starfall Castle where they will keep charge of the relic as they always have.

A dark thought crosses my mind, and I know others are thinking the same. Avalon may be called upon again, should we fail Rhea in this lifetime and need to imbue the challis with the Immortal power of the goddess again.

I pinch the bridge of my nose, and exhaustion washes over me like the waves that lap up the sandy beach in the never-ending push and pull of the realm.

Leaning against Medusa's bar, she slaps down Athena's green journal and gives me an expectant look, making me grin.

"You found it, huh?" I pick up the journal I gifted the Goddess of War and thumb through the pages.

"And what is this?" She asks. "It has memories of *us* in it."

The leather-bound journal is filled with pages of poems and stories of the two former mates.

"Athena had regular sessions with me trying to restore her memories." I think back to my time with my old friend. "She would hold a small ball and squeeze it hard until the pain got to be too much, then she would drop the ball as a signal to stop. I was afraid the sessions weren't working until I saw a drawing of you, scratched on a piece of parchment and left on her desk."

"What was the drawing?" Medusa's green eyes shine with hope.

"The first time she saw you, deposited on the floor of the castle in Atlantis, when Hermes delivered you here from Tartarus."

Medusa joins me with her back against the bar and we watch Achilles tell an animated story to Mor and Hypnos. They listen on, smiling with Lucas, Hermes, and Rhea. Callie stands to the side with Flora and Zephyr, catching up on their search for a good place to hide away from the eyes and ears of the Council.

"So, I had an idea, and I gave her the journal. I told her to write in it, any time she had a good memory of you. The bad memories were always too terrible, so outlandishly cruel, they were hard for her to bear. But the good ones, they seemed to come at the most random of times and would pop into her head and then be gone again.

"I thought, if she could recall enough good memories, they would start to win out over the bad ones. I was hoping she would begin to clear herself of the spell."

Medusa looks at the green leather bindings and places her hand over it.

"There was still love there," I tell Medusa softly.

She doesn't look at me, but she nods, keeping her expression even. Maybe Medusa doesn't want to allow herself to believe it, but I do.

"Thanks." She remains locked on the journal before standing. "I'm going to clean up." She tucks the book under her arm and leaves as Hecate joins me, taking her place.

With a deep sigh, Hecate rolls her neck, obviously tired from the long ordeal of capturing Demeter and keeping me out of the Void.

"You should have Flora or Rhea heal you."

"No. I want to feel the pain. I deserve it." She looks at me, wisdom fills her dark eyes, and gives me a weary smile. "I'm glad you're back." Hecate bumps me with her shoulder.

"You and me both." We watch the younger Immortals, enjoying the company of each other as they laugh with hope in the gleam of their eyes.

"You know what this means," Hecate says.

As I study Rhea, a shiver runs down my spine at the thought of her power shielding my Immortal soul as she transferred me back to my body.

"I do."

"So, how do we tell her?"

Thinking for a moment, I watch as Hermes' Light flare.

"Delicately."

In a flash, he disappears with Rhea, Mor and Hypnos as they guard Demeter. They will return them to Avalon and escort the treacherous queen back for her trial. The moon seems to dim as the goddess moves through the realm as if it wants to track her with its light, yearning for her to need its Lumos.

"How else can you tell her she is the Titan of Death, Chaos returned?" I ask my friend of many years.

"Delicately indeed." She answers.

Carrying me in his arms, Hermes kicks open the door to his home on Mount Olympus. Stalking over the threshold, he slams it shut with a wave of his aura. My fingers thread his dark locks as he marches to the bedroom.

"Hermes." His name is a whisper on my lips...

To Be Continued...

Acknowledgements

How am I already here, writing another page of "thank you's"?

Less than a year ago, I announced I was going to self-publish a ten-year long dream. And I did.

I finally did it. The Forgotten Goddess made her debut to the world, August 29, 2023 and to my surprise....people actually wanted to read it. (Yes, I'm still shocked by this....don't give me that look!)

Then, I did it again.

The Unforgotten Flame joined the literary world, December 27, 2023.

Here we are, less than twelve short months later, and my third book has sprung from my imagination and into the hands of readers.

Admittedly, my acknowledgements for The Forgotten Goddess were sufficient, albeit sparse, largely devoid of any meaningful content. I was still proud to write them, even if they made me a little sad.

My life has become significantly richer since beginning my journey as a self-published, Indie Author and no, it's not buckets of money pouring in but amazing people who have wandered into my orbit and for some reason, they are sticking around. Something I never dreamed would be part of my success story.

And so.... here we go:

First, me. I proud of myself.

Pulling yourself out of total darkness, when there is not a soul around is hard. It's even harder with a few kids in tow. Despite the imposter syndrome, fear of failure and a million other reasons to turn and run away, I did it...again and again. Now, I'm a three time published author...and still going. Some days are better than others are most are still a struggle but... I've got this!

Of course, thank you to my kiddos.

For sitting around and listening to my book-talk, understanding when mom is plugging away at the keyboard each night and being the respite, when a break is needed.

Thank you to my editors!

Suzi Vadori has provided her amazing insight on both books one and two of The Forgotten Goddess series. Her counsel and guidance and critical eye helped me refine the story so wonderfully.

Heather Creed of CreedReads provided the professional polishing and proofing needed to make sure this beauty was as ready for the masses.

To my lovely street team: I can't tell you how much you mean to me.

On July 3rd, 2023, a gang of ruffians gathered together in a group chat and I watched with horror as the first readers in history set their eyes on my work. I held my breath. I don't think I blinked for three days and at the end, we just never shut up. I value our off-the-wall conversations and appreciate your support and friendship so much.

April, Brandi, Bre, Cassie, Christen, Dallas, Hannah, Heather, Holly, Janene, Kalli, Kayla, Kiana, Kim, Kristin, Mollie, Phyllica, Reina, Sarah, Sheena, Shelby, Stormie, Tanesha, and Yesenia – Thank you for being here and sticking with me.

To my author besties: look at us!

To Amber Thoma: I will forever thank a full moon and a subway sandwich for the start of a great friendship. Thank you for helping me make my sad scenes sadder, and my torture scenes more torture-ie. Thanks for letting me talk endlessly about my books and thanks for being my friend.

To 'The Big Three' and 'The Core Four' and my 'Distracted Inklings': I love you ladies. The mutual support and genuine happiness to see each other success is amazing. I cherish you all.

Lastly, I'd be nowhere without the amazing readers, who find solace in books and who decided something within my story was intriguing enough to pick it up. If you stay for a short time, or stick around for the long haul, I'm glad you were here.

So, to the forced friendship and the book bestie, to 2AM text to share tragic scenes and writing sprints shenanigans,

Thank you.

Rebekah Sinclair